SENTIMENTAL TOMMY

THE STORY
OF HIS BOYHOOD

SENTIMENTAL TOMMY

THE STORY
OF HIS BOYHOOD

BY

J. M. BARRIE

CASSELL AND COMPANY
LIMITED
LONDON, PARIS & MELBOURNE
1896

TO MY WIFE

CONTENTS.

SENTIMENTAL TOMMY:

THE STORY OF HIS BOYHOOD.

—✳—

CHAPTER I.

TOMMY CONTRIVES TO KEEP ONE OUT.

THE celebrated Tommy first comes into view on a dirty London stair, and he was in sexless garments, which were all he had, and he was five, and so though we are looking at him, we must do it sideways, lest he sit down hurriedly to hide them. That inscrutable face, which made the clubmen of his later days uneasy, and even puzzled the ladies while he was making love to them, was already his, except when he smiled at one of his pretty thoughts or stopped at an open door to sniff a potful. On his way up and down the stair he often paused to sniff, but he never asked for anything; his mother had warned him against it, and he carried out her injunction with almost unnecessary spirit, declining offers before they were made, as when passing a room, whence came the smell of fried fish, he might call in, " I don't not want none of your fish," or "My mother says I don't not want the littlest bit," or wistfully, "I ain't hungry," or more wistfully still, "My mother says I ain't hungry." His

B

mother heard of this and was angry, crying that
he had let the neighbours know something she
was anxious to conceal, but what he had revealed
to them Tommy could not make out; and when
he questioned her artlessly, she took him with
sudden passion to her flat breast, and often after
that she looked at him long and wofully and
wrung her hands.

The only other pleasant smell known to
Tommy was when the water-carts passed the
mouth of his little street. His street, which
ended in a dead wall, was near the river, but on
the doleful south side of it, opening off a longer
street where the cabs of Waterloo Station sometimes found themselves when they took the
wrong turning; his home was at the top of a
house of four floors, each with accommodation
for at least two families, and here he had lived
with his mother since his father's death six
months ago. There was oil-cloth on the stair as
far as the second floor; there had been oil-cloth
between the second floor and the third—Tommy
could point out pieces of it still adhering to the
wood like remnants of a plaster.

This stair was nursery to all the children
whose homes opened on it, not so safe as
nurseries in the part of London that is chiefly
inhabited by boys in sailor suits, but preferable
as a centre of adventure, and here on an afternoon sat two. They were very busy boasting,
but only the smaller had imagination, and as
he used it recklessly, their positions soon
changed; sexless garments was now prone on a
step, breeches sitting on him.

Shovel, a man of seven, had said, "None on your lip. You weren't never at Thrums yourself."

Tommy's reply was, "Ain't my mother a Thrums woman?"

Shovel, who had but one eye, and that blood-shot, fixed it on him threateningly.

"The Thames is in London," he said.

"'Cos they wouldn't not have it in Thrums," replied Tommy.

"'Amstead 'Eath's in London, I tell yer," Shovel said.

"The cemetery is in Thrums," said Tommy.

"There ain't no queens in Thrums, anyhow."

"There's the auld licht minister."

"Well, then, if you jest see'd Trafalgar Square!"

"If you jest see'd the Thrums townhouse!"

"St. Paul's ain't in Thrums."

"It would like to be."

After reflecting, Shovel said in desperation, "Well, then, my father were once at a hanging."

Tommy replied instantly, "It were my father what was hanged."

There was no possible answer to this save a knock-down blow, but though Tommy was vanquished in body, his spirit remained stanch; he raised his head and gasped, "You should see how they knock down in Thrums!" It was then that Shovel sat on him.

Such was their position when an odd figure in that house, a gentleman, passed them without a word, so desirous was he to make a breath

taken at the foot of the close stair last him
to the top. Tommy merely gaped after this
fine sight, but Shovel had experience, and
"It's a kid or a coffin," he said sharply,
knowing that only birth or death brought a
doctor here.

Watching the doctor's ascent, the two boys
strained their necks over the rickety banisters,
which had been polished black by trousers of the
past, and sometimes they lost him, and then
they saw his legs again.

"Hello, it's your old woman!" cried Shovel.
"Is she a deader?" he asked, brightening, for
funerals made a pleasant stir on the stair.

The question had no meaning for bewildered
Tommy; but he saw that if his mother was a
deader, whatever that might be, he had grown
great in his companion's eye. So he hoped she
was a deader.

"If it's only a kid," Shovel began with such
scorn that Tommy at once screamed, "It ain't!"
and, cross-examined, he swore eagerly that his
mother was in bed when he left her in the morning, that she was still in bed at dinner-time, also
that the sheet was over her face, also that she
was cold.

Then she was a deader and had attained dis-
tinction in the only way possible in that street.
Shovel did not shake Tommy's hand warmly, the
forms of congratulation varying in different parts
of London, but he looked his admiration so
plainly that Tommy's head waggled proudly.
Evidently, whatever his mother had done
redounded to his glory as well as to hers, and

somehow he had become a boy of mark. He
said from his elevation that he hoped Shovel
would believe his tales about Thrums now ; and
Shovel, who had often cuffed Tommy for sticking
to him so closely, cringed in the most snobbish
manner, craving permission to be seen in his
company for the next three days. Tommy, the
upstart, did not see his way to grant this favour
for nothing, and Shovel offered a knife, but did
not have it with him ; it was his sister Ameliar's
knife, and he would take it from her, help his
davy. Tommy would wait there till Shovel
fetched it. Shovel, baffled, wanted to know what
Tommy was putting on hairs for. Tommy
smiled, and asked ;whose mother was a deader.
Then Shovel collapsed, and his wind passed into
Tommy.

The reign of Tommy Sandys, nevertheless,
was among the shortest, for with this question
was he overthrown : "How did yer know she
were cold? "

" Because," replied Tommy triumphantly,
" she tell me herself."

Shovel only looked at him ; but one eye can
be so much more terrible than two that plop,
plop, plop came the balloon softly down the
steps of the throne and at the foot shrank piti-
fully, as if with Ameliar's knife in it.

" It's only a kid arter all ! " screamed Shovel,
furiously. Disappointment gave him eloquence,
and Tommy cowered under his sneers, not understanding them ; but they seemed to amount to
this, that in having a baby he had disgraced the
house.

"But I think," he said, with diffidence, "I think I were once one."

Then all Shovel could say was that he had better keep it dark on that stair.

Tommy squeezed his fist into one eye, and the tears came out at the other. A good-natured impulse was about to make Shovel say that though kids are undoubtedly humiliations, mothers and boys get used to them in time, and go on as brazenly as before; but it was checked by Tommy's unfortunate question, "Shovel, when will it come?"

Shovel, speaking from local experience, replied truthfully that they usually came very soon after the doctor, and at times before him.

"It ain't come before him," Tommy said, confidently.

"How do yer know?"

"'Cos it weren't there at dinner-time, and I been here since dinner-time."

The words meant that Tommy thought it could only enter by way of the stair, and Shovel quivered with delight. "H'st!" he cried, dramatically, and to his joy Tommy looked anxiously down the stair, instead of up it.

"Did you hear it?" Tommy whispered.

Before he could control himself Shovel blurted out: "Do you think as they come on their feet?"

"How then?" demanded Tommy; but Shovel had exhausted his knowledge of the subject. Tommy, who had begun to descend to hold the door, turned and climbed upwards, and his tears were now but the drop left in a cup too hurriedly dried. Where was he off to? Shovel called after him; and he answered, in a determined whisper: "To shove of it out if it tries to come in at the winder."

This was enough for the more knowing urchin, now so full of good things that with another added he must spill, and away he ran for an audience, which could also help him to bait Tommy, that being a game most sportive when there are several to fling at once. At the door he knocked over, and was done with, a laughing little girl who had strayed from a more fashionable street. She rose solemnly, and kissing her muff, to reassure it if it had got a fright, toddled in at the first open door to be out of the way of unmannerly boys.

Tommy, climbing courageously, heard the door slam, and looking down he saw—a strange child. He climbed no higher. It had come.

After a long time he was one flight of stairs nearer it. It was making itself at home on the bottom step; resting, doubtless, before it came hopping up. Another dozen steps, and—It was beautifully dressed in one piece of yellow and brown that reached almost to its feet, with a bit left at the top to form a hood, out of which its pert face peeped impudently; oho, so they came in their Sunday clothes. He drew so near that he could hear it cooing: thought itself as good as upstairs, did it!

He bounced upon her sharply, thinking to carry all with a high hand. "Out you go!" he cried, with the action of one heaving coals.

She whisked round, and, "Oo boy or oo
girl?" she inquired, puzzled by his dress.

"None of your cheek!" roared insulted
manhood.

"Oo boy," she said, decisively.

With the effrontery of them when they are
young, she made room for him on her step, but
he declined the invitation, knowing that her
design was to skip up the stair the moment he
was off his guard.

"You don't needn't think as we'll have you,"
he announced, firmly.   "You had best go away
to—go to—"   His imagination failed him.
"You had best go back," he said.

She did not budge, however, and his next
attempt was craftier.   "My mother," he assured
her, "ain't living here now;" but mother was a
new word to the girl, and she asked gleefully,
"Oo have mother?" expecting him to produce
it from his pocket.   To coax him to give her a
sight of it she said, plaintively, "Me no have
mother."

"You won't not get mine," replied Tommy
doggedly.

She pretended not to understand what was
troubling him, and it passed through his head
that she had to wait there till the doctor came
down for her.   He might come at any moment.

A boy does not put his hand into his pocket
until every other means of gaining his end has
failed, but to that extremity had Tommy now
come.   For months his only splendid possession
had been a penny despised by trade because of
a large round hole in it, as if (to quote Shovel)

some previous owner had cut a farthing out of it. To tell the escapades of this penny (there are no adventurers like coin of the realm) would be one way of exhibiting Tommy to the curious, but it would be a hardhearted way. At present the penny was doubly dear to him, having been long lost and lately found. In a noble moment he had dropped it into a charity box hanging forlorn against the wall of a shop, where it lay very lonely by itself, so that when Tommy was that way he could hear it respond if he shook the box, as acquaintances give each other the time of day in passing. Thus at comparatively small outlay did he spread his benevolence over weeks and feel a glow therefrom, until the glow went, when he and Shovel recaptured the penny with a thread and a bent pin.

This treasure he sadly presented to the girl, and she accepted it with glee, putting it on her finger, as if it were a ring; but instead of saying that she would go now she asked him coolly,

" Oo know tories ? "

" Stories ! " he exclaimed, " I'll—I'll tell you about Thrums," and was about to do it for love, but stopped in time. " This ain't a good stair for stories," he said, cunningly. " I can't not tell stories on this stair, but I—I know a good stair for stories."

The ninny of a girl was completely hood-winked; and see, there they go, each with a hand in the muff, the one leering, oh, so tri-umphantly; the other trusting and gleeful. There was an exuberance of vitality about her as if she lived too quickly in her gladness, which

you may remember in some child who visited
the earth for but a little while.

How superbly Tommy had done it! It had
been another keen brain pitted against his, and
at first he was not winning. Then up came
Thrums, and — But the thing has happened
before; in a word, Blücher. Nevertheless,
Tommy just managed it, for he got the girl out
of the street and on to another stair no more
than in time to escape a ragged rabble, headed
by Shovel, who, finding their quarry gone, turned
on their leader viciously, and had gloomy views
of life till his cap was kicked down a sewer,
which made the world bright again.

Of the tales told by Tommy that day in
words Scotch and cockney, of Thrums, home of
heroes and the arts, where the lamps are lit by a
magician called Leerie-leerie-licht-the-lamps (but
he is also friendly, and you can fling stones at
him), and the merest children are allowed to set
the spinning-wheels a-whirling, and dagont is
the swear, and the stairs are so fine that the
houses wear them outside for show, and you drop
a pail at the end of a rope down a hole, and
sometimes it comes up full of water, and sometimes full of fairies—of these and other wonders,
if you would know, ask not a dull historian, nor
even go to Thrums, but to those rather who
have been boys and girls there and now are
exiles. Such a one Tommy knows, an unhappy
woman, foolish, not very lovable, flung like a
stone out of the red quarry upon a land where it
cannot grip, and tearing her heart for a sight of
the home she shall see no more. From her

Tommy had his pictures, and he coloured them rarely.

Never before had he such a listener. " Oh, dagont, dagont!" he would cry in ecstasy over these fair scenes, and she, awed or gurgling with mirth according to the nature of the last, demanded " 'Nother, 'nother!" whereat he remembered who and what she was, and showing her a morsel of the new one, drew her to more distant parts, until they were so far from his street that he thought she would never be able to find the way back.

His intention had been, on reaching such a spot, to desert her promptly, but she gave him her hand in the muff so confidingly that against his judgment he fell a-pitying the trustful mite who was wandering the world in search of a mother, and so easily diddled on the whole that the chances were against her finding one before morning. Almost unconsciously he began to look about him for a suitable one.

They were now in a street much nearer to his own home than the spurts from spot to spot had led him to suppose. It was new to him, but he recognised it as the acme of fashion by those two sure signs : railings with most of their spikes in place, and cards scored with the word " Apartments." He had discovered such streets as this before when in Shovel's company, and they had watched the toffs go out and in, and it was a lordly sight, for first the toff waggled a rail that was loose at the top and then a girl, called the servant, peeped at him from below, and then he pulled the rail again, and then the door opened from the inside, and you had a glimpse of wonder-land with a place for hanging hats on. He had not contemplated doing anything so handsome for the girl as this, but why should he not establish her here? There were many possible mothers in view, and thrilling with a sense of his generosity he had almost fixed on one, but mistrusted the glint in her eye, and on another when she saved herself by tripping and showing an undarned heel.

He was still of an open mind when the girl of a sudden cried gleefully, " Ma-ma, ma-ma ! " and pointed, with her muff, across the street. The word was as meaningless to Tommy as mother had been to her, but he saw that she was drawing his attention to a woman some thirty yards away.

"Man—man ! " he echoed, chiding her ignorance ; "no, no, you blether, that ain't a man, that's a woman ; that's woman—woman."

" Ooman—ooman," the girl repeated, docilely, but when she looked again, " Ma-ma, ma-ma," she insisted, and this was Tommy's first lesson that however young you catch them they will never listen to reason.

She seemed of a mind to trip off to this woman, and as long as his own mother was safe, it did not greatly matter to Tommy whom she chose ; but if it was this one, she was going the wrong way about it. You cannot snap them up in the street.

The proper course was to track her to her house, which he proceeded to do, and his quarry, who was looking about her anxiously, as if she had lost something, gave him but a short chase. In the next street to the one in which they had first seen her, a street so like it that Tommy might have admired her for knowing the difference, she opened the door with a key and entered, shutting the door behind her. Odd to tell, the child had pointed to this door as the one she would stop at, which surprised Tommy very much.

On the steps he gave her his final instructions, and she dimpled and gurgled, obviously full of admiration for him, which was a thing he approved of, but he would have liked to see her a little more serious.

"That is the door. Well, then, I'll waggle the rail as makes the bell ring, and then I'll run."

That was all, and he wished she had not giggled most of the time. She was sniggering, as if she thought him a very funny boy, even when he rang the bell and bolted.

From a safe place he watched the opening of the door, and saw the frivolous thing lose a valuable second in waving the muff to him. "In you go!" he screamed beneath his breath. Then she entered and the door closed. He waited an hour, or two minutes, or thereabout, and she had not been ejected. Triumph!

With a drum beating inside him Tommy strutted home, where, alas! a boy was waiting to put his foot through it.

CHAPTER II.

BUT THE OTHER GETS IN.

To Tommy, a swaggerer, came Shovel sour-visaged; having now no cap of his own, he exchanged with Tommy, would also have bled the blooming mouth of him, but knew of a revenge that saves the knuckles; announced, with jeers and offensive finger exercise, that "it" had come.

Shovel was a liar. If he only knowed what Tommy knowed!

If Tommy only heard what Shovel had hearn!

Tommy was of opinion that Shovel hadn't not heard anything.

Shovel believed as Tommy didn't know nuthin.

Tommy wouldn't listen to what Shovel had heard.

Neither would Shovel listen to what Tommy knew.

If Shovel would tell what he had heard, Tommy would tell what he knew.

Well, then, Shovel had listened at the door, and heard it mewling.

Tommy knowed it well, and it never mewled.

How could Tommy know it?

'Cos he had been with it a long time.

Gosh! Why, it had only comed a minute ago.

This made Tommy uneasy, and he asked a leading question cunningly. A boy, wasn't it?

No, Shovel's old woman had been up helping to hold it, and she said it were a girl.

Shutting his mouth tightly, which was never natural to him, the startled Tommy mounted the stair, listened and was convinced. He did not enter his dishonoured home. He had no intention of ever entering it again. With one salt tear he renounced—a child, a mother.

On his way downstairs he was received by Shovel and party, who planted their arrows neatly. Kids cried steadily, he was told, for the first year. A boy one was bad enough, but a girl one was oh lawks. He must never again expect to get playing with blokes like what they was. Already she had got round his old gal who would care for him no more. What would they say about this in Thrums?

Shovel even insisted on returning him his cup, and, for some queer reason, this cut deepest. Tommy about to charge, with his head down, now walked away so quietly that Shovel, who could not help liking the funny little cuss, felt a twinge of remorse, and nearly followed him with a magnanimous offer: to treat him as if he were still respectable.

Tommy lay down on a distant stair, one of the very stairs where *she* had sat with him. Ladies, don't you dare to pity him now, for he won't stand it. Rage was what he felt, and a man in a rage (as you may know if you are

married) is only to be soothed by the sight of
all womankind in terror of him. But you may
look upon your handiwork, and gloat, an you
will, on the wreck you have made. A young
gentleman trusted one of you ; behold the result.
O! O! O! O! now do you understand why
we men cannot abide you?

If she had told him flat that his mother, and
his alone, she would have, and so there was an
end of it. Ah! catch them taking a straight
road. But to put on those airs of helplessness,
to wave him that gay good-by, and then the
moment his back was turned, to be off through
the air on—perhaps on her muff, to the home he
had thought to lure her from. In a word, to be
diddled by a girl when one flatters himself he is
diddling! S'death, a dashing fellow finds it
hard to bear. Nevertheless, he has to bear it,
for oh, Tommy, Tommy, 'tis the common lot
of man.

His hand sought his pocket for the penny
that had brought him comfort in dark hours
before now ; but, alack, she had deprived him
even of it. Never again should his pinkie
finger go through that warm hole, and at the
thought a sense of his forlornness choked him,
and he cried. You may pity him a little now.

Darkness came and hid him even from himself. He is not found again until a time of the
night that is not marked on ornamental clocks,
but has an hour to itself on the watch which a
hundred thousand or so of London women carry
in their breasts ; the hour when men steal home-
wards trickling at the mouth and drawing back

from their own shadows to the wives they once went a-maying with, or the mothers who had such travail at the bearing of them, as if for great ends. Out of this, the drunkard's hour, rose the wan face of Tommy, who had waked up somewhere clammy cold and quaking, and he was a very little boy, so he ran to his mother.

Such a shabby dark room it was, but it was home, such a weary worn woman in the bed, but he was her son, and she had been wringing her hands because he was so long in coming, and do you think he hurt her when he pressed his head on her poor breast, and do you think she grudged the heat his cold hands drew from her warm face? He squeezed her with a violence that put more heat into her blood than he took out of it.

And he was very considerate, too: not a word of reproach in him, though he knew very well what that bundle in the back of the bed was.

She guessed that he had heard the news and stayed away through jealousy of his sister, and by and by she said, with a faint smile, "I have a present for you, laddie." In the great world without, she used few Thrums words now; you would have known she was Scotch by her accent only, but when she and Tommy were together in that room, with the door shut, she always spoke as if her window still looked out on the bonny Marywellbrae. It is not really bonny, it is gey an' mean an' bleak, and you must not come to see it. It is just a steep wind-swept street, old and wrinkled, like your mother's face.

c

She had a present for him, she said, and Tommy replied, "I knows," with averted face.

"Such a bonny thing."

"Bonny enough," he said bitterly.

"Look at her, laddie."

But he shrank from the ordeal, crying, "No, no, keep her covered up!"

The little traitor seemed to be asleep, and so he ventured to say, eagerly, "It wouldn't not take long to carry all our things to another house, would it? Me and Shovel could near do it ourselves."

"And that's God's truth," the woman said, with a look round the room. "But what for should we do that?"

"Do you no see, mother?" he whispered excitedly. "Then you and me could slip away, and—and leave her—in the press."

The feeble smile with which his mother received this he interpreted thus, "Wherever we go'd to she would be there before us."

"The little besom!" he cried helplessly.

His mother saw that mischievous boys had been mounting him on his horse, which needed only one slap to make it go a mile; but she was a spiritless woman, and replied indifferently, "You're a funny litlin."

Presently a dry sob broke from her, and thinking the child was the cause, soft-hearted Tommy said, "It can't not be helped, mother; don't cry, mother, I'm fond on yer yet, mother; I—I took her away. I found another woman— but she would come."

"She's God's gift, man," his mother said,

but she added, in a different tone, "Ay, but he
hasna sent her keep."

"God's gift!" Tommy shuddered, but he
said sourly, "I wish he would take her back.
Do you wish that, too, mother?"

The weary woman almost said she did, but
her arms—they gripped the baby as if frightened that he had sent for it. Jealous Tommy,
suddenly deprived of his mother's hand, cried,
"It's true what Shovel says, you don't not love
me never again; you jest loves that little
limmer!"

"Na, na," the mother answered, passionate
at last, "she can never be to me what you hae
been, my laddie, for you came to me when my
hame was in hell, and we tholed it thegither,
you and me."

This bewildered though it comforted him.
He thought his mother might be speaking about
the room in which they had lived until six
months ago, when his father was put into the
black box, but when he asked her if this were so,
she told him to sleep, for she was dog tired.
She always evaded him in this way when he
questioned her about his past, but at times his
mind would wander backwards unbidden to
those distant days, and then he saw flitting
dimly through them the elusive form of a child.
He knew it was himself, and for moments he
could see it clearly, but when he moved a step
nearer it was not there. So does the child we
once were play hide-and-seek with us among the
mists of infancy, until one day he trips and falls
into the daylight. Then we seize him, and

c 2

with that touch we two are one. It is the birth of self-consciousness.

Hitherto he had slept at the back of his mother's bed, but to-night she could not have him there, the place being occupied, and rather sulkily he consented to lie crosswise at her feet, undressing by the feeble fire and taking care, as he got into bed, not to look at the usurper. His mother watched him furtively, and was relieved to read in his face that he had no recollection of ever having slept at the foot of a bed before. But soon after he fell asleep he awoke, and was afraid to move lest his father should kick him. He opened his eyes stealthily, and this was neither the room nor the bed he had expected to see.

The floor was bare save for a sheepskin beside the bed. Tommy always stood on the sheepskin while he was dressing because it was warm to the feet, though risky, as your toes sometimes caught in knots in it. There was a deal table in the middle of the floor with some dirty crockery on it and a kettle that would leave a mark, but they had been left there by Shovel's old girl, for Mrs. Sandys usually kept her house clean. The chairs were of the commonest, and the press door would not remain shut unless you stuck a knife between its halves; but there was a gay blue wardrobe, spotted white where Tommy's mother had scraped off the mud that once bespattered it during a lengthy sojourn at the door of a shop ; and on the mantelpiece was a clock in a little brown and yellow house, and on the clock a Bible that had been in

Thrums. But what Tommy was proudest of
was his mother's kist, to which the chests of
Londoners are not to be compared, though like
it in appearance. On the inside of the lid of
this kist was pasted, after a Thrums custom,
something that his mother called her marriage
lines, which she forced Shovel's mother to come
up and look at one day, when that lady had
made an innuendo Tommy did not understand,
and Shovel's mother had looked, and though
she could not read, was convinced, knowing
them by the shape.

Tommy lay at the foot of the bed looking at
this room, which was his home now, and trying
to think of the other one, and by and by the fire
helped him by falling to ashes, when darkness
came in, and packing the furniture in grotesque
cloths, removed it piece by piece, all but the
clock. Then the room took a new shape. The
fireplace was over there instead of here, the torn
yellow blind gave way to one made of spars of
green wood, that were bunched up at one side,
like a lady out for a walk. On a round table
there was a beautiful blue cloth, with very few
gravy marks, and here a man ate beef when a
woman and a boy ate bread, and near the fire
was the man's big soft chair, out of which you
could pull hairs, just as if it were Shovel's sister.

Of this man who was his father he could get
no hold. He could feel his presence, but never
see him. Yet he had a face. It sometimes
pressed Tommy's face against it in order to hurt
him, which it could do, being all short needles
at the chin.

Once in those days Tommy and his mother
ran away and hid from someone. He did not
know from whom nor for how long, though it
was but for a week, and it left only two impressions on his mind, the one that he often asked,
" Is this starving now, mother ? " the other that
before turning a corner she always peered round
it fearfully. Then they went back again to the
man and he laughed when he saw them, but did
not take his feet off the mantelpiece. There
came a time when the man was always in bed,
but still Tommy could not see his face. What
he did see was the man's clothes lying on the
large chair just as he had placed them there
when he undressed for the last time. The black
coat and worsted waistcoat which he could take
off together were on the seat, and the light
trousers hung over the side, the legs on the
hearthrug, with the red socks still sticking in
them : a man without a body.

But the boy had one vivid recollection, of
how his mother received the news of his father's
death. An old man with a white beard and
gentle ways, who often came to give the invalid
physic, was standing at the bedside, and Tommy
and his mother were sitting on the fender. The
old man came to her and said, " It is all over,"
and put her softly into the big chair. She
covered her face with her hands, and he must
have. thought she was crying, for he tried to
comfort her. But as soon as he was gone she
rose, with such a queer face, and went on tiptoe to
the bed, and looked intently at her husband, and
then she clapped her hands joyously three times.

At last Tommy fell asleep with his mouth open, which is the most important thing that has been told of him as yet, and while he slept day came and restored the furniture that night had stolen. But when the boy woke he did not even notice the change; his brain traversed the hours it had lost since he lay down as quickly as you may put on a stopped clock, and with his first tick he was thinking of nothing but the deceiver in the back of the bed. He raised his head, but could only see that she had crawled under the coverlet to escape his wrath. His mother was asleep. Tommy sat up and peeped over the edge of the bed, then he let his eyes wander round the room; he was looking for the girl's clothes, but they were nowhere to be seen. It is distressing to have to tell that what was in his mind was merely the recovery of his penny. Perhaps as they were Sunday clothes she had hung them up in the wardrobe? He slipped on to the floor and crossed to the wardrobe, but not even the muff could he find. Had she been tired, and gone to bed in them? Very softly he crawled over his mother, and pulling the coverlet off the child's face, got the great shock of his childhood.

It was another one!

CHAPTER III.

SHOWING HOW TOMMY WAS SUDDENLY TRANSFORMED INTO A YOUNG GENTLEMAN.

IT would have fared ill with Mrs. Sandys now had her standoffishness to her neighbours been repaid in the same coin, but they were full of sympathy, especially Shovel's old girl, from whom she had often drawn back offensively on the stair, but who nevertheless waddled up several times a day with savoury messes, explaining, when Mrs. Sandys sniffed, that it was not the tapiocar but merely the cup that smelt of gin. When Tommy returned the cups she noticed not only that they were suspiciously clean, but that minute particles of the mess were adhering to his nose and chin (perched there like shipwrecked mariners on a rock, just out of reach of the devouring element), and after this discovery she brought two cupfuls at a time. She was an Irishwoman who could have led the House of Commons, and in walking she seldom raised her carpet shoes from the ground, perhaps because of her weight, for she had an expansive figure that bulged in all directions, and there were always bits of her here and there that she had forgotten to lace. Round the corner was a delightful eating-house, through whose window you were allowed to gaze at the great sweating dumplings, and Tommy thought

Shovel's mother was rather like a dumpling that
had not been a complete success. If he ever
knew her name he forgot it. Shovel, who
probably had another name also, called her his
old girl or his old woman or his old lady, and it
was a sight to see her chasing him across the
street when she was in liquor, and boastful was
Shovel of the way she could lay on, and he was
partial to her too ; and once when she was giving
it to him pretty strong with the tongs, his
father (who followed many professions, among
them that of finding lost dogs) had struck her
and told her to drop it, and then Shovel sauced
his father for interfering, saying she should lick
him as long as she blooming well liked, which
made his father go for him with a dog-collar ;
and that was how Shovel lost his eye.

For reasons less unselfish than his old girl's
Shovel also was willing to make up to Tommy
at this humiliating time. It might be said of
these two boys that Shovel knew everything but
Tommy knew other things, and as the other
things are best worth hearing of, Shovel liked
to listen to them, even when they were about
Thrums, as they usually were. The very first
time Tommy told him of the wondrous spot,
Shovel had drawn a great breath, and said,
thoughtfully :

" I allers knowed as there were sich a beauty
place, but I didn't jest know its name."

" How could yer know ? " Tommy asked
jealously.

" I ain't sure," said Shovel, " p'raps I
dreamed on it."

"That's it," Tommy cried. "I tell yer, everybody dreams on it!" and Tommy was right; everybody dreams of it, though not all call it Thrums.

On the whole, then, the coming of the kid, who turned out to be called Elspeth, did not ostracise Tommy, but he wished that he had let the other girl in, for he never doubted that her admittance would have kept this one out. He told neither his mother nor his friend of the other girl, fearing that his mother would be angry with him when she learned what she had missed, and that Shovel would crow over his blundering, but occasionally he took a side glance at the victorious infant, and a poorer affair, he thought, he had never set eyes on. Sometimes it was she who looked at him, and then her chuckle of triumph was hard to bear. As long as his mother was there, however, he endured in silence, but the first day she went out in a vain search for work (it is about as difficult to get washing as to get into the Cabinet), he gave the infant a piece of his mind, poking up her head with a stick so that she was bound to listen.

"You thinks as it was clever on you, does yer? Oh, if I had been on the stair!

"You needn't not try to get round me. I likes the other one five times better; yes, three times better.

"Thievey, thievey, thief, that's her place you is lying in. What?

"If you puts out your tongue at me again—! What do yer say?

"She was twice bigger than you. You ain't
got no hair, nor yet no teeth. You're the
littlest I ever seed. Eh? Don't not speak
then, sulks!"

Prudence had kept him away from the other
girl, but he was feeling a great want: someone
to applaud him. When we grow older we call
it sympathy. How Reddy (as he called her
because she had beautiful red-brown hair) had
appreciated him! She had a way he liked of
opening her eyes very wide when she looked at
him. Oh, what a difference from that thing in
the back of the bed!

Not the mere selfish desire to see her again,
however, would take him in quest of Reddy.
He was one of those superior characters, was
Tommy, who got his pleasure in giving it, and
therefore gave it. Now, Reddy was a worthy
girl. In suspecting her of overreaching him he
had maligned her: she had taken what he offered,
and been thankful. It was fitting that he
should give her a treat: let her see him again.

His mother was at last re-engaged by her
old employers, her supplanter having proved
unsatisfactory, and as the work lay in a distant
street, she usually took the kid with her, thus
leaving no one to spy on Tommy's movements.
Reddy's reward for not playing him false, however, did not reach her as soon as doubtless she
would have liked, because the first two or three
times he saw her she was walking with the lady
of his choice, and of course he was not such a
fool as to show himself. But he walked behind
them and noted with satisfaction that the lady

seemed to be reconciled to her lot and inclined to let bygones be bygones; when at length Reddy and her patron met, Tommy thought this a good sign too, that Ma-ma (as she would call the lady) had told her not to go farther away than the lamp-post, lest she should get lost again. So evidently she had got lost once already, and the lady had been sorry. He asked Reddy many shrewd questions about how Mama treated her, and if she got the top of the Sunday egg and had the licking of the pan and wore flannel underneath and slept at the back; and the more he inquired, the more clearly he saw that he had got her one of the right kind.

Tommy arranged with her that she should always be on the outlook for him at the window, and he would come sometimes, and after that they met frequently; and she proved a credit to him, gurgling with mirth at his tales of Thrums, and pinching him when he had finished, to make sure that he was really made just like common human beings. He was a thin, pale boy, while she looked like a baby rose full blown in a night because her time was short; and his movements were sluggish, but if she was not walking she must be dancing, and sometimes when there were few people in the street, the little armful of delight that she was jumped up and down like a ball, while Tommy kept the time, singing "Thrummy, Thrummy, Thrum Thrum Thrummy." They must have seemed a quaint pair to the lady as she sat at her window watching them and beckoning to Tommy to come in.

One day he went in, but only because she had come up behind and taken his hand before he could run. Then did Tommy quake, for he knew from Reddy how the day after the mother-making episode Ma-ma and she had sought in vain for his door, and he saw that the object had been to call down curses on his head. So that head was hanging limply now.

You think that Tommy is to be worsted at last, but don't be too sure; you just wait and see. Ma-ma and Reddy (who was clucking rather heartlessly) first took him into a room prettier even than the one he had lived in long ago (but there was no bed in it), and then, because someone they were in search of was not there, into another room without a bed (where on earth did they sleep?) whose walls were lined with books. Never having seen rows of books before except on sale in the streets, Tommy at once looked about him for the barrow. The table was strewn with sheets of paper of the size that they roll a quarter of butter in, and it was an amazing thick table, a solid square of wood, save for a narrow lane down the centre for the man to put his legs in—if he had legs, which unfortunately there was reason to doubt. He was a formidable man, whose beard licked the table while he wrote, and he wore something like a brown blanket, with a rope tied round it at the middle. Even more uncanny than himself were three busts on a shelf, which Tommy took to be deaders, and he feared the blanket might blow open and show that the man also ended at the waist. But he did not, for presently he turned round to see who had come in (the seat of his chair turning with him in the most startling way), and then Tommy was relieved to notice two big feet far away at the end of him.

"This is the boy, dear," the lady said. "I had to bring him in by force."

Tommy raised his arm instinctively to protect his face, this being the kind of man who could hit hard. But presently he was confused, and also, alas, leering a little. You may remember that Reddy had told him she must not go beyond the lamp-post, lest she should be lost again. She had given him no details of the adventure, but he learned now from Ma-ma and Papa (the man's name was Papa) that she had strayed when Ma-ma was in a shop and that some good kind boy had found her and brought her home; and what do you say to this, they thought Tommy was that boy! In his amazement he very nearly blurted out that he was the other boy, but just then the lady asked Papa if he had a shilling, and this abruptly closed Tommy's mouth. Ever afterwards he remembered Papa as the man that was not sure whether he had a shilling until he felt his pockets—a new kind of mortal to Tommy, who grabbed the shilling when it was offered to him, and then looked at Reddy imploringly, he was so afraid she would tell. But she behaved splendidly, and never even shook her head at him. After this, as hardly need be told, his one desire was to get out of the house with his shilling before they discovered their mistake, and it was well that they were unsuspicious people, for he was making strange hissing sounds in his throat, the result of trying hard to keep his sniggers under control.

There were many ways in which Tommy could have disposed of his shilling. He might have been a good boy and returned it next day to Papa. He might have given Reddy half of it for not telling. It could have carried him over the winter. He might have stalked with it into the shop where the greasy puddings were and come rolling out hours afterwards. Some of these schemes did cross his little mind, but he decided to spend the whole shilling on a present to his mother, and it was to be something useful. He devoted much thought to what she was most in need of, and at last he bought her a coloured picture of Lord Byron swimming the Hellespont.

He told her that he got his shilling from two toffs for playing with a little girl, and the explanation satisfied her; but she could have cried at the waste of the money, which would have been such a God-send to her. He cried altogether, however, at the sight of her face, having expected it to look so pleased, and then she told him, with caresses, that the picture was the one thing she had been longing for ever since she came to London. How had he known this, she asked, and he clapped his hands gleefully, and said he just knowed when he saw it in the shop window.

"It was noble of you," she said, "to spend all your siller on me."

"Wasn't it, mother?" he crowed, "I'm
thinking there ain't many as noble as I is!"

He did not say why he had been so good to
her, but it was because she had written no
letters to Thrums since the intrusion of Elspeth;
a strange reason for a boy whose greatest glory
at one time had been to sit on the fender and
exultingly watch his mother write down words
that would be read aloud in the wonderful place.
She was a long time in writing a letter, but that
only made the whole evening romantic, and he
found an arduous employment in keeping his
tongue wet in preparation for the licking of the
stamp.

But she could not write to the Thrums folk
now without telling them of Elspeth, who was at
present sleeping the sleep of the shameless in
the hollow of the bed, and so for his sake,
Tommy thought, she meant to write no more.
For his sake, mark you, not for her own. She
had often told him that some day he should go
to Thrums, but not with her; she would be far
away from him then in a dark place she was awid
to be lying in. Thus it seemed to Tommy that
she denied herself the pleasure of writing to
Thrums lest the sorry news of Elspeth's advent
should spoil his reception when he went north.

So grateful Tommy gave her the picture,
hoping that it would fill the void. But it did
not. She put it on the mantelpiece so that she
might just sit and look at it, she said, and he
grinned at it from every part of the room, but
when he returned to her, he saw that she was
neither looking at it nor thinking of it. She

was looking straight before her, and sometimes
her lips twitched, and then she drew them into
her mouth to keep them still. It is a kind of
dry weeping that sometimes comes to miserable
ones when their minds stray into the happy past,
and Tommy sat and watched her silently for a
long time, never doubting that the cause of all
her woe was that she could not write to
Thrums.

He had seldom seen tears on his mother's
face, but he saw one now. They had been reluctant to come for many a day, and this one
formed itself beneath her eye and sat there like
a blob of blood.

His own began to come more freely. But
she needn't not expect him to tell her to write
nor to say that he didn't care what Thrums
thought of him so long as she was happy.

The tear rolled down his mother's thin cheek
and fell on the grey shawl that had come from
Thrums.

She did not hear her boy as he dragged a
chair to the press and standing on it got something down from the top shelf. She had forgotten him, and she started when presently the
pen was slipped into her hand and Tommy said,
" You can do it, mother, I wants yer to do it,
mother, I won't not greet, mother ! "

When she saw what he wanted her to do she
patted his face approvingly, but without realising
the extent of his sacrifice. She knew that he
had some maggot in his head that made him re-
gard Elspeth as a sore on the family honour, but
ascribing his views to jealousy she had never

D

tried seriously to change them. Her main reason for sending no news to Thrums of late had been but the cost of a stamp, though she was also a little conscience-stricken at the kind of letters she wrote, and the sight of the materials lying ready for her proved sufficient to draw her to the table.

"Is it to your grandmother you is writing the letter?" Tommy asked, for her grandmother had brought Mrs. Sandys up and was her only surviving relative. This was all Tommy knew of his mother's life in Thrums, though she had told him much about other Thrums folk, and not till long afterwards did he see that there must be something queer about herself, which she was hiding from him.

This letter was not for her granny, however, and Tommy asked next, "Is it to Aaron Latta?" which so startled her that she dropped the pen.

"Whaur heard you that name?" she said sharply. "I never spoke it to you."

"I've heard you saying it when you was sleeping, mother."

"Did I say onything but the name? Quick, tell me."

"You said, 'Oh, Aaron Latta, oh, Aaron, little did we think, Aaron,' and things like that. Are you angry with me, mother?"

"No," she said, relieved, but it was some time before the desire to write came back to her. Then she told him "The letter is to a woman that was gey cruel to me," adding, with a complacent pursing of her lips, the curious remark, "That's the kind I like to write to best."

The pen went scrape, scrape, but Tommy did not weary, though he often sighed, because his mother would never read aloud to him what she wrote. The Thrums people never answered her letters, for the reason, she said, that those she wrote to could not write, which seemed to simple Tommy to be a sufficient explanation. So he had never heard the inside of a letter talking, though a postman lived in the house, and even Shovel's old girl got letters; once when her uncle died she got a telegram, which Shovel proudly wheeled up and down the street in a barrow, other blokes keeping guard at the side. To give a letter to a woman who had been cruel to you struck Tommy as the height of nobility.

"She'll be uplifted when she gets it!" he cried.

"She'll be mad when she gets it," answered his mother, without looking up.

This was the letter :—

"My dear Esther, I send you these few scrapes to let you see I have not forgot you, though my way is now grand by yours. A spleet new black silk, Esther, being the second in a twelvemonth, as I'm a living woman. The other is no none tashed yet, but my gudeman fair insisted on buying a new one, for says he, 'Rich folk like us can afford to be mislaird, and nothing's ower braw for my bonny Jean.' Tell Aaron Latta that. When I'm sailing in my silks, Esther, I sometimes picture you turning your wincey again, for I'se uphaud that's all the new frock you've ha'en the year. I dinna want to

p 2

gie you a scunner of your man, Esther, more by
token they said if your mither had not took him
in hand you would never have kent the colour of
his nightcap, but when you are wraxing ower
your kail-pot in a plot of heat, just picture me
ringing the bell for my servant, and saying, with
a wave of my hand, 'Servant, lay the dinner.'
And ony bonny afternoon when your man is
cleaning out stables and you're at the tub in a
short gown, picture my man taking me and the
children out a ride in a carriage, and I sair doubt
your bairns was never in nothing more genteel
than a coal cart. For bairns is yours, Esther,
and children is mine, and that's a burn without
a brig till't.

"Deary me, Esther, what with one thing
and another, namely, buying a sofa, thirty
shillings as I'm a sinner, I have forgot to tell
you about my second, and it's a girl this time,
my man saying he would like a change. We
have christened her Elspeth after my grand-
mamma, and if my auld granny's aye living, you
can tell her that's her. My man is terribly
windy of his two beautiful children, but he says
he would have been the happiest gentleman in
London though he had just had me, and really
his fondness for me, it cows, Esther, sitting aside
me on the bed, two pounds without the blankets,
about the time Elspeth was born, and feeding
me with the fat of the land, namely, tapiocas and
sherry wine. Tell Aaron Latta that.

"I pity you from the bottom of my heart,
Esther, for having to bide in Thrums, but you
have never seen no better, your man having

neither the siller nor the desire to take you
jaunts, and I'm thinking that is just as well, for
if you saw how the like of me lives it might
disgust you with your own bit house. I often
laugh, Esther, to think that I was once like you,
and looked upon Thrums as a bonny place. How
is the old hole? My son makes grand sport of
the onfortunate bairns as has to bide in Thrums,
and I see him doing it the now to his favourite
companion, which is a young gentleman of ladylike manners, as bides in our terrace. So no
more at present, for my man is sitting ganting
for my society, and I daresay yours is crying to
you to darn his old socks. Mind and tell Aaron
Latta."

This letter was posted next day by Tommy,
with the assistance of Shovel, who seems to have
been the young gentleman of ladylike manners
referred to in the text.

CHAPTER IV.

THE END OF AN IDYLL.

TOMMY never saw Reddy again owing to a fright he got about this time, for which she was really to blame, though a woman who lived in his house was the instrument.

It is, perhaps, idle to attempt a summary of those who lived in that house, as one at least will be off, and another in his place, while we are giving them a line apiece. They were usually this kind who lived through the wall from Mrs. Sandys, but beneath her were the two rooms of Hankey, the postman, and his lodger, the dreariest of middle-aged clerks, except when telling wistfully of his ambition, which was to get out of the tea department into the coffee department, where there is an easier way of counting up the figures. Shovel and family were also on this floor, and in the rooms under them was a newly married couple. When the husband was away at his work, his wife would make some change in the furniture, taking the picture from this wall, for instance, and hanging it on that wall, or wheeling the funny chair she had lain in, before she could walk without a crutch, to the other side of the fireplace, or putting a skirt of yellow paper round the flower pot, and when he returned he always jumped back in wonder and exclaimed: "What an

immense improvement!" These two were so
fond of one another that Tommy asked them
the reason, and they gave it by pointing to the
chair with the wheels, which seemed to him to
be no reason at all. What was this young
husband's trade Tommy never knew, but he was
the only prettily dressed man in the house, and
he could be heard roaring in his sleep, "*And
the next article?*" The meanest-looking man
lived next door to him. Every morning this
man put on a clean white shirt, which sounds
like a splendid beginning, but his other clothes
were of the seediest, and he came and went
shivering, raising his shoulders to his ears and
spreading his hands over his chest as if anxious
to hide his shirt rather than to display it. He
and the happy husband were nicknamed Before
and After, they were so like the pictorial adver-
tisement of Man before and after he has tried
Someone's lozenges. But it is rash to judge by
outsides; Tommy and Shovel one day tracked
Before to his place of business, and it proved to
be a palatial eating-house, long, narrow, padded
with red cushions; through the door they saw
the once despised, now in beautiful black clothes,
the waistcoat a mere nothing, as if to give his
shirt a chance at last, a towel over his arm, and
to and fro he darted, saying, "Yessirquitesosir"
to the toffs on the seats, shouting "Twovegonebeef
—onebeeronetartinahurry" to someone invisible,
and pocketing twopences all day long, just like a
lord. On the same floor as Before and After
lived the large family of little Pikes, who
quarrelled at night for the middle place in the

bed, and then chips of ceiling fell into the room
below, tenant Jim Ricketts and parents, lodger
the young woman we have been trying all these
doors for. Her the police snapped up on a
charge that made Tommy want to hide himself
—child-desertion.

Shovel was the person best worth listening
to on the subject (observe him, the centre of half
a dozen boys), and at first he was for the defence,
being a great stickler for the rights of mothers.
But when the case against the girl leaked out,
she need not look to him for help. The police
had found the child in a basket down an area,
and being knowing ones they pinched it to
make it cry, and then they pretended to go
away. Soon the mother, who was watching
hard by to see if it fell into kind hands, stole to
her baby to comfort it, "and just as she were a
kissing on it and blubbering, the perlice copped
her."

"The slut!" said disgusted Shovel, "what
did she hang about for?" and in answer to a
trembling question from Tommy he replied
decisively, "Six months hard."

"Next case" was probably called immediately, but Tommy vanished, as if he had been
sentenced and removed to the cells.

Never again, unless he wanted six months
hard, must he go near Reddy's home, and so he
now frequently accompanied his mother to the
place where she worked. The little room had a
funny fireplace called a stove, on which his
mother made tea and the girls roasted chestnuts,
and it had no other ordinary furniture except a

long form. But the walls were mysterious.
Three of them were covered with long white
cloths, which went to the side when you tugged
them, and then you could see on rails dozens of
garments that looked like nightgowns. Beneath
the form were scores of little shoes, most of
them white or brown. In this house Tommy's
mother spent eight hours daily, but not all of
them in this room. When she arrived the first
thing she did was to put Elspeth on the floor,
because you cannot fall off a floor; then she
went upstairs with a bucket and a broom to a
large bare room, where she stayed so long that
Tommy nearly forgot what she was like.

While his mother was upstairs Tommy
would give Elspeth two or three shoes to eat to
keep her quiet, and then he played with the
others, pretending to be able to count them,
arranging them in designs, shooting them,
swimming among them, saying "bow-wow" at
them and then turning sharply to see who had
said it. Soon Elspeth dropped her shoes and
gazed in admiration at him, but more often than
not she laughed in the wrong place, and then he
said ironically: "Oh, in course I can't do
nothin'; jest let's see you doing of it, then,
cocky!"

By the time the girls began to arrive, singly
or in twos and threes, his mother was back in
the little room, making tea for herself or sewing
bits of them that had been torn as they stepped
out of a cab, or helping them to put on the
nightgowns, or pretending to listen pleasantly
to their chatter and hating them all the time.

There was every kind of them, gorgeous ones and shabby ones, old tired ones and dashing young ones, but whether they were the Honourable Mrs. Something or only Jane Anything, they all came to that room for the same purpose: to get a little gown and a pair of shoes. Then they went upstairs and danced to a stout little lady, called the Sylph, who bobbed about like a ball at the end of a piece of elastic. What Tommy never forgot was that while they danced the Sylph kept saying, "One, two three, four; one, two, three, four," which they did not seem to mind, but when she said "One, two, three, four, *picture!*" they all stopped and stood motionless, though it might be with one foot as high as their head and their arms stretched out towards the floor, as if they had suddenly seen a halfpenny there.

In the waiting-room, how they joked and pirouetted and gossiped, and hugged and scorned each other, and what slang they spoke and how pretty they often looked next moment, and how they denounced the one that had just gone out as a cat with whom you could not get in a word edgeways; and oh, how prompt they were to give a slice of their earnings to any "cat" who was hard up! But still, they said, she had talent, but no genius. How they pitied people without genius!

Have you ever tasted an encore or a reception? Tommy never had his teeth in one, but he heard much about them in that room, and concluded that they were some sort of cake. It was not the girls who danced in groups, but

those who danced alone, that spoke of their
encores and receptions, and sometimes they had
got them last night, sometimes years ago. Two
girls met in the room, one of whom had stolen
the other's reception, and—but it was too
dreadful to write about. Most of them carried
newspaper cuttings in their purses and read them
aloud to the others, who would not listen.
Tommy listened, however, and as it was all
about how one house had risen at the girls and
they had brought another down, he thought
they led the most adventurous lives.

Occasionally they sent him out to buy news-
papers or chestnuts, and then he had to keep a
sharp eye on the police lest they knew about
Reddy. It was a point of honour with all the
boys he knew to pretend that the policeman was
after them. To gull the policeman into thinking
all was well they blackened their faces and wore
their jackets inside out; their occupation was a
constant state of readiness to fly from him, and
when he tramped out of sight, unconscious of
their existence, they emerged from dark places
and spoke in exultant whispers. Tommy had
been proud to join them, but he now resented
their going on in this way; he felt that he
alone had the right to fly from the law. And
once at least while he was flying something
happened to him that he was to remember
better, far better, than his mother's face.

What set him running on this occasion (he
had been sent out to get one of the girls' shoes
soled) was the grandest sight to be seen in
London—an endless row of policemen walking

in single file, all with the right leg in the air at the same time, then the left leg. Seeing at once that they were after him, Tommy ran, ran, ran until in turning a corner he found himself wedged between two legs. He was of just sufficient size to fill the aperture, but after a momentary lock he squeezed through, and they proved to be the gate into an enchanted land.

The magic began at once. "Dagont, you sacket!" cried some wizard.

A policeman's hand on his shoulder could not have taken the wind out of Tommy more quickly. In the act of starting a-running again he brought down his hind foot with a thud and stood stock still. Can anyone wonder? It was the Thrums tongue, and this the first time he had heard it except from his mother.

It was a dull day, and all the walls were dripping wet, this being the part of London where the fogs are kept. Many men and women were passing to and fro, and Tommy, with a wild exultation in his breast, peered up at the face of this one and that; but no, they were only ordinary people, and he played rub-a-dub with his feet on the pavement, so furious was he with them for moving on as if nothing had happened. Draw up, ye carters; pedestrians, stand still; London, silence for a moment, and let Tommy Sandys listen!

Being but a frail plant in the way of a flood, Tommy was rooted up and borne onward, but he did not feel the buffeting. In a passion of grief he dug his fists in his eyes, for the glory had been his for but a moment. It can be compared to nothing save the parcel (attached to a concealed string) which Shovel and he once placed on the stair for Billy Hankey to find, and then whipped away from him just as he had got it under his arm. But so near the crying, Tommy did not cry, for even while the tears were rushing to his aid he tripped on the step of a shop, and immediately, as if that had rung the magic bell again, a voice, a woman's voice this time, said shrilly, "Threepence ha'penny, and them jimply as big as a bantam's! Na, na, but I'll gi'e you five bawbees."

Tommy sat down flop on the step, feeling queer in the head. Was it—was it—was it Thrums? He knew he had been running a long time.

The woman, or fairy, or whatever you choose to call her, came out of the shop and had to push Tommy aside to get past. Oh, what a sweet foot to be kicked by. At the time, he thought she was dressed not unlike the women of his own stair, but this defect in his vision he mended afterward, as you may hear. Of course, he rose and trotted by her side like a dog, looking up at her as if she were a cathedral; but she mistook his awe for impudence and sent him sprawling, with the words, "Tak' that, you glowering partan!"

Do you think Tommy resented this? On the contrary, he screamed from where he lay, "Say it again! say it again!"

She was gone, however, but only, as it were, to let a window open, from which came the cry, "Davit, have you seen my man?"

A male fairy roared back from some invisible place, "He has gone yont to Petey's wi' the dambrod."

" I'll dambrod him ! " said the female fairy, and the window shut.

Tommy was now staggering like one intoxicated, but he had still some sense left him, and he walked up and down in front of this house, as if to take care of it. In the middle of the street some boys were very busy at a game, carts and lorries passing over them occasionally. They came to the pavement to play marbles, and then Tommy noticed that one of them wore what was probably a glengarry bonnet. Could he be a Thrums boy? At first he played in the stupid London way, but by and by he had to make a new ring, and he did it by whirling round on one foot. Tommy knew from his mother that it is only done in this way in Thrums. Oho! Oho!

By this time he was prancing round his discovery, saying, "I'm one, too—so am I— dagont, does yer hear? dagont!" which so alarmed the boy that he picked up his marble and fled, Tommy, of course, after him. Alas! he must have been some mischievous sprite, for he lured his pursuer back into London and then vanished, and Tommy, searching in vain for the enchanted street, found his own door instead.

His mother pooh-poohed his tale, though he described the street exactly as it struck him on reflection, and it bore a curious resemblance to the palace of Aladdin that Reddy had told him about, leaving his imagination to fill in the details, which it promptly did, with a square, a town-house, some outside stairs, and an auld licht kirk. There was no such street, however, his mother assured him; he had been dreaming. But if this were so, why was she so anxious to make him promise never to look for the place again?

He did go in search of it again, daily for a time, always keeping a look-out for bow-legs, and the moment he saw them, he dived recklessly between, hoping to come out into fairyland on the other side. For though he had lost the street, he knew that this was the way in.

Shovel had never heard of the street, nor had Bob. But Bob gave him something that almost made him forget it for a time. Bob was his favourite among the dancing girls, and she—or should it be he? The odd thing about these girls was that a number of them were really boys—or at least were boys at Christmas-time, which seemed to Tommy to be even stranger than if they had been boys all the year round. A friend of Bob's remarked to her one day, "You are to be a girl next winter, ain't you, Bob?" and Bob shook her head scornfully.

"Do you see any green in my eye, my dear?" she inquired.

Her friend did not look, but Tommy looked, and there was none. He assured her of this so earnestly that Bob fell in love with him on the spot, and chucked him under the chin, first with her thumb and then with her toe, which feat was duly reported to Shovel, who could do it by the end of the week.

Did Tommy, Bob wanted to know, still think her a mere woman?

No, he withdrew the charge, but—but——. She was wearing her outdoor garments, and he pointed to them. "Why does yer wear them, then?" he demanded.

"For the matter of that," she replied, pointing at his frock, "why do you wear them?" Whereupon Tommy began to cry.

"I ain't not got no right ones," he blubbered. Harum-scarum Bob, who was a trump, had him in her motherly arms immediately, and the upshot of it was that a blue suit she had worn when she was Sam Something changed owners. Mrs. Sandys "made it up," and that is how Tommy got into trousers.

Many contingencies were considered in the making, but the suit would fit Tommy by-and-by if he grew, or it shrunk, and they did not pass each other in the night. When proud Tommy first put on his suit the most unexpected shyness overcame him, and having set off vaingloriously he stuck on the stair and wanted to hide. Shovel, who had been having an argument with his old girl, came, all boastful bumps, to him, and Tommy just stood still with a self-conscious simper on his face. And Shovel, who could have damped him considerably, behaved in the most honourable manner, initiating him gravely into the higher life, much as you show the new member round your club.

It was very risky to go back to Reddy, whom he had not seen for many weeks: but in trousers! He could not help it. He only meant to walk

up-and-down her street, so that she might see
him from the window, and know that this splendid thing was he; but though he went several
times into the street, Reddy never came to the
window.

The reason he had to wait in vain at Reddy's
door was that she was dead; she had been dead
for quite a long time when Tommy came back to
look for her. You mothers who have lost your
babies, I should be a sorry knave were I to ask
you to cry now over the death of another
woman's child. Reddy had been lent to two
people for a very little while, just as your babies
were, and when the time was up she blew a kiss
to them and ran gleefully back to God, just as
your babies did. The gates of heaven are so
easily found when we are little, and they are
always standing open to let children wander in.

But though Reddy was gone away for ever,
mamma still lived in that house, and on a day
she opened the door to come out. Tommy was
standing there—she saw him there waiting for
Reddy. Dry-eyed this sorrowful woman had
heard the sentence pronounced, dry-eyed she
had followed the little coffin to its grave; tears
had not come even when, waking from illusive
dreams, she put out her hand in bed to a child
who was not there; but when she saw Tommy
waiting at the door for Reddy, who had been
dead for a month, her bosom moved and she
could cry again.

Those tears were sweet to her husband, and
it was he who took Tommy on his knee in the
room where the books were, and told him that

E

there was no Reddy now.   When Tommy knew
that Reddy was a deader he cried bitterly, and
the man said, very gently, " I am glad you were
so fond of her."

" 'Tain't that," Tommy answered with a
knuckle in his eye, " 'tain't that as makes me
cry."   He looked down at his trousers, and in a
fresh outburst of childish grief he wailed, " It's
them !"

Papa did not understand, but the boy explained.   "She can't not never see them now,"
he sobbed, "and I wants her to see them, and
they has pockets !"

It had come to the man unexpectedly.   He
put Tommy down almost roughly, and raised
his hand to his head as if he felt a sudden pain
there.

But Tommy, you know, was only a little
boy.

CHAPTER V.

THE GIRL WITH TWO MOTHERS.

ELSPETH at last did something to win Tommy's respect; she fell ill of an ailment called in Thrums the croop. When Tommy first heard his mother call it croop, he thought she was merely humouring Elspeth, and that it was nothing more distinguished than London whooping-cough, but on learning that it was genuine croop, he began to survey the ambitious little creature with a new interest.

This was well for Elspeth, as she had now to spend most of the day at home with him, their mother, whose health was failing through frequent attacks of bronchitis, being no longer able to carry her through the streets. Of course Elspeth took to repaying his attentions by loving him, and he soon suspected it, and then gloomily admitted it to himself, but never to Shovel. Being but an Englishman, Shovel saw no reason why relatives should conceal their affection for each other, but he played on this Scottish weakness of Tommy's with cruel enjoyment.

"She's fond on yer!" he would say severely.

"You's a liar."

"Gar long! I believe as you're fond on her!"

"You jest take care, Shovel."

"Ain't yer?"

E 2

"Na-o!"

"Will yer swear?"

"So I will swear."

"Let's hear yer."

"Dagont!"

So for a time the truth was kept hidden, and Shovel retired, casting aspersions, and offering to eat all the hair on Elspeth's head for a penny.

This hair was white at present, which made Tommy uneasy about her future, but on the whole he thought he might make something of her if she was only longer. Sometimes he stretched her on the floor, pulling her legs out straight, for she had a silly way of doubling them up, and then he measured her carefully with his mother's old boots. Her growth proved to be distressingly irregular, as one day she seemed to have grown an inch since last night, and then next day she had shrunk two inches.

After her day's work Mrs. Sandys was now so listless that, had not Tommy interfered, Elspeth would have been a backward child. Reddy had been able to walk from the first day, and so of course had he, but this little slow-coach's legs wobbled at the joints, like the blade of a knife without a spring. The question of questions was—How to keep her on end?

Tommy sat on the fender revolving this problem, his head resting on his hand: that favourite position of mighty intellects when about to be photographed. Elspeth lay on her stomach on the floor, gazing earnestly at him, as if she knew she was in his thoughts for some stupendous purpose. Thus the apple may have looked at Newton before it fell.

Hankey, the postman, compelled the flowers in his window to stand erect by tying them to sticks, so Tommy took two sticks from a bundle of fire-wood, and splicing Elspeth's legs to them, held her upright against the door with one hand. All he asked of her to-day was to remain in this position after he said "One, two, three, four, *picture!*" and withdrew his hand, but down she flopped every time, and he said, with scorn—

"You ain't got no genius: you has just talent."

But he had her in bed with the scratches nicely covered up before his mother came home.

He tried another plan with more success. Lost dogs, it may be remembered, had a habit of following Shovel's father, and he not only took the wanderers in, but taught them how to beg and shake hands and walk on two legs. Tommy had sometimes been present at these agreeable exercises, and being an inventive boy he——But as Elspeth was a nice girl, let it suffice to pause here and add shyly, that in time she could walk.

He also taught her to speak, and if you need to be told with what luscious word he enticed her into language you are sentenced to re-read the first pages of his life.

"Thrums," he would say persuasively, "Thrums, Thrums. You opens your mouth like this, and shuts it like this, and that's it." Yet when he had coaxed her thus for many days, what does she do but break her long silence with the word "Tommy!" The recoil knocked her over.

Soon afterward she brought down a bigger bird. No Londoner can say "Auld licht," and Tommy had often crowed over Shovel's "Ol likt." When the testing of Elspeth could be deferred no longer, he eyed her with the look a hen gives the green egg on which she has been sitting twenty days, but Elspeth triumphed, saying the words modestly even, as if nothing inside her told her she had that day done something which would have baffled Shakespeare, not to speak of most of the gentlemen who sit for Scotch constituencies.

"Reddy couldn't say it!" Tommy cried exultantly, and from that great hour he had no more fears for Elspeth.

Next the alphabet knocked for admission; and entered first M and P, which had prominence in the only poster visible from the window. Mrs. Sandys had taught Tommy his letters, but he had got into words by studying posters.

Elspeth being able now to make the perilous descent of the stairs, Tommy guided her through the streets (letting go hurriedly if Shovel hove in sight) and here she bagged new letters daily. With Catlings something, which is the best, she got into capital Cs; ys are found easily when you know where to look for them (they hang on behind); Xs are never found singly, but often three at a time; Q is so aristocratic that even Tommy had only heard of it—doubtless it was there, but indistinguishable among the masses, like a celebrity in a crowd; on the other hand, big *A* and little *e* were so dirt cheap, that these two scholars passed them with something like a sneer.

The printing-press is either the greatest blessing or the greatest curse of modern times, one sometimes forgets which. Elspeth's faith in it was absolute, and as it only spoke to her from placards, here was her religion, at the age of four:

" PRAY WITHOUT CEASING.

HAPPY ARE THEY WHO NEEDING KNOW THE PAINLESS POROUS PLASTER."

Of religion, Tommy had said many fine things to her, embellishments on the simple doctrine taught him by his mother before the miseries of this world made her indifferent to the next. But the meaning of " Pray without ceasing," Elspeth, who was God's child always, seemed to find out for herself, and it cured all her troubles. She prayed promptly for everyone she saw doing wrong, including Shovel, who occasionally had words with Tommy on the subject, and she not only prayed for her mother, but proposed to Tommy that they should buy her a porous plaster. Mrs. Sandys had been down with bronchitis again.

Tommy raised the monetary difficulty.

Elspeth knew where there was some money, and it was her very own.

Tommy knew where there was money, and it was his very own.

Elspeth would not tell how much she had, and it was twopence halfpenny.

Neither would Tommy tell, and it was two-pence.

Tommy would get a surprise on his birthday.

So would Elspeth get a surprise on her birthday.

Elspeth would not tell what the surprise was to be, and it was to be a gun.

Tommy also must remain mute, and it was to be a box of dominoes.

Elspeth did not want dominoes.

Tommy knew that, but he wanted them.

Elspeth discovered that guns cost fourpence, and dominoes threepence halfpenny; it seemed to her, therefore, that Tommy was defrauding her of a halfpenny.

Tommy liked her cheek. You got the dominoes for threepence halfpenny, but the price on the box is fivepence, so that Elspeth would really owe him a penny.

This led to an agonising scene, in which Elspeth wept while Tommy told her sternly about Reddy. It had become his custom to tell the tale of Reddy when Elspeth was obstreperous.

Then followed a scene in which Tommy called himself a scoundrel for frightening his dear Elspeth, and swore that he loved none but her. Result; reconciliation, and agreed, that instead of a gun and dominoes, they should buy a porous plaster. You know the shops where the plasters are to be obtained by great coloured bottles in their windows, and, as it was advisable to find the very best shop, Tommy and Elspeth in their wanderings came under the influence of the bottles, red, yellow, green, and blue, and

colour entered into their lives, giving them many
delicious thrills. These bottles are the first poem
known to the London child, and you chemists
who are beginning to do without them in your
windows should be told that it is a shame.

In the glamour, then, of the romantic
bottles walked Tommy and Elspeth hand in
hand, meeting so many novelties that they
might have spared a tear for the unfortunate
children who sit in nurseries surrounded by all
they ask for, and if the adventures of these
two frequently ended in the middle, they had
probably begun another while the sailor-suit
boy was still holding up his leg to let the
nurse put on his little sock. While they
wandered, they drew near unwittingly to the
enchanted street, to which the bottles are a
coloured way, and at last they were in it, but
Tommy recognised it not; he did not even feel
that he was near it, for there were no outside
stairs, no fairies strolling about; it was a short
street as shabby as his own.

But someone had shouted "Dinna haver,
lassie; you're blethering!"

Tommy whispered to Elspeth, "Be still,
don't speak," and he gripped her hand tighter
and stared at the speaker. He was a boy of
ten, dressed like a Londoner, and his companion
had disappeared. Tommy never doubting but
that he was the sprite of long ago, gripped him
by the sleeve. All the savings of Elspeth and
himself were in his pocket, and yielding to impulse, as was his way, he thrust the fivepence
halfpenny into James Gloag's hand. The new

millionaire gaped, but not at his patron, for the why and wherefore of this gift were trifles to James beside the tremendous fact that he had fivepence halfpenny. "Almichty me!" he cried, and bolted. Presently he returned, having deposited his money in a safe place, and his first remark was perhaps the meanest on record. He held out his hand and said greedily, "Have you ony mair?"

This, you feel certain, must have been the most important event of that evening, but, strange to say, it was not. Before Tommy could answer James's question, a woman in a shawl had pounced upon him and hurried him and Elspeth out of the street. She had been standing at a corner looking wistfully at the window blinds behind which folk from Thrums passed to and fro, hiding her face from people in the street, but gazing eagerly after them. It was Tommy's mother, whose first free act on coming to London had been to find out that street, and many a time since then she had skulked through it or watched it from dark places, never daring to disclose herself, but sometimes recognising familiar faces, sometimes hearing a few words in the old tongue that is harsh and ungracious to you, but was so sweet to her, and bearing them away with her beneath her shawl as if they were something warm to lay over her cold heart.

For a time she upbraided Tommy passionately for not keeping away from this street, but soon her hunger for news of Thrums overcame her prudence, and she consented to let him go back if he promised never to tell that his mother

came from Thrums. "And if onybody wants
to ken your name, say it's Tommy, but dinna let
on that it's Tommy Sandys."

"Elspeth," Tommy whispered that night,
"I'm near sure there's something queer about
my mother and me and you." But he did not
trouble himself with wondering what the something queer might be, so engrossed was he in
the new and exciting life that had suddenly
opened to him.

CHAPTER VI.

THE ENCHANTED STREET.

In Thrums Street, as it ought to have been called, herded at least one-half of the Thrums folk in London, and they formed a colony, of which the grocer at the corner sometimes said wrathfully that not a member would give sixpence for anything except Bibles or whisky. In the streets one could only tell they were not Londoners by their walk, the flagstones having no grip for their feet, or, if they had come south late in life, by their backs, which they carried at the angle on which webs are most easily supported. When mixing with the world they talked the English tongue, which came out of them as broad as if it had been squeezed through a mangle, but when the day's work was done it was only a few of the giddier striplings that remained Londoners. For the majority there was no raking the streets after diversion, they spent the hour or two before bed-time in reproducing the life of Thrums. Few of them knew much of London except the nearest way between this street and their work, and their most interesting visitor was a Presbyterian minister, most of whose congregation lived in much more fashionable parts, but they were almost exclusively servant girls, and when descending area steps to visit them he had been challenged often and jocularly by policemen, which perhaps was what gave him a subdued and furtive appearance.

The rooms were furnished mainly with articles bought in London, but these became as like Thrums dressers and seats as their owners could make them, old Petey, for instance, cutting the back off a chair because he felt most at home on stools. Drawers were used as baking-boards, pails turned into salt-buckets, floors were sanded and hearthstones ca'med, and the popular supper consisted of porter, hot water, and soaked bread, after every spoonful of which they groaned pleasantly, and stretched their legs. Sometimes they played at the dambrod, but more often they pulled down the blinds on London and talked of Thrums in their mother tongue. Nevertheless few of them wanted to return to it, and their favourite joke was the case of James Gloag's father, who being home-sick flung up his situation and took train for Thrums, but he was back in London in three weeks.

Tommy soon had the entry to these homes, and his first news of the inmates was unexpected. It was that they were always sleeping. In broad daylight he had seen Thrums men asleep on beds, and he was somewhat ashamed of them until he heard the excuse. A number of the men from Thrums were bakers, the first emigrant of this trade having drawn others after him, and they slept great part of the day to be able to work all night in a cellar, making nice rolls for rich people. Baker Lumsden, who became a friend of Tommy, had got his

place in the cellar when his brother died, and
the brother had succeeded Matthew Croall when
he died.

They die very soon, Tommy learned from
Lumsden, generally when they are eight and
thirty. Lumsden was thirty-six, and when he
died his nephew was to get the place. The
wages are good.

Then there were several masons, one of whom,
like the first baker, had found work for all the
others, and there were men who had drifted into
trades strange to their birthplace, and there was
usually one at least who had come to London to
"better himself" and had not done it as yet.
The family Tommy liked best was the Whamonds,
and especially he liked old Petey and young
Petey Whamond. They were a large family of
women and men, all of whom earned their living
in other streets except the old man, who kept
house and was a famous knitter of stockings, as
probably his father had been before him. He
was a great one, too, at telling what they would
be doing at that moment in Thrums, every
corner of which was as familiar to him as the ins
and outs of the family hose. Young Petey got
fourteen shillings a week from a hatter, and one
of his duties was to carry as many as twenty
band-boxes at a time through fashionable streets;
it is a matter for elation that dukes and states-
men had often to take the curbstone, because
young Petey was coming. Nevertheless young
Petey was not satisfied, and never would be
(such is the Thrums nature) until he became a
salesman in the shop to which he acted at

present as fetch and carry, and he used to tell Tommy that this position would be his as soon as he could sneer sufficiently at the old hats. When gentlemen came into the shop and buy a new hat, he explained, they put it on, meaning to tell you to send the old one to their address, and the art of being a fashionable hatter lies in this : you must be able to curl your lips so contemptuously at the old hat that they tell you guiltily to keep it, as they have no further use for it. Then they retire ashamed of their want of moral courage and you have made an extra half-guinea.

"But I aye snort," young Petey admitted, "and it should be done without a sound." When he graduated, he was to marry Martha Spens, who was waiting for him at Tillyloss. There was a London seamstress whom he preferred, and she was willing, but it is safest to stick to Thrums.

When Tommy was among his new friends a Scotch word or phrase often escaped his lips, but old Petey and the others thought he had picked it up from them, and would have been content to accept him as a London waif who lived somewhere round the corner. To trick people so simply, however, is not agreeable to an artist, and he told them his name was Tommy Shovel, and that his old girl walloped him, and his father found dogs, all which inventions Thrums Street accepted as true. What is much more noteworthy is that, as he gave them birth, Tommy half believed them also, being already the best kind of actor.

Not that all the talking was done by Tommy when he came home with news, for he seldom mentioned a Thrums name, of which his mother could not tell him something more. But sometimes she did not choose to tell, as when he announced that a certain Elspeth Lindsay, of the Marywellbrae, was dead. After this she ceased to listen, for old Elspeth had been her grandmother, and she had now no kin in Thrums.

"Tell me about the Painted Lady," Tommy said to her. "Is it true she's a witch?" But Mrs. Sandys had never heard of any woman so called: the Painted Lady must have gone to Thrums after her time.

"There ain't no witches now," said Elspeth tremulously; Shovel's mother had told her so.

"Not in London," replied Tommy with contempt; and this is all that was said of the Painted Lady then. It is the first mention of her in these pages.

The people Mrs. Sandys wanted to hear of chiefly were Aaron Latta and Jean Myles, and soon Tommy brought news of them, but at the same time he had heard of the Den, and he said first:

"Oh, mother, I thought as you had told me about all the beauty places in Thrums, and you ain't never told me about the Den."

His mother heaved a quick breath. "It's the only place I hinna telled you o'," she said.

"Had you forgot it, mother?"

Forget the Den! Ah, no, Tommy, your mother had not forgotten the Den.

" And, listen, Elspeth: in the Den there's a bonny spring of water called the Cuttle Well. Had you forgot the Cuttle Well, mother ? "

No, no ; when Jean Myles forgot the names of her children she would still remember the Cuttle Well. Regardless now of the whispering between Tommy and Elspeth, she sat long over the fire, and it is not difficult to fathom her thoughts. They were of the Den and the Cuttle Well.

Into the life of every man, and no woman, there comes a moment when he learns suddenly that he is held eligible for marriage. A girl gives him the jag, and it brings out the perspiration. Of the issue elsewhere of this stab with a bodkin let others speak ; in Thrums its commonest effect is to make the callant's body take a right angle to his legs, for he has been touched in the fifth button, and he backs away broken-winded. By-and-by, however, he is at his work—among the turnip-shoots, say—guffawing and clapping his corduroys, with pauses for uneasy meditation, and there he ripens with the swedes, so that by the back-end of the year he has discovered, and exults to know, that the reward of manhood is neither more nor less than this sensation at the ribs. Soon thereafter, or at worst, sooner or later (for by holding out he only puts the women's dander up), he is led captive to the Cuttle Well. This well has the reputation of being the place where it is most easily said.

The wooded ravine called the Den is in Thrums rather than on its western edge, but is so craftily hidden away that when within a stone's

F

throw you may give up the search for it; it is
also so deep that larks rise from the bottom and
carol overhead, thinking themselves high in the
heavens before they are on a level with Nether
Drumley's farmland. In shape it is almost a
semicircle, but its size depends on you and the
maid. If she be with you, the Den is so large
that you must rest here and there; if you are
after her boldly, you can dash to the Cuttle
Well, which was the trysting-place, in the time
a stout man takes to lace his boots; if you are
of those self-conscious ones who look behind to
see whether jeering blades are following, you
may crouch and wriggle your way onward and
not be with her in half an hour.

Old Petey had told Tommy that, on the
whole, the greatest pleasure in life on a Saturday
evening is to put your back against a stile that
leads into the Den and rally the sweethearts as
they go by. The lads, when they see you, want
to go round by the other stile, but the lasses
like it, and often the sport ends spiritedly with
their giving you a clout on the head.

Through the Den runs a tiny burn, and by
its side is a pink path, dyed this pretty colour,
perhaps, by the blushes the ladies leave behind
them. The burn as it passes the Cuttle Well,
which stands higher and just out of sight, leaps
in vain to see who is making that cooing noise,
and the well, taking the spray for kisses, laughs
all day at Romeo, who cannot get up. Well is
a name it must have given itself, for it is only
a spring in the bottom of a basinful of water,
where it makes about as much stir in the world

as a minnow jumping at a fly. They say that
if a boy, by making a bowl of his hands, should
suddenly carry off all the water, a quick girl
could thread her needle at the spring. But it is
a spring that will not wait a moment.

Men who have been lads in Thrums sometimes go back to it from London or from across
the seas, to look again at some battered little
house and feel the blasts of their bairnhood
playing through the old wynds, and they may
take with them a foreign wife. They show her
everything, except the Cuttle Well; they often
go there alone. The well is sacred to the
memory of first love. You may walk from the
well to the round cemetery in ten minutes. It
is a common walk for those who go back.

First love is but a boy and girl playing at
the Cuttle Well with a bird's egg. They blow
it on one summer evening in the long grass, and
on the next it is borne away on a coarse laugh,
or it breaks beneath the burden of a tear. And
yet——. I once saw an aged woman, a widow of
many years, cry softly at mention of the Cuttle
Well. "John was a good man to you," I said,
for John had been her husband. "He was a
leal man to me," she answered with wistful eyes,
"ay, he was a leal man to me—but it wasna
John I was thinking o'. You dinna ken what
makes me greet so sair," she added, presently,
and though I thought I knew now I was wrong.
"It's because I canna mind his name," she said.

So the Cuttle Well has its sad memories and
its bright ones, and many of the bright memories have become sad with age, as so often

F 2

happens to beautiful things, but the most mournful of all is the story of Aaron Latta and Jean Myles. Beside the well there stood for long a great pink stone, called the Shoaging Stone, because it could be rocked like a cradle, and on it lovers used to cut their names. Often Aaron Latta and Jean Myles sat together on the Shoaging Stone, and then there came a time when it bore these words, cut by Aaron Latta:

"HERE LIES THE MANHOOD OF AARON LATTA,
   A FOND SON, A FAITHFUL FRIEND, AND A
      TRUE LOVER,
   WHO VIOLATED THE FEELINGS OF SEX ON
      THIS SPOT,
   AND IS NOW THE SCUNNER OF GOD AND
      MAN."

Tommy's mother now heard these words for the first time, Aaron having cut them on the stone after she left Thrums, and her head sank at each line, as if someone had struck four blows at her.

The stone was no longer at the Cuttle Well. As the easiest way of obliterating the words, the minister had ordered it to be broken, and of the pieces another mason had made stands for watches, one of which was now in Thrums Street.

"Aaron Latta ain't a mason now," Tommy rattled on: "he is a warper, because he can warp in his own house without looking on mankind or speaking to mankind. Auld Petey said he minded the day when Aaron Latta was a merry loon, and then Andrew McVittie said,

' God behears, to think that Aaron Latta was ever a merry man ! ' and Baker Lumsden said, ' Curse her ! ' "

His mother shrank in her chair, but said nothing, and Tommy explained: " It was Jean Myles he was cursing ; did you ken her, mother ? She ruined Aaron Latta's life."

" Ay, and wha ruined Jean Myles's life ? " his mother cried passionately.

Tommy did not know, but he thought that young Petey might know, for young Petey had said : " If I had been Jean Myles I would have spat in Aaron's face rather than marry him."

Mrs. Sandys seemed pleased to hear this.

" They wouldna tell me what it were she did," Tommy went on ; " they said it was ower ugly a story, but she were a bad one, for they stoned her out of Thrums.   I dinna know where she is now, but she were stoned out of Thrums ! "

" No alane ? ' "

" There was a man with her, and his name was—it was——"

His mother clasped her hands nervously while Tommy tried to remember the name. " His name was Magerful Tam," he said at length.

" Ay," said his mother, knitting her teeth, " that was his name."

" I dinna mind any more," Tommy concluded. " Yes, I mind they aye called Aaron Latta ' Poor Aaron Latta.' "

" Did they ? I warrant, though, there wasna one as said ' Poor Jean Myles ' ? "

She began the question in a hard voice, but

as she said "Poor Jean Myles" something
caught in her throat, and she sobbed, painful
dry sobs.

"How could they pity her when she were
such a bad one?" Tommy answered briskly.

"Is there none to pity bad ones?" said his
sorrowful mother.

Elspeth plucked her by the skirt. "There's
God, ain't there?" she said, inquiringly, and
getting no answer she flopped upon her knees,
to say a babyish prayer that would sound comic
to anybody except to Him to whom it was
addressed.

"You ain't praying for a woman as was a
disgrace to Thrums!" Tommy cried, jealously,
and he was about to raise her by force, when his
mother stayed his hand.

"Let her alane," she said, with a twitching
mouth and filmy eyes. "Let her alane. Let
my bairn pray for Jean Myles."

CHAPTER VII.

COMIC OVERTURE TO A TRAGEDY.

" JEAN MYLES bides in London " was the next remarkable news brought by Tommy from Thrums Street. "And that ain't all, Magerful Tam is her man; and that ain't all, she has a laddie called Tommy; and that ain't all, Petey and the rest has never seen her in London, but she writes letters to Thrums folks and they writes to Petey and tells him what she said. That ain't all neither, they canna find out what street she bides in, but it's on the bonny side of London, and it's grand, and she wears silk clothes, and her Tommy has velvet trousers, and they have a servant as calls him 'sir.' Oh, I would just like to kick him! They often looks for her in the grand streets, but they're angry at her getting on so well, and Martha Scrymgeour said it were enough to make good women like her stop going reg'lar to the kirk."

"Martha said that!" exclaimed his mother, highly pleased. "Heard you anything of a woman called Esther Auld? Her man does the orra work at the Tappit Hen public in Thrums."

"He's head man at the Tappit Hen public now," answered Tommy; "and she wishes she could find out where Jean Myles bides, so as she could write and tell her that she is grand too, and has six hair-bottomed chairs."

"She'll never get the satisfaction," said his mother triumphantly. "Tell me more about her."

"She has a laddie called Francie, and he has yellow curls, and she nearly greets because she canna tell Jean Myles that he goes to a school for the children of gentlemen only. She is so mad when she gets a letter from Jean Myles that she takes to her bed."

"Yea, yea!" said Mrs. Sandys cheerily.

"But they think Jean Myles has been brought low at last," continued Tommy, "because she hasna wrote for a long time to Thrums, and Esther Auld said that if she knowed for certain as Jean Myles had been brought low, she would put a threepenny bit into the kirk plate."

"I'm glad you've telled me that, laddie," said Mrs. Sandys, and next day, unknown to her children, she wrote another letter. She knew she ran a risk of discovery, yet it was probable that Tommy would only hear her referred to in Thrums Street by her maiden name, which he had never heard from her, and as for her husband he had been Magerful Tam to everyone. The risk was great, but the pleasure——

Unsuspicious Tommy soon had news of another letter from Jean Myles, which had sent Esther Auld to bed again.

"Instead of being brought low," he announced, "Jean Myles is grander than ever. Her Tommy has a governess."

"That would be a doush of water in Esther's face?" his mother said, smiling.

"She wrote to Martha Scrymgeour," said

Tommy, " that it ain't no pleasure to her now
to boast as her laddie is at a school for gentlemen's children only. But what made her mad-
dest was a bit in Jean Myles's letter about
chairs. Jean Myles has give all her hair-
bottomed chairs to a poor woman and buyed a
new kind, because hair-bottomed ones ain't
fashionable now. So Esther Auld can't not bear
the sight of her chairs now, though she were
windy of them till the letter went to Thrums."

" Poor Esther ! " said Mrs. Sandys gaily.

" Oh, and I forgot this, mother. Jean Myles's
reason for not telling where she bides in London
is that she's so grand that she thinks if auld
Petey and the rest knowed where the place was
they would visit her and boast as they was her
friends. Auld Petey stamped wi' rage when he
heard that, and Martha Scrymgeour said, ' Oh,
the pridefu' limmer ! ' "

" Ay, Martha," muttered Mrs. Sandys, " you
and Jean Myles is evens now."

But the passage that had made them all
wince the most was one giving Jean's reasons
for making no calls in Thrums Street. " You
can break it to Martha Scrymgeour's father
and mither," the letter said, " and to Petey
Whamond's sisters and the rest as has friends
in London, that I have seen no Thrums faces
here, the low part where they bide not being
for the like of me to file my feet in. Forby
that, I could not let my son mix with their
bairns for fear they should teach him the vulgar
Thrums words and clarty his blue-velvet suit.
I'm thinking you have to dress your laddie in

corduroy, Esther, but you see that would not do for mine. So no more at present, and we all join in compliments, and my little velvets says he wishes I would send some of his toys to your little corduroys. And so maybe I will, Esther, if you'll tell Aaron Latta how rich and happy I am, and if you're feared to say it to his face, tell it to the roaring farmer of Double Dykes, and he'll pass it on."

"Did you ever hear of such a woman?" Tommy said indignantly, when he had repeated as much of this insult to Thrums as he could remember.

But it was information his mother wanted.

"What said they to that bit?" she asked.

At first, it appears, they limited their comments to "Losh, losh," "keeps a'," "it cows," "my certie," "ay, ay," "sal, tal," "dagont" (the meaning of which is obvious). But by-and-by they recovered their breath, and then Baker Lumsden said, wonderingly:

"Wha that was at her marriage could have thought it would turn out so well? It was an eerie marriage that, Petey!"

"Ay, man, you may say so," old Petey answered. "I was there; I was one o' them as went in ahint Aaron Latta, and I'm no likely to forget it."

"I wasna there," said the baker, "but I was standing at the door, and I saw the hearse drive up."

"What did they mean, mother?" Tommy asked, but she shuddered and replied, evasively, "Did Martha Scrymgeour say anything?"

"She said such a lot," he had to confess, "that I dinna mind none on it. But I mind what her father in Thrums wrote to her; he wrote to her that if she saw a carriage go by, she was to keep her eyes on the ground, for likely as not Jean Myles would be in it, and she thought as they were all dirt beneath her feet. But Kirsty Ross—who is she?"

"She's Martha's mother. What about her?"

"She wrote at the end of the letter that Martha was to hang on ahint the carriage and find out where Jean Myles bides."

"Laddie, that was like Kirsty! Heard you what the roaring farmer o' Double Dykes said?"

No, Tommy had not heard him mentioned. And indeed the roaring farmer of Double Dykes had said nothing. He was already lying very quiet on the south side of the cemetery.

Tommy's mother's next question cost her a painful effort. "Did you hear," she asked, "whether they telled Aaron Latta about the letter?"

"Yes, they telled him," Tommy replied, "and he said a queer thing; he said, 'Jean Myles is dead, I was at her coffining.' That's what he aye says when they tell him there's another letter. I wonder what he means, mother?"

"I wonder!" she echoed, faintly. The only pleasure left her was to raise the envy of those who had hooted her from Thrums, but she paid a price for it. Many a stab she had got from the unwitting Tommy as he repeated the gossip of his new friends, and she only won their envy at the cost of their increased ill-will.

They thought she was lording it in London, and so they were merciless; had they known how poor she was, and how ill, they would have forgotten everything save that she was a Thrummy like themselves, and there were few but would have shared their all with her. But she did not believe this, and therefore you may pity her, for the hour was drawing near, and she knew it, when she must appeal to someone for her children's sake, not for her own.

No, not for her own. When Tommy was wandering the pretty parts of London with James Gloag and other boys from Thrums Street in search of Jean Myles, whom they were to know by her carriage and her silk dress and her son in blue velvet, his mother was in bed with bronchitis in the wretched room we know of, or creeping to the dancing-school, coughing all the way.

Some of the fits of coughing were very near being her last, but she wrestled with her trouble, seeming at times to stifle it, and then for weeks she managed to go to her work, which was still hers, because Shovel's old girl did it for her when the bronchitis would not be defied. Shovel's old slattern gave this service unasked and without payment; if she was thanked it was ungraciously, but she continued to do all she could when there was need; she smelled of gin, but she continued to do all she could.

The wardrobe had been put upon its back on the floor, and so converted into a bed for Tommy and Elspeth, who were sometimes wakened in the night by a loud noise, which alarmed them until they learned that it was only the man in the next room knocking angrily on the wall because their mother's cough kept him from sleeping.

Tommy knew what death was now, and Elspeth knew its name, and both were vaguely aware that it was looking for their mother; but if she could only hold out till Hogmanay, Tommy said, they would fleg it out of the house. Hogmanay is the mighty winter festival of Thrums, and when it came round these two were to give their mother a present that would make her strong. It was not to be a porous plaster. Tommy knew of something better than that.

"And I knows too!" Elspeth gurgled, "and I has threepence a'ready, I has."

"Whisht!" said Tommy, in an agony of dread, "she hears you, and she'll guess. We ain't speaking of nothing to give you at Hogmanay," he said to his mother with great cunning. Then he winked at Elspeth and said, with his hand over his mouth, "I hinna twopence!" and Elspeth, about to cry in fright, "Have you spended it?" saw the joke and crowed instead, "Nor yet has I threepence!"

They smirked together, until Tommy saw a change come over Elspeth's face, which made him run her outside the door.

"You was a-going to pray!" he said, severely.

"'Cos it was a lie, Tommy. I does have threepence."

"Well, you ain't a going to get praying about it. She would hear yer."

"I would do it low, Tommy."

"She would see yer."

"Oh, Tommy, let me. God is angry with me."

Tommy looked down the stair, and no one was in sight. "I'll let yer pray here," he whispered, "and you can say I have twopence. But be quick, and do it standing."

Perhaps Mrs. Sandys had been thinking that when Hogmanay came her children might have no mother to bring presents to, for on their return to the room her eyes followed them woefully, and a shudder of apprehension shook her torn frame. Tommy gave Elspeth a look that meant "I'm sure there's something queer about her."

There was also something queer about himself, which at this time had the strangest gallop. It began one day, with a series of morning calls from Shovel, who suddenly popped his head over the top of the door (he was standing on the handle), roared "Roast-beef!" in the manner of a railway porter announcing the name of a station, and then at once withdrew.

He returned presently to say that vain must be all attempts to wheedle his secret from him, and yet again to ask irritably why Tommy was not coming out to hear all about it. Then did Tommy desert Elspeth, and on the stair Shovel showed him a yellow card with this printed on it: "S. R. J. C.—Supper Ticket;" and written beneath, in a lady's hand: "Admit Joseph Salt." The letters, Shovel explained, meant Society for the somethink of Juvenile Criminals,

and the toffs what ran it got hold of you when
you came out of quod. Then if you was willing
to repent they wrote down your name and the
place what you lived at in a book, and one of
them came to see yer and give yer a ticket for
the blow-out night. This was blow-out night,
and that were Shovel's ticket. He had bought
it from Hump Salt for fourpence. What you
get at the blow-out was roast-beef, plum-duff,
and an orange; but when Hump saw the fourpence he could not wait.

A favour was asked of Tommy. Shovel had
been told by Hump that it was the custom of
the toffs to sit beside you and question you about
your crimes, and lacking the imagination that
made Tommy such an ornament to the house,
the chances were that he would flounder in his
answers and be rejected. Hump had pointed
this out to him after pocketing the fourpence.
Would Tommy, therefore, make up things for
him to say; reward, the orange.

This was a proud moment for Tommy, as
Shovel's knowledge of crime was much more
extensive than his own, though they had both
studied it in the pictures of a lively newspaper
subscribed to by Shovel, senior. He became
patronising at once and rejected the orange as
insufficient.

Then suppose, after he got into the hall,
Shovel dropped his ticket out at the window;
Tommy could pick it up, and then it would
admit him also.

Tommy liked this, but foresaw a danger: the
ticket might be taken from Shovel at the door,

just as they took them from you at that singing thing in the church he had attended with young Petey.

So help Shovel's davy, there was no fear of this. They were superior toffs, what trusted to your honour.

Would Shovel swear to this?

He would.

But would he swear dagont?

He swore dagont; and then Tommy had him. As he was so sure of it, he could not object to Tommy's being the one who dropped the ticket out at the window?

Shovel did object for a time, but after a wrangle he gave up the ticket, intending to take it from Tommy when primed with the necessary tale. So they parted until evening, and Tommy returned to Elspeth, secretive but elated. For the rest of the day he was in thought, now waggling his head smugly over some dark, unutterable design and again looking a little scared. In growing alarm she watched his face, and at last she slipped upon her knees, but he had her up at once and said, reproachfully:

"It were me as teached yer to pray, and now yer prays for me! That's fine treatment!"

Nevertheless, after his mother's return, just before he stole out to join Shovel, he took Elspeth aside and whispered to her, nervously:

"You can pray for me if you like, for, oh, Elspeth, I'm thinking as I'll need it sore!"

And sore he needed it before the night was out.

CHAPTER VIII.

THE BOY WITH TWO MOTHERS.

" I love my dear father and my dear mother and
all the dear little kids at 'ome. You are a kind
laidy or gentleman. I love yer. I will never
do it again, so help me bob. Amen."

This was what Shovel muttered to himself
again and again as the two boys made their way
across the lamp-lit Hungerford Bridge, and
Tommy asked him what it meant.

" My old gal learned me that ; she's deep,"
Shovel said, wiping the words off his mouth with
his sleeve.

" But you got no kids at 'ome !" remonstrated Tommy. (Ameliar was now in service.)

Shovel turned on him with the fury of a
mother protecting her young. " Don't you try
for to knock none on it out," he cried, and again
fell a-mumbling.

Said Tommy scornfully : "If you says it all
out at one bang you'll be done at the start."

Shovel sighed.

" And you should blubber when yer says it,"
added Tommy, who could laugh or cry merely
because other people were laughing or crying, or
even with less reason, and so naturally that he
found it more difficult to stop than to begin.
Shovel was the taller by half a head, and
irresistible with his fists, but to-night Tommy
was master.

G

"You jest stick to me, Shovel," he said airily. "Keep a grip on my hand, same as if yer was Elspeth."

"But what was we copped for, Tommy?" entreated humble Shovel.

Tommy asked him if he knew what a butler was, and Shovel remembered, confusedly, that there had been a portrait of a butler in his father's news-sheet.

"Well, then," said Tommy, inspired by this same source, "there's a room a butler has, and it is a pantry, so you and me we crawled through the winder and we opened the door to the gang. You and me was copped. They catched you below the table and me stabbing the butler."

"It was me what stabbed the butler," Shovel interposed, jealously.

"How could you do it, Shovel?"

"With a knife, I tell yer!"

"Why, you didn't have no knife," said Tommy, impatiently.

This crushed Shovel, but he growled sulkily:

"Well, I bit him in the leg."

"Not you," said selfish Tommy. "You forget about repenting, and if I let yer bite him, you would brag about it. It's safer without, Shovel."

Perhaps it was. "How long did I get in quod, then, Tommy?"

"Fourteen days."

"So did you?" Shovel said, with quick anxiety.

"I got a month," replied Tommy, firmly.

Shovel roared a word that would never have

admitted him to the hall. Then, " I'm as game
as you, and gamer," he whined.

"But I'm better at repenting. I tell yer,
I'll cry when I'm repenting." Tommy's face lit
up, and Shovel could not help saying, with a
curious look at it:

"You—you ain't like any other cove I
knows," to which Tommy replied, also in an
awestruck voice :

"I'm so queer, Shovel, that when I thinks
'bout myself I'm—I'm sometimes near feared."

"What makes your face for to shine like
that? Is it thinking about the blow-out?"

No, it was hardly that, but Tommy could not
tell what it was. He and the saying about art
for art's sake were in the streets that night,
looking for each other.

The splendour of the brightly lighted hall,
which was situated in one of the meanest streets
of perhaps the most densely populated quarter in
London, broke upon the two boys suddenly and
hit each in his vital part, tapping an invitation
on Tommy's brain-pan and taking Shovel
coquettishly in the stomach. Now was the
moment when Shovel meant to strip Tommy of
the ticket, but the spectacle in front dazed him,
and he stopped to tell a vegetable barrow how he
loved his dear father and his dear mother, and all
the dear kids at home. Then Tommy darted
forward and was immediately lost in the crowd
surging round the steps of the hall.

Several gentlemen in evening dress stood
framed in the lighted doorway, shouting : "Have
your tickets in your hands, and give them up as

you pass in." They were fine fellows, helping in a splendid work, and their society did much good, though it was not so well organised as others that have followed in its steps; but Shovel, you may believe, was in no mood to attend to them. He had but one thought: that the traitor Tommy was doubtless at that moment boring his way towards them, underground, as it were, and " holding his ticket in his hand." Shovel dived into the rabble and was flung back upside down. Falling with his arms round a full-grown man, he immediately ran up him as if he had been a lamp-post, and was aloft just sufficiently long to see Tommy give up the ticket and saunter into the hall.

The crowd tried at intervals to rush the door. It was mainly composed of ragged boys, but here and there were men, women, and girls, who came into view for a moment under the lights as the mob heaved and went round and round like a boiling potful. Two policemen joined the ticket-collectors, and though it was a good-humoured gathering, the air was thick with such cries as these:

" I lorst my ticket, ain't I telling yer? Gar on, guv'nor, lemme in!"

"Oh, crumpets, look at Jimmy! Jimmy never done nothink, your honour; he's a himpostor."

" I'm the boy what kicked the peeler. Hie, you toff with the choker, ain't I to step up?"

" Tell yer, I'm a genooine criminal, I am. If yer don't lemme in I'll have the lawr on you."

"Let a poor cove in as his father drownded hisself for his country."

"What air yer torking about? Warn't I in larst year, and the cuss as runs the show, he says to me, 'Allers welcome,' he says. None on your sarse, bobby. I demands to see the cuss what runs——"

"Jest keeping on me out 'cos I ain't done nothin'. Ho, this is a encouragement to honesty, I don't think."

Mighty in tongue and knee and elbow was an unknown knight, ever conspicuous; it might be but by a leg waving for one brief moment in the air. He did not want to go in, would not go in though they went on their blooming knees to him; he was after a viper of the name of Tommy. Half an hour had not tired him, and he was leading another assault, when a magnificent lady, such as you see in wax-works, appeared in the vestibule and made some remark to a policeman, who then shouted:

"If so there be hany lad here called Shovel, he can step forrard."

A dozen lads stepped forward at once, but a flail drove them right and left, and the unknown knight had mounted the parapet amid a shower of execrations. "If you are the real Shovel," the lady said to him, "you can tell me how this proceeds, 'I love my dear father and my dear mother——' Go on."

Shovel obeyed tremblingly. "And all the dear little kids at 'ome. You are a kind lady or gentleman. I love yer. I will never do it again, so help me bob. Amen."

"Charming!" chirped the lady, and down pleasant-smelling aisles she led him, pausing to

drop an observation about Tommy to a clergyman: "So glad I came; I have discovered the
most delightful little monster, called Tommy."
The clergyman looked after her half in sadness,
half sarcastically; he was thinking that he had
discovered a monster also.

At present the body of the hall was empty,
but its sides were lively with gorging boys,
among whom ladies moved, carrying platefuls of
good things. Most of them were sweet women,
fighting bravely for these boys, and not at all like
Shovel's patroness, who had come for a sensation. Tommy, falling into her hands, she got it.

Tommy, who had a corner to himself, was
lolling in it like a little king, and he not only
ordered roast-beef for the awe-struck Shovel, but
sent the lady back for salt. Then he whispered,
exultantly: "Quick, Shovel, feel my pocket"
(it bulged with two oranges), "now the inside
pocket" (plum-duff), "now my waistcoat pocket"
(threepence); "look in my mouth" (chocolates).

When Shovel found speech he began
excitedly: "I love my dear father and my
dear——"

"Gach!" said Tommy, interrupting him
contemptuously. "Repenting ain't no go,
Shovel. Look at them other coves; none of
them has got no money, nor full pockets, and I
tell you, it's 'cos they has repented."

"Gar on!"

"It's true, I tells you. That lady as is
my one, she's called her ladyship, and she don't
care a cuss for boys as has repented," which of
course was a libel, her ladyship being celebrated

wherever paragraphs penetrate for having knitted a pair of stockings for the deserving poor.

"When I saw that," Tommy continued brazenly, "I bragged 'stead of repenting, and the wuss I says I am, she jest says, ' You little monster,' and gives me another orange."

"Then I'm done for," Shovel moaned, " for I rolled off that 'bout loving my dear father and my dear mother, blast 'em, soon as I seen her."

He need not let that depress him. Tommy had told her he would say it, but that it was all flam.

Shovel thought the ideal arrangement would be for him to eat and leave the torking to Tommy. Tommy nodded. "I'm full, at any rate," he said, struggling with his waistcoat. " Oh, Shovel, I *am* full!"

Her ladyship returned, and the boys held by their contract, but of the dark character Tommy seems to have been let not these pages bear the record. Do you wonder that her ladyship believed him? On this point we must fight for our Tommy. You would have believed him. Even Shovel, who knew, between the bites, that it was all whoppers, listened as to his father reading aloud. This was because another boy present half believed it for the moment also. When he described the eerie darkness of the butler's pantry, he shivered involuntarily, and he shut his eyes once—ugh!—that was because he saw the blood spouting out of the butler. He was turning up his trousers to show the mark of the butler's boot on his leg when the lady was called away, and then Shovel shook him, saying:

"Darn yer, doesn't yer know as it's all your eye?" which brought Tommy to his senses with a jerk.

"Sure's death, Shovel," he whispered, in awe, "I was thinking I done it, every bit!"

Had her ladyship come back she would have found him a different boy. He remembered now that Elspeth, for whom he had filled his pockets, was praying for him; he could see her on her knees, saying, "Oh, God, I'se praying for Tommy," and remorse took hold of him and shook him on his seat. He broke into one hysterical laugh, and then immediately began to sob. This was the moment when Shovel should have got him quietly out of the hall.

Members of the society discussing him afterward with bated breath said that never till they died could they forget her ladyship's face while he did it. "But did you notice the boy's own face? It was positively angelic." "Angelic, indeed; the little horror was intoxicated." No, there was a doctor present, and according to him it was the meal that had gone to the boy's head; he looked half starved. As for the clergyman, he only said: "We shall lose her subscription; I am glad of it."

Yes, Tommy was intoxicated, but with a beverage not recognised by the faculty. What happened was this: Supper being finished, the time had come for what Shovel called the jawing, and the boys were now mustered in the body of the hall. The limited audience had gone to the gallery, and unluckily all eyes except Shovel's were turned to the platform. Shovel was apprehensive about Tommy, who was not exactly sobbing now; but strange, uncontrollable sounds not unlike the winding of a clock proceeded from his throat; his face had flushed; there was a purposeful look in his usually unreadable eye; his fingers were fidgeting on the board in front of him, and he seemed to keep his seat with difficulty. The personage who was to address the boys sat on the platform with clergymen, members of committee, and some ladies, one of them Tommy's patroness. Her ladyship saw Tommy and smiled to him, but obtained no response. She had taken a front seat, a choice that she must have regretted presently.

The chairman rose and announced that the Rev. Mr. —— would open the proceedings with prayer. The Rev. Mr. —— rose to pray in a loud voice for the waifs in the body of the hall. At the same moment rose Tommy, and began to pray in a squeaky voice for the people on the platform.

He had many Biblical phrases, mostly picked up in Thrums Street, and what he said was distinctly heard in the stillness, the clergyman being suddenly bereft of speech. "Oh," he cried, "look down on them ones there, for, oh, they are unworthy of Thy mercy, and, oh, the worst sinner is her ladyship, her sitting there so brazen in the black frock with yellow stripes, and the worse I said I were the better pleased were she. Oh, make her think shame for tempting of a poor boy, forgetting 'Suffer little children.' Oh, why cumbereth she the ground? Oh——"

He was in full swing before anyone could act. Shovel having failed to hold him in his seat, had done what was perhaps the next best thing, got beneath it himself. The arm of the petrified clergyman was still extended, as if blessing his brother's remarks; the chairman seemed to be trying to fling his right hand at the culprit; but her ladyship, after the first stab, never moved a muscle. Thus for nearly half a minute, when the officials woke up, and squeezing past many knees, seized Tommy by the neck and ran him out of the building. All down the aisle he prayed hysterically, and for some time afterwards to Shovel, who had been cast forth along with him.

At an hour of that night when their mother was asleep, and it is to be hoped they were the only two children awake in London, Tommy sat up softly in the wardrobe to discover whether Elspeth was still praying for him. He knew that she was on the floor in a nightgown some twelve sizes too large for her, but the room was as silent and black as the world he had just left by taking his fingers from his ears and the blankets off his face.

"I see you," he said mendaciously, and in a guarded voice, so as not to waken his mother, from whom he had kept his escapade. This had not the desired effect of drawing a reply from Elspeth, and he tried bluster.

"You needna think as I'll repent, you brat, so there! What?

"I wish I hadna told you about it!"

Indeed, he had endeavoured not to do so, but pride in his achievement had eventually conquered prudence.

"Reddy would have laughed, she would, and said as I was a wonder. Reddy was the kind I like. What?

"You ate up the oranges quick, and the plum-duff too, so you should pray for yoursel' as well as for me. It's easy to say as you didna know how I got them till after you eated them, but you should have found out. What?

"Do you think it was for my own self as I done it. I jest done it to get the oranges and plum-duff to you, I did, and the threepence too. Eh? Speak, you little besom.

"I tell you as I did repent in the hall. I was greeting, and I never knowed I put up that prayer till Shovel told me on it. We were sitting in the street by that time."

This was true. On leaving the hall Tommy had soon dropped to the cold ground and squatted there till he came to, when he remembered nothing of what had led to his expulsion. Like a stream that has run into a pond and only finds itself again when it gets out, he was but a continuation of the boy who when last conscious of himself was in the corner crying remorsefully over his misdeed; and in this humility he would have returned to Elspeth had no one told him of his prayer. Shovel, however, was at hand, not only to tell him all about it, but to applaud, and home strutted Tommy chuckling.

"I am sleeping," he next said to Elspeth, "so you may as well come to your bed."

He imitated the breathing of a sleeper, but it was the only sound to be heard in London, and he desisted fearfully. "Come away, Elspeth," he said, coaxingly, for he was very fond of her and could not sleep while she was cold and miserable.

Still getting no response he pulled his body inch by inch out of the bedclothes, and holding his breath, found the floor with his feet stealthily, as if to cheat the wardrobe into thinking that he was still in it. But his reason was to discover whether Elspeth had fallen asleep on her knees without her learning that he cared to know. Almost noiselessly he worked himself along the floor, but when he stopped to bring his face nearer hers, there was such a creaking of his joints that if Elspeth did not hear it she— she must be dead! His knees played whack on the floor.

Elspeth only gasped once, but he heard, and remained beside her for a minute, so that she might hug him if such was her desire ; and she put out her hand in the darkness so that his should not have far to travel alone if it chanced to be on the way to her. Thus they sat on their knees, each aghast at the hardheartedness of the other.

Tommy put the blankets over the kneeling figure, and presently announced from the wardrobe that if he died of cold before repenting the blame of keeping him out of heaven would be Elspeth's. But the last word was muffled, for the blankets were tucked about him as he spoke, and two motherly little arms gave him the embrace they wanted to withhold. Foiled again, he kicked off the bedclothes and said: "I tell yer I wants to die!"

This terrified both of them, and he added, quickly:

"Oh, God, if I was sure I were to die to-night I would repent at once." It is the commonest prayer in all languages, but down on her knees slipped Elspeth again, and Tommy, who felt that it had done him good, said indignantly: "Surely that is religion. What?"

He lay on his face until he was frightened by a noise louder than thunder in the daytime— the scraping of his eyelashes on the pillow. Then he sat up in the wardrobe, and fired his last three shots.

"Elspeth Sandys, I'm done with yer for ever, I am. I'll take care on yer, but I'll never kiss yer no more.

"When yer boasts as I'm yer brother I'll say you ain't. I'll tell my mother about Reddy the morn, and syne she'll put you to the door smart.

"When you are a grown woman, I'll buy a house to yer, but you'll have jest to bide in it by your lonely self, and I'll come once a year to speir how you are, but I won't come in, I won't —I'll jest cry up the stair."

The effect of this was even greater than he had expected, for now two were in tears instead of one, and Tommy's grief was the more heart-rending, he was so much better at everything than Elspeth. He jumped out of the wardrobe and ran to her, calling her name, and he put his arms round her cold body, and the dear mite, forgetting how cruelly he had used her, cried, "Oh, tighter, Tommy, tighter; you didn't not mean it, did yer? Oh, you is terrible fond on me, ain't yer? And you won't not tell my mother 'bout Reddy, will yer? And you is no done wi' me for ever, is yer? and you won't not put me in a house by myself, will yer? Oh, Tommy, is that the tightest you can do?"

And Tommy made it tighter, vowing, "I never meant it; I was a bad un to say it. If Reddy were to come back wanting for to squeeze you out, I would send her packing quick, I would. I tell yer what, I'll kiss you with folk looking on, I will, and no be ashamed to do it, and if Shovel is one of them what sees me, and he puts his finger to his nose, I'll blood the mouth of him, I will, dagont!"

Then he prayed for forgiveness, and he could always pray more beautifully than Elspeth. Even she was satisfied with the way he did it, and so, alack, was he.

"But you forgot to tell," she said fondly, when once more they were in the wardrobe together—"you forgot to tell as you filled your pockets wif things to me."

"I didn't forget," Tommy replied modestly. "I missed it out on purpose, I did, 'cos I was sure God knows on it without my telling Him, and I thought He would be pleased if I didn't let on as I knowed it was good of me."

"Oh, Tommy," cried Elspeth, worshipping him, "I couldn't have doned that, I couldn't!" She was barely six, and easily taken in, but she would save him from himself if she could.

CHAPTER IX.

AULD LANG SYNE.

WHAT to do with her ladyship's threepence?
Tommy finally decided to drop it into the
charity-box that had once contained his penny.
They held it over the slit together, Elspeth
almost in tears because it was such a large sum
to give away, but Tommy looking noble, he was
so proud of himself; and when he said "Three!"
they let go.

There followed days of excitement centred
round their money-box. Shovel introduced
Tommy to a boy what said as after a bit you
forget how much money was in your box, and
then when you opened it, oh, Lor'! there is
more than you thought, so he and Elspeth gave
this plan a week's trial, affecting not to know
how much they had gathered, but when they
unlocked it, the sum was still only eightpence;
so then Tommy told the liar to come on, and
they fought while the horrified Elspeth prayed,
and Tommy licked him, a result due to one of
the famous Thrums left-handers then on exhibition in that street for the first time, as taught
the victor by Petey Whamond the younger, late
of Tillyloss.

The money did come in, once in spate (twopence from Bob in twenty-four hours), but
usually so slowly that they saw it resting on the

way, and then, when they listened intently, they could hear the thud of Hogmanay. The last halfpenny was a special aggravation, strolling about, just out of reach, with all the swagger of sixpence, but at last Elspeth had it, and after that, the sooner Hogmanay came the better.

They concealed their excitement under too many wrappings, but their mother suspected nothing. When she was dressing on the morning of Hogmanay, her stockings happened to be at the other side of the room, and they were such a long way off that she rested on the way to them. At the meagre breakfast she said what a heavy teapot that was, and Tommy thought this funny, but the salt had gone from the joke when he remembered it afterwards. And when she was ready to go off to her work she hesitated at the door, looking at her bed and from it to her children as if in two minds, and then went quietly downstairs.

The distance seems greater than ever to-day, poor woman, and you stop longer at the corners, where rude men jeer at you. Scarcely can you push open the door of the dancing-school or lift the pail; the fire has gone out, you must again go on your knees before it, and again the smoke makes you cough. Gaunt slattern, fighting to bring up the phlegm, was it really you for whom another woman gave her life, and thought it a rich reward to get dressing you once in your long clothes, when she called you her beautiful, and smiled, and smiling, died? Well, well; but take courage, Jean Myles. The long road still lies straight up hill, but your climbing is near an end. Shrink from the rude men no more, they are soon to forget you, so soon! It is a heavy door, but soon you will have pushed it open for the last time. The girls will babble still, but not to you, not of you. Cheer up, the work is nearly done. Her beautiful! Come, beautiful, strength for a few more days, and then you can leave the key of the leaden door behind you, and on your way home you may kiss your hand joyously to the weary streets, for you are going to die.

Tommy and Elspeth had been to the foot of the stair many times to look for her before their mother came back that evening, yet when she re-entered her home, behold, they were sitting calmly on the fender as if this were a day like yesterday or to-morrow, as if Tommy had not been on a business visit to Thrums Street, as if the hump on the bed did not mean that a glorious something was hidden under the cover-let. True, Elspeth would look at Tommy imploringly every few minutes, meaning that she could not keep it in much longer, and then Tommy would mutter the one word "Bell" to remind her that it was against the rules to begin before the Thrums eight-o'clock bell rang. They also wiled away the time of waiting by inviting each other to conferences at the window where these whispers passed.

"She ain't got a notion, Tommy."

"Dinna look so often at the bed."

"If I could jest get one more peep at it!"

"No, no; but you can put your hand on the top of it as you go by."

H

The artfulness of Tommy lured his unsuspecting mother into telling how they would be holding Hogmanay in Thrums to-night, how cartloads of kebbock cheeses had been rolling into the town all the livelong day ("Do you hear them, Elspeth?"), and in dark closes the children were already gathering, with smeared faces and in eccentric dress, to sally forth as guisers at the clap of eight, when the ringing of a bell lets Hogmanay loose. ("You see, Elspeth?") Inside the houses men and women were preparing (though not by fasting, which would have been such a good way that it is surprising no one ever thought of it) for a series of visits, at every one of which they would be offered a dram and kebbock and bannock, and in the grander houses "bridies," which are a sublime kind of pie.

Tommy had the audacity to ask what bridies were like. And he could not dress up and be a guiser, could he, mother, for the guisers sang a song, and he did not know the words? What a pity they could not get bridies to buy in London, and learn the song and sing it. But of course they could not! ("Elspeth, if you tumble off the fender again, she'll guess.")

Such is a sample of Tommy, but Elspeth was sly also, if in a smaller way, and it was she who said: "There ain't nothin' in the bed, is there, Tommy!" This duplicity made her uneasy, and she added, behind her teeth, "Maybe there is," and then, "O God, I knows as there is."

But as the great moment drew near there were no more questions; two children were staring at the clock, and listening intently for the peal of a bell nearly five hundred miles away.

The clock struck. "Whist! It's time, Elspeth! They've begun! Come on!"

A few minutes afterwards Mrs. Sandys was roused by a knock at the door, followed by the entrance of two mysterious figures. The female wore a boy's jacket turned outside in, the male a woman's bonnet and a shawl, and to make his disguise the more impenetrable he carried a poker in his right hand. They stopped in the middle of the floor and began to recite, rather tremulously,

> Get up good wife, and binna sweir,
> And deal your bread to them that's here,
> For the time will come when you'll be dead,
> And then you'll need neither ale nor bread.

Mrs. Sandys had started, and then turned piteously from them; but when they were done she tried to smile, and said, with forced gaiety, that she saw they were guisers, and it was a fine night, and would they take a chair. The male stranger did so at once, but the female said, rather anxiously: "You are sure as you don't know who we is?" Their hostess shook her head, and then he of the poker offered her three guesses, a daring thing to do, but all went well, for her first guess was Shovel and his old girl; second guess, Before and After; third guess, Napoleon Buonaparte and the Auld Licht minister. At each guess the smaller of the intruders clapped her hands gleefully, but when, with the third, she was unmuzzled, she putted

H 2

with her head at Mrs. Sandys and hugged her,
screaming, "It ain't none on them; it's jest me,
mother, it's Elspeth!" and even while their
astounded hostess was asking could it be true,
the male conspirator dropped his poker noisily
(to draw attention to himself) and stood revealed
as Thomas Sandys.

Wasn't it just like Thrums, wasn't it just
the very, very same? "Ah, it was wonderful,"
their mother said, but alas, there was one thing
wanting: she had no Hogmanay to give the
guisers.

Had she not? What a pity, Elspeth! What
a pity, Tommy! What might that be in the
bed, Elspeth? It couldn't not be their Hogmanay, could it, Tommy? If Tommy was his
mother he would look and see. If Elspeth was
her mother she would look and see.

Her curiosity thus cunningly aroused, Mrs.
Sandys raised the coverlet of the bed and—there
were three bridies, an oatmeal cake, and a hunk
of kebbock. "And they comed from Thrums!"
cried Elspeth, while Tommy cried, "Petey and
the others got a lot sent from Thrums, and I
bought the bridies from them, and they gave
me the bannock and the kebbock for nuthin'!"
Their mother did not utter the cry of rapture
which Tommy expected so confidently that he
could have done it for her; instead, she pulled
her two children toward her, and the great
moment was like to be a tearful rather than an
ecstatic one, for Elspeth had begun to whimper,
and even Tommy—but by a supreme effort he
shouldered reality to the door.

"Is this my Hogmanay, guidwife?" he asked in the nick of time, and the situation thus being saved, the luscious feast was partaken of, the guisers listening solemnly as each bite went down. They also took care to address their hostess as "guidwife" or "mistress," affecting not to have met her lately, and inquiring genially after the health of herself and family. "How many have you?" was Tommy's masterpiece, and she answered in the proper spirit, but all the time she was hiding great part of her bridie beneath her apron, Hogmanay having come too late for her.

Everything was to be done exactly as they were doing it in Thrums Street, and so presently Tommy made a speech; it was the speech of old Petey, who had rehearsed it several times before him. "Here's a toast," said Tommy, standing up and waving his arms, "here's a toast that we'll drink in silence, one that maun have sad thoughts at the back o't to some of us, but one, my friends, that keeps the hearts of Thrums folk green and ties us all thegither, like as it were wi' twine. It's to all them, wherever they may be the night, wha' have sat as lads and lasses at the Cuttle Well."

To one of the listeners it was such an un-expected ending that a faint cry broke from her, which startled the children, and they sat in silence looking at her. She had turned her face from them, but her arm was extended as if entreating Tommy to stop.

"That was the end," he said, at length, in a tone of expostulation; "it's auld Petey's speech."

"Are you sure," his mother asked wistfully, "that Petey was to say *all* them as have sat at the Cuttle Well? He made no exception, did he?"

Tommy did not know what exception was, but he assured her that he had repeated the speech, word for word. For the remainder of the evening she sat apart by the fire, while her children gambled for crack-nuts, young Petey having made a teetotum for Tommy and taught him what the letters on it meant. Their mirth rang faintly in her ear, and they scarcely heard her fits of coughing; she was as much engrossed in her own thoughts as they in theirs, but hers were sad and theirs were jocund—Hogmanay, like all festivals, being but a bank from which we can only draw what we put in. So an hour or more passed, after which Tommy whispered to Elspeth, "Now's the time; they're at it now," and each took a hand of their mother, and she woke from her reverie to find that they had pulled her from her chair and were jumping up and down, shouting excitedly, "For Auld Lang Syne, my dear, for Auld Lang Syne, Auld Lang Syne, my dear, Auld Lang Syne!" She tried to sing the words with her children, tried to dance round with them, tried to smile, but——

It was Tommy who dropped her hand first. "Mother," he cried, "your face is wet; you're greeting sair, and you said you had forgot the way."

"I mind it now, man, I mind it now," she said, standing helplessly in the middle of the room.

Elspeth nestled against her, crying, "My mother was thinking about Thrums, wasn't she Tommy?"

"I was thinking about the part o't I'm most awid to be in," the poor woman said, sinking back into her chair.

"It's the Den," Tommy told Elspeth.

"It's the Square," Elspeth told Tommy.

"No, it's Monypenny."

"No, it's the Commonty."

But it was none of these places. "It's the cemetery," the woman said, "it's the hamely, quiet cemetery on the hillside. Oh, there's mony a bonny place in my nain bonny toon, but there's nain so hamely like as the cemetery." She sat shaking in the chair, and they thought she was to say no more, but presently she rose excitedly, and with a vehemence that made them shrink from her, she cried, "I winna lie in London! tell Aaron Latta that; I winna lie in London!"

For a few more days she trudged to her work, and after that she seldom left her bed. She had no longer strength to coax up the phlegm, and a doctor brought in by Shovel's mother warned her that her days were near an end. Then she wrote her last letter to Thrums, Tommy and Elspeth standing by to pick up the pen when it fell from her feeble hand, and in the intervals she told them that she was Jean Myles.

"And if I die and Aaron hasna' come," she said, "you maun just gang to auld Petey and tell him wha you are."

"But how can you be Jean Myles?" asked astounded Tommy. "You ain't a grand lady and——"

His mother looked at Elspeth. "No' afore her," she besought him; but before he set off to post the letter she said: "Come canny into my bed the night, when Elspeth's sleeping, and syne I'll tell you all there is to tell about Jean Myles."

"Tell me now whether the letter is to Aaron Latta?"

"It's for him," she said, "but it's no' to him. I'm feared he might burn it without opening it if he saw my write on the cover, so I've wrote it to a friend of his wha will read it to him."

"And what's inside, mother?" the boy begged, inquisitively. "It must be queer things if they'll bring Aaron Latta all the way from Thrums."

"There's but little in it, man," she said, pressing her hand hard upon her chest. "It's no muckle mair than 'Auld Lang Syne, my dear, for Auld Lang Syne.'"

CHAPTER X.

THE FAVOURITE OF THE LADIES.

THAT night the excited boy was wakened by a tap-tap, as of someone knocking for admittance, and stealing to his mother's side, he cried, "Aaron Latta has come; hearken to him chapping at the door!"

It was only the man through the wall, but Mrs. Sandys took Tommy into bed with her, and while Elspeth slept told him the story of her life. She coughed feebly now, but the panting of the dying is a sound that no walls can cage, and the man continued to remonstrate at intervals. Tommy never recalled his mother's story without seeming, through the darkness in which it was told, to hear Elspeth's peaceful breathing and the angry tap-tap on the wall.

"I'm sweer to tell it to you," she began, "but tell I maun, for though it's just a warning to you and Elspeth no' to be like them that brought you into the world, it's all I have to leave you. Ay, and there's another reason: you may soon be among folk wha ken but half the story, and put a waur face on it than I deserve."

She had spoken calmly, but her next words were passionate.

"They thought I was fond of him," she cried; "oh, they were blind, blind! Frae the first I could never thole the sight o' him.

"Maybe that's no' true," she had to add. "I aye kent he was a black, but yet I couldna put him out o' my head; he took sudden grips o' me like an evil thought. I aye ran frae him, and yet I sair doubt that I went looking for him too."

"Was it Aaron Latta?" Tommy asked.

"No, it was your father. The first I ever saw of him was at Cullew, four lang miles from Thrums. There was a ball after the market, and Esther Auld and me went to it. We went in a cart, and I was wearing a pink print, wi' a white bonnet, and blue ribbons that tied aneath the chin. I had a shawl abune, no' to file them. There wasna a more innocent lassie in Thrums, man, no, nor a happier one; for Aaron Latta— Aaron came half the way wi' us, and he was hauding my hand aneath the shawl. He hadna speired me at that time, but I just kent.

"It was an auld custom to choose a queen of beauty at the ball, but that night the men couldna 'gree wha should be judge, and in the tail-end they went thegither to look for one, determined to mak' judge o' the first man they met, though they should have to tear him off a horse and bring him in by force. You wouldna believe, to look at me now, man, that I could have had any thait o' being made queen, but I was fell bonny, and I was as keen as the rest. How simple we were, all pretending to one another that we didna want to be chosen! Esther Auld said she would hod ahint the tent till a queen was picked, and at the very time she said it, she was in a palsy, through

no being able to decide whether she looked
better in her shell necklace or wanting it. She
put it on in the end, and syne when we heard
the tramp o' the men, her mind misgave her,
and she cried: 'For the love o' mercy, keep
them out till I get it off again!'" So we were
a' laughing when they came in.

"Laddie, it was your father and Elspeth's
that they brought wi' them, and he was a
stranger to us, though we kent something about
him afore the night was out. He was finely
put on, wi' a gold chain, and a free w'y of
looking at women, and if you mind o' him ava,
you ken that he was fair and buirdly, wi' a
full face, and aye a laugh ahint it. I tell ye,
man, that when our een met, and I saw that
triumphing laugh ahint his face, I took a fear
of him, as if I had guessed the end.

"For years and years after that night I
dreamed it ower again, and aye I heard mysel'
crying to God to keep that man awa' frae me.
But I doubt I put up no sic prayer at the time;
his masterful look fleid me, and yet it drew me
against my will, and I was trembling wi' pride
as well as fear when he made me queen. We
danced thegither and fought thegither a' through
the ball, and my will was no match for his, and
the warst o't was I had a kind o' secret pleasure
in being mastered.

"Man, he kissed me. Lads had kissed me
afore that night, but never since first I went wi'
Aaron Latta to the Cuttle Well. Aaron hadna
done it, but I was never to let none do it again
except him. So when your father did it I struck

him, but ahint the redness that came ower his
face I saw his triumphing laugh, and he whispered
that he liked me for the blow. He said, 'I prefer
the sweer anes, and the more you struggle, my
beauty, the better pleased I'll be.'   Almost his
hinmost words to me was, 'I've been hearing of
your Aaron, and that pleases me too!'   I fired
up at that and telled him what I thought of him,
but he said, 'If you canna abide me, what made
you dance wi' me so often?' and, oh, laddie,
that's a question that has sung in my head since
syne.

"I've telled you that we found out wha he
was, and 'deed he made no secret of it. Up to
the time he was twal year auld he had been a
kent face in that part, for his mither was a
Cullew woman called Mag Sandys—ay, and a
single woman. She was a hard ane too, for
when he was twelve year auld he flung oot o'
the house saying he would ne'er come back, and
she said he shouldna run awa' wi' thae new boots
on, so she took the boots off him and let him go.

"He was a grown man when more was heard
o' him, and syne stories came saying he was at
Redlintie, playing queer games wi' his father.
His father was gauger there, that's exciseman, a
Mr. Cray, wha got his wife out o' Thrums, and
even when he was courting her (so they say) had
the heart to be ower chief with this other woman.
Weel, Magerful Tam, as he was called through
being so masterful, cast up at Redlintie frae none
kent where, gey desperate for siller, but wi' a
black coat on his back, and he said that all he
wanted was to be owned as the gauger's son.

Mr. Cray said there was no proof that he was his son, and syne the queer sport began. Your father had noticed he was like Mr. Cray, except in the beard, and so he had his beard clippit the same, and he got haud o' some weel-kent claethes o' the gauger's that had been presented to a poor body, and he learned up a' the gauger's tricks o' speech and walking, especially a droll w'y he had o' taking snuff and syne flinging back his head. They were as like as buckies after that, and soon there was a town about it, for one day ladies would find that they had been bowing to the son thinking he was the father, and the next they wouldna speak to the father, mistaking him for the son; and a report spread to the head office o' the excise that the gauger of Redlintie spent his evenings at a public-house, singing ' The De'il's awa' wi' the Exciseman.' Tam drank nows and nans, and it ga'e Mr. Cray a turn to see him come rolling yont the street, just as if it was himsel in a looking-glass. He was a sedate-living man now, but chiefly because his wife kept him in good control, and this sight brought back auld times so vive to him, that he a kind of mistook which ane he was, and took to dropping, forgetful-like, into public-houses again. It was high time Tam should be got out of the place, and they did manage to bribe him into leaving, though no easily, for it had been fine sport to him, and to make a sensation was what he valued above all things. We heard that he went back to Redlintie a curran years after, but both the gauger and his wife were dead, and I ken that he didna trouble the twa daughters. They were

Miss Ailie and Miss Kitty, and as they werena left as well off as was expected they came to Thrums, which had been their mother's town, and started a school for the gentry there. I dinna doubt but what it's the school that Esther Auld's laddie is at.

"So, after being long lost sight of, he turned up at Cullew, wi' what looked to simple folk a fortune in his pouches, and half a dozen untrue stories about how he made it. He had come to make a show o' himsel' afore his mither, and I dare say to give her some gold, for he was aye ready to give when he had, I'll say that for him; but she had flitted to some unkent place, and so he bade on some weeks at the Cullew public. He caredna whether the folk praised or blamed him so long as they wondered at him, and queer stories about his doings was aye on the road to Thrums. One was that he gave wild suppers to whaever would come; another that he went to the kirk just for the glory of flinging a sovereign into the plate wi' a clatter; another that when he lay sleeping on twa chairs, gold and silver dribbled oot o' his trouser pouches to the floor.

"There was an ugly story, too, about a lassie, that led to his leaving the place and coming to Thrums, after he had near killed the Cullew smith in a fight. The first I heard o' his being in Thrums was when Aaron Latta walked into my granny's house and said there was a strange man at the Tappit Hen public, standing drink to any that would tak', and boasting that he had but to waggle his finger to make me give Aaron up. I went wi' Aaron and looked in at the

window, but I kent wha it was afore I looked.
If Aaron had just gone in and struck him! All
decent women, laddie, has a horror of being
fought about. I'm no sure but what that's just
the difference atween good ones and ill ones, but
this man had a power ower me; and if Aaron
had just struck him! Instead o' meddling he
turned white, and I couldna help contrasting
them, and thinking how masterful your father
looked. Fine I kent he was a brute, and yet
I couldna help admiring him for looking so
magerful.

"He bade on at the Tappit Hen, flinging his
siller about in the way that made him a king at
Cullew, but no molesting Miss Ailie and Miss
Kitty, which all but me thought was what he
had come to Thrums to do. Aaron and me was
cried for the first time the Sabbath after he
came, and the next Sabbath for the second time,
but afore that he was aye getting in my road
and speaking to me, but I ran frae him and hod
frae him when I could, and he said the reason I
did that was because I kent his will was stronger
than mine. He was aye saying things that
made me think he saw down to the bottom o'
my soul; what I didna understand was that in
mastering other women he had been learning to
master me. Ay, but though I thought ower
muckle about him, never did I speak him fair.
I loo'ed Aaron wi' all my heart, and your father
kent it; and that, I doubt, was what made him
so keen, for, oh, but he was vain!

"And now we've come to the night I'm so
sweer to speak about. She was a good happy

lassie that gaed into the Den that moonlight night wi' Aaron's arm round her, but it was another woman that came out. We thought we had the Den to oursel's, and as we sat on the Shoaging Stane at the Cuttle Well, Aaron wrote wi' a stick on the ground, 'Jean Latta,' and prigged wi' me to look at it, but I spread my hands ower my face, and he didna ken that I was keeking at it through my fingers all the time. We was so ta'en up with oursel's that we saw nobody coming, and all at once there was your father by the side o' us! 'You've written the wrong name, Aaron,' he said, jeering and pointing with his foot at the letters; 'it should be Jean Sandys.'

"Aaron said not a word, but I had a presentiment of ill, and I cried, 'Dinna let him change the name, Aaron!' Your father had been to change it himsel', but at that he had a new thait, and he said, 'No, I'll no do it; your brave Aaron shall do it for me.'

"Laddie, it doesna do for a man to be a coward afore a woman that's fond o' him. A woman will thole a man's being anything except like hersel'. When I was sure Aaron was a coward I stood still as death, waiting to ken wha's I was to be.

"Aaron did it. He was loath, but your father crushed him to the ground, and said do it he should, and warned him, too, that if he did it he would lose me, bantering him and cowing him and advising him no' to shame me, all in a breath. He kent so weel, you see, what was in my mind, and aye there was that triumphing

laugh about his face. If Aaron had fought and
been beaten, even if he had just lain there and
let the man strike away, if he had done onything
except what he was bidden, he would have won,
for it would have broken your father's power
ower me. But to write the word ! It was like
dishonouring me to save his ain skin, and your
father took good care he should ken it. You've
heard me crying to Aaron in my sleep, but it
wasna for him I cried, it was for his fireside.
All the love I had for him, and it was muckle,
was skailed forever that night at the Cuttle
Well. Without a look ahint me away I went
wi' my master, and I had no more will to resist
him—and oh, man, man, when I came to mysel'
next morning I wished I had never been born !

"The men folk saw that Aaron had shamed
them, and they werena quite so set agin me as
the women, wha had guessed the truth, though
they couldna be sure o't. Sair I pitied mysel',
and sair I grat, but only when none was looking.
The mair they miscalled me the higher I held
my head, and I hung on your father's arm as if
I adored him, and I boasted about his office and
his clerk in London till they believed what I
didna believe a word o' mysel'.

"But though I put sic a brave face on't, I
was near demented in case he shouldna marry
me, and he kent that and jokit me about it.
Dinna think I was fond o' him; I hated him
now. And dinna think his masterfulness had
ony more power ower me ; his power was broken
forever when I woke up that weary morning.
But that was ower late, and to wait on by mysel'

I

in Thrums for what might happen, and me a
single woman—I daredna! So I flattered at
him, and flattered at him, till I got the fool side
o' him, and he married me.

" My granny let the marriage take place in
her house, and he sent in so muckle meat and
drink that some folk was willing to come. One
came that wasna wanted. In the middle o' the
marriage Aaron Latta, wha had refused to speak
to onybody since that night, walked in wearing
his blacks, wi' crape on them, as if it was a
funeral, and all he said was that he had come to
see Jean Myles coffined. He went away quietly
as soon as we was married, but the crowd outside
had fathomed his meaning, and abune the
minister's words I could hear them crying, 'Ay,
it's mair like a burial than a marriage!'

" My heart was near breaking wi' woe, but
oh, I was awid they shouldna ken it, and the
bravest thing I ever did was to sit through the
supper that night, making muckle o' your father,
looking fond-like at him, laughing at his coarse
jokes, and secretly hating him down to my very
marrow a' the time. The crowd got word o' the
on-goings, and they took a cruel revenge. A
carriage had been ordered for nine o'clock to take
us to Tilliedrum, where we should get the train to
London, and when we heard it, as we thought,
drive up to the door, out we went, me on your
father's arm laughing, but wi' my teeth set.
But Aaron's words had put an idea into their
heads, though he didna intend it, and they had
got out the hearse. It was the hearse they had
brought to the door instead of a carriage.

" We got awa' in a carriage in the tailend, and the stanes hitting it was all the good luck flung after me. It had just one horse, and I mind how I cried to Esther Auld, wha had been the first to throw, that when I came back it would be in a carriage and pair.

" Ay, I had pride! In the carriage your father telled me as a joke that he had got away without paying the supper, and that about all the money he had now, forby what was to pay our tickets to London, was the half-sovereign on his watch-chain. But I was determined to have Thrums think I had married grand, and as I had three pounds six on me, the savings o' all my days, I gave two pounds to Malcolm Crabb, the driver, unbeknown to your father, but pretending it was frae him, and telled him to pay for the supper and the carriage with it. He said it was far ower muckle, but I just laughed, and said wealthy gentlemen like Mr. Sandys couldna be bothered to take back change, so Malcolm could keep what was ower. Malcolm was the man Esther Auld had just married, and I counted on this maddening her and on Malcolm's spreading the story through the town. Laddie, I've kent since syne what it is to be without bite or sup, but I've never grudged that siller."

The poor woman had halted many times in her tale, and she was glad to make an end. " You've forgotten what a life he led me in London," she said, " and it could do you no good to hear it, though it might be a lesson to thae lassies at the dancing-school wha think so much o' masterful men. It was by betting at horse-races that your father made a living, and whiles he was large o' siller, but that didna last, and I question whether he would have stuck to me if I hadna got work. Well, he's gone, and the Thrums folk'll soon ken the truth about Jean Myles now."

She paused, and then cried, with extraordinary vehemence, "Oh, man, how I wish I could keep it frae them for ever and ever!"

But presently she was calm again, and she said: "What I've been telling you, you can understand little o' the now, but some of it will come back to you when you're a grown man, and if you're magerful and have some lassie in your grip, may be for the memory of her that bore you, you'll let the poor thing awa'."

And she asked him to add this to his nightly prayer: "O God, keep me from being a magerful man!" and to teach this other prayer to Elspeth: "O God, whatever is to be my fate, may I never be one of them that bow the knee to magerful men, and if I was born like that and canna help it, O take me up to heaven afore I'm fil't."

The wardrobe was invisible in the darkness, but they could still hear Elspeth's breathing as she slept, and the exhausted woman listened long to it, as if she would fain carry away with her to the other world the memory of that sweet sound.

"If you gang to Thrums," she said at last, "you may hear my story frae some that winna spare me in the telling; but should Elspeth be wi' you at sic times, dinna answer back; just slip quietly awa' wi' her. She's so young that she'll soon forget all about her life in London and all about me, and that'll be best for her. I would like her lassiehood to be bright and free frae cares, as if there had never been sic a woman as me. But laddie, oh, my laddie, dinna you forget me; you and me had him to thole thegither, dinna you forget me! Watch ower your little sister by day and hap her by night, and when the time comes that a man wants her—if he be magerful, tell her my story at once. But gin she loves one that is her ain true love, dinna rub off the bloom, laddie, with a word about me. Let her and him gang to the Cuttle Well, as Aaron and me went, kenning no guile and thinking none, and with their arms round one another's waist. But when her wedding-day comes round——"

Her words broke in a sob and she cried: " I see them, I see them standing up thegither afore the minister! Oh! you lad, you lad that's to be married on my Elspeth, turn your face and let me see that you're no' a magerful man!"

But the lad did not turn his face, and when she spoke next it was to Tommy.

"In the bottom o' my kist there's a little silver teapot. It's no' real silver, but it's fell bonny. I bought it for Elspeth twa or three months back when I saw I couldna last the winter. I bought it to her for a marriage present. She's no' to see it till her wedding-day comes round. Syne you're to give it to her, man, and say it's with her mother's love. Tell her all about me, for it canna harm her then.

Tell her of the fool lies I sent to Thrums, but
dinna forget what a bonny place I thought it all
the time, nor how I stood on many a driech
night at the corner of that street, looking so
waeful at the lighted windows, and hungering
for the wring of a Thrums hand or the sound of
the Thrums word, and all the time the shrewd
blasts cutting through my thin trails of claithes.
Tell her, man, how you and me spent this night,
and how I fought to keep my hoast down so as
no' to waken her. Mind that whatever I have
been, I was aye fond o' my bairns, and slaved for
them till I dropped. She'll have long forgotten
what I was like, and it's just as well, but yet—
Look at me, Tommy, look long, long, so as you'll
be able to call up my face as it was on the far-
back night when I telled you my mournful
story. Na, you canna see in the dark, but haud
my hand, haud it tight, so that, when you tell
Elspeth, you'll mind how hot it was, and the
skin loose on it; and put your hand on my
cheeks, man, and feel how wet they are wi'
sorrowful tears, and lay it on my breast, so that
you can tell her how I was shrunk awa'. And if
she greets for her mother a whiley, let her
greet."

The sobbing boy hugged his mother. "Do
you think I'm an auld woman?" she said to
him.

"You're gey auld, are you no'?" he
answered.

"Ay," she said, "I'm gey auld; I'm nine
and twenty. I was seventeen on the day when
Aaron Latta went half-road in the cart wi' me to

Cullew, hauding my hand aneath my shawl. He hedna spiered me, but I just kent."

Tommy remained in his mother's bed for the rest of the night, and so many things were buzzing in his brain that not for an hour did he think it time to repeat his new prayer. At last he said reverently: "O God, keep me from becoming a magerful man!" Then he opened his eyes to let God see that his prayer was ended, and added to himself: "But I think I would fell like it."

CHAPTER XI.

AARON LATTA.

THE Airlie post had dropped the letters for
outlying farms at the Monypenny smithy and
trudged on. The smith having wiped his hand
on his hair, made a row of them, without looking
at the addresses, on his window-sill, where, happening to be seven in number, they were
almost a model of Monypenny, which is within
hail of Thrums, but round the corner from it,
and so has ways of its own. With the next
clang on the anvil the middle letter fell flat, and
now the likeness to Monypenny was absolute.

Again all the sound in the land was the
melancholy sweet kink, kink, kink of the smith's
hammer.

Across the road sat Dite Deuchars, the
mole catcher, a solitary figure, taking his pleasure on the dyke. Behind him was the flour-
miller's field, and beyond it the den, of which
only some tree-tops were visible. He looked
wearily east the road, but no one emerged from
Thrums; he looked wearily west the road, which
doubled out of sight at Aaron Latta's cottage,
little more than a stone's throw distant. On
the inside of Aaron's window an endless procession seemed to be passing, but it was only the
warping mill going round. It was an empty
day, but Dite, the accursed, was used to them;

nothing ever happened where he was, but many things as soon as he had gone.

He yawned and looked at the houses opposite. They were all of one story; the smith's had a rusty plough stowed away on its roof; under a window stood a pew and bookboard, bought at the roup of an old church, and thus transformed into a garden-seat. There were many of them in Thrums that year. All the doors, except that of the smithy, were shut, until one of them blew ajar, when Dite knew at once, from the smell which crossed the road, that Blinder was in the bunk pulling the teeth of his potatoes. May Ann Irons, the blind man's niece, came out at this door to beat the cistern with a bass, and she gave Dite a wag of her head. He was to be married to her if she could get nothing better.

By-and-by the Painted Lady came along the road. She was a little woman, brightly dressed, so fragile that a collie might have knocked her over with his tail, and she had a beautiful white-and-pink face, the white ending of a sudden in the middle of her neck, where it met skin of a duller colour. As she tripped along with mincing gait, she was speaking confidentially to herself, but when she saw Dite grinning, she seemed, first, afraid, and then sorry for herself, and then she tried to carry it off with a giggle, cocking her head impudently at him. Even then she looked childish, and a faded guilelessness, with many pretty airs and graces, still lingered about her, like innocent birds loath to be gone from the spot where their nest has been.

When she had passed monotony again reigned, and Dite crossed to the smithy window, though none of the letters could be for him. He could read the addresses on six of them, but the seventh lay on its back, and every time he rose on his tip-toes to squint down at it, the spout pushed his bonnet over his eyes.

"Smith," he cried in at the door, "to gang hame afore I ken wha that letter's to is more than I can do."

The smith good-naturedly brought the letter to him, and then glancing at the address was dumfounded. "God behears," he exclaimed, with a sudden look at the distant cemetery, "it's to Double Dykes!"

Dite also shot a look at the cemetery. "He'll never get it," he said, with mighty conviction.

The two men gazed at the cemetery for some time, and at last Dite muttered, "Ay, ay, Double Dykes, you was aye fond o' your joke!"

"What has that to do wi' 't?" rapped out the smith, uncomfortably.

Dite shuddered. "Man," he said, "does that letter no bring Double Dykes back terrible vive again! If we was to see him climbing the cemetery dyke the now, and coming stepping down the fields in his moleskin waistcoat wi' the pearl buttons——"

Auchterlonie stopped him with a nervous gesture.

"But it couldna be the pearl buttons," Dite added thoughtfully, "for Betty Finlayson has been wearing them to the kirk this four year. Ay, ay, Double Dykes, that puts you farther awa' again."

The smith took the letter to a neighbour's house to ask the advice of old Irons, the blind tailor, who when he lost his sight had given himself the name of Blinder for bairns to play with.

"Make your mind easy, smith," was Blinder's counsel. "The letter is meant for the Painted Lady. What's Double Dykes? It's but the name of a farm, and we gave it to Sanders because he was the farmer. He's dead, and them that's in the house now become Double Dykes in his place."

But the Painted Lady only had the house, objected Dite; Nether Drumgley was farming the land, and so he was the real Double Dykes. True, she might have pretended to her friends that she had the land also.

She had no friends, the smith said, and since she came to Double Dykes from no one could find out where, though they knew her furniture was bought in Tilliedrum, she had never got a letter. Often, though, as she passed his window she had keeked sideways at the letters, as bairns might look at parlys. If he made a tinkle with his hammer at such times off she went at once, for she was as easily flichtered as a field of crows, that take wing if you tap your pipe on the loof of your hand. It was true she had spoken to him once; when he suddenly saw her standing at his smiddy door, the surprise near made him fall over his brot. She looked so neat and ladylike that he gave his hair a respectful pull before he remembered the kind of woman she was.

And what was it she said to him? Dite asked eagerly.

She had pointed to the letters on the window-sill, and said she, "Oh, the dear loves!" It was a queer say, but she had a bonny English word. The English word was no doubt prideful, but it melted in the mouth like a lick of sirup. She offered him sixpence for a letter, any letter he liked, but of course he refused it. Then she prigged with him just to let her hold one in her hands, for said she, bairnlike, "I used to get one every day." It so happened that one of the letters was to Mysy Robbie; and Mysy was of so little importance that he thought there would be no harm in letting the Painted Lady hold her letter, so he gave it to her, and you should have seen her dawting it with her hand and holding it to her breast like a lassie with a pigeon. "Isn't it sweet?" she said, and before he could stop her she kissed it. She forgot it was no letter of hers, and made to open it, and then she fell a-trembling and saying she durst not read it, for you never know whether the first words might not break your heart. The envelope was red where her lips had touched it, and yet she had an innocent look beneath the paint. When he took the letter from her, though, she called him a low, vulgar fellow for presuming to address a lady. She worked herself into a fury, and said far worse than that; a perfect guller of clarty language came pouring out of her. He had heard women curse many a time without turning a hair, but he felt wae when she did it, for she just spoke it like a bairn that had been in ill company.

The smith's wife, Suphy, who had joined the company, thought that men were easily taken in, especially smiths. She offered, however, to convey the letter to Double Dykes. She was anxious to see the inside of the Painted Lady's house, and this would be a good opportunity. She admitted that she had crawled to the east window of it before now, but that dour bairn of the Painted Lady's had seen her head and whipped down the blind.

Unfortunate Suphy! she could not try the window this time, as it was broad daylight, and the Painted Lady took the letter from her at the door. She returned crestfallen, and for an hour nothing happened. The mole-catcher went off to the square, saying, despondently, that nothing would happen until he was round the corner. No sooner had he rounded the corner than something did happen.

A girl who had left Double Dykes with a letter was walking quickly towards Monypenny. She wore a white pinafore over a magenta frock, and no one could tell her whether she was seven or eight, for she was only the Painted Lady's child. Some boys, her natural enemies, were behind; they had just emerged from the Den, and she heard them before they saw her, and at once her little heart jumped and ran off with her. But the halloo that told her she was discovered

checked her running. Her teeth went into her
underlip; now her head was erect. After her
came the rabble with a rush, flinging stones that
had no mark and epithets that hit. Grizel dis-
dained to look over her shoulder. Little hunted
child, where was succour to come from if she
could not fight for herself?

Though under the torture she would not
cry out. "What's a father?" was their
favourite jeer, because she had once innocently
asked this question of a false friend. One tried
to snatch the letter from her, but she flashed him
a look that sent him to the other side of the
dyke, where, he said, did she think he was afraid
of her? Another strutted by her side, mimicking her in such diverting manner that presently
the others had to pick him out of the ditch.
Thus Grizel moved onward defiantly until she
reached Monypenny, where she tossed the letter
in at the smithy door and immediately returned
home. It was the letter that had been sent to
her mother, now sent back, because it was meant
for the dead farmer after all.

The smith read Jean Myles's last letter, with
a face of growing gravity. "Dear Double
Dykes," it said, " I send you these few scrapes
to say I am dying, and you and Aaron Latta
was seldom sindry, so I charge you to go to him
and say to him 'Aaron Latta, it's all lies Jean
Myles wrote to Thrums about her grandeur, and
her man died mony year back, and it was the
only kindness he ever did her, and if she doesna
die quick, her and her starving bairns will be
flung out into the streets.' If that doesna move

him, say, 'Aaron Latta, do you mind yon day
at Inverquharity and the cushie doos?' likewise,
'Aaron Latta, do you mind yon day at the
Kaims of Airlie?' likewise, 'Aaron Latta, do
you mind that Jean Myles was ower heavy for
you to lift? Oh, Aaron, you could lift me so
pitiful easy now.' And syne says you solemnly
three times, 'Aaron Latta, Jean Myles is lying
dying all alone in a foreign land; Aaron Latta,
Jean Myles is lying dying all alone in a foreign
land; Aaron Latta, Jean Myles is lying dying all
alone in a foreign land.' And if he's sweer to
come, just say, 'Oh, Aaron, man, you micht; oh,
Aaron, oh, Aaron, are you coming?'"

The smith had often denounced this woman,
but he never said a word against her again. He
stood long reflecting, and then took the letter to
Blinder and read it to him.

"She doesna say, 'Oh, Aaron Latta, do you
mind the Cuttle Well?'" was the blind man's
first comment.

"She was thinking about it," said
Auchterlonie.

"Ay, and he's thinking about it," said
Blinder, "night and day, night and day. What
a town there'll be about that letter, smith!"

"There will. But I'm to take it to Aaron
afore the news spreads. He'll never gang to
London though."

"I think he will, smith."

"I ken him well."

"Maybe I ken him better."

"You canna see the ugly mark it left on
his brow."

" I can see the uglier marks it has left in his breast."

" Well, I'll take the letter; I can do no more."

When the smith opened the door of Aaron's house he let out a draught of hot air that was glad to be gone from the warper's restless home. The usual hallan, or passage, divided the but from the ben, and in the ben a great revolving thing, the warping-mill, half filled the room. Between it and a pile of webs that obscured the light, a little silent man was sitting on a box turning a handle. His shoulders were almost as high as his ears, as if he had been caught for ever in a storm, and though he was barely five and thirty, he had the tattered, dishonoured beard of black and white that comes to none till the glory of life has gone.

Suddenly the smith appeared round the webs. "Aaron," he said awkwardly, "do you mind Jean Myles?"

The warper did not for a moment take his eyes off a contrivance with pirns in it that was climbing up and down the whirring mill.

"She's dead," he answered.

"She's dying," said the smith.

A thread broke, and Aaron had to rise to mend it.

"Stop the mill and listen," Auchterlonie begged him, but the warper returned to his seat and the mill again revolved.

"This is her dying words to you," continued the smith. "Did you speak?"

"I didna, but I wish you would take your arm off the haik."

"She's loath to die without seeing you. Do you hear, man? You shall listen to me, I tell you."

"I am listening, smith," the warper replied, without rancour. "It's but right that you should come here to take your pleasure on a shamed man." His calmness gave him a kind of dignity.

"Did I ever say you was a shamed man, Aaron?"

"Am I not?" the warper asked quietly; and Auchterlonie hung his head.

Aaron continued, still turning the handle, "You're truthful, and you canna deny it. Nor will you deny that I shamed you and every other mother's son that night. You try to hod it out o' pity, smith, but even as you look at me now, does the man in you no rise up against me?"

"If so," the smith answered reluctantly, "if so, it's against my will."

"It is so," said Aaron in the same measured voice, "and it's right that it should be so. A man may thieve or debauch or murder, and yet no be so very different frae his fellow-men, but there's one thing he shall not do without their wanting to spit him out o' their mouths, and that is, violate the feelings of sex."

The strange words in which the warper described his fall had always an uncomfortable effect on those who heard him use them, and Auchterlonie could only answer in distress, "Maybe that's what it is."

"That's what it is. I have had twal lang

j

years sitting on this box to think it out. I blame none but mysel'."

"Then you'll have pity on Jean in her sair need," said the smith. He read slowly the first part of the letter, but Aaron made no comment, and the mill had not stopped for a moment.

"She says," the smith proceeded, doggedly— "she says to say to you, 'Aaron Latta, do you mind yon day at Inverquharity and the cushie doos?'"

Only the monotonous whirr of the mill replied.

"She says, 'Aaron Latta, do you mind that Jean Myles was ower heavy for you to lift? Oh, Aaron, you could lift me so pitiful easy now.'"

Another thread broke and the warper rose with sudden fury.

"Now that you've eased your conscience, smith," he said, fiercely, "make your feet your friend."

"I'll do so," Auchterlonie answered, laying the letter on the webs, "but I leave this ahint me."

"Wap it in the fire."

"If that's to be done, you do it yoursel'. Aaron, she treated you ill, but——"

"There's the door, smith."

The smith walked away, and had only gone a few steps when he heard the whirr of the mill again. He went back to the door.

"She's dying, man!" he cried.

"Let her die!" answered Aaron.

In an hour the sensational news was through

half of Thrums, of which Monypenny may be regarded as a broken piece, left behind, like the dot of quicksilver in the tube, to show how high the town once rose. Some could only rejoice at first in the down-come of Jean Myles, but most blamed the smith (and himself among them) for not taking notice of her address, so that Thrums Street could be informed of it and sent to her relief. For Blinder alone believed that Aaron would be softened.

"It was twa threads the smith saw him break," the blind man said, "and Aaron's good at his work. He'll go to London, I tell you."

"You forget, Blinders, that he was warping afore I was a dozen steps frae the door."

"Ay, and that just proves he hadna burned the letter, for he hadna time. If he didna do it at the first impulse, he'll no do it now."

Every little while the boys were sent along the road to look in at Aaron's end window and report.

At seven in the evening Aaron had not left his box, and the blind man's reputation for seeing farther than those with eyes was fallen low.

"It's a good sign," he insisted, nevertheless. "It shows his mind's troubled, for he usually louses at six."

By eight the news was that Aaron had left his mill and was sitting staring at his kitchen fire.

"He's thinking of Inverquharity and the cushie doos," said Blinder.

"More likely," said Dite Deuchars, "he's thinking o' the Cuttle Well."

Corp Shiach clattered along the road about nine to say that Aaron Latta was putting on his blacks as if for a journey.

At once the blind man's reputation rose on stilts. It fell flat, however, before the ten-o'clock bell rang, when three of the Auchterlonie children, each pulling the other back that he might arrive first, announced that Aaron had put on his corduroys again, and was back at the mill.

"That settles it," was everyone's good-night to Blinder, but he only answered thought-fully, "There's a fierce fight going on, my billies."

Next morning when his niece was shaving the blind man, the razor had to travel over a triumphant smirk which would not explain itself to womankind, Blinder being a man who could bide his time. The time came when the smith looked in to say, "Should I gang yont to Aaron's and see if he'll give me the puir woman's address?"

"No, I wouldna advise that," answered Blinder, cleverly concealing his elation, "for Aaron Latta's awa' to London."

"What! How can you ken?"

"I heard him go by in the night."

"It's no possible!"

"I kent his foot."

"You're sure it was Aaron?"

Blinder did not consider this question worth answering, his sharpness at recognising friends by their tread being proved. Sometimes he may have carried his pretensions too far. Many granted that he could tell when a doctor went by, when a lawyer, when a thatcher, when a herd, and this is conceivable, for all callings have their walk. But he was regarded as uncanny when he claimed not only to know ministers in this way, but to be able to distinguish between the steps of the different denominations.

He had made no mistake about the warper, however. Aaron was gone, and ten days elapsed before he was again seen in Thrums.

CHAPTER XII.

A CHILD'S TRAGEDY.

No one in Thrums ever got a word from Aaron Latta about how he spent those ten days, and Tommy and Elspeth, whom he brought back with him, also tried to be reticent, but some of the women were too clever for them. Jean and Aaron did not meet again. Her first intimation that he had come she got from Shovel, who said that a little high-shouldered man in black had been inquiring if she was dead, and was now walking up and down the street like one waiting. She sent her children out to him, but he would not come up. He had answered Tommy roughly, but when Elspeth slipped her hand into his, he let it stay there, and he instructed her to tell Jean Myles that he would bury her in the Thrums cemetery and bring up her bairns. Jean managed once to go to the window and look down at him, and by-and-by he looked up and saw her. They looked long at each other, and then he turned away his head and began to walk up and down again.

At Tilliedrum the coffin was put into a hearse and thus conveyed to Monypenny, Aaron and the two children sitting on the box-seat. Someone said, " Jean Myles boasted that when she came back to Thrums it would be in her carriage and pair, and she has kept her word," and the saying is still preserved in that Bible for week-days of which all little places have their unwritten copy, one of the wisest of books, but nearly every text in it has cost a life.

About a score of men put on their blacks and followed the hearse from the warper's house to the grave. Elspeth wanted to accompany Tommy, but Aaron held her back, saying, quietly, " In this part, it's only men that go to burials, so you and me maun bide at hame," and then she cried, no one understood why, except Tommy. It was because he would see Thrums first; but he whispered to her, " I promise to keep my eyes shut and no look once," and so faithfully did he keep his promise on the whole that the smith held him by the hand most of the way, under the impression that he was blind.

But he had opened his eyes at the grave, when a cord was put into his hand, and then he wept passionately, and on his way back to Monypenny, whether his eyes were open or shut, what he saw was his mother being shut up in a black hole and trying for ever and ever to get out. He ran to Elspeth for comfort, but in the meantime she had learned from Blinder's niece that graves are dark and cold, and so he found her sobbing even like himself. Tommy could never bear to see Elspeth crying, and he revealed his true self in his way of drying her tears.

" It will be so cold in that hole," she sobbed.

" No," he said, " it's warm."

" It will be dark."

" No, it's clear."

" She would like to get out,"

"No, she was terrible pleased to get in."

It was characteristic of him that he soon had Elspeth happy by arguments not one of which he believed himself; characteristic also that his own grief was soothed by the sound of them. Aaron, who was in the garret preparing their bed, had told the children that they must remain indoors to-day out of respect to their mother's memory (to-morrow morning they could explore Thrums); but there were many things in that kitchen for them to look at and exult over. It had no commonplace ceiling, the couples, or rafters, being covered with the loose flooring of a romantic garret, and in the rafters were several great hooks, from one of which hung a ham, and Tommy remembered, with a thrill which he communicated to Elspeth, that it is the right of Thrums children to snip off the ham as much as they can remove with their finger nails and roast it on the ribs of the fire. The chief pieces of furniture were a dresser, a corner cupboard with diamond panes, two tables, one of which stood beneath the other, but would have to come out if Aaron tried to bake, and a bed with a door. These two did not know it, but the room was full of memories of Jean Myles. The corner cupboard had been bought by Aaron at a roup because she said she would like to have one; it was she who had chosen the six cups and saucers with the blue spots on them. A razor-strop, now hard as iron, hung on a nail on the wall; it had not been used since the last time Aaron strutted through the Den with his sweetheart. One day later he had opened the door of the bird-cage, which still stood in the window, and let the yellow yite go. Many things were where no woman would have left them: clothes on the floor with the nail they had torn from the wall; on a chair a tin basin, soapy water and a flannel rag in it; horn spoons with whistles at the end of them were anywhere—on the mantelpiece, beneath the bed; there were drawers that could not be opened because their handles were inside. Perhaps the windows were closed hopelessly also, but this must be left doubtful; no one had ever tried to open them.

The garret where Tommy and Elspeth were to sleep was reached by a ladder from the hallan; when you were near the top of the ladder your head hit a trap-door and pushed it open. At one end of the garret was the bed, and at the other end were piled sticks for firewood and curious dark-coloured slabs whose smell the children disliked, until Tommy said, excitedly, "Peat!" and then they sniffed reverently.

It was Tommy, too, who discovered the tree-tops of the Den, and Elspeth seeing him gazing in a transport out at the window cried, "What is it Tommy? Quick!"

"Promise no to scream," he replied, warningly. "Well, then, Elspeth Sandys, that's where the Den is!"

Elspeth blinked with awe, and anon said, wistfully. "Tommy, do you see that there? That's where the Den is!"

"It were me what told you," cried Tommy, jealously.

" But let me tell you, Tommy! "

" Well, then, you can tell me."

" That there is the Den, Tommy! "

" Dagont! "

Oh, that to-morrow were here! Oh, that Shovel could see these two to-morrow!

Here is another splendid game, T. Sandys, inventor. The girl goes into the bed, the boy shuts the door on her, and imitates the sound of a train in motion. He opens the door and cries, "Tickets, please." The girl says, " What is the name of this place? " The boy replies, " It's Thrums! " There is more to follow, but the only two who have played the game always roared so joyously at this point that they could get no farther.

" Oh, to-morrow, come quick, quick! "

" Oh, poor Shovel! "

To-morrow came, and with it two eager little figures rose and gulped their porridge, and set off to see Thrums. They were dressed in the black clothes Aaron Latta had bought for them in London, and they had agreed just to walk, but when they reached the door and saw the tree-tops of the Den they—they ran. Would you not like to hold them back? It is a child's tragedy.

They went first into the Den, and the rocks were dripping wet, all the trees, save the firs, were bare, and the mud round a tiny spring pulled off one of Elspeth's boots.

" Tommy," she cried, quaking, " that narsty puddle can't not be the Cuttle Well, can it? "

" No, it ain't," said Tommy, quickly, but he feared it was.

"It's c-c-colder here than London," Elspeth said, shivering, and Tommy was shivering too, but he answered, "I'm—I'm—I'm warm."

The Den was strangely small, and soon they were on a shabby brae where women in short gowns came to their doors and men in night-caps sat down on the shafts of their barrows to look at Jean Myles's bairns.

"What does yer think?" Elspeth whispered very doubtfully.

"They're beauties," Tommy answered, deter-minedly.

Presently Elspeth cried, "Oh, Tommy, what a ugly stair! Where is the beauty stairs as is wore outside for show?"

This was one of them and Tommy knew it. "Wait till you see the west town end," he said bravely; "it's grand." But when they were in the west town end, and he had to admit it, "Wait till you see the square," he said, and when they were in the square, "Wait," he said huskily, "till you see the town-house." Alas, this was the town-house facing them, and when they knew it, he said hurriedly, "Wait till you see the Auld Licht Kirk."

They stood long in front of the Auld Licht Kirk, which he had sworn was bigger and love-lier than St. Paul's, but—well, it is a different style of architecture, and had Elspeth not been there with tears in waiting, Tommy would have blubbered. "It's—it's littler than I thought," he said desperately, "but—the minister, oh, what a wonderful big man he is!"

"Are you sure?" Elspeth squeaked.

" I swear he is."

The church door opened and a gentleman came out, a little man, boyish in the back, with the eager face of those who live too quickly. But it was not at him that Tommy pointed reassuringly ; it was at the monster church key, half of which protruded from his tail pocket and waggled like the hilt of a sword.

Speaking like an old residenter, Tommy explained that he had brought his sister to see the church. " She's ta'en aback," he said, picking out Scotch words carefully, " because it's littler than the London kirks, but I told her—I told her that the preaching is better."

This seemed to please the stranger, for he patted Tommy on the head while inquiring, " How do you know that the preaching is better ? "

" Tell him, Elspeth," replied Tommy modestly.

" There ain't nuthin' as Tommy don't know," Elspeth explained. " He knows what the minister is like too."

" He's a noble sight," said Tommy.

" He can get anything from God he likes," said Elspeth.

" He's a terrible big man," said Tommy.

This seemed to please the little gentleman less. " Big ! " he exclaimed, irritably ; " why should he be big ? "

" He is big," Elspeth almost screamed, for the minister was her last hope.

" Nonsense ! " said the little gentleman. " He is—well, I am the minister."

"You!" roared Tommy, wrathfully.

"Oh, oh, oh!" sobbed Elspeth.

For a moment the Rev. Mr. Dishart looked as if he would like to knock two little heads together, but he walked away without doing it.

"Never mind," Tommy whispered hoarsely to Elspeth. "Never mind, Elspeth, you have me yet."

This consolation seldom failed to gladden her, but her disappointment was so sharp to-day that she would not even look up.

"Come away to the cemetery, it's grand," he said; but still she would not be comforted.

"And I'll let you hold my hand—as soon as we're past the houses," he added.

"I'll let you hold it now," he said eventually; but even then Elspeth cried dismally, and her sobs were hurting him more than her.

He knew all the ways of getting round Elspeth, and when next he spoke it was with a sorrowful dignity. "I didna think," he said, "as yer wanted me never to be able to speak again; no, I didna think it, Elspeth."

She took her hands from her face and looked at him inquiringly.

"One of the stories mamma told me and Reddy," he said, "were about a man what saw such a beauty thing that he was struck dumb with admiration. Struck dumb is never to be able to speak again, and I wish I had been struck dumb when you wanted it."

"But I didn't want it!" Elspeth cried.

"If Thrums had been one little bit beautier than it is," he went on solemnly, "it would

have struck me dumb. It would have hurt
me sore, but what about that, if it pleased
you!"

Then did Elspeth see what a wicked girl she
had been, and when next the two were observed
by the curious (it was on the cemetery road),
they were once more looking cheerful. At the
smallest provocation they exchanged notes of
admiration, such as, "Oh, Tommy, what a
bonny barrel!" or "Oh, Elspeth, I tell yer
that's a dyke, and there's just walls in London,"
but sometimes Elspeth would stoop hastily, pretending that she wanted to tie her bootlace, but
really to brush away a tear, and there were
moments when Tommy hung very limp. Each
was trying to deceive the other for the other's
sake, and one of them was never good at decep-
tion. They saw through each other, yet kept
up the chilly game, because they could think of
nothing better, and perhaps the game was worth
playing, for love invented it.

They sat down on their mother's grave. No
stone was ever erected to the memory of Jean
Myles, but it is enough for her that she lies
at home. That comfort will last her to the
Judgment Day.

The man who dug the grave sent them away,
and they wandered to the hill, and thence down
the Roods, where there were so many outside
stairs not put there for show that it was well
Elspeth remembered how susceptible Tommy
was to being struck dumb. For her sake he
said, "They're bonny," and for his sake she replied, "I'm glad they ain't bonnier."

When within one turn of Monypenny they came suddenly upon some boys playing at capey-dykey, a game with marbles that is only known in Thrums. There are thirty-five ways of playing marbles, but this is the best way, and Elspeth knew that Tommy was hungering to look on, but without her, lest he should be accused of sweethearting. So she offered to remain in the background.

Was she sure she shouldn't mind?

She said falteringly that of course she would mind a little, but——

Then Tommy was irritated, and said he knew she would mind, but if she just pretended she didn't mind, he could leave her without feeling that he was mean.

So Elspeth affected not to mind, and then he deserted her, conscience at rest, which was his nature. But he should have remained with her. The players only gave him the side of their eye, and a horrid fear grew on him that they did not know he was a Thrums boy. "Dagont!" he cried to put them right on that point, but though they paused in their game, it was only to laugh at him uproariously. Let the historian use an oath for once; dagont, Tommy had said the swear in the wrong place!

How fond he had been of that word! Many a time he had fired it in the face of Londoners, and the flash had often blinded them and always him. Now he had brought it home, and Thrums would have none of it; it was as if these boys were jeering at their own flag. He tottered away from them until he came to a trance, or passage, where he put his face to the wall and forgot even Elspeth.

He had not noticed a girl pass the mouth of the trance, trying not very successfully to conceal a brandy bottle beneath her pinafore, but presently he heard shouts, and looking out he saw Grizel, the Painted Lady's child, in the hands of her tormentors. She was unknown to him, of course, but she hit back so courageously that he watched her with interest, until—until suddenly he retreated farther into the trance. He had seen Elspeth go on her knees, obviously to ask God to stay the hands and tongues of these cruel boys.

Elspeth had disgraced him, he felt. He was done with her for ever. If they struck her, serve her right.

Struck her! Struck little Elspeth! His imagination painted the picture with one sweep of its brush. Take care, you boys, Tommy is scudding back.

They had not molested Elspeth as yet. When they saw and heard her praying they had bent forward, agape, as if struck suddenly in the stomach. Then one of them, Francie Crabb, the golden-haired son of Esther Auld, recovered and began to knead Grizel's back with his fists, less in viciousness than to show that the prayer was futile. Into this scene sprang Tommy, and he thought that Elspeth was the kneaded one. Had he taken time to reflect he would probably have used the Thrums feint, and then in with a left-hander, which is not very efficacious in its own country; but being in a hurry he let out with Shovel's favourite, and down went Francie Crabb.

"Would you!" said Tommy, threateningly, when Francie attempted to rise.

He saw now that Elspeth was untouched, that he had rescued an unknown girl, and it cannot be pretended of him that he was the boy to squire all ladies in distress. In ordinary circumstances he might have left Grizel to her fate, but having struck for her, he felt that he would like to go on striking. He had also the day's disappointments to avenge. It is startling to reflect that the little minister's height, for instance, put an extra kick in him.

So he stood stridelegs over Francie, who whimpered, "I wouldna have struck this one if that one hadna prayed for me. It wasna likely I would stand that."

"You shall stand it," replied Tommy, and turning to Elspeth, who had risen from her knees, he said: "Pray away, Elspeth."

Elspeth refused, feeling that there would be something wrong in praying from triumph, and Tommy, about to be very angry with her, had a glorious inspiration. "Pray for yourself," he said to Francie, "and do it out loud."

The other boys saw that a novelty promised, and now Francie need expect no aid from them. At first he refused to pray, but he succumbed when Tommy had explained the consequences and illustrated them.

Tommy dictated: "Oh, God, I am a sinner Go on."

Francie not only said it, but looked it.

K

"And I pray to you to repent me, though I ain't worthy," continued Tommy.

"And I pray to you to repent me, though I ain't worthy," growled Francie. (It was the arrival of ain't in Thrums.)

Tommy considered, and then: "I thank Thee, O God," he said, "for telling this girl—this lassie—to pray for me."

Two gentle taps helped to knock this out of Francie.

Being an artist, Tommy had kept his best for the end (and made it up first). "And lastly," he said, "I thank this boy for thrashing me—I mean this here laddie. Oh, may he allus be near to thrash me when I strike this other lassie again. Amen."

When it was all over Tommy looked around triumphantly, and though he liked the expression on several faces, Grizel's pleased him best. "It ain't no wonder you would like to be me, lassie!" he said, in an ecstasy.

"I don't want to be you, you conceited boy," retorted the Painted Lady's child hotly, and her heat was the greater because the clever little wretch had read her thoughts aright. But it was her sweet voice that surprised him.

"You're English!" he cried.

"So are you," broke in a boy offensively, and then Tommy said to Grizel loftily, "Run away; I'll not let none on them touch you."

"I am not afraid of them," she rejoined, with scorn, "and I shall not let you help me, and I won't run." And run she did not; she walked off leisurely with her head in the air, and her dignity was beautiful, except once when she made the mistake of turning round to put out her tongue.

But, alas! in the end someone ran. If only they had not called him "English." In vain he fired a volley of Scotch; they pretended not to understand it. Then he screamed that he and Shovel could fight the lot of them. Who was Shovel? they asked derisively. He replied that Shovel was a bloke who could lick any two of them—and with one hand tied behind his back.

No sooner had he made this proud boast than he went white, and soon two disgraceful tears rolled down his cheeks. The boys saw that for some reason unknown his courage was gone, and even Francie Crabb began to turn up his sleeves and spit upon his hands.

Elspeth was as bewildered as the others, but she slipped her hand into his and away they ran ingloriously, the foe too much astounded to jeer. She sought to comfort him by saying (and it brought her a step nearer womanhood), "You wasn't feared for yourself, you wasn't; you was just feared they would hurt me."

But Tommy sobbed in reply, "That ain't it. I bounced so much about the Thrums folk to Shovel, and now the first day I'm here I heard myself bouncing about Shovel to Thrums folk, and it were that what made me cry. Oh, Elspeth, it's—it's not the same what I thought it would be!"

Nor was it the same to Elspeth, so they sat down by the roadside and cried with their arms round each other, and any passer-by could look

K 2

who had the heart. But when night came, and they were in their garret bed, Tommy was once more seeking to comfort Elspeth with arguments he disbelieved, and again he succeeded. As usual, too, the make-believe made him happy also.

"Have you forgot," he whispered, " that my mother said as she would come and see us every night in our bed? If yer cries, she'll see as we're terrible unhappy, and that will make her unhappy too."

"Oh, Tommy, is she here now?"

"Whisht! She's here, but they don't like living ones to let on as they knows it."

Elspeth kept closer to Tommy, and with their heads beneath the blankets, so as to stifle the sound, he explained to her how they could cheat their mother. When she understood, he took the blankets off their faces and said in the darkness in a loud voice:

"It's a grand place, Thrums!"

Elspeth replied in a similar voice, "Ain't the town-house just big?"

Said Tommy, almost chuckling, "Oh, the bonny, bonny Auld Licht Kirk!"

Said Elspeth, "Oh, the beauty outside stairs!"

Said Tommy, "The minister is so long!"

Said Elspeth, "The folk is so kind!"

Said Tommy, "Especially the laddies!"

"Oh, I is so happy!" cried Elspeth.

"Me too!" cried Tommy.

"My mother would be so chirpy if she could jest see us!" Elspeth said, quite archly.

"But she canna!" replied Tommy, slyly pinching Elspeth in the rib.

Then they dived beneath the blankets, and the whispering was resumed.

"Did she hear, does yer think?" asked Elspeth.

"Every word," Tommy replied. "Elspeth, we've done her!"

CHAPTER XIII.

SHOWS HOW TOMMY TOOK CARE OF ELSPETH.

THUS the first day passed, and others followed in which women, who had known Jean Myles, did her children kindnesses, but could not do all they would have done, for Aaron forbade them to enter his home, except on business, though it was begging for a housewife all day. Had Elspeth at the age of six now settled down to domestic duties she would not have been the youngest housekeeper ever known in Thrums, but she was never very good at doing things, only at loving and being loved, and the observant neighbours thought her a backward girl; they forgot, like most people, that service is not necessarily a handicraft. Tommy discovered what they were saying, and to shield Elspeth he took to housewifery with the blind down; but Aaron, entering the kitchen unexpectedly, took the besom from him, saying:

"It's an ill thing for men folk to ken ower muckle about women's work."

"You do it yoursel'," Tommy argued.

"I said men folk," replied Aaron, quietly.

The children knew that remarks of this sort had reference to their mother, of whom he never spoke more directly; indeed he seldom spoke to them at all, and save when he was cooking or giving the kitchen a slovenly cleaning they saw

little of him. Monypenny had predicted that
their presence must make a new man of him,
but he was still unsociable and morose and sat as
long as ever at the warping-mill, of which he
seemed to have become the silent wheel. Tommy
and Elspeth always dropped their voices when
they spoke of him, and sometimes when his mill
stopped he heard one of them say to the other
" Whisht, he's coming!" Though he seldom
spoke sharply to them, his face did not lose its
loneliness at sight of them. Elspeth was his
favourite (somewhat to the indignation of both);
they found this out without his telling them or
even showing it markedly, and when they
wanted to ask anything of him she was deputed
to do it, but she did it quavering, and after
drawing farther away from him instead of going
nearer. A dreary life would have lain before
them had they not been sent to school.

There were at this time three schools in
Thrums; the chief of them ruled over by the
terrible Cathro (called Knuckly when you were
a street away from him). It was a famous
school, from which a band of three or four or
even six marched every autumn to the universities
as determined after bursaries as ever were High-
landmen to lift cattle, and for the same reason,
that they could not do without.

A very different kind of dominie was Cursing
Ballingall, who had been dropped at Thrums by
a travelling circus, and first became familiar to
the town as, carrying two carpet shoes, two
books, a pillow and a saucepan, which were
all his belongings, he wandered from manse

to manse offering to write sermons for the ministers at circus prices. That scheme failing, he was next seen looking in at windows in search of a canny calling, and eventually he cut one of his braces into a pair of tawse, thus with a single stroke of the knife, making himself a schoolmaster and lop-sided for life. His fee was but a penny a week, "with a bit o' the swine when your father kills," and sometimes there were so many pupils on a form that they could only rise as one. During the first half of the scholastic day Ballingall's shouts and pounces were for parents to listen to, but after his dinner of crowdy, which is raw meal and hot water, served in a cogie, or wooden bowl, languor overcame him and he would sleep, having first given out a sum in arithmetic and announced :

"The one as finds out the answer first, I'll give him his licks."

Last comes the Hanky School, which was for the genteel and for the common who contemplated soaring. You were not admitted to it in corduroys or barefooted, nor did you pay weekly ; no, your father called four times a year with the money in an envelope. He was shown into the blue-and-white room, and there, after business had been transacted, very nervously on Miss Ailie's part, she offered him his choice between ginger wine and what she falteringly called wh-wh-whisky. He partook in the polite national manner, which is thus :

"You will take something, Mr. Cortachy ? "

"No, I thank you, ma'am."

"A little ginger wine ? "

" It agrees ill with me."

" Then a little wh-wh-whisky ? "

" You are ower kind."

" Then may I ? "

" I am not heeding."

" Perhaps, though, you don't take ? "

" I can take it or want it."

" Is that enough ? "

" It will do perfectly."

" Shall I fill it up ? "

" As you please, ma'am."

Miss Ailie's relationship to the magerful man may be remembered ; she shuddered to think of it herself, for in middle age she retained the mind of a young girl, but when duty seemed to call, this schoolmistress could be brave, and she offered to give Elspeth her schooling free of charge. Like the other two hers was a "mixed" school, but she did not want Tommy, because she had seen him in the square one day, and there was a leer on his face that reminded her of his father.

Another woman was less particular. This was Mrs. Crabb, of the Tappit Hen, the Esther Auld whom Jean Myles's letters had so frequently sent to bed. Her Francie was still a pupil of Miss Ailie, and still he wore the golden hair, which, despite all advice, she would not crop. It was so beautiful that no common boys could see it without wanting to give it a tug in passing, and partly to prevent this, partly to show how high she had risen in the social scale, Esther usually sent him to school under the charge of her servant lass. She now proposed to Aaron that this duty should devolve on Tommy, and for the service she would pay his fees at the Hanky School.

"We maun all lend a hand to poor Jean's bairns," she said, with a gleam in her eye. "It would have been well for her, Aaron, if she had married you."

"Is that all you have to say?" asked the warper, who had let her enter no farther than the hallan.

"I would expect him to lift Francie ower the pools in wet weather; and it might be as well if he called him Master Francie."

"Is that all?"

"Ay, I ask no more, for we maun all help Jean's bairns. If she could only look down, Aaron, and see her little velvets, as she called him, lifting my little corduroys ower the pools!"

Aaron flung open the door. "Munt!" he said, and he looked so dangerous that she retired at once. He sent Tommy to Ballingall's, and accepted Miss Ailie's offer for Elspeth, but this was an impossible arrangement, for it was known to the two persons primarily concerned that Elspeth would die if she was not where Tommy was. The few boys he had already begun to know were at Cathro's or Ballingall's, and as they called Miss Ailie's a lassie school he had no desire to attend it, but where he was there also must Elspeth be. Daily he escaped from Ballingall's and hid near the Dovecot, as Miss Ailie's house was called, and every little while he gave vent to Shovel's whistle, so that Elspeth might know of his proximity and be

cheered. Thrice was he carried back, kicking, to
Ballingall's by urchins sent in pursuit, stern
ministers of justice on the first two occasions ;
but on the third they made him an offer : if he
would hide in Couthie's henhouse they were
willing to look for him everywhere else for
two hours.

Tommy's behaviour seemed beautiful to the
impressionable Miss Ailie, but it infuriated
Aaron, and on the fourth day he set off for the
parish school, meaning to put the truant in the
hands of Cathro, from whom there was no escape.
Vainly had Elspeth implored him to let Tommy
come to the Dovecot, and vainly apparently was
she trotting at his side now, looking up appealingly in his face. But when they reached the
gate of the parish school-yard he walked past it
because she was tugging him, and always when
he seemed about to turn she took his hand again,
and he seemed to have lost the power to resist
Jean Myles's bairn. So they came to the Dovecot, and Miss Ailie gained a pupil who had been
meant for Cathro. Tommy's arms were stronger
than Elspeth's, but they could not have done as
much for him that day.

Thus did the two children enter upon the
genteel career, to the indignation of the other
boys and girls of Monypenny, all of whom were
commoners.

CHAPTER XIV.

THE HANKY SCHOOL.

THE Dovecot was a prim little cottage standing back from the steepest brae in Thrums and hidden by high garden walls, to the top of which another boy's shoulders were, for apple-lovers, but one step up. Jargonelle trees grew against the house, stretching their arms round it as if to measure its girth, and it was also remarkable for several "dumb" windows with the most artful blinds painted on them. Miss Ailie's fruit was famous, but she loved her flowers best, and for long a notice board in her garden said, appealingly: "Persons who come to steal the fruit are requested not to walk on the flower-beds." It was that old bachelor, Dr. McQueen, who suggested this inscription to her, and she could never understand why he chuckled every time he read it.

There were seven rooms in the house, but only two were of public note, the school-room, which was downstairs, and the blue-and-white room above. The school-room was so long that it looked very low in the ceiling, and it had a carpet, and on the walls were texts as well as maps. Miss Ailie's desk was in the middle of the room, and there was another desk in a corner; a cloth had been hung over it, as one covers a cage to send the bird to sleep. Perhaps Miss

Ailie thought that a bird had once sung there, for this had been the desk of her sister, Miss Kitty, who died years before Tommy came to Thrums. Dainty Miss Kitty, Miss Kitty with the roguish curls, it is strange to think that you are dead, and that only Miss Ailie hears you singing now at your desk in the corner! Miss Kitty never sang there, but the playful ringlets were once the bright thing in the room, and Miss Ailie sees them still, and they are a song to her.

The pupils had to bring handkerchiefs to the Dovecot, which led to its being called the Hanky School, and in time these handkerchiefs may be said to have assumed a religious character, though their purpose was merely to protect Miss Ailie's carpet. She opened each scholastic day by reading fifteen verses from the Bible, and then she said sternly, "Hankies!" whereupon her pupils whipped out their handkerchiefs, spread them on the floor and kneeled on them while Miss Ailie repeated the Lord's Prayer. School closed at four o'clock, again with hankies.

Only on great occasions were the boys and girls admitted to the blue-and-white room, when they were given shortbread, but had to eat it with their heads flung back so that no crumbs should fall. Nearly everything in this room was blue or white, or both. There were white blinds and blue curtains, a blue table-cover and a white crumb-cloth, a white sheepskin with a blue foot-stool on it, blue chairs dotted with white buttons. Only white flowers came into this room, where there were blue vases for them, not a book was to be seen without a blue alpaca cover. Here Miss Ailie received visitors in her white with the blue braid, and enrolled new pupils in blue ink with a white pen. Some laughed at her, others remembered that she must have something to love after Miss Kitty died.

Miss Ailie had her romance, as you may hear by and by, but you would not have thought it as she came forward to meet you in the blue-and-white room, trembling lest your feet had brought in mud, but too much a lady to ask you to stand on a newspaper, as she would have liked dearly to do. She was somewhat beyond middle-age, and stoutly, even squarely, built, which gave her a masculine appearance; but she had grown so timid since Miss Kitty's death that when she spoke you felt that either her figure or her manner must have been intended for someone else. In conversation she had a way of ending a sentence in the middle which gave her a reputation of being "thro'ither," though an artificial tooth was the cause. It was slightly loose, and had she not at times shut her mouth suddenly, and then done something with her tongue, an accident might have happened. This tooth fascinated Tommy, and once when she was talking he cried excitedly, "Quick, it's coming!" whereupon her mouth snapped close, and she turned pink in the blue-and-white room.

Nevertheless Tommy became her favourite, and as he had taught himself to read, after a fashion, in London, where his lesson-books were chiefly placards and the journal subscribed to by Shovel's father, she often invited him after school

hours to the blue-and-white room, where he sat
on a kitchen chair (with his boots off) and read
aloud, very slowly, while Miss Ailie knitted.
The volume was from the Thrums Book Club,
of which Miss Ailie was one of the twelve
members. Each member contributed a book
every year, and as their tastes in literature dif-
fered, all sorts of books came into the club, and
there was one member who invariably gave a
ro-ro-romance. He was double-chinned and
forty, but the school-mistress called him the
dashing young banker, and for months she
avoided his dangerous contribution. But always
there came a black day when a desire to read the
novel seized her, and she hurried home with it
beneath her rokelay. This year the dashing
banker's choice was a lady's novel called " I Love
My Love with an A," and it was a frivolous
tale, those being before the days of the new
fiction with its grand discovery that women have
an equal right with men to grow beards. The
hero had such a way with him and was so young
(Miss Ailie could not stand them a day more
than twenty) that the school-mistress was en-
raptured and scared at every page, but she fondly
hoped that Tommy did not understand. However, he discovered one day what something
printed thus, " D—n," meant, and he immediately said the word with such unction that
Miss Ailie let fall her knitting. She would
have ended the readings then had not Agatha
been at that point in the arms of an officer who,
Miss Ailie felt almost certain, had a wife in
India, and so how could she rest till she knew

for certain? To track the officer by herself was not to be thought of, to read without knitting being such shameless waste of time, and it was decided to resume the readings on a revised plan: Tommy to say "stroke" in place of the "D—ns," and "word we have no concern with" instead of "Darling" and "Little One."

Miss Ailie was not the only person at the Dovecot who admired Tommy. Though in duty bound, as young patriots, to jeer at him for having been born in the wrong place, the pupils of his own age could not resist the charm of his reminiscences; even Gav Dishart, a son of the manse, listened attentively to him. His great topic was his birthplace, and whatever happened in Thrums, he instantly made contemptible by citing something of the same kind, but on a larger scale, that had happened in London; he turned up his nose almost farther than was safe when they said Catlaw was a stiff mountain to climb. ("Oh, Gav, if you just saw the London mountains!") Snow! why they didn't know what snow was in Thrums. If they could only see St. Paul's or Hyde Park or Shovel! he couldn't help laughing at Thrums, he couldn't —Larfing, he said at first, but in a short time his Scotch was better than theirs, though less unconscious. His English was better also, of course, and you had to speak in a kind of English when inside the Hanky School; you got your revenge at "minutes." On the whole, Tommy irritated his fellow-pupils a good deal, but they found it difficult to keep away from him.

He also contrived to enrage the less genteel

boys of Monypenny. Their leader was Corp
Shiach, three years Tommy's senior, who had
never been inside a school except once, when he
broke hopefully into Ballingall's because of a
stirring rumour (nothing in it) that the dominie
had hangit himself with his remaining brace;
then in order of merit came Birkie Fleemister;
then, perhaps, the smith's family, called the
Haggerty-Taggertys, they were such slovens.
When school was over Tommy frequently stepped
out of his boots and stockings, so that he no
longer looked offensively genteel, and then
Monypenny was willing to let him join in spyo,
smuggle bools, kickbonnety, peeries, the preens,
suckers, pilly, or whatever game was in season,
even to the baiting of the Painted Lady, but
they would not have Elspeth, who should have
been content to play dumps with the female
Haggerty-Taggertys, but could enjoy no game
of which Tommy was not the larger half. Many
times he deserted her for manlier joys, but
though she was out of sight he could not forget
her longing face, and soon he sneaked off to her;
he upbraided her, but he stayed with her.
They bore with him for a time, but when they
discovered that she had persuaded him (after
prayer) to put back the spug's eggs which he
had brought home in triumph, then they drove
him from their company, and for a long time
afterward his deadly enemy was the hard-hitting
Corp Shiach.

Elspeth was not invited to attend the readings
of "I Love My Love with an A," perhaps because there were so many words in it that she had

L

no concern with, but she knew they ended as
the eight o'clock bell began to ring, and it was
her custom to meet Tommy a few yards from
Aaron's door.   Farther she durst not venture in
the gloaming through fear of the Painted Lady,
for Aaron's house was not far from the fearsome
lane that led to Double Dykes, and even the big
boys who made faces at this woman by day ran
from her in the dusk.   Creepy tales were told of
what happened to those on whom she cast a
blighting eye before they could touch cold iron,
and Tommy was one of many who kept a bit of
cold iron from the smithy handy in his pocket.
On his way home from the readings he never had
occasion to use it, but at these times he sometimes met Grizel, who liked to do her shopping
in the evenings when her persecutors were more
easily eluded, and he forced her to speak to him.
Not her loneliness appealed to him, but that look
of admiration she had given him when he was
astride of Francie Crabb.   For such a look he
could pardon many rebuffs ; without it no praise
greatly pleased him ; he was always on the outlook for it.

"I warrant," he said to her one evening,
"you want to have some man body to take care
of you the way I take care of Elspeth."

"No, I don't," she replied, promptly.

"Would you no like somebody to love
you ? "

"Do you mean kissing ? " she asked.

"There's better things in it than that," he
said guardedly ; "but if you want kissing, I—I
—Elspeth'll kiss you."

"Will she want to do it?" inquired Grizel, a little wistfully.

"I'll make her do it," Tommy said.

"I don't want her to do it," cried Grizel, and he could not draw another word from her. However, he was sure she thought him a wonder, and when next day they met he challenged her with it.

"Do you not now?"

"I won't tell you," answered Grizel, who was never known to lie.

"You think I'm a wonder," Tommy persisted, "but you dinna want me to know you think it."

Grizel rocked her arms, a quaint way she had when excited, and she blurted out, "How do you know?"

The look he liked had come back to her face, but he had no time to enjoy it, for just then Elspeth appeared, and Elspeth's jealousy was easily aroused.

"I dinna ken you, lassie," he said coolly to Grizel, and left her stamping her foot at him. She decided never to speak to Tommy again, but the next time they met he took her into the Den and taught her how to fight.

It is painful to have to tell that Miss Ailie was the person who provided him with the opportunity. In the readings they arrived one evening at the scene in the conservatory, which has not a single Stroke in it, but it is so full of Words We have no Concern with that Tommy reeled home blinking, and next day so disgracefully did he flounder in his lessons that the gentle school-mistress cast up her arms in despair.

"I don't know what to say to you," she exclaimed.

"Fine I know what you want to say," he retorted, and unfortunately she asked, "What?"

"Stroke!" he replied, leering horridly.

"I Love My Love with an A" was returned to the club forthwith (whether he really did have a wife in India Miss Ailie never knew) and "Judd on the Shorter Catechism" took its place. But mark the result. The readings ended at a quarter to eight now, at twenty to eight, at half-past seven, and so Tommy could loiter on the way home without arousing Elspeth's suspicion. One evening he saw Grizel cutting her way through the Haggerty-Taggerty group, and he offered to come to her aid if she would say "Help me." But she refused.

When, however, the Haggerty - Taggertys were gone she condescended to say, "I shall never, never ask you to help me, but—if you like—you can show me how to hit without biting my tongue."

"I'll learn you Shovel's curly ones," replied Tommy, cordially, and he adjourned with her to the Den for that purpose. He said he chose the Den so that Corp Shiach and the others might not interrupt them, but it was Elspeth he was thinking of.

"You are like Miss Ailie with her cane when she is pandying," he told Grizel. "You begin well, but you slacken just when you are going to hit."

"It is because my hand opens," Grizel said.

"And then it ends in a shove," said her mentor, severely. "You should close your fists like this, with the thumbs inside, and then play dab, this way, that way, yon way. That's what Shovel calls, 'You want it, take it, you've got it.'"

Thus did the hunted girl get her first lesson in scientific warfare in the Den, and neither she nor Tommy saw the pathos of it. Other lessons followed, and during the rests Grizel told Tommy all that she knew about herself. He had won her confidence at last by—by swearing dagont that he was English also.

CHAPTER XV.

THE MAN WHO NEVER CAME.

"Is it true that your mother's a bonny swearer?"

Tommy wanted to find out all about the Painted Lady, and the best way was to ask.

"She does not always swear," Grizel said eagerly. "She sometimes says sweet, sweet things."

"What kind of things?"

"I won't tell you."

"Tell me one."

"Well, then, 'Beloved.'"

"Word We have no Concern with," murmured Tommy. He was shocked, but still curious. "Does she say 'Beloved' to you?" he inquired.

"No, she says it to him."

"Him! Wha is he?" Tommy thought he was at the beginning of a discovery, but she answered, uncomfortably,

"I don't know."

"But you've seen him?"

"No, he—he is not there."

"Not there! How can she speak to him if he's no there?"

"She thinks he is there. He—he comes on a horse."

"What is the horse like?"

" There is no horse."

" But you said——"

" She just thinks there is a horse.   She hears it."

" Did you ever hear it?"

" No."

The girl was looking imploringly into Tommy's face as if begging it to say that these things need not terrify her, but what he wanted was information.

" What does the Painted Lady do," he asked, " when she thinks she hears the horse?"

" She blows kisses, and then—then she goes to the Den."

" What to do?"

" She walks up and down the Den, talking to the man."

" And him no there?" cried Tommy, scared.

" No, there is no one there."

" And syne what do you do?"

" I won't tell you."

Tommy reflected, and then he said, " She's daft."

" She is not always daft," cried Grizel. " There are whole weeks when she is just sweet."

" Then what do you make of her being so queer in the Den?"

" I am not sure, but I think—I think there was once a place like the Den at her own home in England, where she used to meet the man long ago, and sometimes she forgets that it is not long ago now."

" I wonder wha the man was?"

"I think he was my father."

"I thought you didna ken what a father was?"

"I know now. I think my father was a Scotsman."

"What makes you think that?"

"I heard a Thrums woman say it would account for my being called Grizel, and I think we came to Scotland to look for him, but it is so long, long ago."

"How long?"

"I don't know. We have lived here four years, but we were looking for him before that. It was not in this part of Scotland we looked for him. We gave up looking for him before we came here."

"What made the Painted Lady take a house here, then?"

"I think it was because the Den is so like the place she used to meet him in long ago."

"What was his name?"

"I don't know."

"Does the Painted Lady no tell you about yoursel'?"

"No; she is angry if I ask."

"Her name is Mary, I've heard?"

"Mary Gray is her name, but—but I don't think it is her real name."

"How, does she no use her real name?"

"Because she wants her own mamma to think she is dead."

"What makes her want that?"

"I am not sure, but I think it is because there is me. I think it was naughty of me to be born. Can you help being born?"

Tommy would have liked to tell her about Reddy, but forbore, because he still believed that he had acted criminally in that affair, and so for the time being the inquisition ended. But though he had already discovered all that Grizel knew about her mother and nearly all that curious Thrums ever ferreted out, he returned to the subject at the next meeting in the Den.

"Where does the Painted Lady get her money?"

"Oh," said Grizel, "that is easy. She just goes into that house called the bank, and asks for some, and they give her as much as she likes."

"Ay, I've heard that, but——"

The remainder of the question was never uttered. Instead,

"Hod ahint a tree!" cried Tommy, hastily, and he got behind one himself; but he was too late; Elspeth was upon them; she had caught them together at last.

Tommy showed great cunning. "Pretend you have eggs in your hand," he whispered to Grizel, and then, in a loud voice, he said: "Think shame of yoursel', lassie, for harrying birds' nests. It's a good thing I saw you, and brought you here to force you to put them back. Is that you, Elspeth? I catched this limmer wi' eggs in her hands (and the poor birds sic bonny singers, too!), and so I was forcing her to——"

But it would not do. Grizel was ablaze with indignation. "You are a horrid story-teller," she said, "and if I had known you were ashamed of being seen with me, I should never have spoken to you. Take him," she cried, giving Tommy a push towards Elspeth, "I don't want the mean little story-teller."

"He's not mean!" retorted Elspeth.

"Nor yet little!" roared Tommy.

"Yes, he is," insisted Grizel, "and I was not harrying nests. He came with me here because he wanted to."

"Just for the once," he said, hastily.

"This is the sixth time," said Grizel, and then she marched out of the Den. Tommy and Elspeth followed slowly, and not a word did either say until they were in front of Aaron's house. Then by the light in the window Tommy saw that Elspeth was crying softly, and he felt miserable.

"I was just teaching her to fight," he said humbly.

"You looked like it!" she replied, with the scorn that comes occasionally to the sweetest lady.

He tried to comfort her in various tender ways, but none of them sufficed this time. "You'll marry her as soon as you're a man," she insisted, and she would not let this tragic picture go. It was a case for his biggest efforts, and he opened his mouth to threaten instant self-destruction unless she became happy at once. But he had threatened this too frequently of late, even shown himself drawing the knife across his throat.

As usual the right idea came to him at the right moment. "If you just kent how I did it for your sake," he said, with gentle dignity, "you wouldna blame me; you would think me noble."

She would not help him with a question, and after waiting for it he proceeded. "If you just kent wha she is! And I thought she was dead! What a start it gave me when I found out it was her!"

"Wha is she?" cried Elspeth, with a sudden shiver.

"I was trying to keep it frae you," replied Tommy, sadly.

She seized his arm. "Is it Reddy?" she gasped, for the story of Reddy had been a terror to her all her days.

"She doesna ken I was the laddie that diddled her in London," he said, "and I promise you never to let on, Elspeth. I—I just went to the Den with her to say things that would put her off the scent. If I hadna done that she might have found out and ta'en your place here and tried to pack you off to the Painted Lady's."

Elspeth stared at him, the other grief already forgotten, and he thought he was getting on excellently, when she cried with passion, "I don't believe as it is Reddy!" and ran into the house.

"Dinna believe it, then!" disappointed Tommy shouted, and now he was in such a rage with h'mself that his heart hardened against her. He sought the company of old Blinder.

Unfortunately Elspeth had believed it, and

her woe was the more pitiful because she saw at once, what had never struck Tommy, that it would be wicked to keep Grizel out of her rights. " I'll no win to Heaven now," she said, despairingly to herself, for to offer to change places with Grizel was beyond her courage, and she tried some childish ways of getting round God, such as going on her knees and saying, " I'm so little, and I hinna no mother ! " That was not a bad way.

Another way was to give Grizel everything she had, except Tommy. She collected all her treasures, the bottle with the brass top that she had got from Shovel's old girl, the " housewife " that was a present from Miss Ailie, the tee-totum, the pretty buttons Tommy had won for her at the game of buttony, the witchy marble, the twopence she had already saved for the Muckley, these and some other precious trifles she made a little bundle of and set off for Double Dykes with them, intending to leave them at the door. This was Elspeth, who in ordinary circumstances would not have ventured near that mysterious dwelling even in daylight and in Tommy's company. There was no room for vulgar fear in her bursting little heart to-night.

Tommy went home anon, meaning to be whatever kind of boy she seemed most in need of, but she was not in the house, she was not in the garden ; he called her name, and it was only Birkie Fleemister, mimicking her, who answered, " Oh, Tommy, come to me ! " But Birkie had news for him.

"Sure as death," he said in some awe, "I saw Elspeth ganging yont the double dykes, and I cried to her that the Painted Lady would do her a mischief, but she just ran on."

Elspeth in the double dykes—alone—and at night! Oh, how Tommy would have liked to strike himself now! She must have believed his wicked lie after all, and being so religious she had gone to—— He gave himself no time to finish the thought. The vital thing was that she was in peril; he seemed to hear her calling to him, "Oh, Tommy, come quick! oh, Tommy, oh, Tommy!" and in an agony of apprehension he ran after her. But by the time he got to the beginning of the double dykes he knew that she must be at the end of them, and in the Painted Lady's maw, unless their repute by night had blown her back. He paused on the Coffin Brig, which is one long narrow stone; and along the funnel of the double dykes he sent the lonely whisper, "Elspeth, are you there?" He tried to shout it, but no boy could shout there after nightfall in the Painted Lady's time, and when the words had travelled only a little way along the double dykes, they came whining back to him, like a dog despatched on uncanny work. He heard no other sound save the burn stealing on tiptoe from an evil place, and the uneasy rustling of tree-tops, and his own breathing.

The Coffin Brig remains, but the double dykes have fallen bit by bit into the burn, and the path they made safe is again as naked as when the Kingoldrum Jacobites filed along it,

and sweer they were, to the support of the Pretender.   It traverses a ridge and is streaked
with slippery beech-roots which like to fling you
off your feet, on the one side into a black burn
twenty feet below, on the other down a pleasant
slope.   The double dykes were built by a farmer
fond of his dram, to stop the tongue of a water-
kelpie which lived in a pool below and gave
him a turn every night he staggered home by
shouting, " Drunk again, Peewitbrae ! " and announcing, with a smack of the lips, that it had
a bed ready for him in the burn.   So Peewitbrae
built two parallel dykes two feet apart and two
feet high, between which he could walk home
like a straight man.   His cunning took the
heart out of the brute, and water-kelpies have
not been seen near Thrums since about that time.

By day even girls played at palaulays here,
and it was a favourite resort of boys, who knew
that you were a man when you could stand on
both dykes at once.   They also stripped boldly
to the skin and then looked doubtfully at the
water.   But at night !   To test your nerves you
walked alone between the double dykes, and the
popular practice was to start off whistling, which
keeps up the courage.   At the point where you
turned to run back (the Painted Lady after you,
or so you thought) you dropped a marked stone,
which told next day how far you had ventured.
Corp Shiach long held the championship, and
his stone was ostentatiously fixed in one of the
dykes with lime.   Tommy had suffered at his
hands for saying that Shovel's mark was thirty
yards farther on.

With head bent to the level of the dykes, though it was almost a mirk night beneath the trees, and one arm outstretched before him straight as an elvint, Tommy faced this fearful passage, sometimes stopping to touch cold iron, but on the whole hanging back little, for Elspeth was in peril. Soon he reached the paling that was not needed to keep boys out of the Painted Lady's garden, one of the prettiest and best-tended flower-gardens in Thrums, and crawling through where some spars had fallen, he approached the door as noiseless as an Indian brave after scalps. There he crouched, with a heart that was going like a shuttle on a loom, and listened for Elspeth's voice.

On a night he had come nearly as far as this before, but in the tail of big fellows with a turnip lantern. Into the woodwork of the east window they had thrust a pin, to which a button was tied, and the button was also attached to a long string. They hunkered afar off and pulled this string, and then the button tapped the death-rap on the window, and the sport was successful, for the Painted Lady screamed. But suddenly the door opened and they were put to flight by the fierce barking of a dog. One said that the brute nabbed him in the leg, another saw the vive tongue of it, a third played lick at it with the lantern; this was before they discovered that the dog had been Grizel imitating one, brave Grizel, always ready to protect her mother, and never allowed to cherish the childish fears that were hers by birthright.

Tommy could not hear a sound from within,

but he had startling proof that Elspeth was
near. His foot struck against something at the
door, and, stooping, he saw that it was a little
bundle of the treasures she valued most. So she
had indeed come to stay with the Painted Lady
if Grizel proved merciless! Oh, what a black
he had been!

Though originally a farm-house, the cottage
was no larger than Aaron's, and of its two front
windows only one showed a light, and that
through a blind. Tommy sidled round the
house in the hope that the small east window
would be more hospitable, and just as he saw
that it was blindless something that had been
crouching rose between him and it.

"Let go!" he cried, feeling the Painted
Lady's talons in his neck.

"Tommy!" was the answer.

"It's you, Elspeth?"

"Is it you, Tommy?"

"Of course. Whisht!"

"But say it is."

"It is."

"Oh, Tommy, I'm so fleid!"

He drew her farther from the window and
told her it had all been a wicked lie, and she
was so glad that she forgot to chide him; but he
denounced himself, and he was better than
Elspeth even at that. However, when he learned
what had brought her here he dried his eyes
and skulked to the door again and brought
back her belongings, and then she wanted him
to come away at once. But the window fascinated him; he knew he should never find

courage to come here again, and he glided
towards it, signing to Elspeth to accompany
him. They were now too near Double Dykes
for speaking to be safe, but he tapped his head
as a warning to her to remove her hat, for a
woman's head-gear always reaches a window in
front of its wearer, and he touched his cold iron
and passed it to her as if it were a snuff-mull.
Thus fortified, they approached the window
fearfully, holding hands and stepping high, like
a couple in a minuet.

CHAPTER XVI.

THE PAINTED LADY.

IT had been the ordinary dwelling room of the unknown poor, the mean little "end"—ah, no, no, the noblest chamber in the annals of the Scottish nation. Here on a hard anvil has its character been fashioned and its history made at rush-lights and its God ever most prominent. Always within reach of hands which trembled with reverence as they turned its broad page could be found the Book that is compensation for all things, and that was never more at home than on bare dressers and worm-eaten looms. If you were brought up in that place and have forgotten it, there is no more hope for you.

But though still recalling its past, the kitchen into which Tommy and Elspeth peered was trying successfully to be something else. The plate-rack had been a fixture, and the coffin-bed and the wooden bole, or board in the wall, with its round hole through which you thrust your hand when you wanted salt, and instead of a real mantelpiece there was a quaint imitation one painted over the fireplace. There were some pieces of furniture too, such as were usual in rooms of the kind, but most of them, perhaps in ignorance, had been put to novel uses like the plate-rack, where the Painted Lady kept her many pretty shoes instead of her crockery.

Gossip said she had a looking-glass of such prodigious size that it stood on the floor, and Tommy nudged Elspeth to signify, " There it is!" Other nudges called her attention to the carpet, the spinet, a chair that rocked like a cradle, and some smaller oddities, of which the queerest was a monster velvet glove hanging on the nail that by rights belonged to the bellows. The Painted Lady always put on this glove before she would touch the coals, which diverted Tommy, who knew that common folk lift coals with their bare hands, while society uses the fringe of its second petticoat.

It might have been a boudoir through which a kitchen and bedroom had wandered, spilling by the way, but though the effect was tawdry, everything had been rubbed clean by that passionate housewife, Grizel. She was on her knees at present ca'ming the hearthstone a beautiful blue, and sometimes looking round to address her mother, who was busy among her plants and cut flowers. Surely they were know-nothings who called this woman silly, and blind who said she painted. It was a little face all of one colour, dingy pale, not chubby, but retaining the soft contours of a child's face, and the features were singularly delicate. She was clad in a soft grey, and her figure was of the smallest; there was such an air of youth about her that Tommy thought she could become a girl again by merely shortening her frock, not such a girl as gaunt Grizel though, who would have looked a little woman had she let her frock down. In appearance indeed the Painted Lady resembled her

M 2

plain daughter not at all, but in manner in a score of ways, as when she rocked her arms joyously at sight of a fresh bud, or tossed her brown hair from her brows with a pretty gesture that ought, God knows, to have been for some man to love. The watchers could not hear what she and Grizel said, but evidently it was pleasant converse, and mother and child, happy in each other's company, presented a picture as sweet as it is common, though some might have complained that they were doing each other's work. But the Painted Lady's delight in flowers was a scandal in Thrums, where she would stand her ground if the roughest boy approached her with roses in his hand, and she gave money for them, which was one reason why the people thought her daft. She was tending her flowers now with experienced eye, smelling them daintily, and every time she touched them it was a caress.

The watchers retired into the field to compare impressions, and Elspeth said emphatically, " I like her, Tommy, I'm not none fleid at her."

Tommy had liked her also, but being a man he said, " You forget that she's an ill one."

" She looks as if she didna ken that hersel'," answered Elspeth, and these words of a child are the best picture we can hope to get of the Painted Lady.

On their return to the window they saw that Grizel had finished her ca'ming and was now sitting on the floor nursing a doll. Tommy had not thought her the kind to shut her eyes to the truth about dolls, but she was hugging this one passionately. Without its clothes it was of the nine-pin formation, and the painted eyes and mouth had been incorporated long since in loving Grizel's system; but it became just sweet as she swaddled it in a long yellow frock and slipped its bullet head into a duck of a pink bonnet. These articles of attire and the others that you begin with had all been made by Grizel herself out of the coloured tissue-paper that shopkeepers wrap round brandy bottles. The doll's name was Griselda, and it was exactly six months old, and Grizel had found it, two years ago, lying near the Coffin Brig, naked and almost dead.

It was making the usual fuss at having its clothes put on, and Grizel had to tell it frequently that of all the babies—which shamed it now and again, but kept her so occupied that she forgot her mother. The Painted Lady had sunk into the rocking-chair, and for a time she amused herself with it, but by and by it ceased to rock, and as she sat looking straight before her a change came over her face. Elspeth's hand tightened its clutch on Tommy's; the Painted Lady had begun to talk to herself.

She was not speaking aloud, for evidently Grizel, whose back was toward her, heard nothing, but her lips moved and she nodded her head and smiled and beckoned, apparently to the wall, and the childish face rapidly became vacant and foolish. This mood passed, and now she was sitting very still, only her head moving, as she looked in apprehension and perplexity this way and that, like one who no longer knew where she was, nor who was the child by the fire

When at last Grizel turned and observed the change, she may have sighed, but there was no fear in her face; the fear was on the face of her mother, who shrank from her in unmistakable terror and would have screamed at a harsh word or a hasty movement. Grizel seemed to know this, for she remained where she was, and first she nodded and smiled reassuringly to her mother, and then leaning forward, took her hand and stroked it softly and began to talk. She had laid aside her doll, and with the act become a woman again.

The Painted Lady was soothed, but her bewildered look came and went, as if she only caught at some explanation Grizel was making to lose it in a moment. Yet she seemed most eager to be persuaded. The little watchers at this queer play saw that Grizel was saying things to her which she repeated docilely and clung to and lost hold of. Often Grizel illustrated her words by a sort of pantomime, as when she sat down on a chair and placed the doll in her lap, then sat down on her mother's lap; and when she had done this several times Tommy took Elspeth into the field to say to her:

"Do you no see? She means as she is the Painted Lady's bairn just the same as the doll is her bairn."

If the Painted Lady needed to be told this every minute she was daft indeed, and Elspeth could peer no longer at the eerie spectacle. To leave Tommy, however, was equally difficult, so she crouched at his feet when he returned to

the window, drawn there hastily by the sound
of music.

The Painted Lady could play on the spinet
beautifully, but Grizel could not play, though it
was she who was trying to play now. She was
running her fingers over the notes, producing
noises from them, while she swayed grotesquely
on her seat and made comic faces. Her object
was to capture her mother's mind, and she
succeeded for a short time, but soon it floated
away from all control, and the Painted Lady
fell a-shaking violently. Then Grizel seemed to
be alarmed, and her arms rocked despairingly,
but she went to her mother and took loving
hold of her, and the woman clung to her child
in a way pitiful to see. She was on Grizel's
knee now, but she still shivered as if in a deadly
chill, and her feet rattled on the floor, and her
arms against the sides of the chair. Grizel
pinned the trembling arms with her own, and
twisted her legs round her mother's, and still
the Painted Lady's tremors shook them both,
so that to Tommy they were as two people
wrestling.

The shivering slowly lessened and at last
ceased, but this seemed to make Grizel no less
unhappy. To her vehement attempt to draw
her mother's attention she got no response; the
Painted Lady was hearkening intently for some
sound other than Grizel's voice, and only once
did she look at her child. Then it was with
cruel, ugly eyes, and at the same moment she
shoved Grizel aside so viciously that it was
almost a blow. Grizel sat down sorrowfully

beside her doll, like one aware that she could do
no more, and her mother at once forgot her.
What was she listening for so eagerly? Was
it for the gallop of a horse? Tommy strained
his ears.

"Elspeth—speak low—do you hear anything?"

"No; I'm ower fleid to listen."

"Whisht! do you no hear a horse?"

"No, everything's terrible still. Do you
hear a horse?"

"I—I think I do, but far awa'."

His imagination was on fire. Did he hear a
distant galloping or did he only make himself
hear it? He had bent his head, and Elspeth,
looking affrighted into his face, whispered, "I
hear it too, oh, Tommy, so do I!"

And the Painted Lady had heard it. She
kissed her hand toward the Den several times,
and each time Tommy seemed to hear that distant galloping. All the sweetness had returned
to her face now, and with it a surging joy, and
she rocked her arms exultantly, but quickly
controlled them lest Grizel should see. For
evidently Grizel must be cheated, and so the
Painted Lady became very sly. She slipped off
her shoes to be able to make her preparations
noiselessly, and though at all other times her
face expressed the rapture of love, when she
glanced at her child it was suspiciously and with
a gleam of hatred. Her preparations were for
going out. She was long at the famous mirror,
and when she left it her hair was elaborately
dressed and her face so transformed that first

Tommy exclaimed "Bonny!" and then corrected himself with a scornful "Paint!" On her feet she put a foolish little pair of red shoes, on her head a hat too gay with flowers, and across her shoulders a flimsy white shawl at which the night air of Thrums would laugh. Her every movement was light and cautious and accompanied by side-glances at Grizel, who occasionally looked at her, when the Painted Lady immediately pretended to be tending her plants again. She spoke to Grizel sweetly to deceive her, and shot baleful glances at her next moment. Tommy saw that Grizel had taken up her doll once more and was squeezing it to her breast. She knew very well what was going on behind her back.

Suddenly Tommy took to his heels, Elspeth after him. He had seen the Painted Lady coming on her tiptoes to the window. They saw the window open and a figure in a white shawl creep out of it, as she had doubtless escaped long ago by another window when the door was barred. They lost sight of her at once.

"What will Grizel do now?" Tommy whispered, and he would have returned to his watching place, but Elspeth pointed to the window. Grizel was there closing it, and next moment the lamp was extinguished. They heard a key turn in the lock, and presently Grizel, carrying warm wraps, passed very near them and proceeded along the Double Dykes, not anxious apparently to keep her mother in view, but slowly, as if she knew where to find her.

She went into the Den, where Tommy dared not follow her, but he listened at the stile and in the awful silence he fancied he heard the neighing of a horse.

The next time he met Grizel he was yearning to ask her how she spent that night, but he knew she would not answer; it would be a long time before she gave him her confidence again. He offered her his piece of cold iron, however, and explained why he carried it, whereupon she flung it across the road, crying, " You horrid boy, do you think I am frightened at my mamma ! " But when he was out of sight she came back and slipped the cold iron into her pocket.

CHAPTER XVII.

IN WHICH TOMMY SOLVES THE WOMAN PROBLEM.

PITY made Elspeth want to like the Painted Lady's child now, but her own rules of life were all from a book never opened by Grizel, who made her religion for herself and thought God a swear; she also despised Elspeth for being so dependent on Tommy, and Elspeth knew it. The two great subjects being barred thus, it was not likely that either girl, despite some attempts on Elspeth's part, should find out the best that was in the other, without which friendship has no meaning, and they would have gone different ways had not Tommy given an arm to each. He, indeed, had as little in common with Grizel, for most conspicuous of his traits was the faculty of stepping into other people's shoes and remaining there until he became someone else; his individuality consisted in having none, while she could only be herself and was without tolerance for those who were different; he had at no time in his life the least desire to make other persons like himself, but if they were not like Grizel she rocked her arms and cried, " Why, why, why ? " which is the mark of the " womanly " woman. But his tendency to be anyone he was interested in implied enormous sympathy (for the time being), and though Grizel spurned his overtures, this only fired his pride of conquest. We can

all get whatever we want if we are quite determined to have it (though it be a king's daughter),
and in the end Tommy vanquished Grizel.
How ? By offering to let her come into Aaron's
house and wash it and dust it and ca'm it, "just
as if you were our mother," an invitation she
could not resist. To you this may seem an easy
way, but consider the penetration he showed in
thinking of it. It came to him one day when
he saw her lift the smith's baby out of the
gutter and hug it with a passionate delight in
babies.

"She's so awid to do it," he said basely to
Elspeth, "that we needna let on how much we
want it done." And he also mentioned her
eagerness to Aaron as a reason why she should
be allowed to do it for nothing.

For Aaron to hold out against her admittance would have been to defraud himself, for
she transformed his house. When she saw the
brass lining of the jelly-pan discoloured and that
the stockings hanging from the string beneath
the mantelpiece had given way where the
wearers were hardest on them ; when she found
dripping adhering to a cold frying-pan instead
of in a "pig," and the pitcher leaking and the
carrot-grater stopped—when these and similar
discoveries were made by Grizel, was it a squeal
of horror she gave that such things should be,
or a cry of rapture because to her had fallen the
task of setting them right ?

"She just made a jump for the besom," was
Tommy's graphic description of how it all
began.

You should have seen Grizel on the hoddy-table knocking nails into the wall. The hoddy-table is so-called because it goes beneath the larger one at night, like a chicken under its mother, and Grizel, with the nails in her mouth, used them up so quickly that you would have sworn she swallowed half of them; yet she rocked her arms because she could not be at all four walls at once. She rushed about the room until she was dizzy, and Tommy knew the moment to cry "Grip her, she'll tumble!" when he and Elspeth seized her and put her on a stool.

It is on the hoddy-table that you bake and iron. "There's not a baking-board in the house," Elspeth explained. "There is!" cried Grizel, there and then converting a drawer into one.

Between her big bannocks she made baby ones, for no better reason than that she was so fond of babies, and she kissed the baby ones and said, "Oh, the loves, they are just sweet!" and she felt for them when Tommy took a bite. She could go so quickly between the board and the girdle that she was always at one end of the course or the other, but never gave you time to say at which end, and on the limited space round the fire she could balance such a number of bannocks that they were as much a wonder as the Lord's Prayer written on a sixpence. Such a vigilant eye she kept on them, too, that they dared not fall. Yet she had never been taught to bake; a good-natured neighbour had now and again allowed her to look on.

Then her ironing! Even Aaron opened his mouth on this subject, Blinder being his confidant. "I thought there was a smell o' burning," he said, "and so I went butt the house; but man, as soon as my een lighted on her I minded of my mother at the same job. The crittur was so busy with her work that she looked as if, though the last trumpet had blawn, she would just have cried, 'I canna come till my ironing's done!' Ay, I went ben without a word."

But best of all was to see Grizel "redding-up" on a Saturday afternoon. Where were Tommy and Elspeth then? They were shut up in the coffin-bed to be out of the way, and could scarce have told whether they fled thither or were wapped into it by her energetic arms. Even Aaron dared not cross the floor until it was sanded. "I believe," he said, trying to jest, "you would like to shut me up in the bed too!" "I should just love it," she cried, eagerly; "will you go?" It is an inferior woman who has a sense of humour when there is a besom in her hand.

Thus began great days to Grizel, "sweet" she called them, for she had many of her mother's words, and a pretty way of emphasising them with her plain face that turned them all into superlatives. But though Tommy and Elspeth were her friends now, her mouth shut obstinately the moment they mentioned the Painted Lady; she regretted ever having given Tommy her confidence on that subject and was determined not to do so again. He did not dare

tell her that he had once been at the east
window of her home, but often he and Elspeth
spoke to each other of that adventure, and sometimes they woke in their garret bed thinking
they heard the horseman galloping by. Then
they crept closer to each other, and wondered
whether Grizel was cosey in her bed or stalking
an eerie figure in the Den.

Aaron said little, but he was drawn to the
girl, who had not the self-consciousness of
Tommy and Elspeth in his presence, and sometimes he slipped a penny into her hand. The
pennies were not spent, they were hoarded for
the fair, or Muckle Friday, or Muckley, great
day of the year in Thrums. If you would know
how Tommy was making ready for this mighty
festival, listen.

One of his sources of income was the *Mentor*,
a famous London weekly paper, which seemed to
visitors to be taken in by every person of position
in Thrums. It was to be seen not only in
parlours, but on the arm-chair at the Jute Bank,
in the gauger's gig, in the Spital factor's dog-
cart, on a shoemaker's form, protruding from Dr.
McQueen's tail pocket and from Mr. Duthie's
oxter pocket, on Cathro's school-desk, in the
Rev. Mr. Dishart's study, in half a dozen farms.
Miss Ailie compelled her little servant, Gavinia,
to read the *Mentor*, and stood over her while she
did it; the phrase, " this week's," meant this
week's *Mentor*. Yet the secret must be told:
only one copy of the paper came to Thrums
weekly; it was subscribed for by the whole
reading public between them, and by Miss Ailie's

influence Tommy had become the boy who
carried it from house to house.

This brought him a penny a week, but so
heavy were his incidental expenses that he could
have saved little for the Muckley had not another
organisation given him a better chance. It was
a society, newly started, for helping the deserving
poor; they had to subscribe not less than a
penny weekly to it, and at the end of the year
each subscriber was to be given fuel, etc., to the
value of double what he or she had put in.
"The three Ps" was a nickname given to the
society by Dr. McQueen, because it claimed to
distribute "Peats and Potatoes with Propriety,"
but he was one of its heartiest supporters nevertheless. The history of this society in the first
months of its existence not only shows how
Tommy became a moneyed man, but gives a
glimpse into the character of those it benefited.

Miss Ailie was treasurer, and the pennies
were to be brought to her on Monday evenings
between the hours of seven and eight. The
first Monday evening found her ready in the
school-room, in her hand the famous pencil that
wrote red with the one end, and blue with the
other; by her side her assistant, Mr. T. Sandys,
a pen balanced on his ear. For a whole hour did
they wait, but though many of the worthiest
poor had been enrolled as members, the few who
appeared with their pennies were notoriously
riff-raff. At eight Miss Ailie disconsolately
sent Tommy home, but he was back in five
minutes.

"There's a mask of them," he told her, ex-

citedly, "hanging about, but feared to come in
because the others would see them. They're
ashamed to have it kent that they belong to a
charity society, and Meggie Robbie is wandering
round the Dovecot wi' her penny wrapped in a
paper, and Watty Rattray and Ronny-On is
walking up and down the brae pretending they
dinna ken one another, and auld Connacher's
Jeanie Ann says she has been four times round
the town waiting for Kitty Elshioner to go
away, and there's a one-leggit man hodding in
the ditch, and Tibbie Birse is out wi' a lantern
counting them."

Miss Ailie did not know what to do.
"Here's Jeanie Ann's penny," Tommy continued, opening his hand, "and this is three
bawbees frae Kitty Elshioner, and you and me is
no to tell a soul they've joined."

A furtive tapping was heard at the door. It
was Ronny-On, who had skulked forward with
twopence, but Gavinia answered his knock, so he
just said, "Ay, Gavinia, it's yoursel'. Well, I'll
be stepping," and would have retired had not
Miss Ailie caught him. Even then he said,
"Three bawbees is to you to lay by, and one
bawbee to Gavinia no to tell."

To next Monday evening Miss Ailie now
looked with apprehension, but Tommy lay awake
that night, until, to use a favourite crow of his,
he "found a way." He borrowed the school-
mistress's blue-and-red pencil and sought the
houses of the sensitive poor with the following
effect. One sample will suffice; take him at the
door of Meggie Robbie in the West Muir, which

N

he flung open with the effrontery of a tax-collector.

"You're a three P," he said, with a wave of his pencil.

"I'm no sic thing!" cried the old lady.

"It winna do, woman," Tommy said sternly. "Miss Ailie told me you paid in your first penny on the chap of ten." He wetted the pencil on his tongue to show that it was vain to trifle with him, and Meggy bowed her head.

"It'll be through the town that I've joined," she moaned, but Tommy explained that he was there to save her.

"I'm willing to come to your house," he said, "and collect the money every week, and not a soul will I tell except the committee."

"Kitty Elshioner would see you coming," said Meggy.

"No, no, I'll creep yont the hedge and climb the hen-house."

"But it would be a' found out at any rate," she remembered, "when I go for the peats and things at Hogmanay."

"It needna be," eagerly replied Tommy. "I'll bring them to you in a barrow in the dead o' night."

"Could you?" she cried passionately, and he promised he would, and it may be mentioned here that he did.

"And what for yoursel'?" she inquired.

"A bawbee," he said, "the night afore the Muckley."

The bargain was made, but before he could get away, "Tell me, laddie," said Meggy, coax-

ingly, "has Kitty Elshioner joined?" They
were all as curious to know who had joined as
they were anxious to keep their own member-
bership a secret; but Tommy betrayed none, at
least none who agreed to his proposal. There
were so many of these that on the night before
the Muckley he had thirteen pence.

"And you was doing good all the time
you was making the thirteen pence," Elspeth
said, fondly. "I believe that was the reason
you did it."

"I believe it was!" Tommy exclaimed. He
had not thought of this before, but it was easy
to him to believe anything.

CHAPTER XVIII.

THE MUCKLEY.

EVERY child in Thrums went to bed on the night before the Muckley hugging a pirly, or, as the vulgar say, a money-box; and all the pirlies were ready for to-morrow, that is to say, the mouths of them had been widened with gully knives by owners now so skilful at the jerk which sends their contents to the floor that pirlies they were no longer. "Disgorge!" was the universal cry, or, in the vernacular, "Out you come, you sweer deevils!"

Not a coin but had its history, not a boy who was unable to pick out his own among a hundred. The black one came from the 'Sosh, the bent lad he got for carrying in Ronny-On's sticks. Oh michty me, sure as death he had nearly forgotten the one with the warts on it. Which to spend first? The goldy one? Na faags, it was ower ill to come by. The scartit one? No, no, it was a lucky. Well, then, the one found in the rat's hole. (That was a day!) Ay, dagont, ay, we'll make the first blatter with it.

It was Tommy's first Muckley, and the report that he had thirteen pence brought him many advisers about its best investment. Even Corp Shiach (five pence) suspended hostilities for this purpose. "Mind this," he said solemnly,

" there's none o' the candies as sucks so lang as
Californy's Teuch and Tasty. Other kinds may
be sweeter, but Teuch and Tasty lasts the
langest, and what a grip it has! It pulls out
your teeth!" Corp seemed to think that this
was a recommendation.

" I'm nane sure o' Teuch and Tasty," Birkie
said. " If you dinna keep a watch on it, it slips
ower when you're swallowing your spittle."

" Then you should tie a string to it,"
suggested Tommy, who was thought more of
from that hour.

Beware of pickpockets ! Had it not been for
placards with this glorious announcement (it is
the State's first printed acknowledgment that
boys and girls form part of the body politic) you
might have thought that the night before the
Muckley was absurdly like other nights. Not a
show had arrived, not a strange dog, no romantic
figures were wandering the streets in search of
lodgings, no stands had sprung up in the square.
You could pass hours in pretending to fear that
when the morning came there would be no fairyland. And all the time you *knew.*

About ten o'clock Ballingall's cat was observed washing its face, a deliberate attempt
to bring on rain. It was immediately put to
death.

Tommy and Elspeth had agreed to lie awake
all night; if Tommy nipped Elspeth, Elspeth
would nip Tommy. Other children had made
the same arrangement, though the experienced
ones were aware that it would fail. If it was
true that all the witches were dead, then the

streets of stands and shows and gaming-tables
and shooting-galleries were erected by human
hands, and it followed that were you to listen
through the night you must hear the hammers.
But always in the watches the god of the
Muckley came unseen and glued your eyes, as if
with Teuch and Tasty, and while you slept—Up
you woke with a start. What was it you were
to mind as soon as you woke? Listen! That's
a drum beating! It's the Muckley! They are
all here! It has begun! Oh, michty, michty,
michty, whaur's my breeks?

When Tommy, with Elspeth and Grizel, set
off excitedly for the town, the country folk were
already swarming in. The Monypenny road
was thick with them, braw loons in blue bonnets
with red bobs to them, tartan waistcoats, scarfs
of every colour, woollen shirts as gay, and the
strutting wearers in two minds—whether to
take off the scarf to display the shirt, or hide
the shirt and trust to the scarf. Came lassies,
too, in wincey bodices they were like to burst
through, and they were listening apprehensively
as they ploughed onward for a tearing at the
seams. There were red-headed lasses, yellow-
chy-headed and black-headed, blue-shawled and
red-shawled lasses; boots on every one of them,
stockings almost as common, the skirt kilted up
for the present, but down it should go when
they were in the thick of things, and then it
must take care of itself. All were solemn and
sheepish as yet, but wait a bit.

The first-known face our three met was
Corp. He was only able to sign to them,

because Californy's specialty had already done
its work and glued his teeth together. He was
off to the smithy to be melted, but gave them to
understand that though awkward it was glorious.
Then came Birkie, who had sewn up the mouths
of his pockets, all but a small slit in each, as a
precaution against pickpockets, and was now at
his own request being held upside down by the
Haggerty-Taggertys on the chance that a halfpenny which had disappeared mysteriously might
fall out. A more tragic figure was Francie
Crabb (one and seven pence), who, like a mad,
mad thing, had taken all his money to the fair
at once. In ten minutes he had bought fourteen musical instruments.

Tommy and party had not yet reached the
celebrated corner of the west town end where
the stands began, but they were near it, and he
stopped to give Grizel and Elspeth his final
instructions: "(1) Keep your money in your
purse, and your purse in your hand, and your
hand in your pocket; (2) if you lose me, I'll
give Shovel's whistle, and syne you maun
squeeze and birse your way back to me."

Now, then, are you ready? Bang! They
were in it. Strike up, ye fiddlers; drums,
break; tooters, fifers, at it for your lives;
trumpets, blow; bagpipes, skirl; music-boxes,
all together now—Tommy has arrived.

Even before he had seen Thrums, except
with his mother's eye, Tommy knew that the
wise begin the Muckley by measuring its extent.
That the square and adjoining wynds would be
crammed was a law of nature, but boyhood drew

imaginary lines across the Roods, the west town
end, the east town end, and the brae, and if the
stands did not reach these there had been
retrogression. Tommy found all well in two
quarters, got a nasty shock on the brae, but
medicine for it in the Roods; on the whole,
yelled a hundred children, by way of greeting to
each other, a better Muckley than ever.

From those who loved them best, the more
notable Muckleys got distinctive names for
convenience of reference. As shall be ostentatiously shown in its place, there was a
Muckley called (and by Corp Shiach, too) after
Tommy, but this, his first, was dubbed Sewster's
Muckley, in honour of a seamstress who hanged
herself that day in the Three-cornered Wood.
Poor little sewster, she had known joyous
Muckleys too, but now she was up in the Three-
cornered Wood hanging herself, aged nineteen.
I know nothing more of her, except that in
her maiden days when she left the house her
mother always came to the door to look proudly
after her.

How to describe the scene, when owing to
the throng a boy could only peer at it between
legs or through the crook of a woman's arm?
Shovel would have run up ploughmen to get his
bird's-eye view, and he could have told Tommy
what he saw, and Tommy could have made a
picture of it in his mind, every figure ten feet
high. But perhaps to be lost in it was best.
You had but to dive and come up anywhere to
find something amazing; you fell over a box
of jumping-jacks into a new world.

Everyone to his taste. If you want Tommy's sentiments, here they are, condensed : " The shows surpass everything else on earth. Four streets of them in the square ! The best is the menagerie, because there is the loudest roaring there. Kick the caravans and you increase the roaring. Admission, however, prohibitive (three-pence). More economical to stand outside the show of the ' Mountain Maid and the Shepherd's Bride' and watch the merriman saying funny things to the monkey. Take care you don't get in front of the steps, else you will be pressed up by those behind and have to pay before you have decided that you want to go in. When you fling pennies at the Mountain Maid and the Shepherd's Bride they stop play-acting and scramble for them. Go in at night when there are drunk ploughmen to fling pennies. The Fat Wife with the Golden Locks lets you put your fingers in her arms, but that is soon over. ' The Slave-driver and his Victims.' Not worth the money; they are not blooding. To Jerusalem and Back in a Jiffy. This is a swindle. You just keek through holes."

But Elspeth was of a different mind. She liked To Jerusalem and Back best, and gave the Slave-driver and his Victims a penny to be Christians. The only show she disliked was the wax-work, where was performed the "Tragedy of Tiffano and the Haughty Princess." Tiffano loved the woodman's daughter, and so he would not have the Haughty Princess, and so she got a magician to turn him into a pumpkin, and then she ate him. What distressed Elspeth was that Tiffano could never get to Heaven now, and all the consolation Tommy, doing his best, could give her was "He could go, no doubt he could go, but he would have to take the Haughty Princess wi' him, and he would be sweer to do that."

Grizel reflected: "If I had a whip like the one the slave-driver has, shouldn't I lash the boys who hoot my mamma! I wish I could turn boys into pumpkins. The Mountain Maid wore a beautiful muslin with gold lace, but she does not wash her neck."

Lastly, let Corp have his say: "I looked at the outside of the shows, but always landed back at Californy's stand. Sucking is better nor near anything. The Teuch and Tasty is stickier than ever. I have lost twa teeth. The Mountain Maid is biding all night at Tibbie Birse's, and I went in to see her. She had a bervie and a boiled egg to her tea. She likes her eggs saft wi' a lick of butter in them. The Fat Wife is the ane I like best. She's biding wi' Shilpit Kaytherine on the Tanage Brae. She weighs Jeems and Kaytherine and the sma' black swine. She had an ingin to her tea. The Slave-driver's a fushinless body. One o' the Victims gives him his licks. They a' bide in the caravan. You can stand on the wheel and keek in. They had herrings wi' the rans to their tea. I cut a hole in Jerusalem and Back, and there was no Jerusalem there. The man as ocht Jerusalem greets because the Fair Circassian winna take him. He is biding a' night wi' Blinder. He likes a dram in his tea."

Elspeth's money lasted till four o'clock. For Aaron, almost the only man in Thrums who shunned the revels that day, she bought a gingerbread house; and the miraculous powder which must be taken on a sixpence was to make Blinder see again, but unfortunately he forgot about putting it on the sixpence. And of course there was something for a certain boy. Grizel had completed her purchases by five o'clock, when Tommy was still heavy with threepence halfpenny. They included a fluffy pink shawl, she did not say for whom, but the Painted Lady wore it afterwards, and for herself another doll.

"But that doll's leg is broken," Tommy pointed out.

"That was why I bought it," she said warmly, "I feel so sorry for it, the darling," and she carried it carefully so that the poor thing might suffer as little pain as possible.

Twice they rushed home for hasty meals and were back so quickly that Tommy's shadow strained a muscle in turning with him. Night came on, and from a hundred strings stretched along stands and shows there now hung thousands of long tin things like trumpets. One burning paper could set a dozen of these ablaze, and no sooner were they lit than a wind that had been biding its time rushed in like the merriman, making the lamps swing on their strings, so that the flaring lights embraced, and from a distance Thrums seemed to be on fire.

Even Grizel was willing to hold Tommy's hand now, and the three could only move this way and that as the roaring crowd carried them.

They were not looking at the Muckley, they were part of it, and at last Thrums was all Tommy's fancy had painted it. This intoxicated him, so that he had to scream at intervals, "We're here, Elspeth, I tell you, we're here!" and he became pugnacious and asked youths twice his size whether they denied that he was here, and if so, would they come on. In this frenzy he was seen by Miss Ailie, who had stolen out in a veil to look for Gavinia, but just as she was about to reprove him, dreadful men asked her was she in search of a lad, whereupon she fled home and barred the door, and later in the evening warned Gavinia, through the key-hole, taking her for a roystering blade, that there were policemen in the house, to which the astounding reply of Gavinia, then aged twelve, was, "No sic luck."

With the darkness, too, crept into the Muckley certain devils in the colour of the night who spoke thickly and rolled braw lads in the mire, and egged on friends to fight and cast lewd thoughts into the minds of the women. At first the men had been bashful swains. To the women's "Gie me my faring, Jock," they had replied, "Wait, Jean, till I'm fee'd," but by night most had got their arles, with a dram above it, and he who could only guffaw at Jean a few hours ago had her round the waist now, and still an arm free for rough play with other kimmers. The Jeans were as boisterous as the Jocks, giving them leer for leer, running from them with a giggle, waiting to be caught and rudely kissed. Grand, patient, long-suffering fellows these men were, up at five, summer and winter, foddering their horses, maybe, hours before there would be food for themselves, miserably paid, housed liked cattle, and when the rheumatism seized them, liable to be flung aside like a broken graip. As hard was the life of the women : coarse food, chaff beds, damp clothes their portion; their sweethearts in the service of masters who were reluctant to fee a married man. Is it to be wondered that these lads who could be faithful until death drank soddenly on their one free day, that these girls, starved of opportunities for womanliness, of which they could make as much as the finest lady, sometimes woke after a Muckley to wish that they might wake no more?

Our three brushed shoulders with the devils that had been let loose, but hardly saw them; they heard them, but did not understand their tongue. The eight o'clock bell had rung long since ; and though the racket was as great as ever, it was only because every reveller left now made the noise of two. Mothers were out fishing for their bairns. The Haggerty-Taggertys had straggled home hoarse as crows; every one of them went to bed that night with a stocking round his throat. Of Monypenny boys, Tommy could find none in the square but Corp, who, with another tooth missing, had been going about since six o'clock with his pockets hanging out, as a sign that all was over. An awkward silence had fallen on the trio ; the reason, that Tommy had only threepence left and the smallest of them cost threepence. The reference of course is to

the wondrous gold-paper packets of sweets (not
unlike crackers in appearance) which are only
seen at the Muckley, and are what every girl
claims of her lad or lads. Now, Tommy had
vowed to Elspeth—But he had also said to
Grizel—In short, how could he buy for both
with threepence?

Grizel, as the stranger, ought to get—But he
knew Elspeth too well to believe that she would
dry her eyes with that.

Elspeth being his sister—But he had promised
Grizel, and she had been so ill brought up that
she said nasty things when you broke your word.

The gold packet was bought. That is it
sticking out of Tommy's inside pocket. The
girls saw it, and knew what was troubling him,
but not a word was spoken now between the
three. They set off for home self-consciously,
Tommy the least agitated on the whole, because
he need not make up his mind for another
ten minutes. But he wished Grizel would not
look at him sideways and then rock her arms
in irritation. They passed many merry-makers
homeward bound, many of them following a
tortuous course, for the Scottish toper gives
way first in the legs, the Southron in the other
extremity, and thus between them could be
constructed a man wholly sober and another
as drunk as Chloe. But though the highway
clattered with many feet, not a soul was in the
Double Dykes, and at the easy end of that formidable path Grizel came to a determined stop.

"Good-night," she said, with such a dis-
dainful glance at Tommy.

He had not made up his mind yet, but he saw that it must be done now, and to take a decisive step was always agony to him, though once taken it ceased to trouble. To dodge it for another moment he said, weakly: " Let's—let's sit down a whiley on the dyke."

But Grizel, while coveting the packet, because she had never got a present in her life, would not shilly-shally, " Are you to give it to Elspeth ? " she asked, with the horrid directness that is so trying to an intellect like Tommy's.

" N-no," he said.

" To Grizel ? " cried Elspeth.

" N-no," he said again.

It was an undignified moment for a great boy, but the providence that watched over Tommy until it tired of him came to his aid in the nick of time. It took the form of the Painted Lady, who appeared suddenly out of the gloom of the Double Dykes. Two of the children jumped, and the third clenched her little fists to defend her mamma if Tommy cast a word at her. But he did not; his mouth remained foolishly open. The Painted Lady had been talking cheerfully to herself, but she drew back apprehensively, with a look of appeal on her face, and then—and then Tommy " saw a way." He handed her the gold packet. " It's to you," he said ; " it's—it's your Muckley ! "

For a moment she was afraid to take it, but when she knew that this sweet boy's gift was genuine, she fondled it and was greatly flattered, and dropped him the quaintest courtesy and then looked defiantly at Grizel. But Grizel did not

take it from her. Instead she flung her arms
impulsively round Tommy's neck; she was so
glad, glad, glad.

As Tommy and Elspeth walked away to
their home, Elspeth could hear him breathing
heavily, and occasionally he gave her a furtive
glance.

"Grizel needna have done that," she said,
sharply.

"No," replied Tommy.

"But it was noble of you," she continued,
squeezing his hand, "to give it to the Painted
Lady. Did you mean to give it to her a' the
time?"

"Oh, Elspeth!"

"But did you?"

"Oh, Elspeth!"

"That's no you greeting, is it?" she asked,
softly.

"I'm near the greeting," he said truthfully,
"but I'm no sure what about." His sympathy
was so easily aroused that he sometimes cried
without exactly knowing why.

"It's because you're so good," Elspeth told
him; but presently she said, with a complete
change of voice, "No, Grizel needna have done
that."

"It was a shameful thing to do," Tommy
agreed, shaking his head. "But she did it!"
he added triumphantly; "you saw her do it,
Elspeth!"

"But you didna like it?" Elspeth asked, in
terror.

"No, of course I didna like it, but——"

"But what, Tommy?"

"But I liked her to like it," he admitted,
and by-and-by he began to laugh hysterically.
"I'm no sure what I'm laughing at," he said,
"but I think it's at mysel'." He may have
laughed at himself before, but this Muckley is
memorable as the occasion on which he first
caught himself doing it. The joke grew with
the years, until sometimes he laughed in his
most emotional moments, suddenly seeing himself
in his true light. But it had become a bitter
laugh by that time.

CHAPTER XIX.

CORP IS BROUGHT TO HEEL—GRIZEL DEFIANT.

CORP SHIACH was a bare-footed colt of a boy,
of ungainly build, with a nose so thick and
turned up that it was a certificate of character,
and his hands were covered with warts, which
he had a trick of biting till they bled. Then he
rubbed them on his trousers, which were the
picturesque part of him, for he was at present
" serving " to the masons (he had " earned his
keep " since long before he could remember), and
so wore the white or yellow ducks which the
dust of the quarry stains a rarer orange colour
than is known elsewhere. The orange of the
masons' trousers, the blue of the hearthstones,
these are the most beautiful colours to be seen
in Thrums, though of course Corp was unaware
of it. He was really very good-natured, and
only used his fists freely because of imagination
he had none, and thinking made him sweat, and
consequently the simplest way of proving his
case was to say " I'll fight you." What might
have been the issue of a conflict between him
and Shovel was a problem for Tommy to puzzle
over. Shovel was as quick as Corp was deliberate, and would have danced round him,
putting in unexpected ones, but if he had remained just one moment too long within Corp's
reach——

They nicknamed him Corp because he took fits, when he lay like one dead. He was proud of his fits, was Corp, but they were a bother to him, too, because he could make so little of them. They interested doctors and other carriage folk, who came to his aunt's house to put their fingers into him, and gave him sixpence, and would have given him more, but when they pressed him to tell them what he remembered about his fits, he could only answer dejectedly, " Not a damned thing."

" You might as well no have them ava," his wrathful aunt, with whom he lived, would say, and she thrashed him until his size forbade it.

Soon after the Muckley came word that the Lady of the Spittal was to be brought to see Corp by Mr. Ogilvy, the schoolmaster of Glen Quharity, and at first Corp boasted of it, but as the appointed day drew near he became uneasy.

" The worst o't," he said to anyone who would listen, " is that my auntie is to be away frae hame, and so they'll put a' their questions to me."

The Haggerty-Taggertys and Birkie were so jealous that they said they were glad *they* never had fits, but Tommy made no such pretence.

" Oh, Corp, if I had thae fits of yours ! " he exclaimed greedily.

" If they were mine to give awa'," replied Corp sullenly, " you could have them and welcome." Grown meek in his trouble, he invited Tommy to speak freely, with the result that his eyes were partially opened to the superiority of that boy's attainments. Tommy told him a

o 2

number of interesting things to say to Mr. Ogilvy
and the lady about his fits—about how queer he
felt just before they came on, and the visions he
had while he was lying stiff. But though the
admiring Corp gave attentive ear, he said hopelessly next day, "Not a dagont thing do I
mind. When they question me about my fits
I'll just say I'm sometimes in them and sometimes out o' them, and if they badger me more,
I can aye kick."

Tommy gave him a look that meant, "Fits
are just wasted on you," and Corp replied with
another that meant "I ken they are." Then
they parted, one of them to reflect.

"Corp," he said excitedly, when next they
met, "has Mr. Ogilvy or the lady ever come to
see you afore?"

They had not, and Corp was able to swear
that they did not even know him by sight.

"They dinna ken me either," said Tommy.

"What does that matter?" asked Corp, but
Tommy was too full to speak. He had "found
a way."

The lady and Mr. Ogilvy found Corp such a
success that the one gave him a shilling, and
the other took down his reminiscences in a note-
book. But if you would hear of the rings of
blue and white and yellow Corp saw, and of
the other extraordinary experiences he described
himself as having when in a fit, you need not
search that note-book, for the page has been
torn out. Instead of making inquiries of
Mr. Ogilvy, try any other dominie in the dis-
trict, Mr. Cathro, for instance, who delighted to

tell the tale.   This of course was when it leaked
out that Tommy had personated Corp, by arrangement with the real Corp, who was listening
in rapture beneath the bed.

Tommy, who played his part so well that he
came out of it in a daze, had Corp at heel from
that hour.   He told him what a rogue he had
been in London, and Corp cried admiringly,
"Oh, you deevil! oh, you queer little deevil!"
and sometimes it was Elspeth who was narrator,
and then Tommy's noble acts were the subject;
but still Corp's comment was "Oh, the deevil!
oh, the queer little deevil!"   Elspeth was
flattered by his hero-worship, but his language
shocked her, and after consulting Miss Ailie
she advised him to count twenty when he felt
an oath coming, at the end of which exercise
the desire to swear would have passed away.
Good-natured Corp willingly promised to try
this, but he was never hopeful; and as he explained to Tommy, after a failure, "It just made
me waur than ever; for when I had counted the
twenty I said a big Damn, thoughtful-like, and
syne out jumpit three little damns, like as if
the first ane had cleckit in my mouth."

It was fortunate that Elspeth liked Corp on
the whole, for during the three years now to be
rapidly passed over, Tommy took delight in his
society, though he never treated him as an equal;
Corp indeed did not expect that, and was humbly
grateful for what he got.   In summer, fishing
was their great diversion.   They would set off
as early as four in the morning, fishing wands in
hand, and scour the world for trout, plodding

home in the gloaming with stones in their
fishing basket to deceive those who felt its
weight. In the long winter nights they liked
best to listen to Blinder's tales of the Thrums
Jacobites, tales never put into writing, but
handed down from father to son, and proved
true in the oddest of ways, as by Blinder's trick
of involuntarily holding out his hands to a fire
when he found himself near one, though he
might be sweating to the shirt and the time
a July forenoon. "I make no doubt," he told
them, "as I do that because my forbear, Buchan
Osler (called Buchan wi' the Haap after the wars
was ower), had to hod so lang frae the troopers,
and them so greedy for him that he daredna
crawl to a fire once in an eight days."

The Lord of the Spittal and handsome
Captain Body (whose being "out" made all the
women anxious) marched through the Den, flap-
ping their wings at the head of a fearsome
retinue, and the Thrums folk looked so glum at
them that gay Captain Body said he should kiss
every lass who did not cheer for Charlie, and
none cheered, but at the same time none ran
away. Few in Thrums cared a doit for Charlie,
but some hung on behind this troop till there
was no turning back for them, and one of these
was Buchan. He forced his wife to give Captain
Body a white rose from her bush by the door,
but a thorn in it pricked the gallant, and the
blood from his fingers fell on the bush, and from
that year it grew red roses.

"If you dinna believe me," Blinder said,
"look if the roses is no red on the bush at

Pyotdykes, which was a split frae Buchan's, and speir whether they're no named the blood rose."

" I believe you," Tommy would say breathlessly : " go on."

Captain Body was back in the Den by-and-by, but he had no thought of preeing lasses' mouths now. His face was scratched and haggard and his gay coat torn, and when he crawled to the Cuttle Well he caught some of the water in his bonnet and mixed meal with it, stirring the precious compound with his finger and using the loof of his hand as a spoon. Every stick of furniture Buchan and the other Thrums rebels possessed was seized by the Government and rouped in the market-place of Thrums, but few would bid against the late owners, for whom the things were secretly bought back very cheaply.

To these and many similar stories Tommy listened open-mouthed, seeing the scene far more vividly than the narrator, who became alarmed at his quick loud breathing, and advised him to forget them and go back to his lessons. But his lessons never interested Tommy, and he would go into the Den instead, and repeat Blinder's legends, with embellishments which made them so real, that Corp and Elspeth and Grizel were afraid to look behind them lest the spectre of Captain Body should be standing there, leaning on a ghostly sword.

At such times Elspeth kept a firm grip of Tommy's hand, but one evening as they all ran panic-stricken from some imaginary alarm, she

lost him near the Cuttle Well, and then, as it
seemed to her, the Den became suddenly very
dark and lonely. At first she thought she had
it to herself, but as she stole timidly along the
pink path she heard voices, and cried "Tommy!"
joyously. But no answer came, so it could not
be Tommy. Then she thought it must be a
pair of lovers, but next moment she stood trans-
fixed with fear, for it was the Painted Lady,
who was coming along the path talking aloud
to herself. No, not to herself—to someone she
evidently thought was by her side; she called
him darling and other sweet names, and waited
for his replies and nodded pleased assent to them,
or pouted at them, and terrified Elspeth knew
that she was talking to the man who never
came.

When she saw Elspeth she stopped irreso-
lutely, and the two stood looking in fear at each
other. "You are not my brat, are you?" the
Painted Lady asked.

"N-no," the child gasped.

"Then why don't you call me nasty
names?"

"I dinna never call you names," Elspeth
replied, but the woman still looked puzzled.

"Perhaps you are naughty also?" she said
doubtfully, and then, as if making up her mind
that it must be so, she came closer and said, with
a voice full of pity: "I am so sorry."

Elspeth did not understand half of it, but
the pitying voice, which was of the rarest sweetness, drove away much of her fear, and she said:
"Do you no mind me? I was wi' Tommy

when he gave you the gold packet on Muckley night."

Then the Painted Lady remembered. "He took such a fancy to me," she said, with a pleased simper, and then she looked serious again.

"Do you love him?" she asked, and Elspeth nodded.

"But is he all the world to you?"

"Yes," Elspeth said.

The Painted Lady took her by the arm and said impressively, "Don't let him know."

"But he does know," said Elspeth.

"I am so sorry," the Painted Lady said again. "When they know too well, then they have no pity."

"But I want Tommy to know," Elspeth insisted.

"That is the woful thing," the Painted Lady said, rocking her arms in a way that reminded the child of Grizel. "We want them to know; we cannot help liking them to know!"

Suddenly she became confidential. "Do you think I showed my love too openly?" she asked eagerly. "I tried to hide it, you know. I covered my face with my hands, but he pulled them away, and then, of course, he knew."

She went on, "I kissed his horse's nose, and he said I did that because it was his horse. How could he know? When I asked him how he knew, he kissed me, and I pretended to be angry and ran away. But I was not angry, and I said to myself, 'I am glad, I am glad, I am glad!'

"I wanted so to be good, but—it is so

difficult to refuse when you love him very much, don't you think ? "

The pathos of that was lost on the girl, and the Painted Lady continued sadly : " It would be so nice, would it not, if they liked us to be good? I think it would be sweet." She bent forward and whispered emphatically, " But they don't, you know—it bores them. Never bore them—and they are so easily bored ! It bores them if you say you want to be married. I think it would be sweet to be married, but you should never ask for a wedding. They give you everything else, but if you say you want a wedding, they stamp their feet and go away. Why are you crying, girl? You should not cry ; they don't like it. Put on your prettiest gown and laugh and pretend you are happy, and then they will tell you naughty stories and give you these." She felt her ears and looked at her fingers, on which there may once have been jewels, but there were none now.

" If you cry, you lose your complexion, and then they don't love you any more. I had always such a beautiful skin. Some ladies when they lose their complexion, paint. Horrid, isn't it ? I wonder they can do such a thing."

She eyed Elspeth suspiciously. " But of course you might do it just a little," she said pleadingly—" just to make them go on loving you, don't you think ?

" When they don't want to come any more they write you a letter, and you run with it to your room and kiss it, because you don't know what is inside. Then you open it, and that breaks your heart, you know." She nodded her head sagaciously and smiled with tears in her eyes. "Never, never, never open the letter. Keep it unopened on your breast, and then you can always think that he may come to-morrow. And if—— "

Someone was approaching, and she stopped and listened. "My brat!" she cried furiously, "she is always following me," and she poured forth a torrent of filthy abuse of Grizel, in the midst of which Tommy (for it was he) appeared and carried Elspeth off hastily. This was the only conversation either child ever had with the Painted Lady, and it bore bad fruit for Grizel. Elspeth told some of the Monypenny women about it, and they thought it their duty to point out to Aaron that the Painted Lady and her child were not desirable acquaintances for Tommy and Elspeth.

"I dinna ken," he answered sharply, "whether Tommy's a fit acquaintance for Grizel, but I'm very sure o' this, that she's more than a fit acquaintance for him. And look at what she has done for this house. I kenna what we should do if she didna come in nows and nans."

"You ken well, Aaron," they said, "that onything we could do in the way o' keeping your house in order we should do gladly."

"Thank you," he replied ungraciously, "but I would rather have her."

Nevertheless he agreed that he ought to forbid any intercourse with the Painted Lady, and unfortunately Grizel heard of this. Probably there never would have been any such

intercourse; Grizel guarded against it more than
anyone, for reasons she never spoke of, but she
resented this veto proudly.

"Why must you not speak to my mamma?"
she demanded of Tommy and Elspeth.

"Because—because she is a queer one,"
he said.

"She is not a queer one—she is just sweet."

He tried to evade the question by saying
weakly, "We never see her to speak to at ony
rate, so it will make no difference. It's no as if
you ever asked us to come to Double Dykes."

"But I ask you now," said Grizel, with
flashing eyes.

"Oh, I darena!" cried Elspeth.

"Then I won't ever come into your house
again," said Grizel, decisively.

"No to redd up?" asked Tommy, incredu-
lously. "No to bake nor to iron? You
couldna help it."

"Yes, I could."

"Think what you'll miss!"

Grizel might have retorted, "Think what
you will miss!" but perhaps the reply she did
make had a sharper sting in it. "I shall never
come again," she said loftily, "and my reason
for not coming is that—that my mamma thinks
your house is not respectable!" She flung this
over her shoulder as she stalked away, and it
may be that the tears came when there were
none to see them, but hers was a resolute mind,
and though she continued to be friendly with
Tommy and Elspeth out of doors she never
again crossed their threshold.

"The house is in a terrible state for want o'
you," Tommy would say, trying to wheedle her.
"We hinna sanded the floor for months, and the
box-iron has fallen ahint the dresser, and my
grey sark is rove up the back, and oh, you
should just see the holes in Aaron's stockings!"

Then Grizel rocked her arms in agony, but
no, she would not go in.

CHAPTER XX.

THE SHADOW OF SIR WALTER.

TOMMY was in Miss Ailie's senior class now,
though by no means at the top of it, and her
mind was often disturbed about his future. On
this subject Aaron had never spoken to anyone,
and the problem gave Tommy himself so little
trouble that all Elspeth knew was that he was to
be great and that she was to keep his house.
So the schoolmistress braved an interview with
Aaron for the sake of her favourite.

"You know he is a remarkable boy," she
said.

"At his lessons, ma'am?" asked Aaron,
quietly.

Not exactly at his lessons, she had to admit.

"In what way, then, ma'am?"

Really Miss Ailie could not say. There was
something wonderful about Tommy, you felt it,
but you could not quite give it a name. The
warper must have noticed it himself.

"I've heard him saying something o' the
kind to Elspeth," was Aaron's reply.

"But sometimes he is like a boy inspired,"
said the schoolmistress. "You must have seen
that."

"When he was thinking o' himsel'," answered
Aaron.

"He has such noble sentiments."

"He has."

"And I think, I really think," said Miss Ailie, eagerly, for this was what she had come to say, "that he has got great gifts for the ministry."

"I'm near sure o't," said Aaron, grimly.

"Ah, I see you don't like him."

"I dinna," the warper acknowledged quietly, "but I've been trying to do my duty by him for all that. It's no every laddie that gets three years' schooling straight on end."

This was true, but Miss Ailie used it to press her point. "You have done so well by him," she said, "that I think you should keep him at school for another year or two, and so give him a chance of carrying a bursary. If he carries one it will support him at college ; if he does not—well, then I suppose he must be apprenticed to some trade."

"No," Aaron said, decisively ; "if he gets the chance of a college education and flings it awa', I'll waste no more siller on his keep. I'll send him straight to the herding."

"And I shall not blame you," Miss Ailie declared eagerly.

"Though I would a hantle rather," continued the warper, " waur my money on Elspeth."

"What you spend on him," Miss Ailie argued, "you will really be spending on her, for if he rises in the world he will not leave Elspeth behind. You are prejudiced against him, but you cannot deny that."

"I dinna deny but what he's fond o' her," said Aaron, and after considering the matter for some days he decided that Tommy should get his chance. The schoolmistress had not acted selfishly, for this decision, as she knew, meant that the boy must now be placed in the hands of Mr. Cathro, who was a Greek and Latin scholar. She taught Latin herself, it is true, but as cautiously as she crossed a plank bridge, and she was never comfortable in the dominie's company, because even at a tea-table he would refer familiarly to the ablative absolute instead of letting sleeping dogs lie.

"But Elspeth couldna be happy if we were at different schools," Tommy objected instantly.

"Yes, I could," said Elspeth, who had been won over by Miss Ailie; "it will be so fine, Tommy, to see you again after I hinna seen you for three hours."

Tommy was little known to Mr. Cathro at this time, except as the boy who had got the better of a rival teacher in the affair of Corp, which had delighted him greatly. "But if the sacket thinks he can play any of his tricks on me," he told Aaron, "there is an awakening before him," and he began the cramming of Tommy for a bursary with perfect confidence.

But before the end of the month, at the mere mention of Tommy's name, Mr. Cathro turned red in the face, and the fingers of his laying-on hand would clutch an imaginary pair of tawse. Already Tommy had made him self-conscious. He peered covertly at Tommy, and Tommy had caught him at it every time, and then each quickly looked another way, and Cathro vowed never to look again, but did it next minute, and

what enraged him most was that he knew
Tommy noted his attempts at self-restraint as
well as his covert glances. All the other pupils
knew that a change for the worse had come over
the dominie's temper. They saw him punish
Tommy frequently without perceptible cause,
and that he was still unsatisfied when the
punishment was over. This apparently was
because Tommy gave him a look before returning to his seat. When they had been
walloped they gave Cathro a look also, but it
merely meant, "Oh, that this was a dark road
and I had a divot in my hand!" while his look
was unreadable—that is, unreadable to them, for
the dominie understood it and writhed. What
it said was, "You think me a wonder, and therefore I forgive you."

"And sometimes he fair beats Cathro!" So
Tommy's schoolmates reported at home, and the
dominie had to acknowledge its truth to Aaron.
"I wish you would give that sacket a thrashing
for me," he said, half furiously, yet with a grin
on his face, one day when he and the warper
chanced to meet on the Monypenny road.

"I'll no lay a hand on bairn o' Jean Myles,"
Aaron replied. "Ay, and I understood you to
say that he should meet his match in you."

"Did I ever say that, man? Well, well,
we live and learn."

"What has he been doing now?"

"What has he been doing!" echoed Cathro.
"He has been making me look foolish in my
own class-room. Yes, sir, he has so completely
got the better of me (and not for the first time)

P

that when I tell the story of how he diddled Mr. Ogilvy, Mr. Ogilvy will be able to cap it with the story of how the little whelp diddled me. Upon my soul, Aaron, he is running away with all my self-respect and destroying my sense of humour."

What had so crushed the dominie was the affair of Francie Crabb. Francie was now a pupil, like Gavin Dishart and Tommy, of Mr. Cathro's, who detested the boy's golden curls, perhaps because he was bald himself. They were also an incentive to evil-doing on the part of other boys, who must give them a tug in passing, and on a day the dominie said, in a fury, "Give your mother my compliments, Francie, and tell her I'm so tired of seeing your curls that I mean to cut them off to-morrow morning."

"Say he shall not," whispered Tommy.

"You shanna!" blurted out Francie.

"But I will," said Cathro; "I would do it now if I had the shears."

It was only an empty threat, but an hour afterward the dominie caught Tommy wagering in witchy marbles and other coin that he would not do it, and then instead of taking the tawse to him he said, "Keep him to his bargains, laddies, for whatever may have been my intention at the time, I mean to be as good as my word now."

He looked triumphantly at Tommy, who, however, instead of seeming crestfallen, continued to bet, and now the other boys were eager to close with him, for great was their faith in Cathro. These transactions were carried out on the sly, but the dominie knew what was going on, and despite his faith in himself he had his twitches of uneasiness.

"However, the boy can only be trusting to fear of Mrs. Crabb restraining me," he decided, and he marched into the school-room next morning ostentatiously displaying his wife's largest scissors. His pupils crowded in after him, and though he noticed that all were strangely quiet and many wearing scared faces, he put it down to the coming scene. He could not resist giving one triumphant glance at Tommy, who, however, instead of returning it, looked modestly down. Then — "Is Francie Crabb here?" asked Mr. Cathro, firmly.

"He's hodding ahint the press," cried a dozen voices.

"Come forward, Francie," said the dominie, clicking the shears to encourage him.

There was a long pause, and then Francie emerged in fear from behind the press. Yes, it was Francie, but his curls were gone!

The shears fell to the floor. "Who did this?" roared the terrible Cathro.

"It was Tommy Sandys," blurted out Francie, in tears.

The schoolmaster was unable to speak, and alarmed at the stillness, Francie whined, "He said it would be done at onyrate, and he promised me half his winnings."

It is still remembered by bearded men and married women who were at school that day how Cathro leaped three forms to get at

P 2

Tommy, and how Tommy cried under the
tawse and yet laughed ecstatically at the same
time, and how subsequently he and Francie
collected so many dues that the pockets of them
stood out like brackets from their little persons.

The dominie could not help grinning a little
at his own discomfiture as he told this story,
but Aaron saw nothing amusing in it. "As I
told you," he repeated, "I winna touch him,
so if you're no content wi' what you've done
yoursel', you had better put Francie's mither
on him."

"I hear she has taken him in hand already,"
Mr. Cathro replied dryly. "But, Aaron, I
wish you would at least keep him closer to his
lessons at night, for it is seldom he comes to
the school well prepared."

"I see him sitting lang ower his books,"
said Aaron.

"Ay, maybe, but is he at them?" responded
the dominie with a shake of the head that made
Aaron say, with his first show of interest in
the conversation, "You have little faith in his
carrying a bursary, I see."

But this Mr. Cathro would not admit, for
if he thought Tommy a numskull the one day
he often saw cause to change his mind the next,
so he answered guardedly, "It's too soon to
say, Aaron, for he has eighteen months' stuffing
to undergo yet before we send him to Aberdeen
to try his fortune, and I have filled some gey
toom wimes in eighteen months. But you must
lend me a hand."

The weaver considered, and then replied

stubbornly, "No, I give him his chance, but I'll have nocht to do wi' his use o't. And, dominie, I want you not to say another word to me about him atween this and examination time, for my mind's made up no to say a word to him. It's well kent that I'm no more fit to bring up bairns than to have them (dinna conter me, man, for the thing was proved lang syne at the Cuttle Well), and so till that time I'll let him gang his ain gait. But if he doesna carry a bursary, to the herding he goes. I've said it, and I'll stick to it."

So, as far as Aaron was concerned, Tommy was left in peace to the glory of collecting his winnings from those who had sworn by Cathro, and among them was Master Gavin Ogilvy Dishart, who now found himself surrounded by a debt of sixpence, a degrading position for the son of an Auld Licht minister.

Tommy would not give him time, but was willing to take his copy of " Waverley " as full payment.

Gavin offered him "Ivanhoe" instead, because his mother had given a read of " Waverley " to Gavinia, Miss Ailie's servant, and she read so slowly, putting her finger beneath each word, that she had not yet reached the middle. Also, she was so enamoured of the work that she would fight anyone who tried to take it from her.

Tommy refused "Ivanhoe," as it was not about Jacobites, but suggested that Gavinia should be offered it in lieu of " Waverley," and told that it was a better story.

The suggestion came too late, as Gavinia

had already had a loan of "Ivanhoe," and read
it with rapture, inch by inch. However, if
Tommy would wait a month, or——

Tommy was so eager to read more about the
Jacobites that he found it trying to wait
five minutes. He thought Gavin's duty was
to get his father to compel Gavinia to give
the book up.

Was Tommy daft? Mr. Dishart did not
know that his son possessed these books. He
did not approve of story-books, and when Mrs.
Dishart gave them to Gavin on his birthday
she—she had told him to keep them out of his
father's sight. (Mr. and Mrs. Dishart were
very fond of each other, but there were certain
little matters that she thought it unnecessary to
trouble him about.)

So if Tommy was to get "Waverley" at
once, he must discover another way. He reflected, and then set off to Miss Ailie's (to whom
he still read sober works of an evening, but
novels never), looking as if he had found a way.

For some time Miss Ailie had been anxious
about her red-armed maid, who had never before
given pain unless by excess of willingness, as
when she offered her garter to tie Miss Ailie's
parcels with. Of late, however, Gavinia had
taken to blurting out disquieting questions, to
the significance of which she withheld the key,
such as :

"Is there ony place nowadays, ma'am,
where there's tourniements? And could an
able-bodied lassie walk to them; and what
might be the charge to win in?"

Or, " Would you no like to be so michty beautiful, ma'am, that as soon as the men saw your bonny face they just up wi' you in their arms and ran ? "

Or again, " What's the heaviest weight o' a woman a grand lusty man could carry in his arms as if she were an infant ? "

This method of conveyance seemed to have a peculiar fascination for Gavinia, and she got herself weighed at the flesher's. On another occasion she broke a glass candlestick, and all she said to the pieces was, " Wha carries me wears me."

This mystery was troubling the school-mistress sadly when Tommy arrived with the key to it. "I'm doubting Gavinia's reading ill books on the sly," he said.

" Never ! " exclaimed Miss Ailie, " she reads nothing but the *Mentor*."

Tommy shook his head, like one who would fain hope so, but could not overlook facts. " I've been hearing," he said, " that she reads books as are full o' Strokes and Words We have no Concern with."

Miss Ailie could not believe it, but she was advised to search the kitchen, and under Gavinia's mattress was found the dreadful work.

" And you are only fifteen ! " said Miss Ailie, eyeing her little maid sorrowfully.

" The easier to carry," replied Gavinia, darkly.

" And you named after a minister ! " Miss Ailie continued, for her maid had been christened Gavinia because she was the first child baptised

in his church after the Rev. Gavin Dishart came
to Thrums. "Gavinia, I must tell him of
this. I shall take this book to Mr. Dishart this
very day."

"The right man to take it to," replied the
maid, sullenly, "for it's his ain."

"Gavinia!"

"Well, it was Mrs. Dishart that lended it
to me."

"I—I never saw it on the manse shelves."

"I'm thinking," said the brazen Gavinia,
"as there's hoddy corners in manses as well as
in—blue-and-white rooms."

This dark suggestion was as great a shock
to the gentle schoolmistress as if out of a clear
sky had come suddenly the word—

Stroke!

She tottered with the book that had so demoralised the once meek Gavinia into the blue-
and-white room, where Tommy was restlessly
awaiting her; and when she had told him all, he
said, with downcast eyes:

"I was never sure o' Mrs. Dishart. When
I hand her the *Mentor* she looks as if she didna
care a stroke for't——"

"Tommy!"

"I'm doubting," he said sadly, "that she's
ower fond o' Words We have no Concern with."

Miss Ailie would not listen to such talk, but
she approved of the suggestion that "Waverley"
should be returned not to the minister, but to
his wife, and she accepted gratefully Tommy's
kindly offer to act as bearer. Only happening
to open the book in the middle, she——

"I'm waiting," said Tommy, after ten minutes.

She did not hear him.

"I'm waiting," he said again, but she was now in the next chapter.

"Maybe you would like to read it yoursel'!" he cried, and then she came to, and with a shudder, handed him the book. But after he had gone she returned to the kitchen to reprove Gavinia at greater length; and in the midst of the reproof she said faintly: "You did not happen to look at the end, did you?"

"That I did," replied Gavinia.

"And did she—did he——"

"No," said Gavinia, sorrowfully.

Miss Ailie sighed. "That's what I think too," said Gavinia.

"Why didn't they?" asked the school-mistress.

"Because he was just a sumph," answered Gavinia, scornfully. "If he had been like Fergus, or like the chield in 'Ivanhoe,' he wouldna have ta'en a 'No.' He would just have whipped her up in his arms and away wi' her. That's the kind for me, ma'am."

"There is a fascination about them," murmured Miss Ailie.

"A what?"

But again Miss Ailie came to. "For shame, Gavinia, for shame!" she said, severely; "these are disgraceful sentiments."

In the meantime Tommy had hurried with the book, not to the manse, but to a certain garret, and as he read, his imagination went on

fire. Blinder's stories had made him half a
Jacobite, and now "Waverley" revealed to him
that he was born neither for the ministry nor
the herding, but to restore to his country its
rightful king. The first to whom he confided
this was Corp, who immediately exclaimed:
"Michty me! But what will the police say?"

"I ken a wy," answered Tommy, sternly.

CHAPTER XXI.

THE LAST JACOBITE RISING.

ON the evening of the Queen's birthday, bridies were eaten to her honour in a hundred Thrums homes, and her health was drunk in toddy—Scotch toddy and Highland toddy. Patullo, the writer, gave a men's party, and his sole instructions to his maid were, "Keep running back and forrit wi' the hot water." At the bank there was a ladies' party and ginger wine. From Cathro's bedroom-window a flag was displayed with *Vivat Regina* on it, the sentiment composed by Cathro, the words sewn by the girls of his McCulloch class. The eight o'clock bell rang for an hour, and a loyal crowd had gathered in the square to shout. To a superficial observer, such as the Baron Bailie or Todd, the new policeman, all seemed well and fair.

But a very different scene was being enacted at the same time in the fastnesses of the Den, where three resolute schemers had met by appointment. Their trysting-place was the Cuttle Well, which is most easily reached by the pink path made for that purpose; but the better to further their dark and sinister design, the plotters arrived by three circuitous routes—one descending the Reekie Broth Pot, a low but dangerous waterfall; the second daring the perils of the crags; and the third walking stealthily up the burn.

"Is that you, Tommy?"

"Whist! Do you mind the password?"

"Stroke!"

"Right. Have you heard Gav Dishart coming?"

"I hinna. I doubt his father had grippit him as he was slinking out o' the manse."

"I fear it, Corp. I'm thinking his father is in the Woman's pay."

"What woman?"

"The Woman of Hanover."

"That's the queen, is it no?"

"She'll never get me to call her queen."

"Nor yet me. I think I hear Gav coming."

Gav Dishart was the one who had come by the burn, and his boots were cheeping like a field of mice. He gave the word "Stroke," and the three then looked at each other firmly. The lights of the town were not visible from the Cuttle Well, owing to an arm of cliff that is outstretched between, but the bell could be distinctly heard, and occasionally a shout of revelry.

"They little ken!" said Tommy darkly.

"They hinna a notion," said Corp, but he was looking somewhat perplexed himself.

"It's near time I was back for family exercise," said Gav, uneasily, "so we had better do it quick, Tommy."

"Did you bring the wineglasses?" Tommy asked him.

"No," Gav said; "the press was lockit, but I've brought egg-cups."

"Stand round, then."

The three boys now presented a picturesque appearance, but there was none save the man in the moon to see them. They stood round the Cuttle Well, each holding an egg-cup; and though the daring nature of their undertaking and the romantic surroundings combined to excite them, it was not fear but soaring purpose that paled their faces and caused their hands to tremble, when Tommy said solemnly, "Afore we do what we've come to do, let's swear."

"Stroke!" he said.

"Stroke!" said Gav.

"Stroke!" said Corp.

They then filled their cups, and holding them over the Well, so that they clinked, they said:

"To the king ower the water!"

"To the king ower the water!"

"To the king ower the water!"

When they had drunk, Tommy broke his cup against a rock, for he was determined that it should never be used to honour a meaner toast, and the others followed his example, Corp briskly, though the act puzzled him, and Gav with a gloomy look because he knew that the cups would be missed to-morrow.

"Is that a' now?" whispered Corp, wiping his forehead with his sleeve.

"All!" cried Tommy. "Man, we've just begood."

As secretly as they had entered it, they left the Den, and anon three figures were standing in a dark trance, cynically watching the revellers in the square.

"If they just kent!" muttered the smallest,

who was wearing his jacket outside-in to escape observation.

"But they little ken!" said Gav Dishart.

"They hinna a notion!" said Corp, contemptuously, but still he was a little puzzled, and presently he asked softly: "Lads, what just is it that they dinna ken?"

Had Gav been ready with an answer he could not have uttered it, for just then a terrible little man in black, who had been searching for him in likely places, seized him by the cuff of the neck, and, turning his face in an easterly direction, ran him to family worship. But there was still work to do for the other two. Walking home alone that night from Mr. Patullo's party, Mr. Cathro had an uncomfortable feeling that he was being dogged. When he stopped to listen, all was at once still, but the moment he moved onward he again heard stealthy steps behind. He retired to rest as soon as he reached his house, to be wakened presently by a slight noise at the window, whence the flag-post protruded. It had been but a gust of wind, he decided, and turned round to go to sleep again, when crash! the post was plucked from its place and cast to the ground. The dominie sprang out of bed, and while feeling for a light, thought he heard skurrying feet, but when he looked out at the window no one was to be seen; *Vivat Regina* lay ignobly in the gutters. That it could have been the object of an intended theft was not probable, but the open window might have tempted thieves, and there was a possible though risky way up by the spout. The affair was a good deal talked about at the time, but it remained shrouded in a mystery which even we have been unable to penetrate.

On the heels of the Queen's birthday came the Muckley, the one that was to be known to fame, if fame was willing to listen to Corp, as Tommy's Muckley. Unless he had some grand aim in view never was a boy who yielded to temptations more blithely than Tommy, but when he had such aim never was a boy so firm in withstanding them. At this Muckley he had a mighty reason for not spending money, and with ninepence in his pocket clamouring to be out he spent not one halfpenny. There was something uncanny in the sight of him stalking unscathed between rows of stands and shows, everyone of them aiming at his pockets. Corp and Gav, of course, were in the secret and did their humble best to act in the same unnatural manner, but now and again a show made a successful snap at Gav, and Corp had gloomy fears that he would lose his head in presence of the Teuch and Tasty, from which humiliation indeed he was only saved by the happy idea of requesting Tommy to shout "Deuteronomy!" in a warning voice, every time they drew nigh Californy's seductive stand.

Was there nothing for sale, then, that the three thirsted to buy? There were many things, among them weapons of war, a pack of cards, more properly called Devil's books, blue bonnets suitable for Highland gentlemen, feathers for the bonnets, a tin lantern, yards of tartan cloth, which the deft fingers of Grizel would convert

into warriors' sashes. Corp knew that these
purchases were in Tommy's far-seeing eye, but
he thought the only way to get them was to
ask the price and then offer half. Gav, the
scholar, who had already reached daylight
through the first three books of Euclid, and
took a walk every Saturday morning with his
father and Herodotus, even Gav, the scholar,
was as thick-witted as Corp.

"We'll let other laddies buy them," Tommy
explained in his superior way, "and then after
the Muckley is past, we'll buy them frae them."

The others understood now. After a Muckley
there was always a great dearth of pence, and a
moneyed man could become owner of Muckley
purchases at a sixth part of the Muckley price.

"You crittur!" exclaimed Corp, in abject
admiration.

But Gav saw an objection. "The feck of
them," he pointed out, "will waur their siller
on shows and things to eat, instead of on what
we want them to buy."

"So they will, the nasty sackets!" cried
Corp.

"You couldna blame a laddie for buying
Teuch and Tasty," continued Gav with triumph,
for he was a little jealous of Tommy.

"You couldna," agreed Corp; "no, I'll be
dagont, if you could," and his hand pressed his
money feverishly.

"Deuteronomy!" roared Tommy, and Corp's
hand jumped as if it had been caught in some
other person's pocket.

"But how are we to do?" he asked. "If

you like, I'll take Birkie and the Haggerty-Taggertys round the Muckley and fight ilka ane that doesna buy——"

"Corp," said Tommy, calmly, "I wonder at you. Do you no ken yet that the best plan is to leave a' thing to me?"

"Blethering gowks that we are, of course it is!" cried Corp, and he turned almost fiercely upon Gav. "Lippen all to him," he said with grand confidence, "he'll find a wy."

And Tommy found a way. Birkie was the boy who bought the pack of cards. He saw Tommy looking so woe-begone, that it was necessary to ask the reason.

"Oh, Birkie, lend me threepence," sobbed Tommy, "and I'll give you sixpence the morn."

"You're daft," said Birkie, "there's no a laddie in Thrums that will have one single lonely bawbee the morn."

"Him that buys the cards," moaned Tommy, "will never be without siller, for you tell auld folks' fortunes on them at a penny every throw. Lend me threepence, Birkie. They cost a sic, and I have just——"

"Na, na," said greedy Birkie, "I'm not to be catched wi' chaff. If it's true what you say, I'll buy the cards mysel'."

Having thus got hold of him, Tommy led Birkie to a stand where the King of Egypt was telling fortunes with cards, and doing a roaring trade among the Jocks and Jennys. He also sold packs at sixpence each, and the elated Birkie was an immediate purchaser.

Q

"You're no so clever as you think yoursel'!" he said triumphantly to Tommy, who replied with his inscrutable smile. But to his satellites he said, "Not a soul will buy a fortune frae Birkie. I'll get thae cards for a penny afore next week's out."

Francie Crabb found Tommy sniggering to himself in the back wynd. "What are you goucking at?" asked Francie, in surprise, for as a rule, Tommy only laughed behind his face.

"I winna tell you," chuckled Tommy; "but what a bar; oh, what a divert!"

"Come on, tell me."

"Well it's at the man as is swallowing swords ahint the menagerie."

"I see nothing to laugh at in that."

"I'm no laughing at that. I'm laughing at him for selling the swords for ninepence the piece. Oh, what ignorant he is; oh, what a bar!"

"Ninepence is a mislaird price for a soord," said Francie. "I never gave ninepence."

Tommy looked at him in the way that always made boys fidget with their fists.

"You're near as big a bar as him," he said scornfully. "Did you ever see the sword that's hanging on the wall in the back room at the post-office?"

"No, but my father has told me about it. It has a grand name."

"It's an Andrea Ferrara, that's what it is."

"Ay, I mind the name now; there has been folk killed wi' that soord."

This was true, for the post-office Andrea
Ferrara has a stirring history, but for the
present its price was the important thing.
"Dr. McQueen offered a pound note for it,"
said Tommy.

"I ken that, but what has it to do wi' the
soord-swallower?"

"Just this; that the swords he is selling for
ninepence are Andrea Ferraras, the same as the
post-office ones, and he could get a pound a piece
for them if he kent their worth. Oh, what a
bar; oh, what——"

Francie's eyes lit up greedily, and he looked
at his two silver shillings, and took two steps
in the direction of the sword-swallower's, and
faltered and could not make up his agitated
mind. Tommy set off toward the square at a
brisk walk.

"Whaur are you aff to?" asked Francie,
following him.

"To tell the man what his swords is worth.
It would be ill done no to tell him." To clinch
the matter, off went Tommy at a run, and off
went Francie after him. As a rule Tommy
was the swifter, but on this occasion he lagged
of fell purpose, and reached the sword-
swallower's tent just in time to see Francie
emerge elated therefrom, carrying two Andrea
Ferraras. Francie grinned when they met.

"What a bar!" he crowed.

"What a bar!" agreed Tommy, and
sufficient has now been told to show that he
had found a way. Even Gav acknowledged a
master, and when the accoutrements of war

Q 2

were bought at second-hand as cheaply as
Tommy had predicted, applauded him with
eyes and mouth for a full week, after which
he saw things in a new light. Gav of course
was to enter the bursary lists anon, and he
had supposed that Cathro would have the last
year's schooling of him; but no, his father
decided to send him for the grand final grind
to Mr. Ogilvy of Glen Quharity, a famous
dominie between whom and Mr. Dishart ex-
isted a friendship that none had ever got at
the root of. Mr. Cathro was more annoyed
than he cared to show, Gav being of all the
boys of that time the one likeliest to do his
teacher honour at the University competitions;
but Tommy, though the decision cost him an
adherent, was not ill-pleased, for he had discovered that Gav was one of those irritating
boys who like to be leader. Gav, as has
been said, suddenly saw Tommy's victory over
Messrs. Birkie, Francie, etc., in a new light;
this was because when he wanted back the
shilling which he had contributed to the funds
for buying their purchases, Tommy replied
firmly:

"I canna give you the shilling, but I'll
give you the lantern and the tartan cloth we
bought wi' it."

"What use could they be to me at Glen
Quharity?" Gav protested.

"Oh, if they are no use to you," Tommy
said sweetly, "me and Corp is willing to buy
them off you for threepence."

Then Gav became a scorner of duplicity,

but he had to consent to the bargain and
again Corp said to Tommy, "Oh you crittur!"
But he was sorry to lose a fellow-conspirator.
"There's just the twa o' us now," he sighed.

"Just twa!" cried Tommy. "What are
you havering about, man? There's as many
as I like to whistle for."

"You mean Grizel and Elspeth, I ken,
but——"

"I wasna thinking of the women-folk,"
Tommy told him, with a contemptuous wave of
the hand. He went closer to Corp, and said, in
a low voice, "The McKenzies are waiting!"

"Are they, though?" said Corp, perplexed,
as he had no notion who the McKenzies
might be.

"And Lochiel has twa hunder spearsmen."

"Do you say so?"

"Young Kinnordy's ettling to come out, and
I meet Lord Airlie when the moon rises at the
Loups o' Kenny, and auld Bradwardine's as
spunky as ever, and there's fifty wild Highland-
men lying ready in the muckle cave of Clova."

He spoke so earnestly that Corp could only
ejaculate, "Michty me!"

"But of course they winna rise," continued
Tommy, darkly, " till he lands."

"Of course no," said Corp, "but—wha is
he?"

"Himsel'," whispered Tommy, "the Chevalier!"

Corp hesitated. "But, I thought," he said
diffidently, "I thought you——"

"So I am," said Tommy.

" But you said he hadna landed yet ? "

" Neither he has."

" But you——"

" Well ? "

" You're here, are you no ? "

Tommy stamped his foot in irritation. " You're slow in the uptak," he said. " I'm no here. How can I be here when I'm at St. Germains ? "

" Dinna be angry wi' me," Corp begged. " I ken you're ower the water, but when I see you, I kind of forget; and just for the minute I think you're here."

" Well, think afore you speak."

" I'll try, but that's teuch work. When do you come to Scotland ? "

" I'm no sure; but as soon as I'm ripe."

At nights Tommy now sometimes lay among the cabbages of the school-house watching the shadow of Black Cathro on his sitting-room blind. Cathro never knew he was there. The reason Tommy lay among the cabbages was that there was a price upon his head.

" But if Black Cathro wanted to get the blood-money," Corp said apologetically, " he could nab you any day. He kens you fine."

Tommy smiled meaningly. " Not him," he answered, " I've cheated him bonny; he hasna a notion wha I am. Corp, would you like a good laugh ? "

" That I would."

" Weel, then, I'll tell you wha he thinks I am. Do you ken a little house yont the road a bitty frae Monypenny ? "

"I ken no sic house," said Corp, "except Aaron's."

"Aaron's the man as bides in it," Tommy continued hastily; "at least I think that's the name. Well, as you ken the house, you've maybe noticed a laddie that bides there too?"

"There's no laddie," began Corp, "except——"

"Let me see," interrupted Tommy, "what was his name? Was it Peter? No. Was it Willie! Stop, I mind, it was Tommy."

He glared so that Corp dared not utter a word. "Have you notitched him?"

"I've—I've seen him," Corp gasped.

"Well, this is the joke," said Tommy, trying vainly to restrain his mirth, "Cathro thinks I'm that laddie! Ho! ho! ho!"

Corp scratched his head, then he bit his warts, then he spat upon his hands, then he said "Damn."

The crisis came when Cathro, still ignorant that the heather was on fire, dropped some disparaging remarks about the Stuarts to his history class. Tommy said nothing, but—but one of the school-windows was without a snib, and next morning when the dominie reached his desk he was surprised to find on it a little cotton glove. He raised it on high, greatly puzzled, and then, as ever when he suspected knavery, his eyes sought Tommy, who was sitting on a form, his arms proudly folded. That the whelp had put the glove there, Cathro no longer doubted, and he would have liked to know why, but was reluctant to give him the satisfaction of

asking. So the gauntlet—for gauntlet it was—
was laid aside, the while Tommy, his head bum-
ming like a beeskep, muttered triumphantly
through his teeth, "But he lifted it, he lifted
it!" and at closing time it was flung in his face
with this fair tribute:

"I'm no a rich man, laddie, but I would
give a pound note to know what you'll be at
ten years from now."

There could be no mistaking the dire meaning of these words, and Tommy hurried, pale
but determined, to the quarry, where Corp, with
a barrow in his hands, was learning strange
phrases by heart, and finding it a help to call
his warts after the new swears.

"Corp," cried Tommy, firmly, "I've set sail!"

On the following Saturday evening Charles
Edward landed in the Den. In his bonnet was
the white cockade, and round his waist a tartan
sash; though he had long passed man's allotted
span his face was still full of fire, his figure
lithe and even boyish. For state reasons he had
assumed the name of "Captain Stroke." As he
leapt ashore from the bark, the *Dancing Shovel*,
he was received right loyally by Corp and other
faithful adherents, of whom only two, and these
of a sex to which his House was ever partial,
were visible, owing to the gathering gloom.
Corp of that Ilk sank on his knees at the water's
edge, and kissing his royal master's hand said,
fervently, "Welcome, my prince, once more
to bonny Scotland!" Then he rose and whispered, but with scarcely less emotion, "There's
an egg to your tea."

CHAPTER XXII.

THE SIEGE OF THRUMS.

THE man in the moon is a native of Thrums, who was put up there for hacking sticks on the Sabbath, and as he sails over the Den his interest in the bit placey is still sufficient to make him bend forward and cry "Boo!" at the lovers. When they jump apart you can see the aged reprobate grinning. Once out of sight of the Den, he cares not a boddle how the moon travels, but the masterful crittur enrages him if she is in a hurry here, just as he is cleverly making out whose children's children are courting now. "Slow, there!" he cries to the moon, but she answers placidly that they have the rest of the world to view to-night. "The rest of the world be danged!" roars the man, and he cranes his neck for a last glimpse of the Cuttle Well, until he nearly falls out of the moon.

Never had the man such a trying time as during the year now before him. It was the year when so many scientific magnates sat up half the night in their shirts, spying at him through telescopes. But every effort to discover why he was in such a fidget failed because the spy-glasses were never levelled at the Thrums Den. Through the whole of the incidents now to tell, you may conceive the man (on whom sympathy would be wasted) dagoning horribly, because he was always carried past the Den before he could make head or tail of the change that had come over it.

The spot chosen by the ill-fated Stuart and his gallant remnant for their last desperate enterprise was eminently fitted for their purpose. Being round the corner from Thrums, it was commanded by no fortified place save the farm of Nether Drumgley; and on a recent goustie night nearly all the trees had been blown down, making a hundred hiding-places for bold climbers, and transforming the Den into a scene of wild and mournful grandeur. In no bay more suitable than the flooded field called the Silent Pool could the hunted prince have cast anchor, for the Pool is not only sheltered from observation, but so little troubled by gales that it had only one drawback: at some seasons of the year it was not there. This, however, did not vex Stroke, as it is cannier to call him, for he burned his boats on the night he landed (and a dagont, tedious job it was, too), and pointed out to his followers that the drouth which kept him in must also keep the enemy out. Part of the way to the lair they usually traversed in the burn, because water leaves no trace, and though they carried turnip lanterns and were armed to the teeth, this was often a perilous journey owing to the lovers close at hand on the pink path, from which the trees had been cleared, for lads and lassies must walk whate'er betide. Ronny-On's Jean and Peter Scrymgeour, little Lisbeth Doak and long Sam'l from Pyotdykes were pairing that year, and never knew how near they were to being dirked by Corp of Corp, who lurking in the burn till there were no tibbits in his toes, muttered fiercely, "Cheep one single cheep, and it will be thy hinmost, methinks!" under the impression that Methinks was a Jacobite oath.

For this voluntary service, Stroke clapped Corp of Corp on the shoulder with a naked sword, and said, "Rise, Sir Joseph!" which made Corp more confused than ever, for he was already Corp of Corp, Him of Muckle Kenny, Red McNeil, Andrew Ferrara, and the Master of Inverquharity (Stroke's names), as well as Stab-in-the-Dark, Grind-them-to-Mullins and Warty Joe (his own), and which he was at any particular moment he never knew, till Stroke told him, and even then he forgot and had to be put in irons.

The other frequenters of the lair on Saturday nights (when alone the rebellion was active) were the proud Lady Grizel and Widow Elspeth. It had been thought best to make Elspeth a widow, because she was so religious.

The lair was on the right bank of the burn, near the waterfall, and you climbed to it by ropes, unless you preferred an easier way. It is now a dripping hollow, down which water dribbles from beneath a sluice, but at that time it was hidden on all sides by trees and the huge clods of sward they had torn from the earth as they fell. Two of these clods were the only walls of the lair, which had at times a ceiling not unlike Aaron Latta's bed coverlets, and the chief furniture was two barrels, marked "Usquebach" and "Powder." When the darkness of Stroke's

fortunes sat like a pall upon his brow, as
happened sometimes, he sought to drive it away
by playing cards on one of these barrels with
Sir Joseph, but the approach of the widow made
him pocket them quickly with a warning sign
to his trusty knight, who did not understand,
and asked what had become of them, whereupon
Elspeth cried, in horror:

"Cards! Oh, Tommy, you promised——"

But Stroke rode her down with, "Cards!
Wha has been playing cards? You, Muckle
Kenny, and you, Sir Joseph, after I forbad it!
Hie, there, Inverquharity, all of you, seize those
men."

Then Corp blinked, came to his senses and
marched himself off to the prison on the lonely
promontory called the Queen's Bower, saying
ferociously, "Jouk, Sir Joseph, and I'll blaw
you into posterity."

It is sable night when Stroke and Sir Joseph
reach a point in the Den whence the glimmering
lights of the town are distinctly visible. Neither
speaks. Presently the distant eight o'clock bell
rings, and then Sir Joseph looks anxiously at his
warts, for this is the signal to begin, and as
usual he has forgotten the words.

"Go on," says someone in a whisper. It
cannot be Stroke, for his head is brooding on his
breast. This mysterious voice haunted all the
doings in the Den, and had better be confined in
brackets.

("Go on.")

"Methinks," says Sir Joseph, "methinks the
borers——"

("Burghers.")

"Methinks the burghers now cease from their labours."

"Ay," replied Stroke, "'tis so, would that they ceased from them forever!"

"Methinks the time is at hand."

"Ha!" exclaims Stroke, looking at his lieutenant curiously, "what makest thou say so? For three weeks these fortifications have defied my cannon, there is scarce a breach yet in the walls of yonder town."

"Methinks thou will find a way."

"It may be so, my good Sir Joseph, it may be so, and yet, even when I am most hopeful of success, my schemes go a gley."

"Methinks thy dark——"

("Dinna say Methinks so often.")

("Tommy, I maun. If I dinna get that to start me off, I go through other.")

("Go on.")

"Methinks thy dark spirit lies on thee to-night."

"Ay, 'tis too true. But canst thou blame me if I grow sad? The town still in the enemy's hands, and so much brave blood already spilt in vain. Knowest thou that the brave Kinnordy fell last night? My noble Kinnordy!"

Here Stroke covers his face with his hands, weeping silently, and—and there is an awkward pause.

("Go on—'Still have me.'")

("So it is.") "Weep not, my royal scone——"

("Scion.")

"Weep not, my royal scion, havest thou not still me?"

"Well said, Sir Joseph," cries Stroke, dashing the sign of weakness from his face. "I still have many brave fellows, and with their help I shall be master of this proud town."

"And then ghost we to fair Edinburgh?"

"Ay, 'tis so, but, Sir Joseph, thinkest thou these burghers love the Stuart not?"

"Nay, methinks they are true to thee, but their starch commander—(give me my time, this is a lang ane)—but their arch commander is thy bitterest foe. Vile spoon that he is! (It's no spoon, it's spawn.)"

"Thou meanest the craven Cathro?"

"Methinks ay. (I like thae short anes.)"

"'Tis well!" says Stroke, sternly. "That man hath ever slipped between me and my right. His time will come."

"He floppeth thee—he flouteth thee from the battlements."

"Ha, 'tis well!"

("You've said that already.")

("I say it twice.")

("That's what aye puts me wrang.) Ghost thou to meet the proud Lady Grizel to-night?"

"Ay."

"Ghost thou alone?"

"Ay."

"(What easy anes you have!) I fear it is not chancey for thee to go."

"I must dree my dreed."

"These women is kittle cattle."

"The Stuart hath ever a soft side for them.

Ah, my trusty foster-brother, knowest thou not what it is to love?"

"Alas! I too have had my fling. (Does Grizel kiss your hand yet?)"

("No, she winna, the limmer.) Sir Joseph, I go to her."

"Methinks she is a haughty onion. I prithee go not to-night."

"I have given my word."

"Thy word is a band."

"Adieu, my friend."

"Methinks thou ghost to thy damn. (Did we no promise Elspeth there should be no swearing?)"

The raft Vick Ian Vohr is dragged to the shore, and Stroke steps on board, a proud solitary figure. "Farewell!" he cries hoarsely, as he seizes the oar.

"Farewell, my leech," answers Corp, and then helps him to disembark. Their hands chance to meet, and Stroke's is so hot that Corp quails.

"Tommy," he says, with a shudder, "do you —you dinna think it's a' true, do you?" But the ill-fated prince only gives him a warning look and plunges into the mazes of the forest. For a long time silence reigns over the Den. Lights glint fitfully, a human voice imitates the plaintive cry of the peewit, cautious whistling follows, comes next the clash of arms, and the scream of one in the death-throes, and again silence falls. Stroke emerges near the Reekie Broth Pot, wiping his sword and muttering, "Faugh! it drippeth!" At the same moment the air is filled with music of more than mortal

—well, the air is filled with music. It seems to come from but a few yards away, and pressing his hand to his throbbing brow the chevalier presses forward till, pushing aside the branches of a fallen fir, he comes suddenly upon a scene of such romantic beauty that he stands rooted to the ground. Before him, softly lit by a half-moon (the man in it perspiring with curiosity), is a miniature dell behind which rise threatening rocks, overgrown here and there by grass, heath and bracken, while in the centre of the dell is a bubbling spring called the Cuttle Well, whose water, as it overflows a natural basin, soaks into the surrounding ground and so finds a way into the picturesque stream below. But it is not the loveliness of the spot which fascinates the prince; rather is it the exquisite creature who sits by the bubbling spring, a reed from a hand-loom in her hands, from which she strikes mournful sounds, the while she raises her voice in song. A pink scarf and a blue ribbon are crossed upon her breast, her dark tresses kiss her lovely neck, and as she sits on the only dry stone, her face raised as if in wrapt communion with the heavens, and her feet tucked beneath her to avoid the mud, she seems not a human being, but the very spirit of the place and hour. The royal wanderer remains spellbound, while she strikes her lyre and sings (with but one trivial alteration) the song of Mac-Murrough:

Awake on your hills, on your islands awake,
Brave sons of the mountains, the frith and the lake!
'Tis the bugle—but not for the chase is the call;
'Tis the pibroch's shrill summons—but not to the hall.

'Tis the summons of heroes for conquest or death,
When the banners are blazing on mountain and heath;
They call to the dirk, the claymore and the targe,
To the march and the muster, the line and the charge.

Be the brand of each Chieftain like Stroke's in his ire!
May the blood through his veins flow like currents of fire!
Burst the base foreign yoke as your sires did of yore,
Or die like your sires, and endure it no more.

As the fair singer concluded, Stroke, who had been deeply moved, heaved a great sigh, and immediately, as if in echo of it, came a sigh from the opposite side of the dell. In a second of time three people had learned that a certain lady had two lovers. She starts to her feet, still carefully avoiding the puddles, but it is not she who speaks.

("Did you hear me?")
("Ay.")
("You're ready?")
("Ca' awa'.")

Stroke dashes to the girl's side, just in time to pluck her from the arms of a masked man. The villain raises his mask and reveals the face of—it looks like Corp, but the disguise is thrown away on Stroke.

"Ha, Cathro," he exclaims joyfully, "so at last we meet on equal terms!"

"Back, Stroke, and let me pass."

"Nay, we fight for the wench."

"So be it. The prideful onion is his who wins her."

"Have at thee, caitiff!"

A terrible conflict ensues. Cathro draws first blood. 'Tis but a scratch. Ha! well

R

thrust, Stroke. In vain Cathro girns his teeth. Inch by inch he is driven back, he slips, he recovers, he pants, he is apparently about to fling himself down the steep bank and so find safety in flight, but he comes on again.

("What are you doing? You run now.")

("I ken, but I'm sweer!")

("Off you go.")

Even as Stroke is about to press home, the cowardly foe flings himself down the steep bank and rolls out of sight. He will give no more trouble to-night; and the victor turns to the Lady Grizel, who had been repinning the pink scarf across her breast, while the issue of the combat was still in doubt.

("Now, then, Grizel, you kiss my hand.")

("I tell you I won't.")

("Well, then, go on your knees to me.")

("You needn't think it.")

("Dagon you! Then ca' awa' standing.")

"My liege, thou hast saved me from the wretch Cathro."

"May I always be near to defend thee in time of danger, my pretty chick."

("Tommy, you promised not to call me by those silly names.")

("They slip out, I tell you. That was aye the way wi' the Stuarts.")

("Well, you must say 'Lady Grizel.') Good, my prince, how can I thank thee?"

"By being my wife. (Not a word of this to Elspeth.)"

"Nay, I summoned thee here to tell thee that can never be. The Grizels of Grizel are of ancient lineage, but they mate not with monarchs. My sire, the nunnery gates will soon close on me for ever."

"Then at least say thou lovest me."

"Alas! I love thee not."

("What haver is this? I telled you to say 'Charles, would that I loved thee less.'")

("And I told you I would not.")

("Well, then, where are we now?")

("We miss out all that about my wearing your portrait next my heart, and put in the rich apparel bit, the same as last week.")

("Oh! Then I go on?) Bethink thee, fair jade——"

("Lady.")

"Bethink thee, fair lady, Stuart is not so poor but that, if thou come with him to his lowly lair, he can deck thee with rich apparel and ribbons rare."

"I spurn thy gifts, unhappy man, but if there are holes in——"

("Miss that common bit out. I canna thole it.")

("I like it.) If there are holes in the garments of thy loyal followers, I will come and mend them, and I have a needle and thread in my pocket. (Tommy, there is another button off your shirt! Have you got the button?")

("It's down my breeks.) So be it, proud girl, come!"

It was Grizel who made masks out of tin rags, picked up where tinkers had passed the night, and musical instruments out of broken reeds that smelled of caddis, and Jacobite head-

R 2

gear out of weavers' night-caps; and she kept
the lair so clean and tidy as to raise a fear that
intruders might mistake its character. Elspeth
had to mind the pot, which Aaron Latta never
missed, and Corp was supposed to light the fire
by striking sparks from his knife, a trick which
Tommy considered so easy that he refused to
show how it was done. Many strange sauces
were boiled in that pot, a sort of potato-turnip
pudding often coming out even when not expected, but there was an occasional rabbit that
had been bowled over by Corp's unerring hand,
and once Tommy shot a—a haunch of venison,
having first, with Corp's help, howked it out of
Ronny-On's swine, then suspended head down-
ward, and open like a book at the page of contents, steaming, dripping, a tub beneath, boys
with bladders in the distance. When they had
supped they gathered round the fire, Grizel
knitting a shawl for they knew whom, but the
name was never mentioned, and Tommy told
the story of his life at the French court, and
how he fought in the '45 and afterwards hid in
caves, and so did he shudder, as he described
the cold of his bracken beds, and so glowed his
face, for it was all real to him, that Grizel let
the wool drop on her knee, and Corp whispered
to Elspeth, "Dinna be fleid for him; I'se
uphaud he found a wy." Those quiet evenings
were not the least pleasant spent in the Den.

But sometimes they were interrupted by a
fierce endeavour to carry the lair, when boys from
Cathro's climbed to it up each other's backs, the
rope, of course, having been pulled into safety at

the first sound, and then that end of the Den
rang with shouts, and deeds of valour on both
sides were as common as pine needles, and once
Tommy and Corp were only saved from captors
who had them down, by Grizel rushing into the
midst of things with two flaring torches, and
another time bold Birkie, most daring of the
storming party, was seized with two others and
made to walk the plank. The plank had been
part of a gate, and was suspended over the bank
of the Silent Pool, so that, as you approached
the farther end, down you went. It was not a
Jacobite method, but Tommy feared that rows
of bodies, hanging from the trees still standing
in the Den, might attract attention.

CHAPTER XXIII.

GRIZEL PAYS THREE VISITS.

LESS alarming but more irritating was the attempt of the youth of Monypenny and the West town end, to establish a rival firm of Jacobites (without even being sure of the name). They started business (Francie Crabb leader, because he had a kilt) on a flagon of porter and an ounce of twist, which they carried on a stick through the Den, saying "Bowf!" like dogs, when they met anyone, and then laughing doubtfully. The twist and porter were seized by Tommy and his followers, and Haggerty-Taggerty, Major, arrived home with his head so firmly secured in the flagon that the solder had to be melted before he saw the world again. Francie was in still worse plight, for during the remainder of the evening he had to hide in shame among the brackens, and Tommy wore a kilt.

One cruel revenge the beaten rivals had. They waylaid Grizel, when she was alone, and thus assailed her, she answering not a word.

" What's a father? "

" She'll soon no have a mither either! "

" The Painted Lady needs to paint her cheeks no langer! "

" Na, the red spots comes themsels now."

" Have you heard her hoasting? "

"Ay, it's the hoast o' a dying woman."

"The joiner heard it, and gave her a look, measuring her wi' his eye for the coffin. 'Five and a half by one and a half would hold her snod,' he says to himsel'."

"Ronny-On's auld wife heard it, and says she, 'Dinna think, my leddy, as you'll be buried in consecrated ground.'"

"Na, a'body kens she'll just be hauled at the end o' a rope to the hole where the witches was shooled in."

"Wi' a paling spar through her, to keep her down on the day o' judgment."

Well, well, these children became men and women in time, one of them even a bit of a hero, though he never knew it.

Are you angry with them? If so, put the cheap thing aside, or think only of Grizel, and perhaps God will turn your anger into love for her.

Great-hearted, solitary child! She walked away from them without flinching, but on reaching the Den, where no one could see her, she lay down on the ground, and her cheeks were dry, but little wells of water stood in her eyes.

She would not be the Lady Grizel that night. She went home instead, but there was something she wanted to ask Tommy now, and the next time she saw him she began at once. Grizel always began at once, often in the middle, she saw what she was making for so clearly.

"Do you know what it means when there are red spots in your cheeks, that used not to be there?"

Tommy knew at once to whom she was referring, for he had heard the gossip of the youth of Monypenny, and he hesitated to answer.

"And if, when you cough, you bring up a tiny speck of blood?"

"I would get a bottle frae the doctor," said Tommy, evasively.

"She won't have the doctor," answered Grizel, unguardedly, and then with a look dared Tommy to say that she spoke of her mother.

"Does it mean you are dying?"

"I—I—oh, no, they soon get better."

He said this because he was so sorry for Grizel. There never was a more sympathetic nature than Tommy's. At every time of his life his pity was easily aroused for persons in distress, and he sought to comfort them by shutting their eyes to the truth as long as possible. This sometimes brought relief to them, but it was useless to Grizel, who must face her troubles.

"Why don't you answer truthfully?" she cried, with vehemence. "It is so easy to be truthful!"

"Well, then," said Tommy, reluctantly, "I think they generally die."

Elspeth often carried in her pocket a little Testament, presented to her by the Rev. Mr. Dishart for learning by heart one of the noblest of books, the Shorter Catechism, as Scottish children do or did, not understanding it at the time, but its meaning comes long afterwards, and suddenly, when you have most need of it.

Sometimes Elspeth read aloud from her Testament to Grizel, who made no comment, but this same evening, when the two were alone, she said abruptly:

"Have you your Testament?"

"Yes," Elspeth said, producing it.

"Which is the page about saving sinners?"

"It's all about that."

"But the page when you are in a hurry?"

Elspeth read aloud the story of the Crucifixion, and Grizel listened sharply until she heard what Jesus said to the malefactor: "To-day shalt thou be with me in Paradise."

"And was he?"

"Of course."

"But he had been wicked all his life, and I believe he was only good, just that minute, because they were crucifying him. If they had let him come down——"

"No, he repented, you know. That means he had faith, and if you have faith you are saved. It doesna matter how bad you have been. You have just to say 'I believe' before you die, and God lets you in. It's so easy, Grizel," cried Elspeth, with shining eyes.

Grizel pondered. "I don't believe it is so easy as that," she said decisively.

Nevertheless she asked presently what the Testament cost, and when Elspeth answered "Fourpence," offered her the money.

"I don't want to sell it," Elspeth remonstrated.

"If you don't give it to me, I shall take it from you," said Grizel determinedly.

"You can buy one."

"No, the shop people would guess."

"Guess what?"

"I won't tell you."

"I'll lend it to you."

"I won't take it that way." So Elspeth had to part with her Testament, saying wonderingly, "Can you read?"

"Yes, and write too. Mamma taught me."

"But I thought she was daft," Elspeth blurted out.

"She is only daft now and then," Grizel replied, without her usual spirit. "Generally she is not daft at all, but only timid."

Next morning the Painted Lady's child paid three calls, one in town, two in the country. The adorable thing is that once having made up her mind, she never flinched, not even when her hand was on the knocker.

The first gentleman received her in his lobby. For a moment he did not remember her; then suddenly the colour deepened on his face, and he went back and shut the parlour door.

"Did anybody see you coming here?" he asked quickly.

"I don't know."

"What does she want?"

"She did not send me; I came myself."

"Well?"

"When you come to our house——"

"I never come to your house."

"That is a lie."

"Speak lower."

"When you come to our house you tell

me to go out and play. But I don't. I go
and cry."

No doubt he was listening, but his eyes were
on the parlour door.

" I don't know why I cry, but you know, you
wicked man !   Why is it ? "

"Why is it ? " she demanded again, like a
queen-child, but he could only fidget with his gold
chain and shuffle uneasily in his parnella shoes.

" You are not coming to see my mamma
again."

The gentleman gave her an ugly look.

" If you do," she said at once, " I shall come
straight here and open that door you are looking
at, and tell your wife."

He dared not swear.   His hand——

" If you offer me money," said Grizel, " I
shall tell her now."

He muttered something to himself.

" Is it true ? " she asked, " that mamma is
dying ? "

This was a genuine shock to him, for he had
not been at Double Dykes since winter, and then
the Painted Lady was quite well.

" Nonsense ! " he said, and his obvious dis-
belief brought some comfort to the girl. But
she asked, " Why are there red spots on her
cheeks, then ? "

" Paint," he answered.

" No," cried Grizel, rocking her arms, " it is
not paint now. I thought it might be, and I
tried to rub it off while she was sleeping, but it
will not come off. And when she coughs there
is blood on her handkerchief."

He looked alarmed now, and Grizel's fears came back. "If mamma dies," she said determinedly, "she must be buried in the cemetery."

"She is not dying, I tell you."

"And you must come to the funeral."

"Are you gyte?"

"With crape on your hat."

His mouth formed an emphatic "No."

"You must," said Grizel, firmly, "you shall! If you don't——" She pointed to the parlour door.

Her remaining two visits were to a similar effect, and one of the gentlemen came out of the ordeal somewhat less shamefully than the first, the other worse, for he blubbered and wanted to kiss her. It is questionable whether many young ladies have made such a profound impression in a series of morning calls.

The names of these gentlemen are not known, but you shall be told presently where they may be found. Every person in Thrums used to know the place, and many itched to get at the names, but as yet no one has had the nerve to look for them.

Not at this time did Grizel say a word of these interviews to her friends, though Tommy had to be told of them later, and she never again referred to her mother at the Saturday evenings in the Den. But the others began to know a queer thing, nothing less than this, that in their absence the lair was sometimes visited by a person or persons unknown, who made use of their stock of firewood. It was a startling discovery, but when they discussed it in council, Grizel never contributed a word. The affair remained a mystery until one Saturday evening, when Tommy and Elspeth, reaching the lair first, found in it a delicate white shawl. They both recognised in it the pretty thing the Painted Lady had pinned across her shoulders on the night they saw her steal out of Double Dykes, to meet the man of long ago.

Even while their eyes were saying this, Grizel climbed in without giving the password, and they knew from her quick glance around that she had come for the shawl. She snatched it out of Tommy's hand with a look that prohibited questions.

"It's the pair o' them," Tommy said to Elspeth at the first opportunity, "that sometimes comes here at nights and kindles the fire and warms themselves at the gloze. And the last time they came they forgot the shawl."

"I dinna like to think the Painted Lady has been up here, Tommy."

"But she has. You ken how when she has a daft fit, she wanders the Den trysting the man that never comes. Has she no been seen at all hours o' the night, Grizel following a wee bit ahint, like as if to take tent o' her?"

"They say that, and that Grizel canna get her to go home till the daft fit has passed."

"Well, she has that kechering hoast and spit now, and so Grizel brings her up here out o' the blasts."

"But how could she be got to come here, if she winna go home?"

"Because frae here she can watch for the man."

Elspeth shuddered. "Do you think she's here often, Tommy?" she asked.

"Just when she has a daft fit on, and they say she's wise sax days in seven."

This made the Jacobite meetings eerie events for Elspeth, but Tommy liked them the better; and what were they not to Grizel, who ran to them with passionate fondness every Saturday night? Sometimes she even outdistanced her haunting dreads, for she knew that her mother did not think herself seriously ill; and had not the three gentlemen made light of that curious cough? So there were nights when the lair saw Grizel go riotous with glee, laughing, dancing, and shouting over-much, like one trying to make up for a lost childhood. But it was also noticed that when the time came to leave the Den, she was very loath, and kissed her hands to the places where she had been happiest, saying wistfully, and with pretty gestures that were foreign to Thrums, "Good-night, dear Cuttle Well!" "Good-bye, sweet, sweet Lair!" as if she knew it could not last. Those weekly risings in the Den were most real to Tommy, but it was Grizel who loved them best.

CHAPTER XXIV.

A ROMANCE OF TWO OLD MAIDS AND A STOUT BACHELOR.

CAME Gavinia, a burgess of the besieged city, along the south shore of the Silent Pool. She was but a maid seeking to know what love might be, and as she wandered on, she nibbled dreamily at a hot sweet-smelling bridie, whose gravy oozed deliciously through a bursting paper-bag.

It was a fit night for dark deeds.

"Methinks she cometh to her damn!"

The speaker was a masked man who had followed her—he was sniffing ecstatically—since she left the city walls.

She seemed to possess a charmed life. He would have had her in Shovel Gorge, but just then Ronny-On's Jean and Peter Scrymgeour turned the corner.

Suddenly Gavinia felt an exquisite thrill; a man was pursuing her. She slipped the paper-bag out of sight, holding it dexterously against her side with her arm, so that the gravy should not spurt out, and ran. Lights flashed, a kingly voice cried "Now!" and immediately a petticoat was flung over her head. (The Lady Griselda looked thin that evening.)

Gavinia was dragged to the Lair, and though many a time they bumped her, she tenderly nursed the paper-bag with her arm, or fondly thought she did so, for when unmuffled she discovered that it had been removed, as if by painless surgery. And her captors' tongues were sweeping their chins for stray crumbs.

The wench was offered her choice of Stroke's gallant fellows, but "Wha carries me wears me," said she promptly, and not only had he to carry her from one end of the Den to the other, but he must do it whistling as if barely conscious that she was there. So after many attempts (for she was always willing to let them have their try) Corp of Corp, speaking for Sir Joseph and the others, announced a general retreat.

Instead of taking this prisoner's life, Stroke made her his tool, releasing her on condition that every seventh day she appeared at the Lair with information concerning the doings in the town. Also, her name was Agnes of Kingoldrum, and, if she said it was not, the plank. Bought thus, Agnes proved of service, bringing such bags of news that Stroke was often occupied now in drawing diagrams of Thrums and its strongholds, including the residence of Cathro, with dotted lines to show the direction of proposed underground passages.

And presently came by this messenger disquieting rumours indeed. Another letter, being the third in six months, had reached the Dovecot, addressed, not to Miss Ailie, but to Miss Kitty. Miss Kitty had been dead fully six years, and Archie Piatt, the post, swore that this was the eighteenth, if not the nineteenth, letter he had delivered to her name since that time. They were all in the same hand, a man's, and there had been similar letters while she was alive, but of these he kept no record. Miss Ailie always took these letters with a trembling hand, and then locked herself in her bedroom, leaving the key in such a position in its hole that you might just as well go straight back to the kitchen. Within a few hours of the arrival of these ghostly letters, tongues were wagging about them, but to the two or three persons who (after passing a sleepless night) bluntly asked Miss Ailie from whom they came, she only replied by pursing her lips. Nothing could be learned at the post-office save that Miss Ailie never posted any letters there, except to two Misses and a Mrs., all resident in Redlintie. The mysterious letters came from Australy or Manchester, or some such part.

What could Stroke make of this? He expressed no opinion, but oh, his face was grim. Orders were immediately given to double the sentinels. A barrel was placed in the Queen's Bower. Sawdust was introduced at immense risk into the Lair. A paper containing this writing, "248xho317Oxh4591AWS3 14dd5," was passed round and then solemnly burned. Nothing was left to chance.

Agnes of Kingoldrum (Stroke told her) did not know Miss Ailie, but she was commanded to pay special attention to the gossip of the town regarding this new move of the enemy. By next Saturday the plot had thickened. Previous letters might have reddened Miss Ailie's eyes for an hour or two, but they

s

gladdened her as a whole. Now she sat crying all evening with this one on her lap; she gave up her daily walk to the Berlin wool shop, with all its romantic possibilities; at the clatter of the tea-things she would start apprehensively; she had let a red shawl lie for two days in the blue-and-white room.

Stroke never blanched. He called his faithful remnant around him, and told them the story of Bell the Cat, with its application in the records of his race. Did they take his meaning? This Miss Ailie must be watched closely. In short, once more in Scottish history, someone must bell the cat. Who would volunteer?

Corp of Corp and Sir Joseph stepped forward as one man.

"Thou couldst not look like Gavinia," the prince said, shaking his head.

"Wha wants him to look like Gavinia?" cried an indignant voice.

"Peace, Agnes!" said Stroke.

"Agnes, why bletherest thou?" said Sir Joseph.

"If onybody's to watch Miss Ailie," insisted the obstinate woman, "surely it should be me?"

"Ha!" Stroke sprang to his feet, for something in her voice, or the outline of her figure, or perhaps it was her profile, had given him an idea. "A torch!" he cried eagerly, and with its aid he scanned her face until his own shone triumphant.

"He kens a wy, methinks!" exclaimed one of his men.

Sir Joseph was right. It had been among

the prince's exploits to make his way into
Thrums in disguise, and mix with the people
as one of themselves, and on several of these
occasions he had seen Miss Ailie's attendant.
Agnes's resemblance to her now struck him for
the first time. It should be Agnes of Kingoldrum's honourable though dangerous part to take
this Gavinia's place.

But how to obtain possession of Gavinia's
person? Agnes made several suggestions, but
was told to hold her prating peace. It could
only be done in one way. They must kidnap
her. Sir Joseph was ordered to be ready to
accompany his liege on this perilous enterprise
in ten minutes. "And mind," said Stroke,
gravely, "we carry our lives in our hands."

"In our hands!" gasped Sir Joseph, greatly
puzzled, but he dared ask no more, and when
the two set forth (leaving Agnes of Kingoldrum
looking very uncomfortable), he was surprised
to see that Stroke was carrying nothing. Sir
Joseph carried in his hand his red hanky,
mysteriously knotted.

"Where is yours?" he whispered.

"What meanest thou?"

Sir Joseph replied, "Oh, nothing," and
thought it best to slip his handkerchief into
his trouser-pocket, but the affair bothered him
for long afterwards.

When they returned through the Den there
still seemed (to the unpiercing eye) to be but
two of them; nevertheless, Stroke re-entered
the Lair to announce to Agnes and the others
that he had left Gavinia below in charge of Sir

Joseph. She was to walk the plank anon, but
first she must be stripped that Agnes might
don her garments. Stroke was every inch a
prince, so he kept Agnes by his side, and sent
down the Lady Griselda and Widow Elspeth to
strip the prisoner, Sir Joseph having orders to
stand back fifty paces. (It is a pleasure to have
to record this.)

The signal having been given that this
delicate task was accomplished, Stroke whistled
shrilly, and next moment was heard from far
below a thud, as of a body falling in water, then
an agonising shriek, and then again all was
still, save for the heavy breathing of Agnes of
Kingoldrum.

Sir Joseph (very wet) returned to the Lair,
and Agnes was commanded to take off her
clothes in a retired spot and put on those of
the deceased, which she should find behind a
fallen tree.

"I winna be called the deceased," cried
Agnes hotly, but she had to do as she was
bid, and when she emerged from behind the
tree she was the very image of the ill-fated
Gavinia. Stroke showed her a plan of Miss
Ailie's back-door, and also gave her a kitchen
key (when he produced this, she felt in her
pockets and then snatched it from him), after
which she set out for the Dove-cot in a scare
about her own identity.

"And now, what dost thou think about it
a'?" inquired Sir Joseph, eagerly, to which
Stroke made answer, looking at him fixedly—

"The wind is in the west!"

Sir Joseph should have kept this a secret, but soon Stroke heard Inverquharity prating of it, and he called his lieutenant before him. Sir Joseph acknowledged humbly that he had been unable to hide it from Inverquharity, but he promised not to tell Muckle Kenny, of whose loyalty there were doubts. Henceforth, when the faithful fellow was Muckle Kenny, he would say doggedly to himself, "Dinna question me, Kenny. I ken nocht about it."

Dark indeed were now the fortunes of the Pretender, but they had one bright spot. Miss Ailie had been taken in completely by the trick played on her, and thus Stroke now got full information of the enemy's doings. Cathro having failed to dislodge the Jacobites, the seat of war had been changed by Victoria to the Dove-cot, whither her despatches were now forwarded. That this last one, of which Agnes of Kingoldrum tried in vain to obtain possession, doubled the price on the Pretender's head, there could be no doubt; but as Miss Ailie was a notorious Hanoverian, only the hunted prince himself knew why this should make her cry.

He hinted with a snigger something about an affair he had once had with the lady.

The Widow and Sir Joseph accepted this explanation, but it made Lady Griselda rock her arms in irritation.

The reports about Miss Ailie's behaviour became more and more alarming. She walked up and down her bedroom now in the middle of the night. Every time the knocker clanked she held herself together with both hands.

Agnes had orders not to answer the door until her mistress had keeked through the window.

"She's expecting a veesitor, methinks," said Corp. This was his bright day.

"Ay," answered Agnes, "but is't a man-body, or just a woman-body?"

Leaving the rebels in the Lair stunned by Victoria's latest move, we now return to Thrums, where Miss Ailie's excited state had indeed been the talk of many. Even the gossips, however, had under-estimated her distress of mind, almost as much as they misunderstood its cause. You must listen now (will you?) to so mild a thing as the long thin romance of two maiden ladies and a stout bachelor, all beginning to be old the day the three of them first drank tea together, and that was ten years ago.

Miss Ailie and Miss Kitty, you may remember, were not natives of Thrums. They had been born and brought up at Redlintie, and on the death of their parents they had remained there, the gauger having left them all his money, which was just sufficient to enable them to live like ladies, if they took tiny Magenta Cottage, and preferred an inexperienced maid. At first their life was very quiet, the walk from eleven to one for the good of fragile Miss Kitty's health, its outstanding feature. When they strolled together on the cliffs, Miss Ailie's short thick figure, straight as an elvint, cut the wind in two, but Miss Kitty was swayed this way and that, and when she shook her curls at the wind, it blew them roguishly in her face, and had another shot at them, as soon as they were put to rights. If the two walked by the shore (where the younger sometimes bathed her feet, the elder keeping a sharp eye on land and water), the sea behaved like the wind, dodging Miss Ailie's ankles and snapping playfully at Miss Kitty's. Thus even the elements could distinguish between the sisters, who nevertheless had so much in common that at times Miss Ailie would look into her mirror and sigh to think that some day Miss Kitty might be like this. How Miss Ailie adored Miss Kitty! She trembled with pleasure if you said Miss Kitty was pretty, and she dreamed dreams in which she herself walked as bridesmaid only. And just as Miss Ailie could be romantic, Miss Kitty, the romantic, could be prim, and the primness was her own as much as the curls, but Miss Ailie usually carried it for her, like a cloak in case of rain.

Not often have two sweeter women grown together on one stem. What were the men of Redlintie about? The sisters never asked each other this question, but there were times when, apparently without cause, Miss Ailie hugged Miss Kitty vehemently, as if challenging the world, and perhaps Miss Kitty understood.

Thus a year or more passed uneventfully, until the one romance of their lives befell them. It began with the reappearance in Redlintie of Magerful Tam, who had come to torment his father into giving him more money, but finding he had come too late, did not harass the sisters. This is perhaps the best thing that can be told of him, and, as if he knew this, he had often told it himself to Jean Myles, without however telling her what followed. For something to his advantage did follow, and it was greatly to the credit of Miss Ailie and Miss Kitty, though they went about it as timidly as if they were participating in a crime. Ever since they learned of the sin which had brought this man into the world their lives had been saddened, for on the same day they realised what a secret sorrow had long lain at their mother's heart. Alison Sibbald was a very simple gracious lady, who never recovered from the shock of discovering that she had married a libertine; yet she had pressed her husband to do something for his son, and been greatly pained when he refused with a coarse laugh. The daughters were very like her in nature, and though the knowledge of what she had suffered increased manyfold their love for her, so that in her last days their passionate devotion to her was the talk of Redlintie, it did not blind them to what seemed to them to be their duty to the man. As their father's son, they held, he had a right to a third of the gauger's money, and to withhold it from him, now that they knew his whereabouts, would have been a form of theft. But how to give T. his third? They called him T. from delicacy, and they had never spoken to him. When he passed them in the streets, they turned pale, and, thinking of their mother, looked another way. But they knew he winked.

At last looking red in one street, and white in another, but resolute in all, they took their business to the office of Mr. John McLean, the writer, who had once escorted Miss Kitty home from a party without anything coming of it, so that it was quite a psychological novel in several volumes. Now Mr. John happened to be away at the fishing, and a reckless maid showed them into the presence of a strange man, who was no other than his brother Ivie, home for a year's holiday from India, and naturally this extraordinary occurrence so agitated them that Miss Ailie had told half her story before she realised that Miss Kitty was titting at her dress. Then indeed she sought to withdraw, but Ivie, with the alarming yet not unpleasing audacity of his sex, said he had heard enough to convince him that in this matter he was qualified to take his brother's place. But he was not, for he announced, " My advice to you is, not to give T. a halfpenny," which showed that he did not even understand what they had come about.

They begged permission to talk to each other behind the door, and presently returned, troubled but brave. Miss Kitty whispered " Courage ! " and this helped Miss Ailie to the deed.

" We have quite made up our minds to let T. have the money," she said, " but—but the difficulty is the taking it to him. Must we take it in person ? "

" Why not ? " asked Ivie, bewildered.

" It would be such a painful meeting to us," said Miss Ailie.

" And to him," added simple Miss Kitty.

" You see, we have thought it best not to— not to know him," said Miss Ailie, faintly.

"Mother——" faltered Miss Kitty, and at the word the eyes of both ladies began to fill.

Then, of course, Mr. McLean discovered the object of their visit, and promised that his brother should take this delicate task off their hands, and as he bowed them out he said, "Ladies, I think you are doing a very foolish thing, and I shall respect you for it all my life." At least Miss Kitty insisted that respect was the word, Miss Ailie thought he said esteem.

That was how it began, and it progressed for nearly a year at a rate that will take away your breath. On the very next day he met Miss Kitty in High Street, a most awkward encounter for her ("for, you know, Ailie, we were never introduced, so how could I decide all in a moment what to do?"), and he raised his hat (the Misses Croall were at their window and saw the whole thing). But we must galop, like the friendship. He bowed the first two times, the third time he shook hands (by a sort of providence Miss Kitty had put on her new mittens), the fourth, fifth, and sixth times he conversed, the seventh time he—they replied that they really could not trouble him so much, but he said he was going that way at any rate; the eighth time, ninth time, and tenth time the figures of two ladies and a gentleman might have been observed, etc., and either the eleventh or twelfth time ("Fancy our not being sure, Ailie"—"It has all come so quickly, Kitty") he took his first dish of tea at Magenta Cottage.

There were many more walks after this, often along the cliffs to a little fishing village, over

which the greatest of magicians once stretched
his wand, so that it became famous for ever, as
all the world saw except himself; and tea at the
cottage followed, when Ivie asked Miss Kitty to
sing "The Land o' the Leal," and Miss Ailie
sat by the window, taking in her merino, that it
might fit Miss Kitty, cutting her sable muff
(once Alison Sibbald's) into wristbands for Miss
Kitty's astrakhan; they did not go quite all the
way round, but men are blind.

Ivie was not altogether blind.   The sisters,
it is to be feared, called him the dashing
McLean, but he was at this time nearly forty
years old, an age when bachelors like to take a
long rest from thinking of matrimony, before beginning again.   Fifteen years earlier he had been
in love, but the girl had not cared to wait for him,
and, though in India he had often pictured himself returning to Redlintie to gaze wistfully at
her old home, when he did come back he never
went, because the house was a little out of the
way.   But unknown to him two ladies went, to
whom he had told this as a rather dreary joke.
They were ladies he esteemed very much, though
having a sense of humour he sometimes chuckled
on his way home from Magenta Cottage, and he
thought out many ways of adding little pleasures
to their lives.   It was like him to ask Miss Kitty
to sing and play, though he disliked music.   He
understood that it is a hard world for single
women, and knew himself for a very ordinary
sort of man.   If it ever crossed his head that
Miss Kitty would be willing to marry him, he
felt genuinely sorry at the same time that she

had not done better long ago. He never flattered himself that he could be accepted now, save for the good home he could provide (he was not the man to blame women for being influenced by that), for like most of his sex he was unaware that a woman is never too old to love, or to be loved; if they do know it, the mean ones among them make a jest of it, at which (God knows why) their wives laugh. Mr. McLean had been acquainted with the sisters for months before he was sure even that Miss Kitty was his favourite. He found that out one evening when sitting with an old friend, whose wife and children were in the room, gathered round a lamp and playing at some child's game. Suddenly Ivie McLean envied his friend, and at the same moment he thought tenderly of Miss Kitty. But the feeling passed. He experienced it next and as suddenly when arriving at Bombay, where some women were waiting to greet their husbands.

Before he went away the two gentlewomen knew that he was not to speak. They did not tell each other what was in their minds. Miss Kitty was so bright during those last days, that she must have deceived anyone who did not love her, and Miss Ailie held her mouth very tight, and if possible was straighter than ever, but oh, how gentle she was with Miss Kitty! Ivie's lasts two weeks in the old country were spent in London, and during that time Miss Kitty liked to go away by herself, and sit on a rock and gaze at the sea. Once Miss Ailie followed her and would have called him a——

"Don't, Ailie!" said Miss Kitty, implor-

ingly. But that night, when Miss Kitty was
brushing her hair, she said, courageously, "Ailie,
I don't think I should wear curls any longer.
You know I—I shall be thirty-seven in August."
And after the elder sister had become calm
again, Miss Kitty said timidly, "You don't
think I have been unladylike, do you, Ailie?"

Such a trifle now remains to tell. Miss
Kitty was the better business woman of the two,
and kept the accounts, and understood, as Miss
Ailie could not understand, how their little income was invested, and even knew what Consols
were, though never quite certain whether it was
their fall or rise that is matter for congratulation. And after the ship had sailed, she told
Miss Ailie that nearly all their money was lost,
and that she had known it for a month.

"And you kept it from me! Why?"

"I thought, Ailie, that you, knowing I am
not strong—that you—would perhaps tell him."

"And I would!" cried Miss Ailie.

"And then," said Miss Kitty, "perhaps he,
out of pity, you know!"

"Well, even if he had!" said Miss Ailie.

"I could not, oh, I could not," replied Miss
Kitty, flushing; "it—it would not have been
ladylike, Ailie."

Thus forced to support themselves, the sisters
decided to keep school genteelly, and hearing that
there was an opening in Thrums, they settled
there, and Miss Kitty brushed her hair out
now, and with a twist and a twirl ran it up her
fingers into a net, whence by noon some of it
had escaped through the little windows and was

curls again. She and Miss Ailie were happy in
Thrums, for time took the pain out of the affair
of Mr. McLean, until it became not merely a
romantic memory, but, with the letters he wrote
to Miss Kitty and her answers, the great quiet
pleasure of their lives. They were friendly letters
only, but Miss Kitty wrote hers out in pencil
first and read them to Miss Ailie, who had been
taking notes for them.

In the last weeks of Miss Kitty's life Miss
Ailie conceived a passionate unspoken hatred of
Mr. McLean, and her intention was to write and
tell him that he had killed her darling. But
owing to the illness into which she was flung by
Miss Kitty's death, that unjust letter was never
written.

But why did Mr. McLean continue to write
to Miss Kitty?

Well, have pity or be merciless as you choose.
For several years Mr. McLean's letters had been
the one thing the sisters looked forward to, and
now, when Miss Ailie was without Miss Kitty,
must she lose them also? She never doubted,
though she may have been wrong, that if Ivie
knew of Miss Kitty's death, one letter would
come in answer, and that the last. She could
not tell him. In the meantime he wrote twice
asking the reason of this long silence, and at last
Miss Ailie, whose handwriting was very like her
sister's, wrote him a letter which was posted at
Tilliedrum and signed "Katherine Cray." The
thing seems monstrous, but this gentle lady did
it, and it was never so difficult to do again.
Latterly, it had been easy.

This last letter of Mr. McLean's announced to Miss Kitty that he was about to start for home "for good," and he spoke in it of coming to Thrums to see the sisters, as soon as he reached Redlintie. Poor Miss Ailie! After sleepless nights she trudged to the Tilliedrum post-office with a full confession of her crime, which would be her welcome home to him when he arrived at his brother's house. Many of the words were written on damp blobs. After that she could do nothing but wait for the storm, and waiting she became so meek, that Gavinia, who loved her because she was "that simple," said sorrowfully :

"How is't you never rage at me now, ma'am ? I'm sure it keepit you lightsome, and I likit to hear the bum o't."

"And instead o' the raging I was prigging for," the soft-hearted maid told her friends, "she gave me a flannel petticoat!" Indeed, Miss Ailie had taken to giving away her possessions at this time, like a woman who thought she was on her death-bed. There was something for each of her pupils, including—but the important thing is that there was a gift for Tommy, which had the effect of planting the Hanoverian Woman (to whom he must have given many uneasy moments) more securely on the British Throne.

CHAPTER XXV.

A PENNY PASS-BOOK.

ELSPETH conveyed the gift to Tommy in a brown paper wrapping, and when it lay revealed as an aging volume of *Mamma's Boy*, a magazine for the Home, nothing could have looked more harmless. But, ah, you never know. Hungrily Tommy ran his eye through the bill of fare for something choice to begin with, and he found it.

"The Boy Pirate" it was called. Never could have been fairer promise, and down he sat confidently.

It was a paper on the boys who have been undone by reading pernicious fiction. It gave their names, and the number of pistols they had bought, and what the judge said when he pronounced sentence. It counted the sensational tales found beneath the bed, and described the desolation of the mothers and sisters. It told the colour of the father's hair before and afterward.

Tommy flung the thing from him, picked it up again, and read on uneasily, and when at last he rose he was shrinking from himself. In hopes that he might sleep it off he went early to bed, but his contrition was still with him in the morning. Then Elspeth was shown the article which had saved him, and she, too, shuddered at what she had been, though her remorse was but a poor display beside his, he was so much better at everything than Elspeth. Tommy's distress of mind was so genuine and so keen that it had several hours' start of his admiration of it; and it was still sincere, though he himself had become gloomy, when he told his followers that they were no more. Grizel heard his tale with disdain, and said she hated Miss Ailie for giving him the silly book, but he reproved these unchristian sentiments, while admitting that Miss Ailie had played on him a scurvy trick.

"But you're glad you've repented, Tommy," Elspeth reminded him, anxiously.

"Ay, I'm glad," he answered without heartiness.

"Well, gin you repent I'll repent too," said Corp, always ready to accept Tommy without question.

"You'll be happier," replied Tommy, sourly.

"Ay, to be good's the great thing," Corp growled; "but, Tommy, could we no have just one michty blatter, methinks, to end up wi'?"

This, of course, could not be, and Saturday forenoon found Tommy wandering the streets listlessly, very happy, you know, but inclined to kick at anyone who came near, such, for instance, as the stranger who asked him in the square if he could point out the abode of Miss Ailie Cray.

Tommy led the way, casting some converted looks at the gentleman, and judging him to be the mysterious unknown in whom the late Captain Stroke had taken such a reprehensible interest. He was a stout, red-faced man, stepping firmly into the fifties, with a beard that

T

even the most converted must envy, and a frown
sat on his brows all the way, proving him
possibly ill-tempered, but also one of the notable
few who can think hard about one thing for at
least five consecutive minutes. Many took a
glint at him as he passed, but missed the frown,
they were wondering so much why the fur of
his heavy top-coat was on the inside, where it
made little show, save at blasty corners.

Miss Ailie was in her parlour, trying to give
her mind to a blue-and-white note-book, but
when she saw who was coming up the garden
she dropped the little volume and tottered to her
bedroom. She was there when Gavinia came up
to announce that she had shown a gentleman
into the blue-and-white room, who gave the
name of Ivie McLean. "Tell him—I shall
come down—presently," gasped Miss Ailie, and
then Gavinia was sure this was the man who
was making her mistress so unhappy.

"She's so easily flichtered now," Gavinia
told Tommy in the kitchen, "that for fear o'
starting her I never whistle at my work without
telling her I'm to do't, and if I fall on the stair,
my first thought is to jump up and cry, 'It was
just me tum'ling.' And now I believe this
brute'll be the death o' her."

"But what can he do to her?"

"I dinna ken, but she's greeting sair, and
you can hear how he's rampaging up and down
the blue-and-white room. Listen to his thrawn
feet! He's raging because she's so lang in
coming down, and come she daurna. Oh, the
poor crittur!"

Now, Tommy was very fond of his old school-mistress, and he began to be unhappy with Gavinia.

"She hasna a man-body in the world to take care o' her," sobbed the girl.

"Has she no?" cried Tommy, fiercely, and under one of the impulses that so easily mastered him he marched into the blue-and-white room.

"Well, my young friend, and what may you want?" asked Mr. McLean, impatiently.

Tommy sat down and folded his arms. "I'm going to sit here and see what you do to Miss Ailie," he said determinedly.

Mr. McLean said "Oh!" and then seemed favourably impressed, for he added quietly: "She is a friend of yours, is she? Well, I have no intention of hurting her."

"You had better no," replied Tommy, stoutly.

"Did she send you here?"

"No; I came mysel'."

"To protect her?"

There was the irony in it that so puts up a boy's dander. "Dinna think," said Tommy, hotly, "that I'm fleid at you, though I have no beard—at least, I hinna it wi' me."

At this unexpected conclusion a smile crossed Mr. McLean's face, but was gone in an instant. "I wish you had laughed," said Tommy, on the watch; "once a body laughs he canna be angry no more," which was pretty good even for Tommy. It made Mr. McLean ask him why he was so fond of Miss Ailie.

T 2

"I'm the only man-body she has," he answered.

"Oh? But why are you her man-body?"

The boy could think of no better reason than this : "Because—because she's so sair in need o' ane." (There were moments when one liked Tommy.)

Mr. McLean turned to the window, and perhaps forgot that he was not alone. "Well, what are you thinking about so deeply?" he asked by-and-by.

"I was trying to think o' something that would gar you laugh," answered Tommy, very earnestly, and was surprised to see that he had nearly done it.

The blue-and-white note-book was lying on the floor where Miss Ailie had dropped it. Often in Tommy's presence she had consulted this work, and certainly its effect on her was the reverse of laughter; but once he had seen Dr. McQueen pick it up and roar over every page. With an inspiration Tommy handed the book to Mr. McLean. "It made the doctor laugh," he said persuasively.

"Go away," said Ivie, impatiently ; "I am in no mood for laughing."

"I tell you what," answered Tommy, "I'll go, if you promise to look at it," and to be rid of him the man agreed. For the next quarter of an hour Tommy and Gavinia were very near the door of the blue-and-white room, Tommy whispering dejectedly, "I hear no laughing," and Gavinia replying, "But he has quieted down."

Mr. McLean had a right to be very angry, but God only can say whether he had a right to be as angry as he was. The book had been handed to him open, and he was laying it down unread when a word underlined caught his eye. It was his own name. Nothing in all literature arrests our attention quite so much as that. He sat down to the book. It was just about this time that Miss Ailie went on her knees to pray.

It was only a penny pass-book. On its blue cover had been pasted a slip of white paper, and on the paper was written, in blue ink, "Alison Cray," with a date nearly nine years old. The contents were in Miss Ailie's prim hand-writing; jottings for her own use begun about the time when the sisters, trembling at their audacity, had opened school, and consulted and added to fitfully ever since. Hours must have been spent in erasing the blots and other blemishes so carefully. The tiny volume was not yet full, and between its two last written pages lay a piece of blue blotting-paper neatly cut to the size of the leaf.

Some of these notes were transcripts from books, some contained the advice of friends, others were doubtless the result of talks with Miss Kitty (from whom there were signs that the work had been kept a secret), many were Miss Ailie's own. An entry of this kind was frequent: "If you are uncertain of the answer to a question in arithmetic, it is advisable to leave the room on some pretext and work out the sum swiftly in the passage." Various pretexts were suggested, and this one (which had an insufficient line through it) had been inserted by Dr. McQueen on that day when Tommy saw him chuckling, "You pretend that your nose is bleeding, and putting your handkerchief to it, retire hastily, the supposition being that you have gone to put the key of the blue-and-white room down your back." Evidently these small deceptions troubled Miss Ailie, for she had written, "Such subterfuge is, I hope, pardonable, the object being the maintenance of scholastic discipline." On another page, where the arithmetic was again troubling her, this appeared: "If Kitty were aware that the squealing of the slate-pencils gave me such headaches, she would insist on again taking the arithmetic class, though it always makes her ill. Surely, then, I am justified in saying that the sound does not distress me." To this the doctor had added, "You are a brick."

There were two pages headed NEVER, which mentioned ten things that Miss Ailie must never do; among them, "*Never* let the big boys know you are afraid of them. To awe them stamp with the foot, speak in a loud ferocious voice, and look them unflinchingly in the face."

"Punishments" was another heading, but she had written it small, as if to prevent herself seeing it each time she opened the book. Obviously her hope had been to dispose of Punishment in a few lines, but it would have none of that, and Mr. McLean found it stalking from page to page. Miss Ailie favoured the cane in preference to tawse, which "often flap round your neck as you are about to bring them down."

Except in desperate cases "it will probably be found sufficient to order the offender to bring the cane to you." Then followed a note about rubbing the culprit's hand "with sweet butter or dripping" should you have struck too hard.

Dispiriting item, that on resuming his seat the chastised one is a hero to his fellows for the rest of the day. Item, that Master John James Rattray knows she hurts her own hand more than his. Item, that John James promised to be good throughout the session if she would let him thrash the bad ones. Item, that Master T. Sandys, himself under correction, explained to her (the artistic instinct again) how to give the cane a waggle when descending, which would double its nip. Item, that Elsie Dundas offered to receive Francie Crabb's punishment for two snaps. Item, that Master Gavin Dishart, for what he considered the honour of his school, though aware he was imperilling his soul, fought Hendry Dickie of Cathro's for saying Miss Ailie could not draw blood with one stroke.

The effect on Miss Ailie of these mortifying discoveries could be read in the paragraph headed A MOTHER'S METHOD, which was copied from a newspaper. Mrs. E——, it seems, was the mother of four boys (residing at D——), and she subjected them frequently to corporal chastisement without permanent spiritual result. Mrs. E——, by the advice of another lady, Mrs. K—— (mother of six), then had recourse to the following interesting experiment: Instead of punishing her children physically when they misbehaved, she now in their presence wounded herself by striking her left hand severely with a ruler held in the right. Soon their better natures were touched, and the four implored her to desist, promising with tears never to offend again. From that hour Mrs. E—— had little trouble with her boys.

It was recorded in the blue-and-white book how Miss Ailie gave this plan a fair trial, but her boys must have been darker characters than Mrs. E——'s, for it merely set them to watching each other, so that they might cry out, "Pandy yourself quick, Miss Ailie; Gavin Dishart's drawing the devil on his slate." Nevertheless when Miss Ailie announced a return to more conventional methods, Francie was put up (with threats) to say that he suffered agonies of remorse every time she pandied herself for him, but the thing had been organised in a hurry and Francie was insufficiently primed, and on cross-examination he let out that he thought remorse was a swelling of the hands.

Miss Ailie was very humble-minded, and her entries under THE TEACHER TAUGHT were all admonitions for herself. Thus she chided herself for cowardice because "Delicate private reasons have made me avoid all mention of India in the geography classes. Kitty says quite calmly that this is fair neither to our pupils nor to I—— M——. The courage of Kitty in this matter is a constant rebuke to me." Except on a few occasions Mr. McLean found that he was always referred to as I—— M——.

Quite early in the volume Miss Ailie knew that her sister's hold on life was loosening.

"How bright the world suddenly seems," Mr. McLean read, "when there is the tiniest improvement in the health of an invalid one loves." Is it laughable that such a note as this is appended to a recipe for beef-tea? "It is surely not very wicked to pretend to Kitty that I keep some of it for myself; she would not take it all if she knew I dined on the beef it was made from." Other entries showed too plainly that Miss Ailie stinted herself of food to provide delicacies for Miss Kitty. No doubt her expenses were alarming her when she wrote this: "An interesting article in the *Mentor* says that nearly all of us eat and drink too much. Were we to mortify our stomachs we should be healthier animals and more capable of sustained thought. The word animal in this connection is coarse, but the article is most impressive, and a crushing reply to Dr. McQueen's assertion that the editor drinks. In the school-room I have frequently found my thoughts of late wandering from class-work, and I hastily ascribed it to sitting up during the night with Kitty or to my habit of listening lest she should be calling for me. Probably I had over-eaten, and I must mortify the stomach. A glass of hot water with half a spoonful of sugar in it is highly recommended as a light supper."

"How long ago it may seem since yesterday!" Do you need to be told on what dark day Miss Ailie discovered that? "I used to pray that I should be taken first, but I was both impious and selfish, for how could fragile Kitty have fought on alone?"

In time happiness again returned to Miss
Ailie; of all our friends it is the one most reluctant to leave us on this side of the grave.   It
came at first disguised, in the form of duties, old
and new; and stealthily, when Miss Ailie was not
looking, it mixed with the small worries and
joys that had been events while Miss Kitty
lived, and these it converted once more into
events, where Miss Ailie found it lurking, and at
first she would not take it back to her heart, but
it crept in without her knowing.   And still
there were I—— M——'s letters.   "They are
all I have to look forward to," she wrote in self-
defence.   "I shall never write to I—— M——
again," was another entry, but Mr. McLean
found on the same page, "I have written to
I—— M——, but do not intend posting it,"
and beneath that was, "God forgive me, I have
posted it."

The troubles with arithmetic were becoming
more terrible.   "I am never *really* sure about
the decimals," she wrote.

A Professor of Memory had appeared at the
Muckley, and Miss Ailie admits having given
him half-a-crown to explain his system to her.
But when he was gone she could not remember
whether you multiplied everything by ten before
dividing by five and subtracting a hundred, or
began by dividing and doing something under-
hand with the cube root.   Then Mr. Dishart,
who had a microscope, wanted his boy to be
taught science, and several experiments were
described at length in the book, one of them
dealing with a penny, *H,* and a piston, *X Y,*

and you do things to the piston "and then the penny comes to the surface." "But it never does," Miss Ailie wrote sorrowfully; perhaps she was glad when Master Dishart was sent to another school.

"Though I teach the girls the pianoforte I find that I cannot stretch my fingers as I used to do. Kitty used to take the music, and I often remember this suddenly when superintending a lesson. It is a pain to me that so many wish to acquire 'The Land o' the Leal,' which Kitty sang so often to I—— M—— at Magenta Cottage."

Even the French, of which Miss Ailie had once been very proud, was slipping from her. "Kitty and I kept up our French by translating I—— M——'s letters and comparing our versions; but now that this stimulus is taken away I find that I am forgetting my French. Or is it only that I am growing old? too old to keep school?" This dread was beginning to haunt Miss Ailie, and the pages between which the blotting-paper lay revealed that she had written to the editor of the *Mentor* asking up to what age he thought a needy gentlewoman had a right to teach. The answer was not given, but her comment on it told everything. "I asked him to be severely truthful, so that I cannot resent his reply. But if I take his advice, how am I to live? And if I do not take it, I fear I am but a stumbling-block in the way of true education."

That is a summary of what Mr. McLean read in the blue-and-white book; remember, you

were warned not to expect much. And Tommy
and Gavinia listened, and Tommy said, "I hear
no laughing," and Gavinia answered, "But he
has quieted down," and upstairs Miss Ailie was
on her knees. A time came when Mr. McLean
could find something to laugh at in that little
pass-book, but it was not then, not even when
he reached the end. He left something on the
last page instead. At least, I think it must
have been he: Miss Ailie's tears could not have
been so long a-drying.

You may rise now, Miss Ailie; your prayer
is granted.

CHAPTER XXVI.

TOMMY REPENTS, AND IS NONE THE WORSE FOR IT.

Mr. McLean wrote a few reassuring words to Miss Ailie, and having told Gavinia to give the note to her walked quietly out of the house; he was coming back after he had visited Miss Kitty's grave. Gavinia, however, did not know this, and having delivered the note she returned dolefully to the kitchen to say to Tommy, "His letter maun have been as thraun as himsel', for as soon as she read it, down she plumped on her knees again."

But Tommy was not in the kitchen; he was on the garden-wall, watching Miss Ailie's persecutor.

"Would it no be easier to watch him frae the gate?" suggested Gavinia, who had not the true detective instinct.

Tommy disregarded her womanlike question; a great change had come over him since she went upstairs; his head now wobbled on his shoulders like a little balloon that wanted to cut its connection with earth and soar.

"What makes you look so queer?" cried the startled maid. "I thought you was converted."

"So I am," he shouted; "I'm more converted than ever, and yet I can do it just the same! Gavinia, I've found a wy!"

He was hurrying off on Mr. McLean's trail,

but turned to say, "Gavinia, do you ken wha that man is?"

"Ower weel I ken," she answered, "it's Mr. McLean."

"McLean!" he echoed scornfully, "ay, I've heard that's one of the names he goes by, but hearken, and I'll tell you wha he really is. That's the scoundrel Stroke!"

No wonder Gavinia was flabbergasted. "Wha are you then?" she cried.

"I'm the Champion of Dames," he replied loftily, and before she had recovered from this he was stalking Mr. McLean in the cemetery.

Miss Kitty sleeps in a beautiful hollow called the Basin, but the stone put up to her memory hardly marks the spot now, for with a score of others it was blown on its face by the wind that uprooted so many trees in the Den, and as it fell it lies. From the Basin to the rough road that clings like a belt to the round cemetery dyke is little more than a jump, and shortly after Miss Kitty's grave had been pointed out to him, Mr. McLean was seen standing there hat in hand by a man on the road. This man was Dr. McQueen hobbling home from the Forest Muir; he did not hobble as a rule, but hobble everyone must on that misshapen brae, except Murdoch Gelatley, who being short in one leg elsewhere, is here the only straight man. McQueen's sharp eyes, however, picked out not only the stranger, but Tommy crouching behind Haggart's stone, and him did the doctor's famous crook staff catch in the neck and whisk across the dyke.

"What man is that you're watching, you mysterious loon?" McQueen demanded curiously; but of course Tommy would not divulge so big a secret. Now the one weakness of this large-hearted old bachelor (perhaps it is a professional virtue) was a devouring inquisitiveness, and he would be troubled until he discovered who was the stranger standing in such obvious emotion by the side of an old grave. "Well you must come back with me to the surgery, for I want you to run an errand for me," he said testily, hoping to pump the boy by the way, but Tommy dived beneath his stick and escaped. This rasped the doctor's temper, which was unfortunate for Grizel, whom he caught presently peeping in at his surgery window. A dozen times of late she had wondered whether she should ask him to visit her mamma, and though the Painted Lady had screamed in terror at the proposal, being afraid of doctors, Grizel would have ventured ere now, had it not been for her mistaken conviction that he was a hard man, who would only flout her. It had once come to her ears that he had said a woman like her mamma could demoralise a whole town, with other harsh remarks, doubtless exaggerated in the repetition, and so he was the last man she dared think of going to for help, when he should have been the first. Nevertheless she had come now, and a soft word from him, such as he gave most readily to all who were in distress, would have drawn her pitiful tale from her, but he was in a grumpy mood, and had heard none of the rumours about her mother's being ill, which indeed were only common among the Mony-penny children, and his first words checked her confidences. "What are you hanging about my open window for?" he cried sharply.

"Did you think I wanted to steal anything?" replied the indignant child.

"I won't say but what I had some such thait."

She turned to leave him, but he hooked her with his staff. "As you're here," he said, "will you go an errand for me?"

"No," she told him promptly; "I don't like you."

"There's no love lost between us," he replied, "for I think you're the dourest lassie I ever clapped eyes on, but there's no other litlin handy, so you must do as you are bid, and take this bottle to Ballingall's."

"Is it a medicine bottle?" she asked, with sudden interest.

"Yes, it's medicine. Do you know Ballingall's house in the West town end?"

"Ballingall who has the little school?"

"The same, but I doubt he'll keep school no longer."

"Is he dying?"

"I'm afraid there's no doubt of it. Will you go?"

"I should love to go," she cried.

"Love!" he echoed, looking at her with displeasure. "You can't love to go, so talk no more nonsense, but go, and I'll give you a bawbee."

"I don't want a bawbee," she said. "Do you think they will let me go in to see Ballingall?"

The doctor frowned. "What makes you want to see a dying man?" he demanded.

"I should just love to see him!" she exclaimed, and she added determinedly, "I won't give up the bottle until they let me in."

He thought her an unpleasant, morbid girl, but "that is no affair of mine," he said, shrugging his shoulders, and he gave her the bottle to deliver. Before taking it to Ballingall's, however, she committed a little crime. She bought an empty bottle at the 'Sosh, and poured into it some of the contents of the medicine bottle, which she then filled up with water. She dared try no other way now of getting medicine for her mother, and was too ignorant to know that there are different drugs for different ailments.

Grizel not only contrived to get in to see Ballingall, but stayed by his side for several hours, and when she came out it was night-time. On her way home she saw a light moving in the Den, where she had expected to play no more, and she could not prevent her legs from running joyously toward it. So when Corp, rising out of the darkness, deftly cut her throat, she was not so angry as she should have been.

"I'm so glad we are to play again, after all, Corp," she said; but he replied grandly, "Thou little kennest wha you're speaking to, my gentle jade."

He gave a curious hitch to his breeches, but it only puzzled her. "I wear gallowses no more," he explained, lifting his waistcoat to show that his braces now encircled him as a

U

belt, but even then she did not understand. "Know, then," said Corp, sternly, "I am Ben the Boatswain."

"And am I not the Lady Griselda any more?" she asked.

"I'm no sure," he confessed; "but if you are, there's a price on your head."

"What is Tommy?"

"I dinna ken yet, but Gavinia says he telled her he's Champion of Damns. I kenna what Elspeth'll say to that."

Grizel was starting for the Lair, but he caught her by the skirt.

"Is he not at the Lair?" she inquired.

"We knowest it not," he answered gravely. "We're looking for't," he added with some awe; "we've been looking for't this three year." Then, in a louder voice, "If you can guide us to it, my pretty trifle, you'll be richly rewarded."

"But where is he? Don't you know?"

"Fine I knowest, but it wouldna be mous to tell you, for I kenna whether you be friend or foe. What's that you're carrying?"

"It is a—a medicine bottle."

"Gie me a sook!"

"No."

"Just one," begged Corp, "and I'll tell you where he is."

He got his way, and smacked his lips unctuously.

"Now, where is Tommy?"

"Put your face close to mine," said Corp, and then he whispered hoarsely, "He's in a spleet new Lair, writing out bills wi' a' his

might, offering five hundred crowns' reward for
Stroke's head, dead or alive!"

The new haunt was a deserted house, that
stood, very damp, near a little waterfall to the
east of the Den. Bits of it well planted in the
marsh adhere doggedly together to this day, but
even then the roof was off and the chimney lay
in a heap on the ground, like blankets that have
slipped off a bed.

This was the good ship *Ailie* lying at anchor,
man-of-war, thirty guns, a cart-wheel to steer it
by, T. Sandys commander.

On the following Saturday, Ben the Boatswain piped all hands, and Mr. Sandys delivered
a speech of the bluff, straightforward kind that
sailors love. Here, unfortunately, it must be
condensed. He reminded them that three years
had passed since their gracious queen (cheers)
sent them into these seas to hunt down the Pretender (hisses). Their ship had been christened
the *Ailie*, because its object was to avenge the
insults offered by the Pretender to a lady of
that name for whom every one of them would
willingly die. Like all his race the Pretender,
or Stroke, as he called himself, was a torment to
single women; he had not only stolen all this
lady's wealth, but now he wanted to make her
walk the plank, a way of getting rid of enemies
the mere mention of which set the blood of all
honest men boiling (cheers). As yet they had
not succeeded in finding Stroke's Lair, though
they knew it to be in one of the adjoining
islands, but they had suffered many privations,

twice their gallant vessel had been burned to
the water's edge, once she had been sunk, once
blown into the air, but had that dismayed them?

Here the Boatswain sent round a whisper,
and they all cried loyally, "Ay, ay, sir."

He had now news for them that would warm
their hearts like grog. He had not discovered
the Lair, but he had seen Stroke, he had spoken
to him ! Disguised as a boy, he had tracked the
Jacobite and found him skulking in the house of
the unhappy Ailie. After blustering for a little,
Stroke had gone on his knees and offered not
only to cease persecuting this lady but to return
to France. Mr. Sandys had kicked him into a
standing posture and then left him. But this
clemency had been ill repaid. Stroke had not
returned to France. He was staying at the
Quharity Arms, a Thrums inn, where he called
himself McLean. It had gone through the
town like wildfire that he had written to someone in Redlintie to send him on another suit of
clothes and four dickies. No one suspected his
real character, but all noted that he went to the
unhappy Ailie's house daily, and there was a
town about it. Ailie was but a woman, and
women could not defend themselves ("Boatswain, put Grizel in irons if she opens her
mouth"), and so the poor thing had been forced
to speak to him, and even to go walks with
him. Her life was in danger, and before now
Mr. Sandys would have taken him prisoner, but
the queen had said these words, "Noble Sandys,
destroy the Lair," and the best way to discover
this horrid spot was to follow Stroke night and

day until he went to it. Then they would burn
it to the ground, put him on board the *Ailie*, up
with the jib-boom sail, and away to the Tower
of London.

At the words "Tower of London," Ben
cried "Tumble up there!" which was the signal
for three such ringing cheers as only British tars
are capable of. Three? To be exact, only two
and a half, for the third stopped in the middle,
as if the lid had suddenly been put on.

What so startled them was the unexpected
appearance in their midst of the very man
Tommy had been talking of. Taking a stroll
through the Den, Mr. McLean had been drawn
toward the ruin by the first cheers, and had
arrived in time to learn who and what he really
was.

"Stroke!" gasped one small voice.

The presumptuous man folded his arms.
"So, Sandys," he said, in hollow tones, "we
meet again!"

Even Grizel got behind Tommy, and perhaps
it was this that gave him spunk to say tremulously, "Wh-what are you doing here?"

"I have come," replied the ruddy Pretender,
"to defy you, ay, proud Sandys, to challenge
thee to the deed thou pratest of. I go from
here to my Lair. Follow me, if thou darest!"

He brought his hand down with a bang upon
the barrel, laughed disdainfully, and springing
over the vessel's side was at once lost in the
darkness. Instead of following, all stood trans-
fixed, gazing at the barrel, on which lay five
shillings.

"He put them there when he slammed it!"

"Losh behears! there's a shilling to ilka ane o' us!"

"I winna touch the siller," said Sandys, moodily.

"What?" cried Gavinia.

"I tell you it's a bribe."

"Do you hear him?" screamed Gavinia. 'He says we're no to lay hands on't! Corp, whaur's your tongue?"

But even in that trying moment Corp's trust in Tommy shone out beautiful and strong. "Dinna be feared, Gavinia," he whispered, "he'll find a wy."

"Lights out, and follow Stroke!" was the order, and the crew at once scattered in pursuit, Mr. Sandys remaining behind a moment to—to put something in his pocket.

Mr. McLean gave them a long chase, walking demurely when lovers were in sight, but at other times doubling, jumping, even standing on eminences and crowing insultingly like a cock, and not until he had only breath left to chuckle did the stout man vanish from the Den. Elspeth, now a cabin-boy, was so shaken by the realism of the night's adventures that Gavinia (able seaman) took her home, and when Mr. Sandys and his Boatswain met at the Cuttle Well neither could tell where Grizel was.

"She had no business to munt without my leave," Tommy said sulkily.

"No, she hadna. Is she the Lady Griselda yet?"

"Not her, she's the Commander's wife."

Ben shook his head, for this, he felt, was the one thing Tommy could not do. "Well, then," growled Tommy, "if she winna be that, she'll have to serve before the mast, for I tell you plain I'll have no single women on board."

"And what am I, forby Ben the Boatswain?"

"Nothing. Honest men has just one name."

"What! I'm just one single man?" Corp was a little crestfallen. "It's a come-down," he said, with a sigh; "mind, I dinna grumble, but it's a come-down."

"And you dinna have 'Methinks' now either," Tommy announced pitilessly.

Corp had dreaded this. "I'll be gey an' lonely without it," he said, with some dignity, "and it was the usefullest swear I kent o'. 'Methinks!' I used to roar at Mason Malcolm's collie, and the crittur came in ahint in a swite o' fear. Losh, Tommy, is that you blooding?"

There was indeed an ugly gash on Tommy's hand. "You've been hacking at yoursel' again," said the distressed Corp, who knew that in his enthusiasm Tommy had more than once drawn blood from himself. "When you take it a' so real as that," he said uncomfortably, "I near think we should give it up."

Tommy stamped his foot. "Take tent o' yoursel'!" he cried threateningly. "When I was tracking Stroke I fell in with one of his men, and we had a tussle. He pinked me in the hand, but 'tis only a scratch, bah! He was carrying treasure, and I took it from him."

Ben whistled. "Five shillings?" he asked, slapping his knee.

"How did you know?" demanded Tommy, frowning, and then they tried to stare each other down.

"I thought I saw you pouching it," Corp ventured to say.

"Boatswain!"

"I mean," explained Corp hurriedly, "I mean that I kent you would find a wy. Didest thou kill the Jacobite rebel?"

"He lies but a few paces off," replied Tommy, "and already the vultures are picking his bones."

"So perish all Victoria's enemies," said Ben the Boatswain, loyally, but a sudden fear made him add, with a complete change of voice, "You dinna chance to ken his name?"

"Ay, I had marked him before," answered Tommy, "he was called Corp of Corp."

Ben the Boatswain rose, sat down, rose again. "Tommy," he said, wiping his brow with his sleeve, "come awa' hame!"

CHAPTER XXVII.

THE LONGER CATECHISM.

In the meantime Mr. McLean was walking slowly to the Quharity Arms, fanning his face with his hat, and in the West town end he came upon some boys who had gathered with offensive cries round a girl in a lustre jacket. A wave of his stick put them to flight, but the girl only thanked him with a look, and entered a little house the window of which showed a brighter light than its neighbours. Dr. McQueen came out of this house a moment afterwards, and as the two men now knew each other slightly they walked home together, McLean relating humorously how he had spent the evening. "And though Commander Sandys means to incarcerate me in the Tower of London," he said, "he did me a good service the other day, and I feel an interest in him."

"What did the inventive sacket do?" the doctor asked inquisitively; but McLean, who had referred to the incident of the pass-book, affected not to hear. "Miss Ailie has told me his history," he said, "and that he goes to the University next year."

"Or to the herding," put in McQueen, dryly.

"Yes, I heard that was the alternative, but he should easily carry a bursary; he is a remarkable boy."

"Ay, but I'm no sure that it's the remarkable boys who carry the bursaries. However, if you have taken a fancy to him, you should hear what Mr. Cathro has to say on the subject; for my own part, I have been more taken up with one of his band lately than with himself—a lassie, too."

"She who went into that house just before you came out?"

"The same, and she is the most puzzling bit of womankind I ever fell in with."

"She looked an ordinary girl enough," said Mr. McLean.

The doctor chuckled. "Man," he said, "in my time I have met all kinds of women except ordinary ones. What would you think if I told you that this ordinary girl had been spending three or four hours daily in that house entirely because there was a man dying in it?"

"Someone she had an affection for?"

"My certie, no! I'm afraid it is long since anybody had an affection for shilpit, hirpling, old Ballingall, and as for this lassie Grizel, she had never spoken to him until I sent her on an errand to his house a week ago. He was a single man (like you and me), without women-folk, a schoolmaster of his own making, and in the smallest way, and his one attraction to her was that he was on his death-bed. Most lassies of her age skirl to get away from the presence of death, but she prigged, sir, fairly prigged, to get into it!"

"Ah, I prefer less uncommon girls," McLean said. "They should not have let her have her wish; it can only do her harm."

"That is another curious thing," replied the doctor. "It does not seem to have done her any harm; rather it has turned her from being a dour, silent crittur into a talkative one, and that, I take it, is a sign of grace."

He sighed, and added: "Not that I can get her to talk of herself and her mother. (There is a mystery about them, you understand.) No, the obstinate brat will tell me nothing on that subject; instead of answering my questions she asks questions of me—an endless rush of questions, and all about Ballingall. How did I know he was dying? When you put your fingers on their wrist, what is it you count? which is the place where the lungs are? when you tap their chest, what do you listen for? are they not dying as long as they can rise now and then, and dress and go out? when they are really dying, do they always know it themselves? If they don't know it, is that a sign that they are not so ill as you think them? When they don't know they are dying, is it best to keep it from them in case they should scream with terror? and so on in a spate of questions, till I called her the Longer Catechism."

"And only morbid curiosity prompted her?"

"Nothing else," said the confident doctor; "if there had been anything else, I should have found it out, you may be sure. However, unhealthily minded though she be, the women who took their turn at Ballingall's bedside were glad of her help."

"The more shame to them," McLean remarked warmly; but the doctor would let no one, save himself, miscall the women of Thrums.

"Ca' canny," he retorted. "The women of this place are as overdriven as the men, from the day they have the strength to turn a pirn-wheel to the day they crawl over their bed-board for the last time, but never yet have I said, 'I need one of you to sit up all night wi' an unweel body,' but what there were half a dozen willing to do it. They are a grand race, sir, and will remain so till they find it out themselves."

"But of what use could a girl of twelve or fourteen be to them?"

"Use!" McQueen cried. "Man, she has been simply a treasure, and but for one thing I would believe it was less a morbid mind than a sort of divine instinct for nursing that took her to Ballingall's bedside. The women do their best in a rough - and - ready way; but, sir, it cowed to see that lassie easying a pillow for Ballingall's head, or changing a sheet without letting in the air, or getting a poultice on his back without disturbing the one on his chest. I had just to let her see how to do these things once, and after that Ballingall complained if any other soul touched him."

"Ah," said McLean, "then perhaps I was uncharitable, and the nurse's instinct is the true explanation."

"No, you're wrong again, though I might have been taken in as well as you but for the one thing I spoke of. Three days ago Ballingall had a ghost of a chance of pulling through, I thought, and I told the lassie that if he did, the credit would be mainly hers. You'll scarcely believe it, but, upon my word, she looked disappointed rather than pleased, and she said to me, quite reproachfully, 'You told me he was sure to die!' What do you make of that?"

"It sounds unnatural."

"It does, and so does what followed. Do you know what straiking is?"

"Arraying the corpse for the coffin, laying it out, in short, is it not?"

"Ay, ay. Well, it appears that Grizel had prigged with the women to let her be present at Ballingall's straiking, and they had refused."

"I should think so," exclaimed McLean, with a shudder.

"But that's not all. She came to me in her difficulty, and said that if I didna promise her this privilege she would nurse Ballingall no more."

"Ugh! That shows at least that pity for him had not influenced her."

"No, she cared not a doit for him. I question if she's the kind that could care for anyone. It's plain by her thrawn look when you speak to her about her mother that she has no affection even for her. However, there she was, prepared to leave Ballingall to his fate if I did not grant her request, and I had to yield to her."

"You promised?"

"I did, sore against the grain, but I accept the responsibility. You are pained, but you don't know what a good nurse means to a doctor."

"Well?"

"Well, he died after all, and the straiking is going on now. You saw her go in."

"I think you could have been excused for breaking your word and turning her out."

"To tell the truth," said the doctor, "I had the same idea when I saw her enter, and I tried to shoo her to the door, but she cried, 'You promised, you *can't* break a promise!' and the morbid brat that she is looked so horrified at the very notion of anybody's breaking a promise that I slunk away as if she had right on her side."

"No wonder the little monster is unpopular," was McLean's comment. "The children hereabout seem to take to her as little as I do, for I had to drive away some who were molesting her. I am sorry I interfered now."

"I can tell you why they t'nead her," replied the doctor, and he repeated the little that was known in Thrums of the Painted Lady. "And, you see, the womenfolk are mad because they can find out so little about her, where she got her money, for instance, and who are the 'gentlemen' that are said to visit her at Double Dykes. They have tried many ways of drawing Grizel, from heckle biscuits and parlies to a slap in the face, but neither by coaxing nor squeezing will you get an egg out of a sweer hen, and so they found. 'The dour little limmer,' they say, 'stalking about wi' all her blinds down,' and they are slow to interfere when their laddies call her names. It's a pity for herself that she's not more communicative, for if she would just satisfy the women's curiosity she would find them full of kindness. A terrible thing, Mr. McLean is curiosity. The Bible says that the love of money is the root of all evil, but we must ask Mr. Dishart if love of money is not a misprint for curiosity. And you won't find men boring their way into other folk's concerns; it is a woman's failing, essentially a woman's." This was the doctor's pet topic, and he pursued it until they had to part. He had opened his door and was about to enter when he saw Gavinia passing on her way home from the Den.

"Come here, my lass," he called to her, and then said inquisitively, "I'm told Mr. McLean is at his tea with Miss Ailie every day?"

"And it's true," replied Gavinia, in huge delight, "and what's more, she has given him some presents."

"You say so, lassie! What were they now?"

"I dinna ken," Gavinia had to admit, dejectedly. "She took them out o' the ottoman, and it has aye been kept locked."

McQueen looked very knowingly at her. "Will he, think you?" he asked mysteriously.

The maid seemed to understand, for she replied promptly, "I hope he will."

"But he hasna spiered her as yet, you think?"

"No," she said, "no, but he calls her Ailie, and wi' the gentry it's but one loup frae that to spiering."

"Maybe," answered the doctor, "but it's a loup they often bogle at. I'se uphaud he's close on fifty, Gavinia?"

"There's no denying he is by his best," she said regretfully, and then added, with spirit, "but Miss Ailie's no heavy, and in thae grite arms o' his he could daidle her as if she were an infant."

This bewildered McQueen, and he asked, "What are you blethering about, Gavinia?" to which she replied, regally, "Wha carries me, wears me!" The doctor concluded that it must be Den language.

"And I hope he's good enough for her," continued Miss Ailie's warm-hearted maid, "for she deserves a good ane."

"She does," McQueen agreed heartily, "ay, and I believe he is, for he breathes through his nose instead of through his mouth; and let me tell you, Gavinia, that's the one thing to be sure of in a man before you take him for better or worse."

The astounded maid replied, "I'll ken better things than that about my lad afore I take him," but the doctor assured her that it was the box which held them all, "though you maun tell no one, lassie, for it's my one discovery in five-and-thirty years of practice."

Seeing that, despite his bantering tone, he was speaking seriously, she pressed him for his meaning, but he only replied sadly, "You're like the rest, Gavinia; I see it breaking out on you in spots."

"An illness!" she cried, in alarm.

"Ay, lassie, an illness called curiosity. I had just been telling Mr. McLean that curiosity is essentially a woman's ailment, and up you come ahint to prove it." He shook a finger at her reprovingly, and was probably still reflecting on woman's ways when Grizel walked home at midnight breathing through her nose, and Tommy fell asleep with his mouth open. For Tommy could never have stood the doctor's test of a man. In the painting of him, aged twenty-four, which was exhibited in the Royal Academy, his lips meet firmly, but no one knew save himself how he gasped after each sitting.

CHAPTER XXVIII.

BUT IT SHOULD HAVE BEEN MISS KITTY.

THE ottoman whence, as Gavinia said, Miss
Ailie produced the presents she gave to Mr.
McLean stood near the door of the blue-and-
white room, with a reel of thread between,
to keep them apart forever. Except on washing
days it was of a genteel appearance, for though
but a wooden kist, it had a gay outer garment
with frills, which Gavinia starched, and beneath
this was apparel of a private character that
tied with tapes. When Miss Ailie, pins in her
mouth, was on her knees arraying the ottoman,
it might almost have been mistaken for a female
child.

The contents of the ottoman were a few
trivial articles sewn or knitted by Miss Kitty
during her last illness, "just to keep me out of
languor," she would explain wistfully to her
sister. She never told Miss Ailie that they were
intended for any special person; on the contrary
she said, "Perhaps you may find someone they
will be useful to," but almost without her knowing it they always grew into something that
would be useful to Ivie McLean.

"The remarkable thing is that they are an
exact fit," the man said about the slippers, and
Miss Ailie nodded, but she did not think it
remarkable.

There were also two fluffy little bags, and Miss Ailie had to explain their use. "If you put your feet into them in bed," she faltered, "they—they keep you warm."

McLean turned hastily to something else, a smoking-cap. "I scarcely think this can have been meant for me," he said; "you have forgotten how she used to chide me for smoking."

Miss Ailie had not forgotten. "But in a way," she replied, flushing a little, "we—that is, Kitty—could not help admiring you for smoking. There is something so—so dashing about it."

"I was little worth all the friendship you two gave me, Ailie," he told her humbly, and he was nearly saying something to her then that he had made up his mind to say. The time came a few days later. They had been walking together on the hill, and on their return to the Dove-Cot he had insisted, "in his old imperious way," on coming in to tea. Hearing talking in the kitchen, Miss Ailie went along the passage to discover what company her maid kept; but before she reached the door, which was ajar, she turned as if she had heard something dreadful and hurried upstairs, signing to Mr. McLean, with imploring eyes, to follow her. This at once sent him to the kitchen door.

Gavinia was alone. She was standing in the middle of the floor, with one arm crooked as if making believe that another's arm rested on it, and over her head was a little muslin window-blind, representing a bride's veil. Thus she was two persons, but she was also a third, who addressed them in clerical tones.

v 2

"Ivie McLean," she said, as solemnly as though she were the Rev. Mr. Dishart, "do you take this woman to be thy lawful wedded wife?" With almost indecent haste she answered herself, "I do."

"Alison Cray," she said next, "do you take this man to be thy lawful wedded husband?" "I do."

Just then the door shut softly; and Gavinia ran to see who had been listening, with the result that she hid herself in the coal-cellar.

While she was there, Miss Ailie and Mr. McLean were sitting in the blue-and-white room very self-conscious, and Miss Ailie was speaking confusedly of anything and everything, saying more in five minutes than had served for the previous hour, and always as she slackened she read an intention in his face that started her tongue upon another journey. But, "Timid Ailie," he said at last, "do you think you can talk me down?" and then she gave him a look of reproach that turned treacherously into one of appeal, but he had the hardihood to continue: "Ailie, do you need to be told what I want to say?"

Miss Ailie stood quite still now, a stiff, thick figure, with a soft, plain face and nervous hands. "Before you speak," she said nervously, "I have something to tell you that—perhaps then you will not say it.

"I have always led you to believe," she began, trembling, "that I am forty-nine. I am fifty-one."

He would have spoken, but the look of appeal

came back to her face, asking him to make it easier for her by saying nothing. She took a pair of spectacles from her pocket, and he divined what this meant before she spoke. " I have avoided letting you see that I need them," she said. " You—men don't like—" She tried to say it all in a rush, but the words would not come.

"I am beginning to be a little deaf," she went on. " To deceive you about that, I have sometimes answered you without really knowing what you said."

"Anything more, Ailie ? "

" My accomplishments — they were never great, but Kitty and I thought my playing of classical pieces—my fingers are not sufficiently pliable now. And I—I forget so many things."

" But, Ailie——"

"Please let me tell you. I was reading a book, a story, last winter, and one of the characters, an old maid, was held up to ridicule in it for many little peculiarities that—that I recognised as my own. They had grown upon me without my knowing that they made me ridiculous, and now I—I have tried, but I cannot alter them."

"Is that all, Ailie ? "

" No."

The last seemed to be the hardest to say. Dusk had come on, and they could not see each other well. She asked him to light the lamp, and his back was toward her while he did it, wondering a little at her request. When he turned, her hands rose like cowards to hide her

head, but she pulled them down. " Do you not
see ? " she said.

" I see that you have done something to your
hair," he answered; "I liked it best the other
way."

Most people would have liked it best the
other way. There was still a good deal of it,
but the "bun" in which it ended had gone
strangely small. "The rest was false," said Miss
Ailie, with a painful effort; "at least, it is my
own, but it came out when—when Kitty died."

She stopped, but he was silent. "That is all
now," she said softly, and she waited for him to
speak if he chose. He turned his head away
sharply, and Miss Ailie mistook his meaning. If
she gave one little sob— Well, it was but one,
and then all the glory of womanhood came
rushing to her aid, and it unfurled its flag over
her, whispering, "Now, sweet daughter, now,
strike for me," and she raised her head gallantly,
and for a moment in her life the old school-
mistress was a queen. "I shall ring for tea,"
she said, quietly and without a tremor; "do you
think there is anything so refreshing after a walk
as a dish of tea ? "

She rang the bell, but its tinkle only made
Gavinia recede farther into the cellar, and that
summons has not been answered to this day, and
no one seems to care, for while the wires were
still vibrating Mr. McLean had asked Miss Ailie
to forgive him and marry him.

Miss Ailie said she would, but, " Oh," she
cried, " ten years ago it might have been my
Kitty. I would that it had been Kitty ! "

Miss Ailie was dear to him now, and ten years is a long time, and men are vain. Mr. McLean replied, quite honestly, " I am not sure that I did not always like you best," but that hurt her, and he had to unsay the words.

" I was a thoughtless fool ten years ago," he said bitterly, and Miss Ailie's answer came strangely from such timid lips. " Yes, you were !" she exclaimed passionately, and all the wrath, long pent up, with very different feelings, in her gentle bosom, against the man who should have adored her Kitty, leapt at that reproachful cry to her mouth and eyes, and so passed out of her for ever.

CHAPTER XXIX.

TOMMY THE SCHOLAR.

So Miss Ailie could be brave, but what a poltroon she was also! Three calls did she make on dear friends, ostensibly to ask how a cold was or to instruct them in a new device in Shetland wool, but really to announce that she did not propose keeping school after the end of the term —because—in short, Mr. Ivie McLean and she —that is, he—and so on. But though she had planned it all out so carefully, with at least three capital ways of leading up to it, and knew precisely what they would say, and pined to hear them say it, on each occasion shyness conquered and she came away with the words unspoken. How she despised herself, and how Mr. McLean laughed! He wanted to take the job off her hands by telling the news to Dr. McQueen, who could be depended on to spread it through the town, and Miss Ailie discovered with horror that his simple plan was to say, "How are you, Doctor? I just looked in to tell you that Miss Ailie and I are to be married. Good afternoon." The audacity of this captivated Miss Ailie even while it outraged her sense of decency. To Redlintie went Mr. McLean, and returning next day, drew from his pocket something which he put on Miss Ailie's finger, and then she had the idea of taking off her left glove in church, which

would have announced her engagement as loudly
as though Mr. Dishart had included it in his
pulpit intimations. Religion, however, stopped
her when she had got the little finger out, and
the Misses Finlayson, who sat behind and knew
she had an itchy something inside her glove,
concluded that it was her threepenny for the
plate. As for Gavinia, like others of her class in
those days, she had never heard of engagement
rings, and so it really seemed as if Mr. McLean
must call on the doctor after all. But "No,"
said he, "I hit upon a better notion to-day in
the Den," and to explain this notion he produced
from his pocket a large, vulgar bottle, which
shocked Miss Ailie, and indeed that bottle had
not passed through the streets uncommented on.

Mr. McLean having observed this bottle
afloat on the Silent Pool, had fished it out with
his stick, and its contents set him chuckling.
They consisted of a sheet of paper which stated
that the bottle was being flung into the sea in
lat. 20, long. 40, by T. Sandys, Commander of
the *Ailie*, then among the breakers. Sandys
had little hope of weathering the gale, but he
was indifferent to his own fate so long as his
enemy did not escape, and he called upon what-
soever loyal subjects of the queen should find this
document to sail at once to lat. 20, long. 40, and
there cruise till they had captured the Pretender,
alias Stroke, and destroyed his Lair. A somewhat unfavourable personal description of Stroke
was appended, with a map of the coast, and a
stern warning to all loyal subjects not to delay,
as one Ailie was in the villain's hands, and he

might kill her any day. Victoria Regina would give five hundred crowns for his head. The letter ended in manly style with the writer's sending an affecting farewell message to his wife and little children.

"And so while we are playing ourselves," said Mr. McLean to Miss Ailie, "your favourite is seeking my blood."

"Our favourite" interposed the school-mistress, and he accepted the correction, for neither of them could forget that their present relations might have been very different had it not been for Tommy's faith in the pass-book. The boy had shown a knowledge of the human heart, in Miss Ailie's opinion, that was simply wonderful; inspiration she called it, and though Ivie thought it a happy accident, he did not call it so to her. Tommy's father had been the instrument in bringing these two together originally, and now Tommy had brought them together again; there was fate in it, and if the boy was of the right stuff McLean meant to reward him.

"I see now," he said to Miss Ailie, "a way of getting rid of our fearsome secret and making my peace with Sandys at one fell blow." He declined to tell her more, but presently he sought Gavinia, who dreaded him nowadays because of his disconcerting way of looking at her inquiringly and saying "I do!"

"You don't happen to know, Gavinia," he asked, "whether the good ship *Ailie* weathered the gale of the 15th instant? If it did," he went on, "Commander Sandys will learn something to

his advantage from a bottle that is to be cast
into the ocean this evening."

Gavinia thought she heard the chink of
another five shillings, and her mouth opened so
wide that a chaffinch could have built therein.
" Is he to look for a bottle in the pond ? " she
asked, eagerly.

" I do," replied McLean with such solemnity
that she again retired to the coal-cellar.

That evening Mr. McLean cast a bottle into
the Silent Pool, and subsequently called on Mr.
Cathro, to whom he introduced himself as one
interested in Master Thomas Sandys. He was
heartily received, but at the name of Tommy,
Cathro heaved a sigh that could not pass un-
noticed. " I see you don't find him an angel,"
said Mr. McLean, politely.

" 'Deed, sir, there are times when I wish he
was an angel," the dominie replied so viciously
that McLean laughed. " And I grudge you
that laugh," continued Cathro, " for your Tommy
Sandys has taken from me the most precious
possession a teacher can have—my sense of
humour."

" He strikes me as having a considerable
sense of humour himself."

" Well, he may, Mr. McLean, for he has
gone off with all mine. But bide a wee till I
get in the tumblers, and I'll tell you the latest
about him—if what you want to hear is just the
plain exasperating truth.

" His humour that you spoke of," resumed
the schoolmaster presently, addressing his words
to the visitor and his mind to a toddy-ladle of

horn, "is ill to endure in a school where the understanding is that the dominie makes all the jokes (except on examination day, when the ministers get their yearly fling), but I think I like your young friend worst when he is deadly serious. He is constantly playing some new part—playing is hardly the word though, for into each part he puts an earnestness that cheats even himself, until he takes to another. I suppose you want me to give you some idea of his character, and I could tell you what it is at any particular moment; but it changes, sir, I do assure you, almost as quickly as the circus-rider flings off his layers of waistcoats. A single puff of wind blows him from one character to another, and he may be noble and vicious, and a tyrant and a slave, and hard as granite and melting as butter in the sun, all in one forenoon. All you can be sure of is that whatever he is he will be it in excess."

"But I understood," said McLean, "that at present he is solely engaged on a war of extermination in the Den."

"Ah, those exploits, I fancy, are confined to Saturday nights, and unfortunately his Saturday debauch does not keep him sober for the rest of the week, which we demand of respectable characters in these parts. For the last day or two, for instance, he has been in mourning."

"I had not heard of that."

"No, I daresay not, and I'll give you the facts, if you'll fill your glass first. But perhaps—" here the dominie's eyes twinkled as if a gleam of humour had been left him after all—

"perhaps you have been more used of late to ginger wine?"

The visitor received the shot impassively, as if he did not know he had been hit, and Cathro proceeded with his narrative. "Well, for a day or two Tommy Sandys has been coming to the school in a black jacket with crape on the cuffs, and not only so, he has sat quiet and forlornlike at his desk, as if he had lost some near and dear relative. Now I knew that he had not, for his only relative is a sister whom you may have seen at the Hanky school, and both she and Aaron Latta are hearty. Yet, sir (and this shows the effect he has on me), though I was puzzled and curious, I dared not ask for an explanation."

"But why not?" was the visitor's natural question.

"Because, sir, he is such a mysterious little sacket," replied Cathro, testily, "and so clever at leading you into a hole, that it's not chancey to meddle with him, and I could see through the corner of my eye that for all this woeful face he was proud of it and hoped I was taking note. For though sometimes his emotion masters him completely, at other times he can step aside, as it were, and take an approving look at it. That is a characteristic of him, and not the least maddening one."

"But you solved the mystery somehow, I suppose?"

"I got at the truth to-day by an accident, or rather my wife discovered it for me. She happened to call in at the school on a domestic matter I need not trouble you with (sal, she

needna have troubled me with it either !), and on
her way up the yard she noticed a laddie called
Lewis Doig playing with other ungodly youths
at the game of kickbonnety. Lewis's father, a
gentleman farmer, was buried jimply a fortnight
since, and such want of respect for his memory
made my wife give the loon a dunt on the head
with a pound of sugar, which she had just
bought at the 'Sosh. He turned on her ready
to scart or spit or run, as seemed wisest, and in
a klink her woman's eye saw what mine had
overlooked, that he was not even wearing a
black jacket. Well, she told him what the slap
was for, and his little countenance cleared at
once. 'Oh,' says he, 'that's all right, Tommy
and me has arranged it,' and he pointed blithely
to a corner of the yard where Tommy was hunk-
ering by himself in Lewis's jacket, and wiping
his mournful eyes with Lewis's hanky. I daresay
you can jalouse the rest, but I kept Lewis
behind after the school skailed and got a full
confession out of him. He had tried hard, he
gave me to understand, to mourn fittingly for
his father, but the kickbonnety season being on,
it was uphill work, and he was relieved when
Tommy volunteered to take it off his hands.
Tommy's offer was to swop jackets every morning for a week or two, and thus properly attired
to do the mourning for him."

The dominie paused, and regarded his guest
quizzically. "Sir," he said at length, "laddies
are a queer growth; I assure you, there was no
persuading Lewis that it was not a right and
honourable compact."

"And what payment," asked McLean, laughing, "did Tommy demand from Lewis for this service?"

"Not a farthing, sir—which gives another uncanny glint into his character. When he wants money, there's none so crafty at getting it, but he did this for the pleasure of the thing, or, as he said to Lewis, 'to feel what it would be like.' That, I tell you, is the nature of the sacket; he has a devouring desire to try on other folk's feelings, as if they were so many suits of clothes."

"And from your account he makes them fit him too."

"My certie, he does, and a lippie in the bonnet more than that."

So far the schoolmaster had spoken frankly, even with an occasional grin at his own expense, but his words came reluctantly when he had to speak of Tommy's prospects at the bursary examinations. "I would rather say nothing on that head," he said, almost coaxingly, "for the laddie has a year to reform in yet, and it's never safe to prophesy."

"Still, I should have thought that you could guess pretty accurately how the boys you mean to send up in a year's time are likely to do? You have had a long experience, and, I am told, a glorious one."

"'Deed, there's no denying it," answered the dominie, with a pride he had won the right to wear. "If all the ministers, for instance, I have turned out in this bit school were to come back together, they could hold the General Assembly in the square."

He lay back in his big chair, a complacent dominie again. " Guess the chances of my laddies ! " he cried, forgetting what he had just said, and that there was a Tommy to bother him. " I tell you, sir, that's a matter on which I'm never deceived. I can tell the results so accurately that a wise Senatus would give my lot the bursaries I say they'll carry, without setting them down to examination-papers at all." And for the next half-hour he was reciting cases in proof of his sagacity.

" Wonderful ! " chimed in McLean. " I see it is evident you can tell me how Tommy Sandys will do ; " but at that, Cathro's rush of words again subsided into a dribble.

" He's the worst Latinist that ever had the impudence to think of bursaries," he groaned.

" And his Greek ? " asked McLean, helping on the conversation as far as possible.

" His Greek, sir, could be packed in a pill-box."

" That does not sound promising. But the best mathematicians are sometimes the worst linguists."

" His Greek is better than his mathematics," said Cathro, and he fell into lamentation. " I have had no luck lately," he sighed. " The laddies I have to prepare for college are second-raters, and the vexing thing is, that when a real scholar is reared in Thrums, instead of his being handed over to me for the finishing, they send him to Mr. Ogilvy in Glenquharity. Did Miss Ailie ever mention Gavin Dishart to you—the minister's son ? I just craved to get the teaching of that laddie; he was the kind you can cram with learning till there's no room left for another spoonful, and they bude send him to Mr. Ogilvy, and you'll see he'll stand high above my loons in the bursary list. And then Ogilvy will put on sic airs that there will be no enduring him. Ogilvy and I, sir, we are engaged in an everlasting duel; when we send students to the examinations, it is we two who are the real competitors. But what chance have I, when he is represented by a Gavin Dishart and my man is Tommy Sandys?"

McLean was greatly disappointed. "Why send Tommy up at all if he is so backward?" he said. "You are sure you have not exaggerated his deficiencies?"

"Well, not much at any rate. But he baffles me; one day I think him a perfect numskull, and the next he makes such a show of the small drop of scholarship he has that I'm not sure but what he may be a genius."

"That sounds better. Does he study hard?"

"Study! He is the most careless whelp that ever——"

"But if I were to give him an inducement to study?"

"Such as?" asked Cathro, who could at times be as inquisitive as the doctor.

"We need not go into that. But suppose it appealed to him?"

Cathro considered. "To be candid," he said, "I don't think he could study, in the big meaning of the word. I daresay I'm wrong, but I have a feeling that whatever knowledge

W

that boy acquires he will dig out of himself.
There is something inside him, or so I think at
times, that is his master, and rebels against
book-learning. No, I can't tell what it is;
when we know that, we shall know the real
Tommy."

"And yet," said McLean, curiously, "you
advise his being allowed to compete for a
bursary. That, if you will excuse my saying
so, sounds foolish to me."

"It can't seem so foolish to you," replied
Cathro, scratching his head, "as it seems to me
six days in seven."

"And you know that Aaron Latta has
sworn to send him to the herding if he does
not carry a bursary. Surely the wisest course
would be to apprentice him now to some
trade——"

"What trade would not be the worse ot
him? He would cut off his fingers with a
joiner's saw, and smash them with a mason's
mell; put him in a brot behind a counter, and
in some grand, magnanimous mood he would
sell off his master's things for nothing; make
a clerk of him, and he would only ravel the
figures; send him to the soldiering, and he
would have a sudden impulse to fight on the
wrong side. No, no, Miss Ailie says he has
a gift for the ministry, and we must cling to
that."

In thus sheltering himself behind Miss
Ailie, where he had never skulked before, the
dominie showed how weak he thought his
position, and he added, with a brazen laugh,

"Then if he does distinguish himself at the examinations I can take the credit for it, and if he comes back in disgrace I shall call you to witness that I only sent him to them at her instigation."

"All which," maintained McLean, as he put on his topcoat, "means that somehow, against your better judgment, you think he may distinguish himself after all."

"You've found me out," answered Cathro, half relieved, half sorry. "I had no intention of telling you so much, but as you have found me out I'll make a clean breast of it. Unless something unexpected happens to the laddie— unless he take to playing at scholarship as if it were a Jacobite rebellion, for instance—he shouldna have the ghost of a chance of a bursary; and if he were any other boy as ill-prepared I should be ashamed to send him up, but he is Tommy Sandys, you see, and—it is a terrible thing to say, but it's Gospel truth, it's Gospel truth—I'm trusting to the possibility of his diddling the examiners!"

It was a startling confession for a conscientious dominie, and Cathro flung out his hands as if to withdraw the words, but his visitor would have no tampering with them. "So that sums up Tommy, so far as you know him," he said, as he bade his host good-night. "It does," Cathro admitted grimly; "but if what you wanted was a written certificate of character, I should like to add this, that never did any boy sit on my forms whom I had such a pleasure in thrashing."

w 2

CHAPTER XXX.

END OF THE JACOBITE RISING.

In the small hours of the following night the pulse of Thrums stopped for a moment, and then went on again, but the only watcher remained silent, and the people rose in the morning without knowing that they had lost one of their number while they slept. In the same ignorance they toiled through a long day.

It was a close October day in the end of a summer that had lingered to give the country-side nothing better than a second crop of haws. Beneath the beeches leaves lay in yellow heaps like sliced turnip, and over all the strath was a pink haze; the fields were singed brown except where a recent ploughing gave them a mourning border. From early morn men, women and children (Tommy among them) were in the fields taking up their potatoes, half-a-dozen gatherers at first to every drill, and by noon it seemed a dozen, though the new-comers were but stout sacks, now able to stand alone. By-and-by heavy-laden carts were trailing into Thrums, dog-tired toilers hanging on behind, not to be dragged, but for an incentive to keep them trudging, boys and girls falling asleep on top of the load, and so neglecting to enjoy the ride which was their recompense for lifting. A growing mist mixed with the daylight, and still there

were a few people out, falling over their feet
with fatigue; it took silent possession, and then
the shadowy forms left in the fields were motionless and would remain there until carted to
garrets and kitchen corners and other winter
quarters on Monday morning. There were few
gad-abouts that Saturday night. Washings
were not brought in, though Mr. Dishart had
preached against the unseemly sight of linen
hanging on the line on the Sabbath-day. Innes,
stravaiging the square and wynds in his apple-
cart, jingled his weights in vain, unable to shake
even moneyed children off their stools; and when
at last he told his beast to go home, they took
with them all the stir of the town. Family
exercise came on early in many houses, and as
the gude wife handed her man the Bible she
said entreatingly, "A short ane." After that
one might have said that no earthly knock could
bring them to their doors, yet within an hour
the town was in a ferment.

When Tommy and Elspeth reached the Den
the mist lay so thick that they had to feel their
way through it to the *Ailie*, where they found
Gavinia alone and scared. "Was you peeping
in, trying to fleg me twa three minutes syne?"
she asked eagerly, and when they shook their
heads, she looked cold with fear. "As sure as
death," she said, "there was some living thing
standing there; I couldna see it for the rime,
but I heard it breathing hard."

Tommy felt Elspeth's hand begin to tremble,
and he said "McLean!" hastily, though he
knew that McLean had not yet left the Quharity

Arms.　Next moment Corp arrived with another story as unnerving.

"Has Grizel no come yet?" he asked in a troubled voice. "Tommy, hearken to this, a light has been burning in Double Dykes and the door swinging open a' day! I saw it mysel', and so did Willum Dods."

"Did you go close?"

"Na faags! Willum was hol'ing and I was lifting, so we hadna time in the daylight, and wha would venture near the Painted Lady's house on sic a night?"

Even Tommy felt uneasy, but when Gavinia cried, "There's something uncanny in being out the night; tell us what was in Mr. McLean's bottle, Tommy, and syne we'll run hame," he became Commander Sandys again, and replied blankly, "What bottle?"

"The ane I warned you he was to fling into the water; dinna dare tell me you hinna got it."

"I know not what thou art speaking about," said Tommy; "but it's a queer thing, it's a queer thing, Gavinia"—here he fixed her with his terrifying eye—"that I happen to have found a—another bottle," and still glaring at her he explained that he had found this bottle floating on the horizon. It contained a letter to him, which he now read aloud. It was signed "The Villain Stroke, his mark," and announced that the writer, "tired of this relentless persecution," had determined to reform rather than be killed. "Meet me at the Cuttle Well, on Saturday, when the eight-o'clock bell is ringing," he wrote, "and I shall there make you an offer for my freedom."

The crew received this communication with shouts, Gavinia's cry of "Five shillings, if no ten!" expressing the general sentiment, but it would not have been like Tommy to think with them. "You poor things," he said, "you just believe everything you're telled! How do I know that this is not a trick of Stroke's to bring me here when he is some other gait working mischief?"

Corp was impressed, but Gavinia said short-sightedly, "There's no sign o't."

"There's ower much sign o't," retorted Tommy. "What's this story about Double Dykes? And how do we ken that there hasna been foul work there, and this man at the bottom o't? I tell you, before the world's half an hour older I'll find out," and he looked significantly at Corp, who answered, quaking, "I winna gang by mysel', no, Tommy, I winna!"

So Tommy had to accompany him, saying valiantly, "I'm no feared, and this rime is fine for hodding in," to which Corp replied as firmly, "Neither am I, and we can aye keep touching cauld iron." Before they were half-way down the Double Dykes they got a thrill, for they realised simultaneously that they were being followed. They stopped and gripped each other hard, but now they could hear nothing.

"The Painted Lady!" Corp whispered.

"Stroke!" Tommy replied as cautiously. He was excited rather than afraid, and had the pluck to cry, "Wha's that? I see you!" but no answer came back through the mist, and now the boys had a double reason for pressing forward.

"Can you see the house, Corp?"

"It should be here about, but it's smored in rime."

"I'm touching the paling. I ken the road to the window now."

"Hark! What's that?"

It sounded like devil's music in front of them, and they fell back until Corp remembered, "It maun be the door swinging open, and squealing and moaning on its hinges. Tommy, I take ill wi' that. What can it mean?"

"I'm here to find out." They reached the window where Tommy had watched once before, and looking in together saw the room plainly by the light of a lamp which stood on the spinet. There was no one inside, but otherwise Tommy noticed little change. The fire was out, having evidently burned itself done, the bedclothes were in some disorder. To avoid the creaking door, the boys passed round the back of the house to the window of the other room. This room was without a light, but its door stood open and sufficient light came from the kitchen to show that it also was untenanted. It seemed to have been used as a lumber room.

The boys turned to go, passing near the front of the empty house, where they shivered and stopped, mastered by a feeling they could not have explained. The helpless door, like the staring eyes of a dead person, seemed to be calling to them to shut it, and Tommy was about to steal forward for this purpose when Corp gripped him and whispered that the light had gone out. It was true, though Tommy

disbelieved until they had returned to the east
window to make sure.

"There maun be folk in the hoose, Tommy!"

"You saw it was toom. The lamp had gone
out itself, or else—what's that?"

It was the unmistakable closing of a door,
softly but firmly. "The wind has blown it to,"
they tried to persuade themselves, though aware
that there was not sufficient wind for this. After
a long period of stillness they gathered courage
to go to the door and shake it. It was not only
shut, but locked.

On their way back through the Double
Dykes they were silent, listening painfully, but
hearing nothing. But when they reached the
Coffin Brig, Tommy said, "Dinna say nothing
about this to Elspeth, it would terrify her;" he
was always so thoughtful for Elspeth.

"But what do you think o't a'?" Corp said,
imploringly.

"I winna tell you yet," replied Tommy,
cautiously.

When they boarded the *Ailie*, where the two
girls were very glad to see them again, the eight-
o'clock bell had begun to ring, and thus Tommy
had a reasonable excuse for hurrying his crew to
the Cuttle Well without saying anything of his
expedition to Double Dykes, save that he had
not seen Grizel. At the Well they had not
long to wait before Mr. McLean suddenly appeared out of the mist, and to their astonishment
Miss Ailie was leaning on his arm. She was
blushing and smiling too, in a way pretty to see,
though it spoilt the effect of Stroke's statement.

The first thing Stroke did was to give up his sword to Tommy, and to apologise for its being an umbrella on account of the unsettled state of the weather, and then Corp led three cheers, the captain alone declining to join in, for he had an uneasy feeling that he was being ridiculed.

"But I thought there were five of you," Mr. McLean said; "where is the fifth?"

"You ken best," replied Tommy, sulkily, and sulky he remained throughout the scene, because he knew he was not the chief figure in it. Having this knowledge to depress him, it is to his credit that he bore himself with dignity throughout, keeping his crew so well in hand that they dared not give expression to their natural emotions.

"As you are aware, Mr. Sandys," McLean began solemnly, "I have come here to sue for pardon. It is not yours to give you reply, the Queen alone can pardon, and I grant it; but, sir, is it not well known to all of us that you can get anything out of her you like?"

Tommy's eyes roved suspiciously, but the suppliant proceeded in the same tone. "What are my offences? The first is that I have been bearing arms (unwittingly) against the Throne; the second that I have brought trouble to the lady by my side, who has the proud privilege of calling you her friend. But, Sandys, such amends as can come from an erring man I now offer to make most contritely. Intercede with Her Majesty on my behalf, and on my part I promise to war against her no more. I am willing to settle down in the neighbouring town as a law-abiding citizen, whom you can watch with eagle eye. Say, what more wouldst thou of the unhappy Stuart?"

But Tommy would say nothing; he only looked doubtfully at Miss Ailie, and that set McLean off again. "You ask what reparation I shall make to this lady. Sandys, I tell thee that here also thou hast proved too strong for me. In the hope that she would plead for me with you, I have been driven to offer her my hand in marriage, and she is willing to take me if thou grantest thy consent."

At this Gavinia jumped with joy, and then cried, "Up wi' her!" words whose bearing the schoolmistress fortunately did not understand. All save Tommy looked at Miss Ailie, and she put her arm on Mr. McLean's, and—yes, it was obvious, Miss Ailie was a lover at the Cuttle Well at last, like so many others. She had often said that the Den parade was vulgar, but she never said it again.

It was unexpected news to Tommy, but that was not what lowered his head in humiliation now. In the general rejoicing he had been nigh forgotten, even Elspeth was hanging in Miss Ailie's skirts, Gavinia had eyes for none but lovers, Corp was rapturously examining five half-crowns that had been dropped into his hands for distribution. Had Tommy given an order now, who would have obeyed it? His power was gone, his crew would not listen to another word against Mr. McLean.

"Tommy thought Mr. McLean hated you!" said Elspeth to Miss Ailie.

"It was queer you made sic a mistake!"
said Corp to Tommy.

"Oh, the tattie-doolie!" cried Gavinia.

So they knew that Mr. McLean had only
been speaking sarcastically; of a sudden they
saw through and despised their captain. Tears
of mortification rose in Tommy's eyes, and kind-
hearted Miss Ailie saw them, and she thought it
was her lover's irony that made him smart. She
had said little hitherto, but now she put her
hand on his shoulder, and told them all that she
did indeed owe the supreme joy that had come
to her to him. "No, Gavinia," she said,
blushing, "I will not give you the particulars,
but I assure you that had it not been for
Tommy, Mr. McLean would never have asked
me to marry him."

Elspeth crossed proudly to the side of her
noble brother (who could scarcely trust his ears),
and Gavinia cried in wonder, "What did he
do?"

Now McLean had seen Tommy's tears
also, and being a kindly man he dropped the
satirist and chimed in warmly, "And if I had
not asked Miss Ailie to marry me I should have
lost the great happiness of my life, so you may
all imagine how beholden I feel to Tommy."

Again Tommy was the centre-piece, and
though these words were as puzzling to him as
to his crew, their sincerity was unmistakable,
and once more his head began to waggle complacently.

"And to show how grateful we are," said
Miss Ailie, "we are to give him a—a sort of

marriage present. We are to double the value of
the bursary he wins at the university——" She
could get no further, for now Elspeth was
hugging her, and Corp cheering frantically, and
Mr. McLean thought it necessary to add the
warning, " If he does carry a bursary, you
understand; for, should he fail, I give him
nothing."

" Him fail ! " exclaimed Corp, with whom
Miss Ailie of course agreed. " And he can
spend the money in whatever way he chooses,"
she said. " What will you do with it, Tommy?"

The lucky boy answered instantly, " I'll take
Elspeth to Aberdeen to bide with me," and then
Elspeth hugged him, and Miss Ailie said in a
delighted aside to Mr. McLean, " I told you
so," and he, too, was well pleased.

" It was the one thing needed to make him
work," the schoolmistress whispered. " Is not
his love for his sister beautiful ? "

McLean admitted that it was, but half-
banteringly he said to Elspeth : " What could
you do in lodgings, you excited mite ? "

" I can sit and look at Tommy," she
answered quickly.

" But he will be away for hours at his
classes."

" I'll sit at the window waiting for him,"
said she.

" And I'll run back quick," said Tommy.

All this time another problem had been
bewildering Gavinia, and now she broke in
eagerly : " But what was it he did ? I thought
he was agin Mr. McLean."

"And so did I," said Corp.

"I cheated you grandly," replied Tommy with the audacity he found so useful.

"And a' the time you was pretending to be agin him," screamed Gavinia, "was you—was you bringing this about on the sly?"

Tommy looked up into Mr. McLean's face, but could get no guidance from it, so he said nothing: he only held his head higher than ever. "Oh, the clever little curse!" cried Corp, and Elspeth's delight was as ecstatic, though differently worded. Yet Gavinia stuck to her problem, "How did you do it, what was it you did?" and the cruel McLean said: "You may tell her, Tommy; you have my permission."

It would have been an awkward position for most boys, and even Tommy—but next moment he said quite coolly: "I think you and me and Miss Ailie should keep it to oursels, Gavinia's sic a gossip."

"Oh, how thoughtful of him!" cried Miss Ailie the deceived, and McLean said: "How very thoughtful!" but now he saw in a flash why Mr. Cathro still had hopes that Tommy might carry a bursary.

Thus was the repentant McLean pardoned, and nothing remained for him to do save to show the crew his Lair, which they had sworn to destroy. He had behaved so splendidly that they had forgotten almost that they were the emissaries of justice; but not to destroy the Lair seemed a pity, it would be such a striking way of bringing their adventures in the Den to a close. The degenerate Stuart read this feeling in their faces, and he was ready, he said, to show them his Lair if they would first point it out to him; but here was a difficulty, for how could they do that? For a moment it seemed as if the negotiations must fall through; but Sandys, that captain of resource, invited McLean to step aside for a private conference, and when they rejoined the others McLean said gravely that he now remembered where the Lair was and would guide them to it.

They had only to cross a plank, invisible in the mist until they were close to it, and climb a slippery bank strewn with fallen trees. McLean, with a mock serious air, led the way, Miss Ailie on his arm. Corp and Gavinia followed, weighted and hampered by their new half-crowns, and Tommy and Elspeth in the rear whispered joyously of the coming life. And so, very unprepared for it, they moved toward the tragedy of the night.

CHAPTER XXXI.

A LETTER TO GOD.

"Do you keep a light burning in the Lair?" McLean turned to ask, forgetting for the moment that it was not their domicile, but his.

"No, there's no light," replied Corp, equally forgetful; but even as he spoke he stopped, so suddenly that Elspeth struck against him. For he had seen a light. "This is queer!" he cried, and both he and Gavinia fell back in consternation. McLean pushed forward alone, and was back in a trice, with a new expression on his face. "Are you playing some trick on me?" he demanded suspiciously of Tommy. "There is someone there; I almost ran against a pair of blazing eyes."

"But there's nobody; there can be nobody there," answered Tommy in a bewilderment that was obviously unfeigned, "unless—unless——" He looked at Corp, and the eyes of both finished the sentence. The desolate scene at Double Dykes, which the meeting with McLean and Miss Ailie had driven from their minds, again confronted them, and they seemed once more to hear the whimpering of the Painted Lady's door.

"Unless what?" asked the man impatiently. But still the two boys only stared at each other. "The Den's no mous the night," said Corp at

last in a low voice, and his unspoken fears spread
to the womankind, so that Miss Ailie shuddered
and Elspeth gripped Tommy with both hands
and Gavinia whispered, "Let's awa' hame, we
can come back in the daylight."

But McLean chafed and pressed upward, and
next moment a girl's voice was heard crying:
"It is no business of yours; I won't let you
touch her."

"Grizel!" exclaimed Tommy and his crew
simultaneously, and they had no more fear until
they were inside the Lair. What they saw had
best be described very briefly. A fire was burning
in a corner of the Lair, and in front of it, partly
covered with a sheet, lay the Painted Lady dead.
Grizel stood beside the body guarding it, her
hands clenched, her eyes very strange. "You
sha'n't touch her!" she cried passionately, and
repeated it many times, as if she had lost the
power to leave off, but Corp crept past her and
raised the coverlet.

"She's straikit!" he shouted. "Did you do
it yoursel', Grizel? God behears, she did it
hersel'!"

A very long silence it seemed to be after
that.

Miss Ailie would have taken the motherless
girl to her arms, but first, at Corp's discovery,
she had drawn back in uncontrollable repulsion,
and Grizel, about to go to her, saw it, and turned
from her to Tommy. Her eyes rested on him
beseechingly, with a look he saw only once again
in them until she was a woman; but his first
thought was not for Grizel. Elspeth was clinging

x

to him, terrified and sobbing, and he cried to her, "Shut your een," and then led her tenderly away. He was always good to Elspeth.

There was no lack of sympathy with Grizel when the news spread through the town, and unshod men with their gallowses hanging down and women buttoning as they ran, hurried to the Den. But to all the questions put to her and to all the kindly offers made, as the body was carried to Double Dykes, she only rocked her arms, crying, "I don't want anything to eat. I shall stay all night beside her. I am not frightened at my mamma. I won't tell you why she was in the Den. I am not sure how long she has been dead. Oh, what do these little things matter?"

The great thing was that her mamma should be buried in the cemetery, and not in unconsecrated ground with a stake through her as the boys had predicted; and it was only after she was promised this, that Grizel told her little tale. She had feared for a long time that her mamma was dying of consumption, but she told no one, because everybody was against her and her mamma. Her mamma never knew that she was dying, and sometimes she used to get so much better that Grizel hoped she would live a long time, but that hope never lasted long. The reason she sat so much with Ballingall was just to find out what doctors did to dying people to make them live a little longer, and she watched his straiking to be able to do it to her mamma when the time came. She was sure none of the women would consent to straik her mamma. On the previous night, she could not say at what hour, she had been awakened by a cold wind, and so she knew that the door was open. She put out her hand in the darkness and found that her mamma was not beside her. It had happened before, and she was not frightened. She had hidden the key of the door that night and nailed down the window, but her mamma had found the key. Grizel rose, lit the lamp, and having dressed hurriedly, set off with wraps to the Den. Her mamma was generally as sensible as anybody in Thrums, but sometimes she had shaking fits, and after them she thought it was the time of long ago. Then she went to the Den to meet a man who had promised, she said, to be there, but he never came, and before daybreak Grizel could usually induce her to return home. Latterly she had persuaded her mamma to wait for him in the old Lair, because it was less cold there, and she had got her to do this last night. Her mamma did not seem very unwell, but she fell asleep, and she died sleeping, and then Grizel went back to Double Dykes for linen and straiked her.

Some say in Thrums that a spade was found in the Lair, but that is only the growth of later years. Grizel had done all she could do, and through the long Saturday she sat by the side of the body, helpless and unable to cry. She knew that it could not remain there much longer, but every time she rose to go and confess, fear of the indignities to which the body of her darling mamma might be subjected pulled her back.

The boys had spoken idly; but hunted Grizel, who knew so much less and so much more than any of them, believed it all.

It was she who had stood so near Gavinia in the ruined house. She had only gone there to listen to human voices. When she discovered from the talk of her friends that she had left a light burning at Double Dykes and the door open, fear of the suspicions this might give rise to had sent her to the house on the heels of the two boys, and it was she who had stolen past them in the mist to put out the light and lock the door. Then she had returned to her mamma's side.

The doctor was among the listeners, almost the only dry-eyed one, but he was not dry-eyed because he felt the artless story least. Again and again he rose from his chair restlessly, and Grizel thought he scowled at her when he was really scowling at himself; as soon as she had finished he cleared the room brusquely of all intruders, and then he turned on her passionately.

"Think shame of yoursel'," he thundered, "for keeping me in the dark," and of course she took his words literally, though their full meaning was, "I shall scorn myself from this hour for not having won the poor child's confidence."

Oh, he was a hard man, Grizel thought, the hardest of them all. But she was used to standing up to hard men, and she answered defiantly: "I did mean to tell you; that day you sent me with the bottle to Ballingall, I was waiting at the surgery door to tell you, but you were cruel,

you said I was a thief, and then how could I
tell you?"

This, too, struck home, and the doctor
winced, but what he said was, "You fooled me
for a whole week, and the town knows it; do
you think I can forgive you for that?"

"I don't care whether you forgive me,"
replied Grizel at once.

"Nor do I care whether you care," he rapped
out, all the time wishing he could strike himself; "but I'm the doctor of this place, and
when your mother was ill you should have
come straight to me. What had I done that
you should be afraid of me?"

"I am not afraid of you," she replied, "I am
not afraid of anyone, but mamma was afraid of
you because she knew you had said cruel things
about her, and I thought—I won't tell you what
I thought." But with a little pressing she
changed her mind and told him. "I was not
sure whether you would come to see her, though
I asked you; and if you came, I knew you would
tell her she was dying, and that would have
made her scream. And that is not all. I
thought you might tell her that she would be
buried with a stake through her——"

"Oh, these blackguard laddies!" cried
McQueen, clenching his fists.

"And so I dared not tell you," Grizel concluded calmly; "I am not frightened at you,
but I was frightened you would hurt my dear
darling mamma," and she went and stood
defiantly between him and her mother.

The doctor moved up and down the room,

crying : " How did I not know of this, why was
I not told ? " and he knew that the fault had
been his own, and so was furious when Grizel
told him so.

" Yes, it is," she insisted, " you knew mamma
was an unhappy lady, and that the people
shouted things against her and terrified her ; and
you must have known, for everybody knew, that
she was sometimes silly and wandered about all
night, and you are a big strong man, and so you
should have been sorry for her ; and if you had
been sorry, you would have come to see her and
been kind to her, and then you would have found
it all out."

" Have done, lassie ! " he said, half angrily,
half beseechingly ; but she did not understand
that he was suffering, and she went on relent-
lessly : " And you knew that bad men used to
come to see her at night—they have not come
for a long time—but you never tried to stop
their coming, and I could have stopped it if I
had known they were bad ; but I did not know
at first, and I was only a little girl, and you
should have told me."

" Have done ! " It was all that he could
say, for, like many, he had heard of men visiting
the Painted Lady by stealth, and he had only
wondered, with other gossips, who they were.

He crossed again to the side of the dead
woman. " And Ballingall's was the only corpse
you ever saw straiked ? " he said in wonder, she
had done her work so well. But he was not doubting her ; he knew already that this girl was
clothed in truthfulness.

" Was it you that kept this house so clean ? "
he asked almost irritably, for he himself was the
one undusted, neglected-looking thing in it, and
he was suddenly conscious of his frayed wrist-
band and of buttons hanging by a thread.

" Yes."

" What age are you ? "

" I think I am thirteen."

He looked long at her, vindictively she
thought, but he was only picturing the probable
future of a painted lady's child, and he said
mournfully to himself, " Ay, it does not even
end here; and that's the crowning pity of it."
But Grizel only heard him say, " Poor thing! "
and she bridled immediately.

" I won't let you pity me," she cried.

" You dour brat ! " he retorted. " But you
need not think you are to have everything your
own way still. I must get some Monypenny
woman to take you till the funeral is over, and
after that——"

" I won't go," said Grizel, determinedly; " I
shall stay with mamma till she is buried."

He was not accustomed to contradiction, and
he stamped his foot. " You shall do as you are
told," he said.

" I won't ! " replied Grizel, and she also
stamped her foot.

" Very well, then, you thrawn tid ; but at
any rate I'll send in a woman to sleep with
you."

" I want no one. Do you think I am
afraid ? "

" I think you will be afraid when you wake

up in the darkness and find yourself alone with
—with it."

"I sha'n't; I shall remember at once that she
is to be buried nicely in the cemetery, and that
will make me happy."

"You unnatural——"

"Besides, I sha'n't sleep; I have something
to do."

His curiosity again got the better of the
doctor. "What can you have to do at such a
time?" he demanded, and her reply surprised
him, "I am to make a dress."

"You!"

"I have made them before now," she said
indignantly.

"But at such a time!"

"It is a black dress," she cried; "I don't
have one. I am to make it out of mamma's."

He said nothing for some time, then "When
did you think of this?"

"I thought of it weeks ago, I bought crape
at the corner shop to be ready and——"

She thought he was looking at her in horror,
and stopped abruptly. "I don't care what you
think," she said.

"What I do think," he retorted, taking up
his hat, "is, that you are a most exasperating
lassie. If I bide here another minute, I believe
you'll get round me."

"I don't want to get round you."

"Then what makes you say such things? I
question if I'll get an hour's sleep to-night for
thinking of you."

"I don't want you to think of me!"

He groaned. "What could an untidy, hardened old single man like me do with you in his house?" he said. "Oh, you little limmer, to put such a thought into my head."

"I never did!" she exclaimed indignantly.

"It began, I do believe it began," he sighed, "the first time I saw you easying Ballingall's pillows."

"What began?"

"You brat, you wilful brat, don't pretend ignorance. You set a trap to catch me and——"

"Oh!" cried Grizel, and she opened the door quickly. "Go away, you horrid man," she said.

He liked her the more for this regal action, and therefore it enraged him. Sheer anxiety lest he should succumb to her on the spot was what made him bluster as he strode off, and "That brat of a Grizel," or "The Painted Lady's most unbearable lassie," or "The dour little besom" was his way of referring to her in company for days; but if anyone agreed with him he roared "Don't be a fool, man; she's a wonder, she's a delight," or "You have a dozen yourself, Janet, but I wouldna neifer Grizel for the lot of them." And it was he, still denouncing her so long as he was contradicted, who persuaded the Auld Licht Minister to officiate at the funeral. Then he said to himself, "And now I wash my hands of her; I have done all that can be expected of me." He told himself this a great many times, as if it were a medicine that must be taken frequently; and Grizel heard from Tommy, with whom she had some strange conversations, that he was going about denouncing her "up hill and

down dale." But she did not care, she was so
—so happy.

For a hole was dug for the Painted Lady in
the cemetery, just as if she had been a good
woman, and Mr. Dishart conducted the service in
Double Dykes before the removal of the body,
nor did he say one word that could hurt Grizel,
perhaps because his wife had drawn a promise
from him. A large gathering of men followed
the coffin, three of them because, as you may
remember, Grizel had dared them to stay away,
but all the others out of sympathy with a
motherless child who, as the procession started,
rocked her arms in delight because her mamma
was being buried respectably.

Being a woman, she could not attend the
funeral, and so the chief mourner was Tommy,
as you could see by the position he took at the
grave and by the white bands Grizel had sewn on
his sleeves. He was looking very important, as
if he had something remarkable in prospect; but
little attention was given him until the cords
were dropped into the grave, and a prayer offered
up, when he pulled Mr. Dishart's coat and
muttered something about a paper. Those who
had been making ready to depart swung round
again, and the minister told him if he had anything to say to speak out.

"It's a paper," Tommy said, nervous yet
elated, and addressing all, "that Grizel put in
the coffin. She told me to tell you about it
when the cords fell on the lid."

"What sort of a paper?" asked Mr. Dishart,
frowning.

"It's—it's a letter to God," Tommy gasped.

Nothing was to be heard except the shovelling of earth into the grave. "Hold your spade, John," the minister said to the grave-digger, and then even that sound stopped. "Go on," Mr. Dishart signed to the boy.

"Grizel doesna believe her mother has much chance of getting to heaven," Tommy said, "and she wrote the letter to God, so that when He opens the coffins on the last day He will find it and read about them."

"About whom?" asked the stern minister.

"About Grizel's father, for one. She doesna know his name, but the Painted Lady wore a locket wi' a picture of him on her breast, and it's buried wi' her, and Grizel told God to look at it so as to know him. She thinks her mother will be damned for having her, and that it winna be fair unless God damns her father too."

"Go on," said Mr. Dishart.

"There was three Thrums men—I think they were gentlemen," Tommy continued almost blithely, "that used to visit the Painted Lady in the night-time, afore she took ill. They wanted Grizel to promise no to tell about their going to Double Dykes, and she promised because she was ower innocent to know what they went for— but their names are in the letter."

A movement in the crowd was checked by the minister's uplifted arm. "Go on," he cried.

"She wouldna tell me who they were, because it would have been breaking her promise," said Tommy, "but—" he looked around him inquisitively—"but they're here at the funeral."

The mourners were looking sideways at each other, some breathing hard, but none dared to speak before the minister. He stood for a long time in doubt, but at last he signed to John to proceed with the filling-in of the grave. Contrary to custom, all remained. Not until the grave was again level with the sward did Mr. Dishart speak, and then it was with a gesture that appalled his hearers. "This grave," he said, raising his arm, "is locked till the day of judgment."

Leaving him standing there, a threatening figure, they broke into groups and dispersed, walking slowly at first, and then fast, to tell their wives.

CHAPTER XXXII.

AN ELOPEMENT.

THE solitary child remained at Double Dykes, awaiting the arrival of her father, for the Painted Lady's manner of leaving the world had made such a stir that the neighbours said he must have heard of it, even though he were in London, and if he had the heart of a stone he could not desert his bairn. They argued thus among themselves, less as people who were sure of it than to escape the perplexing question, what to do with Grizel if the man never claimed her? and before her they spoke of his coming as a certainty, because it would be so obviously the best thing for her. In the meantime they overwhelmed her with offers of everything she could need, which was kindly, but not essential, for after the funeral expenses had been paid (Grizel insisted on paying them herself) she had still several gold pieces, found in her mamma's beautiful tortoise-shell purse, and there were nearly twenty pounds in the bank.

But day after day passed, and the man had not come. Perhaps he resented the Painted Lady's ostentatious death; which, if he was nicely strung, must have jarred upon his nerves. He could hardly have acknowledged Grizel now without publicity being given to his private concerns. Or he may never have heard of the

Painted Lady's death; or if he read of it, he may
not have known which painted lady in particular
she was. Or he may have married, and told his
wife all and she had forgiven him, which somehow, according to the plays and the novels, cuts
the past adrift from a man and enables him to
begin again at yesterday. Whatever the reason,
Grizel's father was in no hurry to reveal himself;
and, though not to her, among themselves the
people talked of the probability of his not coming
at all. She could not remain alone at Double
Dykes, they all admitted; but where, then, should
she go? No fine lady in need of a handmaid
seemed to think a painted lady's child would
suit; indeed, Grizel at first sight had not the
manner that attracts philanthropists. Once only
did the problem approach solution ; a woman in
the Denhead was willing to take the child
because (she expressed it) as she had seven she
might as well have eight, but her man said no,
he would not have his bairns fil't. Others would
have taken her cordially for a few weeks or
months, had they not known that at the end of
this time they would be blamed, even by themselves, if they let her go. All, in short, were
eager to show her kindness if one would give her
a home, but where was that one to be found?

Much of this talk came to Grizel through
Tommy, and she told him in the house of Double
Dykes that people need not trouble themselves
about her, for she had no wish to stay with
them. It was only charity they brought her;
no one wanted her for herself. "It is because I
am a child of shame," she told him, dry-eyed,

He fidgeted on his chair, and asked,
"What's that?" not very honestly.

"I don't know," she said, "no one will tell
me, but it is something you can't love."

"You have a terrible wish to be loved," he
said in wonder, and she nodded her head wistfully. "That is not what I wish for most of all,
though," she told him; and when he asked what
she wished for most of all, she said, "To love
somebody—oh, it would be sweet!"

To Tommy, most sympathetic of mortals, she
seemed a very pathetic little figure, and tears
came to his eyes as he surveyed her; he could
always cry very easily. "If it wasna for
Elspeth," he began, stammering, "I could love
you, but you winna let a body do onything on
the sly."

It was a vague offer, but she understood, and
became the old Grizel at once. "I don't want
you to love me," she said indignantly; "I don't
think you know how to love."

"Neither can you know, then," retorted
Tommy, huffily, "for there's nobody for you to
love."

"Yes, there is," she said, "and I do love her
and she loves me."

"But wha is she?"

"That girl." To his amazement she pointed
to her own reflection in the famous mirror the
size of which had scandalised Thrums. Tommy
thought this affection for herself barely respectable, but he dared not say so, lest he should be
put to the door. "I love her ever so much,"
Grizel went on, "and she is so fond of me she

hates to see me unhappy. Don't look so sad,
dearest, darlingest," she cried vehemently; "I
love you, you know, oh, you sweet!" and with
each epithet she kissed her reflection and looked
defiantly at the boy.

"But you canna put your arms round her
and hug her," he pointed out triumphantly, and
so he had the last word after all. Unfortunately
Grizel kept this side of her, new even to Tommy,
hidden from all others, and her unresponsiveness
lost her many possible friends. Even Miss Ailie,
who now had a dressmaker in the blue-and-
white room, sitting on a bedroom chair and
sewing for her life (oh, the agony—or is it the
rapture?—of having to decide whether to marry
in grey with beads or brown plain to the throat),
even sympathetic Miss Ailie, having met with
several rebuffs, said that Grizel had a most
unaffectionate nature, and, "Ay, she's hardy,"
agreed the town, "but it's better, maybe, for
hersel'." There are none so unpopular as the
silent ones.

If only Miss Ailie, or others like her, could
have slipped noiselessly into Double Dykes at
night, they would have found Grizel's pillow
wet. But she would have heard them long
before they reached the door, and jumped to the
floor in terror, thinking it was her father's step
at last. For, unknown to anyone, his coming,
which the town so anxiously desired, was her
one dread. She had told Tommy what she
should say to him if he came, and Tommy had
been awed and delighted, they were such scathing
things; probably, had the necessity arisen, she

would have found courage to say them, but they
were made up in the daytime, and at night they
brought less comfort. Then she listened fearfully
and longed for the morning, wild ideas coursing
through her head of flying before he could seize
her; but when morning came, it brought other
thoughts, as of the strange remarks she had
heard about her mamma and herself during the
past few days. To brood over these was the
most unhealthy occupation she could find, but it
was her only birthright. Many of the remarks
came unguardedly from lips that had no desire
to cause her pain, others fell in a rage because
she would not tell what were the names in her
letter to God. The words that troubled her
most, perhaps, were the doctor's, "She is a brave
lass, but it must be in her blood." They were
not intended for her ears, but she heard.
"What did he mean?" she asked Miss Ailie,
Mrs. Dishart, and others who came to see her,
and they replied with pain that it had only been
a doctor's remark, of no importance to people
who were well. "Then why are you crying?"
she demanded, looking them full in the face with
eyes there was no deceiving.

"Oh, why is everyone afraid to tell me the
truth!" she would cry, beating her palms in
anguish.

She walked into McQueen's surgery and said,
"Could you not cut it out?" so abruptly that
he wondered what she was speaking about.

"The bad thing that is in my blood," she
explained. "Do cut it out; I sha'n't scream. I
promise not to scream."

Y

He sighed and answered, "If it could be cut out, lassie, I would try to do it, though it was the most dangerous of operations."

She looked in anguish at him. "There are cleverer doctors than you, aren't there?" she asked, and he was not offended.

"Ay, a hantle cleverer," he told her, "but none so clever as that. God help you, bairn, if you have to do it yourself some day."

"Can I do it myself?" she cried, brightening. "I shall do it now. Is it done with a knife?"

"With a sharper knife than a surgeon's," he answered, and then regretting he had said so much, he tried to cheer her. But that he could not do. "You are afraid to tell me the truth too," she said, and when she went away he was sorry for her, but not so sorry as she was for herself. "When I am grown up," she announced dolefully to Tommy, "I shall be a bad woman, just like mamma."

"Not if you try to be good," he said.

"Yes, I shall. There is something in my blood that will make me bad, and I so wanted to be good. Oh! oh! oh!"

She told him of the things she had heard people say, but though they perplexed him almost as much as her, he was not so hopeless of learning their meaning, for here was just the kind of difficulty he liked to overcome. "I'll get it out o' Blinder," he said with confidence in his ingenuity, "and then I'll tell you what he says." But however much he might strive to do so, Tommy could never repeat anything without giving it frills and other adornment of his own making, and Grizel knew this. "I must hear what he says myself," she insisted.

"But he winna speak plain afore you."

"Yes, he will, if he does not know I am there."

The plot succeeded, though only partially, for so quick was the blind man's sense of hearing that in the middle of the conversation he said sharply, "Somebody's ahint the dyke!" and he caught Grizel by the shoulder. "It's the Painted Lady's lassie," he said when she screamed, and he stormed against Tommy for taking such advantage of his blindness. But to her he said gently, "I daresay you egged him on to this, meaning well, but you maun forget most of what I've said, especially about being in the blood. I spoke in haste, it doesna apply to the like of you."

"Yes, it does," replied Grizel, and all that had been revealed to her she carried hot to the surgery, Tommy stopping at the door in as great perturbation as herself. "I know what being in the blood is now," she said tragically to McQueen, "there is something about it in the Bible. I am the child of evil passions, and that means that I was born with wickedness in my blood. It is lying sleeping in me just now because I am only thirteen, and if I can prevent its waking when I am grown up I shall always be good, but a very little thing will waken it; it wants so much to be wakened, and if it is once wakened it will run all through me, and soon I shall be like mamma."

It was all horribly clear to her, and she

Y 2

would not wait for words of comfort that could only obscure the truth. Accompanied by Tommy, who said nothing, but often glanced at her, fascinated yet alarmed, as if expecting to see the ghastly change come over her at any moment —for he was as convinced as she, and had the livelier imagination—she returned to Monypenny to beg of Blinder to tell her one thing more. And he told her, not speaking lightly, but because his words contained a solemn warning to a girl who he thought might need it.

"What sort of thing would be likeliest to waken the wickedness?" she asked, holding her breath for the answer.

"Keeping company wi' ill men," said Blinder, gravely.

"Like the man who made mamma wicked, like my father?"

"Ay," Blinder replied; "fly from the like of him, my lass, though it should be to the other end of the world."

She stood quite still, with a most sorrowful face, and then ran away, ran so swiftly that when Tommy, who had lingered for a moment, came to the door she was already out of sight. Scarcely less excited than she, he set off for Double Dykes, his imagination in such a blaze that he looked fearfully in the pools of the burn for a black frock. But Grizel had not drowned herself; she was standing erect in her home, like one at bay, her arms rigid, her hands clenched, and when he pushed open the door she screamed.

"Grizel," said the distressed boy, "did you think I was him come for you?"

"Yes!"

"Maybe he'll no come. The folk think he winna come."

"But if he does, if he does!"

"Maybe you needna go wi' him unless you're willing?"

"I must, he can compel me because he is my father. Oh! oh! oh!" She lay down on the bed, and on her eyes there slowly formed the little wells of water Tommy was to know so well in time. He stood by her side in anguish; for though his own tears came at the first call, he could never face them in others.

"Grizel," he said impulsively, "there's just one thing for you to do. You have money, and you maun run away afore he comes!"

She jumped up at that. "I have thought of it," she answered, "I am always thinking about it, but how can I—oh, how can I? It would not be respectable."

"To run away?"

"To go by myself," said the poor girl, "and I do want to be respectable, it would be sweet."

In some ways Tommy was as innocent as she, and her reasoning seemed to him to be sound. She was looking at him woefully, and entreaty was on her face; all at once he felt what a lonely little crittur she was, and in a burst of manhood—

But, "Dinna prig wi' me to go with you," he said, struggling.

"I have not!" she answered panting; and she had not in words, but the mute appeal was still on her face. "Grizel," he cried, "I'll come!"

Then she seized his hand and pressed it to her breast, saying, "Oh, Tommy, I am so fond of you!"

It was the first time she had admitted it, and his head wagged well content, as if saying for him, "I knew you would understand me some day." But next moment the haunting shadow that so often overtook him in the act of soaring fell cold upon his mind, and "I maun take Elspeth!" he announced, as if Elspeth had him by the leg.

"You sha'n't!" said Grizel's face.

"She winna let go," said Tommy's.

Grizel quivered from top to toe. "I hate Elspeth!" she cried, with curious passion, and the more moral Tommy was ashamed of her. "You dinna ken how fond o' her I am," he said.

"Yes, I do."

"Then you shouldna want me to leave her and go wi' you."

"That is why I want it," Grizel blurted out, and now we are all ashamed of her. But fortunately Tommy did not see how much she had admitted in that hasty cry; and as neither would give way to the other, they parted stiffly, his last words being "Mind, it wouldna be respectable to go by yoursel'," and hers "I don't care, I'm going." Nevertheless it was she who slept easily that night, and he who tossed about almost until cockcrow. She had only one ugly dream, of herself wandering from door to door in a strange town, asking for lodgings, but the

woman who answered her weary knocks—there
were many doors, but invariably the same woman
—always asked suspiciously "Is Tommy with
you?" and Grizel shook her head, and then the
woman drove her away, perceiving that she was
not respectable. This woke her, and she feared
the dream would come true, but she clenched
her fists in the darkness, saying, "I can't help it,
I am going, and I won't have Elspeth," and
after that she slept in peace. In the meantime
Tommy, the imaginative—but that night he was
not Tommy, rather was he Grizel, for he saw her
as we can only see ourselves. Now she—or he,
if you will—had been caught by her father and
brought back, and she turned into a painted
thing like her mother. She brandished a brandy
bottle and a stream of foul words ran lightly
from her mouth, and suddenly stopped, because
she was wailing "I wanted so to be good, it is
sweet to be good!" Now a man with a beard
was whipping her, and Tommy felt each lash on
his own body, so that he had to strike out, and
he started up in bed, and the horrible thing was
that he had never been asleep. Thus it went on
until early morning, when his eyes were red
and his body was damp with sweat.

But now again he was Tommy, and at first
even to think of leaving Elspeth was absurd.
Yet it would be pleasant to leave Aaron, who
disliked him so much. To disappear without a
word would be a fine revenge, for the people
would say that Aaron must have ill-treated him;
and while they searched the pools of the burn
for his body, Aaron would be looking on tremb-

ling, perhaps with a policeman's hand on his shoulder. Tommy saw the commotion as vividly as if the searchers were already out and he in a tree looking down at them; but in a second he also heard Elspeth skirling, and down he flung himself from the tree, crying, "I'm here, Elspeth, dinna greet; oh, what a brute I've been!" No, he could not leave Elspeth. How wicked of Grizel to expect it of him! She was a bad one, Grizel.

But having now decided not to go, his sympathy with the girl who was to lose him returned in a rush, and before he went to school he besought her to—it amounted to this, to be more like himself; that is, he begged her to postpone her departure indefinitely, not to make up her mind until to-morrow—or the day after—or the day after that. He produced reasons, as that she had only four pounds and some shillings now, while by-and-by she might get the Painted Lady's money, at present in the bank; also she ought to wait for the money that would come to her from the roup of the furniture. But Grizel waived all argument aside; secure in her four pounds and shillings she was determined to go to-night, for her father might be here to-morrow; she was going to London because it was so big that no one could ever find her there, and she would never, never write to Tommy to tell him how she fared, lest the letter put her father on her track. He implored her to write once, so that the money owing her might be forwarded, but even this bribe did not move her, and he set off for school most gloomily.

Cathro was specially aggravating that day, nagged him, said before the whole school that he was a numskull, even fell upon him with the tawse, and for no earthly reason except that Tommy would not bother his head with the *oratio obliqua*. If there is any kind of dominie more maddening than another, it is the one who will not leave you alone (ask any thoughtful boy). How wretched the lot of him whose life is cast among fools not capable of understanding him! what was that saying about entertaining angels unawares? London! Grizel had more than sufficient money to take two there, and once in London, a wonder such as himself was bound to do wondrous things. Now that he thought of it, to become a minister was abhorrent to him; to preach would be rather nice; oh, what things he should say (he began to make them up, and they were so grand that he almost wept), but to be good after the sermon was over, always to be good (even when Elspeth was out of the way), never to think queer unsayable things, never to say Stroke, never, in short, to "find a way"—he was appalled. If it had not been for Elspeth——

So even Elspeth did not need him. When he went home from school, thinking only of her, he found that she had gone to the Auld Licht manse to play with little Margaret. Very well, if such was her wish, he would go. Nobody wanted him except Grizel. Perhaps when news came from London of his greatness, they would think more of him. He would send a letter to Thrums, asking Mr. McLean to transfer his kindness to Elspeth. That would show them what a noble fellow he was. Elspeth would really benefit by his disappearance; he was running away for Elspeth's sake. And when he was great, which would be in a few years, he would come back for her.

But no, he——. The dash represents Tommy swithering once more, and he was at one or other end of the swither all day. When he acted sharply it was always on impulse, and as soon as the die was cast he was a philosopher with no regrets. But when he had time to reflect, he jumped miserably back and forward. So when Grizel was ready to start, he did not know in the least what he meant to do.

She was to pass by the Cuttle Well, on her way to Tilliedrum, where she would get the London train, he had been told coldly, and he could be there at the time—if he liked. The time was seven o'clock in the evening on a week-day, when the lovers are not in the Den, and Tommy arrived first. When he stole through the small field that separates Monypenny from the Den, his decision was—but on reaching the Cuttle Well, its nearness to the uncanny Lair chilled his courage, and now he had only come to bid her good-bye. She was very late, and it suddenly struck him that she had already set off. "After getting me to promise to go wi' her!" he said to himself at once.

But Grizel came; she was only late because it had taken her such a long time to say good-bye to the girl in the glass. She was wearing her black dress and lustre jacket, and carried in a bundle the few treasures she was taking with her, and though she did not ask Tommy if he was coming, she cast a quick look round to see if he had a bundle anywhere, and he had none. That told her his decision, and she would have liked to sit down for a minute and cry, but of course she had too much pride, and she bade him farewell so promptly that he thought he had a grievance. " I'm coming as far as the toll-house wi' you," he said sulkily, and so they started together.

At the toll-house Grizel stopped. "It's a fine night," said Tommy almost apologetically, " I'll go as far as the quarry o' Benshee."

When they came to the quarry, he said, " We're no half-roads yet, I'll go wi' you as far as Padanarum." Now she began to wonder and to glance at him sideways, which made him more uncomfortable than ever. To prevent her asking him a question for which he had no answer, he said, " What makes you look so little the day ? "

" I am not looking little," she replied, greatly annoyed, "I am looking taller than usual. I have let down my frock three inches so as to look taller—and older."

" You look younger than ever," he said cruelly.

" I don't! I look fifteen, and when you are fifteen you grow up very quickly. Do say I look older!" she entreated anxiously. " It would make me feel more respectable."

But he shook his head with surprising obstinacy, and then she began to remark on his clothes, which had been exercising her curiosity ever since they left the Den.

"How is it that you are looking so stout?" she asked. "I feel cold, but you are wiping the sweat off your face every minute."

It was true, but he would have preferred not to answer. Grizel's questions, however, were all so straight in the face that there was no dodging them. "I have on twa suits o' clothes, and a' my sarks," he had to admit, sticky and sullen.

She stopped, but he trudged on doggedly. She ran after him and gave his arm an impulsive squeeze with both hands. "Oh, you sweet!" she said.

"No, I'm not," he answered in alarm.

"Yes you are! You are coming with me."

"I'm not!"

"Then why did you put on so many clothes?"

Tommy swithered wretchedly on one foot. "I didna put them on to come wi' you," he explained, "I just put them on in case I should come wi' you."

"And are you not coming?"

"How can I ken?"

"But you must decide!" Grizel almost screamed.

"I needna," he stammered, "till we're at Tilliedrum. Let's speak about some other thing."

She rocked her arms, crying, "It is so easy to make up one's mind."

"It's easy to you that has just one mind," he retorted with spirit, "but if you had as many minds as I have——!"

On they went.

CHAPTER XXXIII.

THERE IS SOMEONE TO LOVE GRIZEL AT LAST.

CORP was sitting on the Monypenny dyke, spitting on a candlestick and then rubbing it briskly against his orange-coloured trousers. The doctor passing in his gig, both of them streaked, till they blended, with the mud of Look-about-you road (through which you should drive winking rapidly all the way), saw him and drew up.

"Well, how is Grizel?" he asked. He had avoided Double Dykes since the funeral, but vain had been his attempts to turn its little inmate out of his mind; there she was, against his will, and there, he now admitted to himself angrily, or with a rueful sigh, she seemed likely to remain until someone gave her a home. It was an almost ludicrous distrust of himself that kept him away from her; he feared that if he went to Double Dykes her lonely face would complete his conquest. For, oh, he was reluctant to be got the better of, as he expressed it to himself. Maggy Ann, his maid, was the ideal woman for a bachelor's house. When she saw him coming she fled, guiltily concealing the hated duster; when he roared at her for announcing that dinner was ready, she left him to eat it half cold; when he spilled matches on the floor and then stepped upon them and set the rug on fire, she let him tell her that she should be more careful;

she did not carry off his favourite boots to the
cobbler because they were down at heel; she did
not fling up her arms in horror and cry that she
had brushed that coat just five minutes ago;
nor did she count the treasured "dottels" on
the mantelpiece to discover how many pipes he
had smoked since morning; nor point out that
he had stepped over the door-mat; nor line her
shelves with the new *Mentor;* nor give him up
his foot for sitting half the night with patients
who could not pay—in short, he knew the ways
of the limmers, and Maggy Ann was a jewel.
But it had taken him a dozen years to bring her
to this perfection, and well he knew that the
curse of Eve, as he called the rage for the duster,
slumbered in her rather than was extinguished.
With the volcanic Grizel in the house, Maggy
Ann would once more burst into flame, and the
horrified doctor looked to right of him, to left of
him, before him and behind him, and everywhere he seemed to see two new brooms bearing
down. No, the brat, he would not have her;
the besom, why did she bother him; the witches
take her, for putting the idea into his head,
nailing it into his head, indeed. But nevertheless he was for ever urging other people to
adopt her, assuring them that they would find
her a treasure, and even shaking his staff at them
when they refused; and he was so uneasy if he
did not hear of her several times a day that he
made Monypenny the way to and from everywhere, so that he might drop into artful talk
with those who had seen her last. Corp,
accordingly, was not surprised at his "How is

Grizel?" now, and he answered, between two
spits, "She's fine; she gave me this."

It was one of the Painted Lady's silver
candlesticks, and the doctor asked sharply why
Grizel had given it to him.

"She said because she liked me," Corp replied, wonderingly. "She brought it to my
auntie's door soon after I loused, and put it into
my hand; ay, and she had a blue shawl, and
she told me to give it to Gavinia, because she
liked her too."

"What else did she say?"

Corp tried to think. "I said, 'This cows,
Grizel, but thank you kindly,'" he answered,
much pleased with his effort of memory, but the
doctor interrupted him rudely. "Nobody wants
to hear what you said, you dotterel; what more
did she say?" And thus encouraged, Corp remembered that she had said she hoped he
would not forget her. "What for should I
forget her when I see her ilka day?" he asked,
and was probably about to divulge that this was
his reply to her, but without waiting for more,
McQueen turned his beast's head and drove to
the entrance to the double dykes. Here he
alighted and hastened up the path on foot, but
before he reached the house he met Dite
Deuchars taking his ease beneath a tree, and
Dite could tell him that Grizel was not at home.
"But there's somebody in Double Dykes," he
said, "though I kenna wha could be there unless
it's the ghost of the Painted Lady hersel."
About an hour syne I saw Grizel come out o' the
house, carrying a bundle, but she hadna gone

many yards when she turned round and waved
her hand to the east window. I couldna see wha
was at it, but there maun have been somebody,
for first the crittur waved to the window and
next she kissed her hand to it, and syne she
went on a bit, and syne she ran back close to the
window and nodded and flung more kisses, and
back and forrit she went a curran times as if
she could hardly tear hersel' awa'. 'Wha's
that you're so chief wi'?' I speired when she
came by me at last, but she just said, 'I won't
tell you,' in her dour wy, and she hasna come
back yet."

Whom could she have been saying good-bye
to so demonstratively, and whither had she
gone? With a curiosity that for the moment
took the place of his uneasiness, McQueen proceeded to the house, the door of which was shut
but not locked. Two glances convinced him
that there was no one here; the kitchen was as
he had seen it last, except that the long mirror
had been placed on a chair close to the east
window. The doctor went to the outside of the
window and looked in; he could see nothing but
his own reflection in the mirror, and was completely puzzled. But it was no time, he felt,
for standing there scratching his head, when
there was reason to fear that the girl had gone.
Gone where? He saw his selfishness now, in
a glaring light, and it fled out of him pursued
by curses.

He stopped at Aaron's door and called for
Tommy, but Tommy had left the house an hour
ago. "Gone with her, the sacket; he very likely

put her up to this," the doctor muttered, and the surmise seemed justified when he heard that Grizel and Tommy had been seen passing the Feus. That they were running away had never struck those who saw them, and McQueen said nothing of his suspicions, but off he went in his gig on their track and ran them down within a mile of Tilliedrum. Grizel scurried on, thinking it was undoubtedly her father, but in a few minutes the three were conversing almost amicably, the doctor's first words had been so "sweet.'

Tommy explained that they were out for a walk, but Grizel could not lie, and in a few passionate sentences she told McQueen the truth. He had guessed the greater part of it, and while she spoke he looked so sorry for her, such a sweet change had come over his manner, that she held his hand.

"But you must go no farther," he told her. "I am to take you back with me," and that alarmed her. "I won't go back," she said determinedly, "he might come."

"There's little fear of his coming," McQueen assured her, gently, "but if he does come I give you my solemn word that I won't let him take you away unless you want to go."

Even then she only wavered, but he got her altogether with this: "And should he come, just think what a piece of your mind you could give him, with me standing by holding your hand."

"Oh, would you do that?" she asked, brightening.

"I would do a good deal to get the chance," he said.

z

"I should just love it!" she cried. "I shall come now," and she stepped light-heartedly into the gig, where the doctor joined her. Tommy, who had been in the background all this time, was about to jump up beside them, but McQueen waved him back, saying maliciously, "There's just room for two, my man, so I won't interfere with your walk."

Tommy, in danger of being left, very hot and stout and sulky, whimpered, "What have I done to anger you?"

"You were going with her, you blackguard," replied McQueen, not yet in full possession of the facts, for whether Tommy was or was not going with her no one can ever know.

"If I was," cried the injured boy, "it wasna because I wanted to go, it was because it wouldna have been respectable for her to go by hersel'."

The doctor had already started his shalt, but at these astonishing words he drew up sharply. "Say that again," he said, as if thinking that his ears must have deceived him, and Tommy repeated his remark, wondering at its effect.

"And you tell me that you were going with her," the doctor repeated, "to make her enterprise more respectable?" and he looked from one to the other.

"Of course I was," replied Tommy, resenting his surprise at a thing so obvious ; and "That's why I wanted him to come," chimed in Grizel.

Still McQueen's glance wandered from the boy to the girl, and from the girl to the boy. "You are a pair!" he said at last, and he signed

in silence to Tommy to mount the gig. But his
manner had alarmed Grizel, ever watching herself lest she should stray into the ways of bad
ones, and she asked anxiously, "There was
nothing wrong in it, was there?"

"No," the doctor answered gravely, laying
his hand on hers, "no, it was just sweet."

What McQueen had to say to her was not
for Tommy's ears, and the conversation was but
a makeshift until they reached Thrums, where
he sent the boy home, recommending him to
hold his tongue about the escapade (and Tommy
of course saw the advisability of keeping it from
Elspeth); but he took Grizel into his parlour
and set her down on the buffet stool by the fire,
where he surveyed her in silence at his leisure.
Then he tried her in his old armchair, then on
his sofa; then he put the *Mentor* into her hand,
and told her to hold it as if it were a duster,
then he sent her into the passage, with instructions to open the door presently and announce
"Dinner is ready"; then he told her to put
some coals on the fire; then he told her to sit
at the window, first with an open book in her
hand, secondly as if she was busy knitting; and
all these things she did wondering exceedingly,
for he gave no explanation except the incom-
prehensible one, "I want to see what it would
be like."

She had told him in the gig why she had
changed the position of the mirror at Double
Dykes; it was to let "that darling" wave good-
bye to her from the window; and now having

z 2

experimented with her in his parlour, he drew her toward his chair, so that she stood between his knees. And he asked her if she understood why he had gone to Double Dykes.

" Was it to get me to tell you what were the names in the letter?" she said wistfully. "That is what everyone asks me, but I won't tell—no, I won't"; and she closed her mouth hard.

He, too, would have liked to hear the names, and he sighed, it must be admitted, at sight of that determined mouth, but he could say truthfully, "Your refusal to break your promise is one of the things that I admire in you."

Admire! Grizel could scarce believe that this gift was for her. "You don't mean that you really like me?" she faltered, but she felt sure all the time that he did, and she cried, "Oh, but why? oh, how can you?"

" For one reason," he said, "because you are so good."

" Good! Oh! oh! oh!" She clapped her hands joyously.

" And, for another—because you are so brave."

" But I am not really brave," she said anxiously, yet resolved to hide nothing; "I only pretend to be brave; I am often frightened, but I just don't let on."

That, he told her, is the highest form of bravery, but Grizel was very, very tired of being brave, and she insisted impetuously, "I don't want to be brave, I want to be afraid, like other girls."

" Ay, it's your right, you little woman," he

answered tenderly; and then again he became
mysterious. He kicked off his shoes to show
her that he was wearing socks that did not
match. "I just pull on the first that come to
hand," he said recklessly.

"Oh!" cried Grizel.

On his dusty book-shelves he wrote, with his
finger, "Not dusted since the year One."

"Oh! oh!" she cried.

He put his fingers through his grey, untidy
hair. "That's the only comb I have that is at
hand when I want it," he went on, regardless of
her agony.

"All the stud-holes in my shirts," he said,
"are now so frayed and large that the studs fall
out, and I find them in my socks at night."

Oh! oh! he was killing her, he was, but
what cared he? "Look at my clothes," said
the cruel man, "I read when I'm eating, and I
spill so much gravy that—that we boil my
waistcoat once a month, and make soup of it!"

To Grizel this was the most tragic picture ever
drawn by man, and he saw that it was time to desist. "And it's all," he said, looking at her sadly,
"it's all because I'm a lonely old bachelor with
no womankind to look after him, no little girl
to brighten him when he comes home dog-tired,
no one to care whether his socks are in holes and
his comb behind the wash-stand, no soft hand to
soothe his brow when it aches, no one to work
for, no one to love, many a one to close the old
bachelor's eyes when he dies, but none to drop a
tear for him, no one to——"

"Oh! oh! oh! That is just like me. Oh!

oh !" cried Grizel, and he pulled her closer to him, saying, "The more reason we should join thegither ; Grizel, if you don't take pity on me, and come and bide with me and be my little housekeeper, the Lord Almighty only knows what is to become of the old doctor."

At this she broke away from him, and stood far back pressing her arms to her sides, and she cried, "It is not out of charity you ask me, is it ?" and then she went a little nearer. "You would not say it if it wasn't true, would you ? "

"No, my dawtie, it's true," he told her, and if he had been pitying himself a little, there was an end of that now.

She remembered something and cried joyously, "And you knew what was in my blood before you asked me, so I don't need to tell you, do I ? And you are not afraid that I shall corrupt you, are you ? And you don't think it a pity I didn't die when I was a tiny baby, do you ? Some people think so—I heard them say it."

"What would have become of me ? " was all he dared answer in words, but he drew her to him again, and when she asked if it was true, as she had heard a woman say, that in some matters men were all alike and did what that one man had done to her mamma, he could reply solemnly, "No, it is not true; it's a lie that has done more harm than any war in any century."

She sat on his knee, telling him many things that had come recently to her knowledge but were not so new to him. The fall of woman was the subject—a strange topic for a girl of

thirteen and a man of sixty. They don't become
wicked in a moment, he learned; if they are
good to begin with, it takes quite a long time to
make them bad. Her mamma was good to
begin with. "I know she was good, because
when she thought she was the girl she used to
be, she looked sweet and said lovely things.
The way the men do is this: they put evil
thoughts into the woman's head, and say them
often to her, till she gets accustomed to them,
and thinks they cannot be bad when the man
she loves likes them, and it is called corrupting
the mind.

"And then a baby comes to them," Grizel
said softly, "and it is called a child of shame.
I am a child of shame."

He made no reply, so she looked up, and his
face was very old and sad. "I am sorry too,"
she whispered, but still he said nothing, and
then she put her fingers on his eyes to discover
if they were wet, and they were wet. And so
Grizel knew that there was someone who loved
her at last.

The mirror was the only article of value that
Grizel took with her to her new home; everything else was rouped at the door of Double
Dykes; Tommy, who should have been at his
books, acting as auctioneer's clerk for sixpence.
There are houses in Thrums where you may still
be told who got the bed and who the rocking-
chair, and how Nether Drumgley's wife dared
him to come home without the spinet; but it is
not by the sales that the roup is best remembered. Curiosity took many persons into Double

Dykes that day, and in the room that had never
been furnished they saw a mournful stack of
empty brandy bottles, piled there by the auctioneer, who had found them in every corner,
beneath the bed, in presses, in boxes, whither
they had been thrust by Grizel's mamma, as if
to conceal their number from herself. The
counting of these bottles was a labour, but it is
not even by them that the roup is remembered.
Among them some sacrilegious hands found a
bundle of papers with a sad blue ribbon round
them. They were the Painted Lady's love-
letters, the letters she had written to the man.
Why or how they had come back to her no
one knew.

Most of them were given to Grizel, but a
dozen or more passed without her leave into the
kists of various people, where often since then
they have been consulted by swains in need of a
pretty phrase; and Tommy's schoolfellows, the
very boys and girls who hooted the Painted
Lady, were in time—so oddly do things turn
out—to be among those whom her letters
taught how to woo. Where the kists did not
let in the damp or careless fingers, the paper
long remained clean, the ink but little faded.
Some of the letters were creased, as if they had
been much folded, perhaps for slipping into
secret hiding-places, but none of them bore any
address or a date. "To my beloved," was
sometimes written on the cover, and inside he
was darling or beloved again. So no one could
have arranged them in the order in which they
were written, though there was a three-cornered

one which said it was the first. There was a
violet in it, clinging to the paper as if they were
fond of each other, and Grizel's mamma had
written, "The violet is me, hiding in a corner
because I am so happy." The letters were in
many moods, playful, reflective, sad, despairing,
arch, but all were written in an ecstasy of the
purest love, and most of them were cheerful, so
that you seemed to see the sun dancing on the
paper while she wrote, the same sun that afterwards showed up her painted cheeks. Why
they came back to her no one ever discovered,
any more than how she who slipped the violet
into that three-cornered one and took it out to
kiss again and wrote, "It is my first love-letter,
and I love it so much I am reluctant to let
it go," became in a few years the derision of the
Double Dykes. Some of these letters may be in
old kists still, but whether that is so or not,
they alone have passed the Painted Lady's
memory from one generation to another, and
they have purified it, so that what she was died
with her vile body, and what she might have
been lived on, as if it were her true self.

CHAPTER XXXIV.

WHO TOLD TOMMY TO SPEAK?

" MISS ALISON CRAY presents her compliments to —— and requests the favour of their company at her marriage with Mr. Ivie McLean, on January 8th, at six o'clock."

Tommy in his Sabbath clothes, with a rose from the Dove Cot hothouse for buttonhole (which he slipped into his pocket when he saw other boys approaching), delivered them at the doors of the aristocracy, where, by the way, he had been a few weeks earlier, with another circular:

" Miss Alison Cray being about to give up school, has pleasure in stating that she has disposed of the goodwill of her establishment to Miss Jessy Langlands and Miss S. Oram, who will enter upon their scholastic duties on January 9th, at Roods Cottage, where she most cordially," and so on.

Here if the writer dared (but you would be so angry) he would introduce at the length of a chapter two brand-new characters, the Misses Langlands and Oram, who suddenly present themselves to him in the most sympathetic light. Miss Ailie has been safely stowed to port, but their little boat is only setting sail, and they are such young ones, neither out of her teens, that he would fain turn for a time

from her to them. Twelve pounds they paid
for the goodwill, and, oh, the exciting discus-
sions, oh, the scraping to get the money
together! If little Miss Langlands had not
been so bold, big Miss Oram must have drawn
back, but if Miss Oram had not had that idea
about a paper partition, of what avail the bold-
ness of Miss Langlands? How these two
trumps of girls succeeded in hiring the Painted
Lady's spinet from Nether Drumgley—in the
absence of his wife, who on her way home from
buying a Cochin-china met the spinet in a cart—
how the mother of one of them, realising in a
klink that she was common no more, henceforth
wore black caps instead of mutches (but the
father dandered on in the old plebeian way);
what the enterprise meant to a young man in
distant Newcastle, whose favourite name was
Jessy; how the news travelled to still more
distant Canada, where a family of emigrants
which had left its Sarah behind in Thrums,
could talk of nothing else for weeks—it is hard
to have to pass on without dwelling on these
things, and indeed—but pass on we must.

The chief figure at the wedding of Miss Ailie
was undoubtedly Mr. T. Sandys. When one
remembers his prominence, it is difficult to think
that the wedding could have taken place without
him. It was he (in his Sabbath clothes again,
and now flaunting his buttonhole brazenly) who
in insulting language ordered the rabble to stand
back there. It was he who dashed out to the
'Sosh to get a hundred ha'pennies for the fifty
pennies Mr. McLean had brought to toss into

the air. It was he who went round in the
carriage to pick up the guests, and whisked them
in and out, and slammed the door, and saw to it
that the minister was not kept waiting, and
warned Miss Ailie that if she did not come now
they should begin without her. It was he who
stood near her with a handkerchief ready in his
hand lest she took to crying on her new brown
silk (Miss Ailie was married in brown silk after
all). As a crown to his audacity, it was he who
told Mr. Dishart, in the middle of a noble
passage, to mind the lamp.

These duties were Dr. McQueen's, the best
man, but either demoralised by the bridegroom,
who went all to pieces at the critical moment
and was much more nervous than the bride, or
in terror lest Grizel, who had sent him to the
wedding speckless and most beautifully starched,
should suddenly appear at the door and cry,
" Oh, oh, take your fingers off your shirt ! " he
was through other till the knot was tied, and
then it was too late, for Tommy had made his
mark. It was Tommy who led the way to the
schoolroom where the feast was ready, it was
Tommy who put the guests in their places (even
the banker cringed to him), it was Tommy who
winked to Mr. Dishart to say grace. As you
will readily believe, Miss Ailie could not endure
the thought of excluding her pupils from the
festivities, and they began to arrive as soon as
the tables had been cleared of all save oranges
and tarts and raisins. Tommy, waving Gavinia
aside, showed them in, and one of them, curious
to tell, was Corp, in borrowed blacks, and

Tommy shook hands with him and called him
Mr. Shiach, both new experiences to Corp, who
knocked over a table in his anxiety to behave
himself, and roared at intervals "Do you see
the little deevil!" and bit his warts and then
politely swallowed the blood.

As if oranges and tarts and raisins were not
enough, came the Punch and Judy show,
Tommy's culminating triumph. All the way
to Redlintie had Mr. McLean sent for the
Punch and Judy show, and nevertheless there
was a probability of no performance, for Miss
Ailie considered the show immoral. Most
anxious was she to give pleasure to her pupils,
and this she knew was the best way, but how
could she countenance an entertainment which
was an encouragement to every form of vice and
crime? To send these children to the Misses
Langlands and Oram, fresh from an introduction
to the comic view of murder! It could not be
done, now could it? Mr. McLean could make
no suggestion. Mr. Dishart thought it would
be advisable to substitute another entertainment; was there not a game called "The
Minister's Cat"? Mrs. Dishart thought they
should have the show and risk the consequences.
So also thought Dr. McQueen. The banker was
consulted, but saw no way out of the difficulty,
nor did the lawyer, nor did the Misses Finlayson. Then Tommy appeared on the scene,
and presently retired to find a way.

He found it. The performance took place,
and none of the fun was omitted, yet neither
Miss Ailie—tuts, tuts, Mrs. McLean—nor Mr.

Dishart could disapprove. Punch did chuck his baby out at the window (roars of laughter) in his jovial, time-honoured way, *but* immediately thereafter up popped the showman to say, "Ah, my dear boys and girls, let this be a lesson to you never to destroy your offsprings. Oh, shame on Punch, for to do the wicked deed; he will be catched in the end, and serve him right." Then when Mr. Punch had wolloped his wife with the stick, amid thunders of applause, up again bobbed the showman: "Ah, my dear boys and girls, what a lesson is this we sees, what goings on is this? He have bashed the head of her as should ha' been the apple of his eye, and he does not care a—he does not care; but mark my words, his home it will now be desolate, no more shall she meet him at his door with kindly smile, he have done for her quite, and now he is a hunted man. Oh, be warned by his sad igsample, and do not bash the head of your loving wife." And there was a great deal more of the same, and simple Mrs. McLean almost wept tears of joy because her favourite's good heart had suggested these improvements.

Grizel was not at the wedding; she was invited, but could not go because she was in mourning. But only her parramatty frock was in mourning, for already she had been the doctor's housekeeper for two full months, and her father had not appeared to plague her (he never did appear, it may be told at once), and so how could her face be woful when her heart leapt with gladness? Never had prisoner pined for the fields more than this reticent girl

to be frank, and she poured out her inmost self
to the doctor, so that daily he discovered something beautiful (and exasperating) about womanhood. And it was his love for her that had
changed her. "You do love me, don't you?"
she would say, and his answer might be, "I have
told you that fifty times already"; to which she
would reply gleefully, "That is not often, I say
it all day to myself."

Exasperating? Yes, that was the word.
Long before summer came, the doctor knew
that he had given himself into the hands of a
tyrant. It was idle his saying that this
irregularity and that carelessness were habits
that had become part of him; she only rocked
her arms impatiently, and if he would not stand
still to be put to rights, then she would follow
him along the street, brushing him as he walked,
a sight that was witnessed several times while he
was in the mutinous stage.

"Talk about masterfulness," he would say,
when she whipped off his coat or made a dart at
the mud on his trousers; "you are the most
masterful little besom I ever clapped eyes on."

But as he said it he perhaps crossed his legs,
and she immediately cried, "You have missed
two holes in lacing your boots!"

Of a morning he would ask her sarcastically
to examine him from top to toe and see if he
would do, and examine him she did, turning him
round, pointing out that he had been sitting
"again" on his tails, that oh, oh, he must have
cut that buttonhole with his knife. He became
most artful in hiding deficiencies from her, but

her suspicions once roused would not sleep, and all subterfuge was vain. "Why have you buttoned your coat up tight to the throat to-day?" she would demand sternly.

"It is such a cold morning," he said.

"That is not the reason," she replied at once (she could see through broadcloth at a glance), "I believe you have on the old necktie again, and you promised to buy a new one."

"I always forget about it when I'm out," he said humbly, and next evening he found on his table a new tie, made by Grizel herself out of her mamma's rokelay.

It was related by one who had dropped in at the doctor's house unexpectedly, that he found Grizel making a new shirt, and forcing the doctor to try on the sleeves while they were still in the pin stage.

She soon knew his every want, and just as he was beginning to want it, there it was at his elbow. He realised what a study she had made of him when he heard her talking of his favourite dishes and his favourite seat, and his way of biting his underlip when in thought, and how hard he was on his left cuff. It had been one of his boasts that he had no favourite dishes, etc., but he saw now that he had been a slave to them for years without knowing it.

She discussed him with other mothers as if he were her little boy, and he denounced her for it. But all the time she was spoiling him. Formerly he had got on very well when nothing was in its place. Now he roared helplessly if he mislaid his razor.

He was determined to make a lady of her, which necessitated her being sent to school; she preferred hemming, baking, and rubbing things till they shone, and not both could have had their way (which sounds fatal for the man), had they not arranged a compromise, Grizel, for instance, to study geography for an hour in the evening with Miss Langlands (go to school in the daytime she would not) so long as the doctor shaved every morning, but if no shave no geography; the doctor to wipe his pen on the blot-sheet instead of on the lining of his coat if she took three lessons a week from Miss Oram on the spinet. How happy and proud she was! Her glee was a constant source of wonder to McQueen. Perhaps she put on airs a little, her walk, said the critical, had become a strut; but how could she help that when the new joyousness of living was dancing and singing within her?

Had all her fears for the future rolled away like clouds that leave no mark behind? The doctor thought so at times, she so seldom spoke of them to him; he did not see that when they came she hid them from him because she had discovered that they saddened him. And she had so little time to brood, being convinced of the sinfulness of sitting still, that if the clouds came suddenly, they never stayed long save once, and then it was, mayhap, as well. The thunderclap was caused by Tommy, who brought it on unintentionally and was almost as much scared by his handiwork as Grizel herself. She and he had been very friendly of late, partly

A A

because they shared with McQueen the secret of
the frustrated elopement, partly because they
both thought that in that curious incident
Tommy had behaved in a most disinterested
and splendid way. Grizel had not been sure of
it at first, but it had grown on Tommy, he had
so thoroughly convinced himself of his intention
to get into the train with her at Tilliedrum that
her doubts were dispelled—easily dispelled, you
say, but the truth must be told, Grizel was very
anxious to be rid of them. And Tommy's were
honest convictions, born full grown of a desire
for happiness to all. Had Elspeth discovered
how nearly he had deserted her, the same sentiment would have made him swear to her with
tears that never should he have gone farther than
Tilliedrum, and while he was persuading her he
would have persuaded himself. Then again,
when he met Grizel—well, to get him in doubt
it would have been necessary to catch him on
the way between these two girls.

So Tommy and Grizel were friends, and finding that it hurt the doctor to speak on a certain
subject to him, Grizel gave her confidences to
Tommy. She had a fear, which he shared on its
being explained to him, that she might meet a
man of the stamp of her father, and grow fond
of him before she knew the kind he was, and as
even Tommy could not suggest an infallible test
which would lay them bare at the first glance,
he consented to consult Blinder once more. He
found the blind man by his fireside, very difficult
to coax into words on the important topic, but
Tommy's "You've said ower much no to tell a

bit more," seemed to impress him, and he
answered the question,—

"You said a woman should fly frae the like
o' Grizel's father though it should be to the
other end of the world, but how is she to ken
that he's that kind?"

"She'll ken," Blinder answered after thinking
it over, "if she likes him and fears him at one
breath, and has a sort of secret dread that he's
getting a power ower her that she canna resist."

These words were a flash of light on a ne-
glected corner to Tommy. "Now I see, now I
ken," he exclaimed, amazed; "now I ken what
my mother meant! Blinder, is that no the kind
of man that's called masterful?"

"It's what poor women find them and call
them to their cost," said Blinder.

Tommy's excitement was prodigious. "Now
I ken, now I see!" he cried, slapping his leg
and stamping up and down the room.

"Sit down!" roared his host.

"I canna," retorted the boy. "Oh, to think
o't, to think I came to speir that question at
you, to think her and me has wondered what
kind he was, and I kent a' the time!" Without staying to tell Blinder what he was blethering about, he hurried off to Grizel, who was
waiting for him in the Den, and to her he poured
out his astonishing news.

"I ken all about them, I've kent since afore
I came to Thrums, but though I generally say
the prayer, I've forgot to think o' what it
means." In a stampede of words he told her all
he could remember of his mother's story as

A A 2

related to him on a grim night in London so long ago, and she listened eagerly. And when that was over, he repeated first his prayer and then Elspeth's, "O God, whatever is to be my fate, may I never be one of them that bow the knee to masterful man, and if I was born like that and canna help it, O take me up to heaven afore I'm fil't." Grizel repeated it after him until she had it by heart, and even as she said it a strange thing happened, for she began to draw back from Tommy, with a look of terror on her face.

"What makes you look at me like that?" he cried.

"I believe—I think—you are masterful," she gasped.

"Me!" he retorted indignantly.

"Now," she went on, waving him back, "now I know why I would not give in to you when you wanted me to be Stroke's wife. I was afraid you were masterful!"

"Was that it?" cried Tommy.

"Now," she proceeded, too excited to heed his interruptions, "now I know why I would not kiss your hand, now I know why I would not say I liked you. I was afraid of you, I——"

"Were you?" His eyes began to sparkle, and something very like rapture was pushing the indignation from his face. "Oh, Grizel, have I a power over you?"

"No, you have not," she cried passionately. "I was just frightened that you might have. Oh, oh, I know you now!"

"To think o't, to think o't!" he crowed, wagging his head, and then she clenched her

fist, crying, " Oh, you wicked, you should cry
with shame ! "

But he had his answer ready, " It canna be
my wite, for I never kent o't till you telled me.
Grizel, it has just come about without either of
us kenning ! "

She shuddered at this, and then seized him
by the shoulders. " It has not come about at
all," she said, " I was only frightened that it
might come, and now it can't come, for I won't
let it."

" But can you help yoursel' ? "

" Yes, I can. I shall never be friends with
you again."

She had such a capacity for keeping her
word that this alarmed him, and he did his best
to extinguish his lights. "I'm no masterful,
Grizel," he said, "and I dinna want to be, it was
just for a minute that I liked the thought."
She shook her head, but his next words had
more effect. " If I had been that kind, would
I have teached you Elspeth's prayer ? "

" N-no, I don't think so," she said slowly,
and perhaps he would have succeeded in soothing
her, had not a sudden thought brought back the
terror to her face.

" What is't now ? " he asked.

" Oh, oh, oh ! " she cried, " and I nearly
went away with you ! " and without another
word she fled from the Den. She never told the
doctor of this incident, and in time it became a
mere shadow in the background, so that she was
again his happy housekeeper, but that was because she had found strength to break with

Tommy. She was only an eager little girl, pathetically ignorant about what she wanted most to understand, but she saw how an instinct had been fighting for her, and now it should not have to fight alone. How careful she became! All Tommy's wiles were vain, she would scarcely answer if he spoke to her; if he had ever possessed a power over her it was gone, Elspeth's prayer had saved her.

Jean Myles had told Tommy to teach that prayer to Elspeth; but who had told him to repeat it to Grizel?

CHAPTER XXXV.

THE BRANDING OF TOMMY.

GRIZEL's secession had at least one good effect: it gave Tommy more time in which to make a scholar of himself. Would you like a picture of Tommy trying to make a scholar of himself?

They all helped him in their different ways: Grizel, by declining his company; Corp, by being far away at Lookaboutyou, adding to the inches of a farm-house; Aaron Latta, by saying nothing, but looking "college or the herding"; Mr. McLean, who had settled down with Ailie at the Dove Cot, by inquiries about his progress; Elspeth by—but did Elspeth's talks with him about how they should live in Aberdeen and afterward (when they were in the big house) do more than send his mind a-galloping (she holding on behind) along roads that lead not to Aberdeen? What drove Tommy oftenest to the weary drudgery was, perhaps, the alarm that came over him when he seemed of a sudden to hear the names of the bursars proclaimed and no Thomas Sandys among them. Then did he shudder, for well he knew that Aaron would keep his threat, and he hastily covered the round table with books and sat for hours sorrowfully pecking at them, every little while to discover that his mind had soared to other things, when he hauled it back, as one draws in a reluctant

kite. On these occasions Aaron seldom troubled
him, except by glances that, nevertheless, brought
the kite back more quickly than if they had
been words of warning. If Elspeth was present
the warper might sit moodily by the fire, but
when the man and the boy were left together one
or other of them soon retired, as if this was the
only way of preserving the peace. Though determined to keep his word to Jean Myles
liberally, Aaron had never liked Tommy, and
Tommy's avoidance of him is easily accounted
for; he knew that Aaron did not admire him,
and unless you admired Tommy he was always a
boor in your presence, shy and self-distrustful.
Especially was this so if you were a lady (how
amazingly he got on in after years with some of
you, what agony others endured till he went
away!), and it is the chief reason why there are
such contradictory accounts of him to-day.

Sometimes Mr. Cathro had hopes of him
other than those that could only be revealed in
a shameful whisper with the door shut. "Not
so bad," he might say to McLean; "if he keeps
it up we may squeeze him through yet, without
trusting to—to what I was fool enough to mention to you. The mathematics are his weak
point, there's nothing practical about him (except when it's needed to carry out his devil's
designs) and he cares not a doit about the line
A B, nor what it's doing in the circle K, but
there's whiles he surprises me when we're at
Homer. He has the spirit o't, man, even when
he bogles at the sense."

But the next time Ivie called for a report— !

In his great days, so glittering, so brief (the days of the Penny Life) Tommy, looking back to this year was sure that he had never really tried to work. But he had. He did his very best, doggedly, wearily sitting at the round table till Elspeth feared that he was killing himself and gave him a melancholy comfort by saying so. An hour afterwards he might discover that he had been far away from his books, looking on at his affecting death and counting the mourners at the funeral.

Had he thought that Grizel's discovery was making her unhappy he would have melted at once, but never did she look so proud as when she scornfully passed him by, and he wagged his head complacently over her coming chagrin when she heard that he had carried the highest bursary. Then she would know what she had flung away. This should have helped him to another struggle with his lexicon, but it only provided a breeze for the kite, which flew so strong that he had to let go the string.

Aaron and the Dominie met one day in the square, and to Aaron's surprise Mr. Cathro's despondency about Tommy was more pronounced than before. "I wonder at that," the warper said, "for I assure you he has been harder at it than ever thae last nights. What's more, he used to look doleful as he sat at his table, but I notice now that he's as sweer to leave off as he's keen to begin, and the face of him is a' eagerness too, and he reads ower to himself what he has wrote and wags his head at it as if he thought it grand."

"Say you so?" asked Cathro, suspiciously; "does he leave what he writes lying about, Aaron?"

"No, but he takes it to you, does he no'?"

"Not him," said the Dominie, emphatically. "I may be mistaken, Aaron, but I'm doubting the young whelp is at his tricks again."

The Dominie was right, and before many days passed he discovered what was Tommy's new and delicious occupation.

For years Mr. Cathro had been in the habit of writing letters for such of the populace as could not guide a pen, and though he often told them not to come deaving him he liked the job, unexpected presents of a hen or a ham occasionally arriving as his reward, while the personal matters thus confided to him, as if he were a safe for the banking of private histories, gave him and his wife gossip for winter nights. Of late the number of his clients had decreased without his noticing it, so confident was he that they could not get on without him, but he received a shock at last from Andrew Dickie, who came one Saturday night with paper, envelope, a Queen's head, and a request for a letter for Bell Birse, now of Tilliedrum.

"You want me to speir in your name whether she'll have you, do you?" asked Cathro, with a flourish of his pen.

"It's no just so simple as that," said Andrew, and then he seemed to be rather at a loss to say what it was. "I dinna ken," he continued presently with a grave face, "whether

you've noticed that I'm a gey queer deevil?
Losh, I think I'm the queerest deevil I ken."

"We are all that," the Dominie assured him.
"But what do you want me to write?"

"Well, it's like this," said Andrew; "I'm
willing to marry her if she's agreeable, but I
want to make sure that she'll take me afore I
speir her. I'm a proud man, Dominie."

"You're a sly one!"

"Am I no!" said Andrew, well pleased.
"Well, could you put the letter in that wy?"

"I wouldna," replied Mr. Cathro, "though
I could, and I couldna though I would. It
would defy the face of clay to do it, you canny
lover."

Now, the Dominie had frequently declined
to write as he was bidden, and had suggested
alterations which were invariably accepted, but
to his astonishment Andrew would not give in.
"I'll be stepping then," he said coolly, "for if
you hinna the knack o't I ken somebody that
has."

"Who?" demanded the irate Dominie.

"I promised no to tell you," replied Andrew,
and away he went. Mr. Cathro expected him
to return presently in humbler mood, but was
disappointed, and a week or two afterwards he
heard Andrew and Mary Jane Proctor cried in
the parish church. "Did Bell Birse refuse
him?" he asked the kirk officer, and was informed that Bell had never got a chance. "His
letter was so cunning," said John, "that without
speiring her, it drew ane frae her in which she let
out that she was centered on Davit Allardyce."

"But who wrote Andrew's letter?" asked Mr. Cathro, sharply.

"I thought it had been yoursel'," said John, and the Dominie chafed, and lost much of the afternoon service by going over in his mind the names of possible rivals. He never thought of Tommy.

Then a week or two later fell a heavier blow. At least twice a year the Dominie had written for Meggy Duff to her daughter in Ireland a long letter founded on this suggestion, "Dear Kaytherine, if you dinna send ten shillings immediately, your puir auld mother will have neither house nor hame. I'm crying to you for't, Kaytherine; hearken and you'll hear my cry across the cauldriff sea." He met Meggy in the Banker's close one day, and asked her pleasantly if the time was not drawing nigh for another appeal.

"I have wrote," replied the old woman, giving her pocket a boastful smack which she thus explained, "And it was the whole ten shillings this time, and you never got more for me than five."

"Who wrote the letter for you?" he asked, lowering.

She, too, it seemed, had promised not to tell.

"Did you promise to tell nobody, Meggy, or just no to tell me," he pressed her, of a sudden suspecting Tommy.

"Just no to tell you," she answered, and at that,

"Da-a-a," began the Dominie, and then saved his reputation by adding "gont." The deriva-

tion of the word dagont has puzzled many, but
here we seem to have it.

It is interesting to know what Tommy wrote.
The general opinion was that his letter must
have been a triumph of eloquent appeal, and
indeed he had first sketched out several masterpieces, all of some length and in different styles,
but on the whole not unlike the concoctions of
Meggy's former secretary; that is, he had dwelt
on the duties of daughters, on the hardness of
the times, on the certainty that if Katherine
helped this time assistance would never be
needed again. This sort of thing had always
satisfied the Dominie, but Tommy, despite his
several attempts, had a vague consciousness that
there was something second-rate about them,
and he tapped on his brain till it responded.
The letter he despatched to Ireland but had the
wisdom not to read aloud even to Meggy contained nothing save her own words, "Dear
Kaytherine, if you dinna send ten shillings
immediately your puir auld mother will have
neither house nor hame. I'm crying to you
for't, Kaytherine; hearken and you'll hear my
cry across the cauldriff sea." It was a call from
the heart which transported Katherine to
Thrums in a second of time, she seemed to see
her mother again, grown frail since last they met
—and so all was well for Meggy. Tommy did
not put all this to himself but he felt it, and
after that he *could not* have written the letter
differently. Happy Tommy! To be an artist is
a great thing, but to be an artist and not know
it is the most glorious plight in the world.

Other fickle clients put their correspondence into the boy's hands, and Cathro found it out but said nothing. Dignity kept him in check; he did not even let the tawse speak for him. So well did he dissemble that Tommy could not decide how much he knew, and dreaded his getting hold of some of the letters, yet pined to watch his face while he read them. This could not last forever. Mr. Cathro was like a haughty kettle which has choked its spout that none may know it has come a-boil, and we all know what in that event must happen sooner or later to the lid.

The three boys who had college in the tail of their eye had certain privileges not for the herd. It was taken for granted that when knowledge came their way they needed no overseer to make them stand their ground, and accordingly for great part of the day they had a back bench to themselves, with half-a-dozen hedges of boys and girls between them and the Dominie. From his chair Mr. Cathro could not see them, but a foot-board was nailed to it, and when he stood on this, as he had an aggravating trick of doing, softly and swiftly, they were suddenly in view. A large fire had been burning all day, and the atmosphere was soporific. Mr. Cathro was so sleepy himself that the sight of a nodding head enraged him like a caricature, and he was on the footboard frequently for the reason that makes bearded men suck peppermints in church. Against his better judgment he took several peeps at Tommy, whom he had lately suspected of writing his letters in school, or at least of

gloating over them on that back bench. To-day
he was sure of it. However absorbing Euclid
may be, even the forty-seventh of the first book
does not make you chuckle and wag your head ;
you can bring a substantive in Virgil back to the
verb that has lost it without looking as if you
would like to exhibit them together in the
square. But Tommy was thus elated until he
gave way to grief of the most affecting kind.
Now he looked gloomily before him as if all was
over, now he buried his face in his hands, next
his eyes were closed as if in prayer. All this the
Dominie stood from him, but when at last he
began to blubber—

At the blackboard was an arithmetic class,
slates in hand, each member adding up aloud in
turn a row of figures. By and by it was known
that Cathro had ceased to listen. "Go on," his
voice rather than himself said, and he accepted
Mary Dundas's trembling assertion that four
and seven make ten. Such was the faith in
Cathro that even boys who could add promptly
turned their eleven into ten, and he did not
catch them at it. So obviously was his mind
as well as his gaze on something beyond, that
Sandy Riach, a wit who had been waiting his
chance for years, snapped at it now, and roared
"Ten and eleven, nineteen" ("Go on," said
Cathro), "and four, twenty," gasped Sandy,
"and eight, sixteen," he added, gaining courage.
"Very good," murmured the Dominie, whereupon Sandy clenched his reputation forever by
saying, in one glorious mouthful, "and six,
eleven, and two, five, and one, nocht."

There was no laughing at it then (though Sandy held a levee in the evening), they were all so stricken with amazement. By one movement they swung round to see what had fascinated Cathro, and the other classes doing likewise, Tommy became suddenly the centre of observation. Big tears were slinking down his face, and falling on some sheets of paper, which emotion prevented his concealing. Anon the unusual stillness in the school made him look up, but he was dazed, like one uncertain of his whereabouts, and he blinked rapidly to clear his eyes, as a bird shakes water from its wings.

Mr. Cathro first uttered what was afterward described as a kind of throttled skirl, and then he roared "Come here!" whereupon Tommy stepped forward heavily, and tried, as commanded, to come to his senses, but it was not easy to make so long a journey in a moment, and several times, as he seemed about to conquer his tears, a wave of feeling set them flowing again.

"Take your time," said Mr. Cathro, grimly, " I can wait," and this had such a helpful effect that Tommy was able presently to speak up for his misdeeds. They consisted of some letters written at home, but brought to the school for private reading, and the Dominie got a nasty jar when he saw that they were all signed "Betsy Grieve." Miss Betsy Grieve, servant to Mr. Duthie, was about to marry, and these letters were acknowledgments of wedding presents. Now, Mr. Cathro had written similar letters for Betsy only a few days before.

"Did she ask you to write these for her?" he demanded, fuming, and Tommy replied demurely that she had. He could not help adding, though he felt the unwisdom of it, "She got some other body to do them first, but his letters didna satisfy her."

"Oh!" said Mr. Cathro, and it was such a vicious "oh" that Tommy squeaked tremblingly, "I dinna know who he was."

Keeping his mouth shut by gripping his underlip with his teeth, the Dominie read the letters, and Tommy gazed eagerly at him, all fear forgotten, soul conquering body. The others stood or sat waiting, perplexed as to the cause, confident of the issue. The letters were much finer productions than Cathro's, he had to admit it to himself as he read. Yet the rivals had started fair, for Betsy was a recent immigrant from Dunkeld way, and the letters were to people known neither to Tommy nor to the Dominie. Also, she had given the same details for the guidance of each. A lady had sent a teapot, which affected to be new, but was not; Betsy recognised it by a scratch on the lid, and wanted to scratch back, but politely. So Tommy wrote, "When you come to see me we shall have a cup of tea out of your beautiful present, and it will be like a meeting of three old friends." That was perhaps too polite, Betsy feared, but Tommy said authoritatively, "No, the politer the nippier."

There was a set of six cups and saucers from Peter something, who had loved Betsy in vain. She had shown the Dominie and Tommy the

ear-rings given her long ago by Peter (they
were bought with Sosh checks) and the poem he
had written about them, and she was most
anxious to gratify him in her reply. All Cathro
could do, however, was to wish Peter well in
some ornate sentences, while Tommy's was a
letter that only a tender woman's heart could
have indited, with such beautiful touches about
the days which are no more, alas! forever, that
Betsy listened to it with heaving breast and
felt so sorry for her old swain that, forgetting
she had never loved him, she all but gave
Andrew the go-by and returned to Peter. As
for Peter, who had been getting over his
trouble, he saw now for the first time what he
had lost, and he carried Betsy's dear letter in
his oxter pocket and was inconsolable.

But the masterpiece went to Mrs. Dinnie,
baker, in return for a flagon bun. Long ago her
daughter, Janet, and Betsy had agreed to marry
on the same day, and many a quip had Mrs.
Dinnie cast at their romantic compact. But
Janet died, and so it was a sad letter that
Tommy had to write to her mother. "I'm
doubting you're no auld enough for this ane,"
soft-hearted Betsy said, but she did not know
her man. "Tell me some one thing the mother
used often to say when she was taking her fun
off the pair of you," he said, and "Where is she
buried?" was a suggestive question, with the
happy tag, "Is there a tree hanging over the
grave?" Thus assisted, he composed a letter
that had a tear in every sentence. Betsy rubbed
her eyes red over it, and not all its sentiments

were allowed to die, for Mrs. Dinnie, touched to the heart, printed the best of them in black licorice on short bread for funeral feasts, at which they gave rise to solemn reflections as they went down.

Nevertheless, this letter affected none so much as the writer of it. His first rough sketch became so damp as he wrote that he had to abandon his pen and take to pencil; while he was revising he had often to desist to dry his eyes on the coverlet of Aaron's bed, which made Elspeth weep also, though she had no notion what he was at. But when the work was finished he took her into the secret and read his letter to her, and he almost choked as he did so. Yet he smiled rapturously through his woe, and she knew no better than to be proud of him, and he woke next morning with a cold, brought on you can see how, but his triumph was worth its price.

Having read the letter in an uncanny silence, Mr. Cathro unbottled Tommy for the details, and out they came with a rush, blowing away the cork discretion. Yet was the Dominie slow to strike; he seemed to find more satisfaction in surveying his young friend with a wondering gaze that had a dash of admiration in it, which Tommy was the first to note.

"I don't mind admitting before the whole school," said Mr. Cathro, slowly, "that if these letters had been addressed to me they would have taken me in."

Tommy tried to look modest, but his chest would have its way.

B B 2

"You little sacket," cried the Dominie, "how did you manage it?"

"I think I thought I was Betsy at the time," Tommy answered, with proper awe.

"She told me nothing about the weeping-willow at the grave," said the Dominie, perhaps in self-defence.

"You hadna speired if there was one, retorted Tommy jealously.

"What made you think of it?"

"I saw it might come in neat." (He had said in the letter that the weeping-willow reminded him of the days when Janet's bonny hair hung down kissing her waist just as the willow kissed the grave.)

"Willows don't hang so low as you seem to think," said the Dominie.

"Yes, they do," replied Tommy; "I walked three miles to see one to make sure. I was near putting in another beautiful bit about weeping-willows."

"Well, why didn't you?"

Tommy looked up with an impudent snigger. "You could never guess," he said.

"Answer me at once," thundered his preceptor. "Was it because——"

"No," interrupted Tommy, so conscious of Mr. Cathro's inferiority that to let him go on seemed waste of time. "It was because, though it is a beautiful thing in itself, I felt a servant lassie wouldna have thought o't. I was sweer," he admitted, with a sigh; then firmly, "but I cut it out."

Again Cathro admired, reluctantly. The

hack does feel the difference between himself
and the artist. Cathro might possibly have had
the idea, he could not have cut it out.

But the hack is sometimes, or usually, or
nearly always the artist's master, and can make
him suffer for his dem'd superiority.

"What made you snivel when you read the
pathetic bits?" asked Cathro, with itching
fingers.

"I was so sorry for Peter and Mrs. Dinnie,"
Tommy answered, a little puzzled himself now.
"I saw them so clear."

"And yet until Betsy came to you, you had
never heard tell of them?"

"No."

"And on reflection you don't care a doit
about them?"

"N-no."

"And you care as little for Betsy?"

"No now, but at the time I a kind of
thought I was to be married to Andrew."

"And even while you blubbered you were
saying to yourself, 'What a clever billie I
am!'"

Mr. Cathro had certainly intended to end the
scene with the strap, but as he stretched out his
hand for it he had another idea. "Do you know
why Nether Drumgley's sheep are branded with
the letters N. D.?" he asked his pupils, and a
dozen replied, "So as all may ken wha they
belong to."

"Precisely," said Mr. Cathro, "and similarly
they used to brand a letter on a felon, so that all
might know whom *he* belonged to." He crossed

to the fireplace, and, picking up a charred stick, wrote with it on the forehead of startled Tommy the letters "S. T."

"Now," said the Dominie complacently, "we know to whom Tommy belongs."

All were so taken aback that for some seconds nothing could be heard save Tommy indignantly wiping his brow; then "Wha is he?" cried one, the mouthpiece of half a hundred.

"He is one of the two proprietors we have just been speaking of," replied Cathro, dryly, and turning again to Tommy, he said, "Wipe away, Sentimental Tommy, try hot water, try cold water, try a knife, but you will never get those letters off you; you are branded for ever and ever."

CHAPTER XXXVI.

OF FOUR MINISTERS WHO AFTERWARDS BOASTED THAT THEY HAD KNOWN TOMMY SANDYS.

BURSARY examination time had come, and to the siege of Aberdeen marched a hungry half-dozen—three of them from Thrums, two from the Glenquharity school. The sixth was Tod Lindertis, a ploughman from the Dubb of Prosen, his place of study the bothy after lousing time (Do you hear the klink of quoits ?) or a one-roomed house near it, his tutor a dogged little woman, who knew not the accusative from the dative, but never tired of holding the book while Tod recited. Him someone greets with the good-natured jeer, "It's your fourth try, is it no, Tod ? " and he answers cheerily, "It is, my lathie, and I'll keep kick, kick, kicking away to the nth time."

"Which means till the door flies open," says the dogged little woman, who is the gallant Tod's no less gallant wife, and already the mother of two. I hope Tod will succeed this time.

The competitors, who were to travel part of the way on their shanks, met soon after daybreak in Cathro's yard, where a little crowd awaited them, parents trying to look humble, Mr. Duthie and Ramsay Cameron thinking of the morning when they set off on the same errand—but the results were different, and Mr. Duthie is now a minister, and Ramsay is in the middle of another wob. Both dominies were present, hating each other for that day only, up to the mouth, where their icy politeness was a thing to shudder at, and each was drilling his detachment to the last moment, but by different methods; for while Mr. Cathro entreated Joe Meldrum for God's sake to mind that about the genitive, and Willie Simpson to keep his mouth shut and drink even water sparingly, Mr. Ogilvy cracked jokes with Gav Dishart and explained them to Lauchlan McLauchlan. "Think of anything now but what is before you," was Mr. Ogilvy's advice. "Think of nothing else," roared Mr. Cathro. But though Mr. Ogilvy seemed outwardly calm it was base pretence; his dickie gradually wriggled through the opening of his waistcoat, as if bearing a protest from his inward parts, and he let it hang crumpled and conspicuous, while Grizel, on the outskirts of the crowd, yearned to put it right.

Grizel was not there, she told several people, including herself, to say good-by to Tommy, and oh, how she scorned Elspeth for looking as if life would not be endurable without him. Knowing what Elspeth was, Tommy had decided that she should not accompany him to the yard (of course she was to follow him to Aberdeen if he distinguished himself—Mr. McLean had promised to bring her), but she told him of her dream that he headed the bursary list, and as this dream coincided with some dreams of his own, though not with all, it seemed to give her such fortitude that he let her come. An expressionless face was Tommy's, so that not even the experienced dominie of Glenquharity, covertly scanning his rival's lot, could tell whether he was gloomy or uplifted; he did not seem to be in need of a long sleep like Willie Simpson, nor were his eyes glazed like Gav Dishart's, who carried all the problems of Euclid before him on an invisible blackboard and dared not even wink lest he displaced them, nor did he, like Tod Lindertis, answer questions about his money pocket or where he had stowed his bread and cheese with

> "After envy, spare, obey,
> The dative put, remember, pray."

Mr. Ogilvy noticed that Cathro tapped his forehead, doubtfully, every time his eyes fell on Tommy, but otherwise shunned him, and he asked, "What are his chances?"

"That's the laddie," replied Mr. Cathro, "who, when you took her ladyship to see Corp Shiach years ago impersona——"

"I know," Mr. Ogilvy interrupted him hastily, "but how will he stand, think you?"

Mr. Cathro coughed. "We'll see," he said guardedly.

Nevertheless Tommy was not to get round the corner without betraying a little of himself, for Elspeth, having borne up magnificently when he shook hands, screamed at the tragedy of his back and fell into the arms of Tod's wife, whereupon Tommy first tried to brazen it out and then kissed her in the presence of a score of witnesses, including Grizel, who stamped her foot, though what right had she to be so angry? "I'm sure," Elspeth sobbed, "that the professor would let me sit beside you; I would just hunker on the floor and hold your foot and no say a word." Tommy gave Tod's wife an imploring look, and she managed to comfort Elspeth with predictions of his coming triumph and the reunion to follow. Grateful Elspeth in return asked Tommy to help Tod when the professors were not looking, and he promised, after which she had no more fear for Tod.

And now, ye drums that we all carry in our breasts, beat your best over the bravest sight ever seen in a small Scotch town of an autumn morning, the departure of its fighting lads for the lists at Aberdeen. Let the tune be the sweet familiar one you found somewhere in the Bible long ago, "The mothers we leave behind us"— leave behind us on their knees. May it dirl through your bones, brave boys, to the end, as you hope not to be damned. And now, quick march.

A week has elapsed, and now—there is no call for music now, for these are but the vanquished crawling back, Joe Meldrum and—and another. No, it is not Tod, he stays on in Aberdeen, for he is a twelve-pound tenner. The two were within a mile of Thrums at three o'clock, but after that they lagged, waiting for the gloaming, when they stole to their homes, ducking as they passed windows without the blinds down. Elspeth ran to Tommy when he appeared in the doorway, and then she got quickly between him and Aaron. The warper was sitting by the fire at his evening meal, and he gave the wanderer a long steady look, then without a word returned to his porridge and porter. It was a less hearty welcome home even than Joe's; his mother was among those who had wept to lose her son, but when he came back to her she gave him a whack on the head with the thieval.

Aaron asked not a question about those days in Aberdeen, but he heard a little about them from Elspeth. Tommy had not excused himself to Elspeth, he had let her do as she liked with his head (this was a great treat to her), and while it lay pressed against hers, she made remarks about Aberdeen professors which it would have done them good to hear. These she repeated to Aaron, who was about to answer roughly, and then suddenly put her on his knee instead.

"They didna ask the right questions," she told him, and when the warper asked if Tommy had said so, she declared that he had refused to say a word against them, which seemed to her to cover him with glory. "But he doubted they would make that mistake afore he started," she said brightly, "so you see he saw through them afore he ever set eyes on them."

Corp would have replied admiringly to this, "Oh, the little deevil!" (when he heard of Tommy's failure he wanted to fight Gav Dishart and Willie Simpson), but Aaron was another kind of confidant, and even when she explained on Tommy's authority that there are two kinds of cleverness, the kind you learn from books and a kind that is inside yourself, which latter was Tommy's kind, he only replied,

"He can take it wi' him to the herding, then, and see if it'll keep the cattle frae stravaiging."

"It's no that kind of cleverness either," said
Elspeth, quaking, and quaked also Tommy, who
had gone to the garret, to listen through the
floor.

"No? I would like to ken what use his
cleverness can be put to, then," said Aaron, and
Elspeth answered nothing, and Tommy only
sighed, for that indeed was the problem. But
though to these three and to Cathro, and to
Mr. and Mrs. McLean and to others more
mildly interested, it seemed a problem beyond
solution, there was one in Thrums who rocked
her arms at their denseness, a girl growing so
long in the legs that twice within the last year
she had found it necessary to let down her
parramatty frock. As soon as she heard that
Tommy had come home vanquished, she put on
the quaint blue bonnet with the white strings,
in which she fondly believed she looked ever so
old (her period of mourning was at an end, but
she still wore her black dress), and forgetting all
except that he was unhappy, she ran to a certain
little house to comfort him. But she did not go
in, for through the window she saw Elspeth
petting him, and that somehow annoyed her. In
the evening, however, she called on Mr. Cathro.

Perhaps you want to know why she, who at
last saw Sentimental Tommy in his true light
and spurned him accordingly, now exerted herself in his behalf instead of going on with the
papering of the surgery. Well, that was the
reason. She had put the question to herself
before—not, indeed, before going to Monypenny,
but before calling on the Dominie—and decided

that she wanted to send Tommy to college, because she disliked him so much that she could not endure the prospect of his remaining in Thrums. Now, are you satisfied?

She could scarcely take time to say good-evening to Mr. Cathro before telling him the object of her visit. "The letters Tommy has been writing for people are very clever, are they not?" she began.

"You've heard of them, have you?"

"Everybody has heard of them," she said injudiciously, and he groaned and asked if she had come to tell him this. But he admitted their cleverness, whereupon she asked, "Well, if he is clever at writing letters, would he not be clever at writing an essay?"

"I wager my head against a snuff mull that he would be, but what are you driving at?"

"I was wondering whether he could not win the prize I heard Dr. McQueen speaking about, the—is it not called the Hugh Blackadder?"

"My head against a buckie that he could! Sit down, Grizel, I see what you mean now. Ay, but the pity is he's not eligible for the Hugh Blackadder. Oh, that he was, oh, that he was! It would make Ogilvy of Glenquharity sing small at last! His loons have carried the Blackadder for the last seven years without a break. The Hugh Blackadder Mortification, the bequest is called, and, 'deed, it has been a sore mortification to me!"

Calming down, he told her the story of the bequest. Hugh Blackadder was a Thrums man who made a fortune in America, and bequeathed the interest of three hundred pounds of it to be competed for yearly by the youth of his native place. He had grown fond of Thrums and all its ways over there, and left directions that the prize should be given for the best essay in the Scots tongue, the ministers of the town and glens to be the judges, the competitors to be boys who were going to college but had not without it the wherewithal to support themselves. The ministers took this to mean that those who carried small bursaries were eligible, and indeed it had usually gone to a bursar.

"Sentimental Tommy would not have been able to compete if he had got a bursary," Mr. Cathro explained, "because however small it was Mr. McLean meant to double it; and he can't compete without it, for McLean refuses to help him now (he was here an hour since, saying the laddie was obviously hopeless), so I never thought of entering Tommy for the Blackadder. No, it will go to Ogilvy's Lauchlan McLauchlan, who is a twelve-pounder, and, as there can be no competitors he'll get it without the trouble of coming back to write the essay."

"But suppose Mr. McLean were willing to do what he promised if Tommy won the Blackadder?"

"It's useless to appeal to McLean. He's hard set against the laddie now and washes his hands of him, saying that Aaron Latta is right after all. He may soften, and get Tommy into a trade to save him from the herding, but send him to college he won't, and indeed he's right, the laddie's a fool."

"Not at writing let——"

"And what is the effect of his letter-writing but to make me ridiculous? Me! I wonder you can expect me to move a finger for him, he has been my torment ever since his inscrutable face appeared at my door."

"Never mind him," said Grizel, cunningly. "But think what a triumph it would be to you if your boy beat Mr. Ogilvy's."

The Dominie rose in his excitement and slammed the table. "My certie, lassie, but it would!" he cried. "Ogilvy looks on the Blackadder as his perquisite, and he's surer of it than ever this year. And there's no doubt but Tommy would carry it. My head to a buckie preen he would carry it, and then, oh, for a sight of Ogilvy's face, oh, for——" He broke off abruptly. "But what's the good of thinking of it?" he said, dolefully. "Mr. McLean's a firm man when he makes up his mind."

Nevertheless, though McLean, who had a Scotchman's faith in the verdict of professors, and had been bitterly disappointed by Tommy's failure, refused to be converted by the Dominie's entreaties, he yielded to them when they were voiced by Ailie (brought into the plot *vice* Grizel retired), and Elspeth got round Aaron, and so it came about that with his usual luck, Tommy was given another chance, present at the competition, which took place in the Thrums school, the Rev. Mr. Duthie, the Rev. Mr. Dishart, the Rev. Mr. Gloag of Noran Side, the Rev. Mr. Lorrimer of Glenquharity (these on hair-bottomed chairs), and Mr. Cathro and Mr. Ogilvy (cane); present also to a less extent

(that is to say, their faces at the windows), Corp
and others who applauded the local champion
when he entered and derided McLauchlan. The
subject of the essay was changed yearly, this
time "A Day in Church" was announced, and
immediately Lauchlan McLauchlan, who had
not missed a service since his scarlet fever year
(and too few then), smote his red head in agony,
while Tommy, who had missed as many as
possible, looked calmly confident. For two
hours the competitors were put into a small
room communicating with the larger one, and
Tommy began at once with a confident smirk
that presently gave way to a most holy expression; while Lauchlan gaped at him and at last
got started also, but had to pause occasionally
to rub his face on his sleeve, for, like Corp, he
was one of the kind who cannot think without
perspiring. In the large room the ministers
gossiped about eternal punishment, and of the
two dominies one sat at his ease, like a passenger
who knows that the coach will reach the goal
without any exertion on his part, while the
other paced the floor, with many a despondent
glance through the open door whence the
scraping proceeded; and the one was pleasantly
cool; and the other in a plot of heat; and the
one made genial remarks about everyday matters,
and the answers of the other stood on their
heads. It was a familiar comedy to Mr. Ogilvy,
hardly a variation on what had happened five
times in six for many years: the same scene, the
same scraping in the little room, the same background of ministers (blackaviced Mr. Lorrimer

had begun to bark again), the same dominies; everything was as it had so often been, except that he and Cathro had changed places; it was Cathro who sat smiling now and Mr. Ogilvy who dolefully paced the floor.

To be able to write! Throughout Mr. Ogilvy's life, save when he was about one and twenty, this had seemed the great thing, and he ever approached the thought reverently, as if it were a maid of more than mortal purity. And it is, and because he knew this she let him see her face, which shall ever be hidden from those who look not for the soul, and to help him nearer to her came assistance in strange guise, the loss of loved ones, dolour unutterable; but still she was beyond his reach. Night by night, when the only light in the glen was the school-house lamp, of use at least as a landmark to solitary travellers—who miss it nowadays, for it burns no more—she hovered over him, nor did she deride his hopeless efforts, but rather as she saw him go from black to grey and from grey to white in her service, were her luminous eyes sorrowful because she was not for him, and she bent impulsively toward him, so that once or twice in a long life he touched her fingers, and a heavenly spark was lit, for he had risen higher than himself, and that is literature.

He knew that oblivion was at hand, ready to sweep away his pages almost as soon as they were filled (Do we not all hear her besom when we pause to dip?), but he had done his best and he had a sense of humour, and perhaps some day would come a pupil of whom he could make

C C

what he had failed to make of himself. That prodigy never did come, though it was not for want of nursing, and there came at least, in succession most maddening to Mr. Cathro, a row of youths who could be trained to carry the Hugh Blackadder. Mr. Ogilvy's many triumphs in this competition had not dulled his appetite for more, and depressed he was at the prospect of a reverse. That it was coming now he could not doubt. McLauchlan, who was to be Rev., had a flow of words (which would prevent his perspiring much in the pulpit), but he could no more describe a familiar scene with the pen than a milkmaid can draw a cow. The Thrums representatives were sometimes as little gifted, it is true, and never were they so well exercised, but this Tommy had the knack of it, as Mr. Ogilvy could not doubt, for the story of his letter-writing had been through the glens.

"Keep up your spirits," Mr. Lorrimer had said to him as they walked together to the fray, "Cathro's loon may compose the better of the two, but, as I understand, the first years of his life were spent in London, and so he may bogle at the Scotch."

But the Dominie replied, "Don't buoy me up on a soap bubble. If there's as much in him as I fear, that should be a help to him instead of a hindrance, for it will have set him a-thinking about the words he uses."

And the satisfaction on Tommy's face when the subject of the essay was given out, with the business-like way in which he set to work, had added to the Dominie's misgivings; if anything was required to dishearten him utterly it was provided by Cathro's confident smile. The two Thrums ministers were naturally desirous that Tommy should win, but the younger of them was very fond of Mr. Ogilvy, and noticing his unhappy peeps through the door dividing the rooms, proposed that it should be closed. He shut it himself, and as he did so he observed that Tommy was biting his pen and frowning, while McLauchlan, having ceased to think, was getting on nicely. But it did not strike Mr. Dishart that this was worth commenting on.

"Are you not satisfied with the honours you have already got, you greedy man?" he said, laying his hand affectionately on Mr. Ogilvy, who only sighed for reply.

"It is well that the prize should go to different localities, for in that way its sphere of usefulness is extended," remarked pompous Mr. Gloag, who could be impartial, as there was no candidate from Noran Side. He was a minister much in request for church soirées, where he amused the congregations so greatly with personal anecdote about himself that they never thought much of him afterwards. There is one such minister in every presbytery.

"And to have carried the Hugh Blackadder seven times running is surely enough for any one locality, even though it be Glenquharity," said Mr. Lorrimer, preparing for defeat.

"There's consolation for you, sir," said Mr. Cathro, sarcastically, to his rival, who tried to take snuff in sheer bravado, but let it slip through his fingers, and after that until the

cc2

two hours were up, the talk was chiefly of how
Tommy would get on at Aberdeen. But it was
confined to the four ministers and one dominie.
Mr. Ogilvy still hovered about the door of communication, and his face fell more and more,
making Mr. Dishart quite unhappy.

"I'm an old fool," the Dominie admitted,
"but I can't help being cast down. The fact is
that—I have only heard the scrape of one pen
for nearly an hour."

"Poor Lauchlan!" exclaimed Mr. Cathro,
rubbing his hands gleefully, and indeed it was
such a shameless exhibition that the Auld Licht
minister said reproachfully, "You forget yourself, Mr. Cathro, let us not be unseemly exalted
in the hour of our triumph."

Then Mr. Cathro sat upon his hands as the
best way of keeping them apart, but the moment
Mr. Dishart's back presented itself, he winked
at Mr. Ogilvy.

He winked a good deal more presently.

For after all—how to tell it! Tommy was
ignominiously beaten, making such a beggarly
show that the judges thought it unnecessary to
take the essays home with them for leisurely
consideration before pronouncing Mr. Lauchlan
McLauchlan winner. There was quite a commotion in the school-room. At the end of the
allotted time the two competitors had been told
to hand in their essays, and how Mr. McLauchlan was sniggering is not worth recording, so
dumbfounded, confused and raging was Tommy.
He clung to his papers, crying fiercely that the
two hours could not be up yet, and Lauchlan

having tried to keep the laugh in too long it exploded in his mouth, whereupon, said he, with a guffaw, "He hasna written a word for near an hour!"

"What! It was you I heard!" cried Mr. Ogilvy gleaming, while the unhappy Cathro tore the essay from Tommy's hands. Essay! It was no more an essay than a twig is a tree, for the gowk had stuck in the middle of his second page. Yes, stuck is the right expression, as his chagrined teacher had to admit when the boy was cross-examined. He had not been "up to some of his tricks," he had stuck, and his explanations, as you will admit, merely emphasised his incapacity.

He had brought himself to public scorn for lack of a word. What word? they asked testily, but even now he could not tell. He had wanted a Scotch word that would signify how many people were in church, and it was on the tip of his tongue but would come no farther. Puckle was nearly the word, but it did not mean so many people as he meant. The hour had gone by just like winking; he had forgotten all about time while searching his mind for the word.

When Mr. Ogilvy heard this he seemed to be much impressed, repeatedly he nodded his head as some beat time to music, and he muttered to himself, "The right word—yes, that's everything," and "'the time went by like winking'—exactly, precisely," and he would have liked to examine Tommy's bumps, but did not, nor said a word aloud, for was he not there in McLauchlan's interest?

The other five were furious; even **Mr.**
Lorrimer, though his man had won, could not
smile in face of such imbecility. " You little
tattie doolie," Cathro roared, " were there not a
dozen words to wile from if you had an ill-will
to puckle ?   What ailed you at manzy, or——"

" I thought of manzy," replied Tommy woefully, for he was ashamed of himself, " but—but
a manzy's a swarm.   It would mean that the
folk in the kirk were buzzing thegither like bees,
instead of sitting still."

" Even if it does mean that," said Mr.
Duthie, with impatience, " what was the need of
being so particular?   Surely the art of essay-
writing consists in using the first word that
comes and hurrying on."

" That's how I did," said the proud Mc-
Lauchlan, who is now leader of a party in the
church, and a figure in Edinburgh during the
month of May.

" I see," interposed Mr. Cloag, " that Mc-
Lauchlan speaks of there being a mask of people
in the church.   Mask is a fine Scotch word."

" Admirable," assented Mr. Dishart.

" I thought of mask," whimpered Tommy,
" but that would mean the kirk was crammed,
and I just meant it to be middling full."

" Flow would have done," suggested Mr.
Lorrimer.

" Flow's but a handful," said Tommy.

" Curran, then, you jackanapes ! "

" Curran's no enough."

Mr. Lorrimer flung up his hands in despair.

" I wanted something between curran and

mask," said Tommy, dogged, yet almost at the crying.

Mr. Ogilvy, who had been hiding his admiration with difficulty, spread a net for him. " You said you wanted a word that meant middling full. Well, why did you not say middling full—or fell mask?"

" Yes, why not?" demanded the ministers, unconsciously caught in the net.

" I wanted one word," replied Tommy, unconsciously avoiding it.

"You jewel!" muttered Mr. Ogilvy under his breath, but Mr. Cathro would have banged the boy's head had not the ministers interfered.

" It is so easy, too, to find the right word," said Mr. Gloag.

" It's no; it's as difficult as to hit a squirrel," cried Tommy, and again Mr. Ogilvy nodded approval.

But the ministers were only pained.

" The lad is merely a numskull," said Mr. Dishart, kindly.

" And no teacher could have turned him into anything else," said Mr. Duthie.

" And so, Cathro, you need not feel sore over your defeat," added Mr. Gloag; but nevertheless Cathro took Tommy by the neck and ran him out of the parish school of Thrums. When he returned to the others he found the ministers congratulating McLauchlan, whose nose was in the air, and complimenting Mr. Ogilvy, who listened to their formal phrases solemnly and accepted their hand-shakes with a dry chuckle.

" Ay, grin away, sir," the mortified dominie

of Thrums said to him sourly, "the joke is on your side."

"You are right, sir," replied Mr. Ogilvy, mysteriously, "the joke is on my side, and the best of it is that not one of you knows what the joke is!"

And then an odd thing happened. As they were preparing to leave the school, the door opened a little and there appeared in the aperture the face of Tommy, tear-stained but excited. "I ken the word now," he cried, "it came to me a' at once; it is hantle!"

The door closed with a victorious bang, just in time to prevent Cathro——

"Oh, the sumph!" exclaimed Mr. Lauchlan McLauchlan, "as if it mattered what the word is now!"

And said Mr. Dishart, "Cathro, you had better tell Aaron Latta that the sooner he sends this nincompoop to the herding the better."

But Mr. Ogilvy giving his Lauchlan a push that nearly sent him sprawling, said in an ecstasy to himself, "He *had* to think of it till he got it —and he got it. The laddie is a genius!" They were about to tear up Tommy's essay, but he snatched it from them and put it in his oxter pocket. "I am a collector of curiosities," he explained, "and this paper may be worth money yet."

"Well," said Cathro, savagely, "I have one satisfaction, I ran him out of my school."

"Who knows," replied Mr. Ogilvy, "but what you may be proud to dust a chair for him when he comes back?"

CHAPTER XXXVII.

THE END OF A BOYHOOD.

CONVINCED of his own worthlessness, Tommy was sufficiently humble now, but Aaron Latta, nevertheless, marched to the square on the following market day and came back with the boy's sentence, Elspeth being happily absent.

"I say nothing about the disgrace you have brought on this house," the warper began without emotion, "for it has been a shamed house since afore you were born, and it's a small offence to skail on a clarty floor. But now I've done more for you than I promised Jean Myles to do, and you had your pick atween college and the herding, and the herding you've chosen twice. I call you no names, you ken best what you're fitted for, but I've seen the farmer of the Dubb of Prosen the day, and he was short-handed through the loss of Tod Lindertis, so you're fee'd to him. Dinna think you get Tod's place, it'll be years afore you rise to that, but it's right and proper that as he steps up, you should step down."

"The Dubb of Prosen!" cried Tommy in dismay. "It's fifteen miles frae here."

"It's a' that."

"But—but—but Elspeth and me never thought of my being so far away that she couldna see me. We thought of a farmer near Thrums."

"The farther you're frae her the better," said Aaron, uneasily, yet honestly believing what he said.

"It'll kill her," Tommy cried fiercely. With only his own suffering to consider he would probably have nursed it into a play through which he stalked as the noble child of misfortune, but in his anxiety for Elspeth he could still forget himself. "Fine you ken she canna do without me," he screamed.

"She maun be weaned," replied the warper, with a show of temper; he was convinced that the sooner Elspeth learned to do without Tommy the better it would be for herself in the end, but in his way of regarding the boy there was also a touch of jealousy, pathetic rather than forbidding. To him he left the task of breaking the news to Elspeth; and Tommy, terrified lest she should swoon under it, was almost offended when she remained calm. But, alas, the reason was that she thought she was going with him.

"Will we have to walk all the way to the Dubb of Prosen?" she asked, quite brightly, and at that Tommy twisted about in misery. "You are no—you canna—" he began, and then dodged the telling. "We—we may get a lift in a cart," he said weakly.

"And I'll sit aside you in the fields, and make chains o' the gowans, will I no? Speak, Tommy!"

"Ay—ay, will you," he groaned.

"And we'll have a wee, wee room to oursels, and——"

He broke down, "Oh, Elspeth," he cried,

"it was ill-done of me no to stick to my books, and get a bursary, and it was waur o' me to bother about that word. I'm a scoundrel, I am, I'm a black, I'm a——"

But she put her hand on his mouth, saying, "I'm fonder o' you than ever, Tommy, and I'll like the Dubb o' Prosen fine, and what does it matter where we are when we're thegither?" which was poor comfort for him, but still he could not tell her the truth, and so in the end Aaron had to tell her. It struck her down, and the doctor had to be called in during the night to stop her hysterics. When at last she fell asleep Tommy's arm was beneath her, and by and by it was in agony, but he set his teeth and kept it there rather than risk waking her.

When Tommy was out of the way, Aaron did his clumsy best to soothe her, sometimes half shamefacedly pressing her cheek to his, and she did not repel him, but there was no response. "Dinna take on in that way, dawtie," he would say, "I'll be good to you."

"But you're no Tommy," Elspeth answered.

"I'm not, I'm but a stunted tree, blasted in my youth, but for a' that, I would like to have somebody to care for me, and there's none to do't, Elspeth, if you winna. I'll gang walks wi' you, I'll take you to the fishing, I'll come to the garret at night to hap you up, I'll—I'll teach you the games I used to play mysel'. I'm no sure but what you might make something o' me yet, bairn, if you tried hard."

"But you're no Tommy," Elspeth wailed

again, and when he advised her to put Tommy
out of her mind for a little and speak of other
things, she only answered innocently, "What
else is there to speak about?"

Mr. McLean had sent Tommy a pound, and
so was done with him, but Ailie still thought
him a dear, though no longer a wonder, and
Elspeth took a strange confession to her, how
one night she was so angry with God that she
had gone to bed without saying her prayers.
She had just meant to keep Him in suspense for
a little, and then say them, but she fell asleep.
And that was not the worst, for when she woke
in the morning, and saw that she was still living,
she was glad she had not said them. But next
night she said them twice.

And this, too, is another flash into her dark
character. Tommy, who never missed saying his
prayers and could say them with surprising
quickness, told her, "God is fonder of lonely
lasses than of any other kind, and every time
you greet it makes Him greet, and when you're
cheerful it makes Him cheerful too." This was
meant to dry her eyes, but it had not that effect,
for, said Elspeth, vindictively, "Well, then, I'll
just make Him as miserable as I can."

When Tommy was merely concerned with
his own affairs he did not think much about God,
but he knew that no other could console Elspeth,
and his love for her usually told him the right
things to say, and while he said them he was
quite carried away by his sentiments and even
wept over them, but within the hour he might
be leering. They were beautiful, and were

repeated of course to Mrs. McLean, who told her husband of them, declaring that this boy's love for his sister made her a better woman.

"But nevertheless," said Ivie, "Mr. Cathro assures me——"

"He is prejudiced," retorted Mrs. McLean warmly, prejudice being a failing which all women marvel at. "Just listen to what the boy said to Elspeth to-day. He said to her, 'When I am away, try for a whole day to be better than you ever were before, and think of nothing else, and then when prayer-time comes you will see that you have been happy without knowing it.' Fancy his finding that out."

"I wonder if he ever tried it himself?" said Mr. McLean.

"Ivie, think shame of yourself!"

"Well, even Cathro admits that he has a kind of cleverness, but——"

"Cleverness!" exclaimed Ailie, indignantly, "that is not cleverness, it is holiness;" and leaving the cynic she sought Elspeth, and did her good by pointing out that a girl who had such a brother should try to save him pain. "He is very miserable, dear," she said, "because you are so unhappy. If you looked brighter, think how that would help him, and it would show that you are worthy of him." So Elspeth went home trying hard to look brighter, but made a sad mess of it.

"Think of getting letters frae me every time the post comes in!" said Tommy, and then indeed her face shone.

And then Elspeth could write to him—yes,

as often as ever she liked! This pleased her
even more. It was such an exquisite thought
that she could not wait, but wrote the first one
before he started, and he answered it across the
table. And Mrs. McLean made a letter bag,
with two strings to it, and showed her how to
carry it about with her in a safer place than a
pocket.

Then a cheering thing occurred. Came Corp,
with the astounding news that, in the Glen
Quharity dominie's opinion, Tommy should have
got the Hugh Blackadder.

"He says he is glad he wasna judge, because
he would have had to give you the prize, and he
laughs like to split at the ministers for giving it
to Lauchlan McLauchlan."

Now, great was the repute of Mr. Ogilvy, and
Tommy gaped incredulous. "He had no word
of that at the time," he said.

"No likely! He says if the ministers was
so doited as to think his loon did best, it wasna
for him to conter them."

"Man, Corp, you ca' me aff my feet! How
do you ken this?"

Corp had promised not to tell, and he thought
he did not tell, but Tommy was too clever for
him. Grizel, it appeared, had heard Mr. Ogilvy
saying this strange thing to the doctor, and she
burned to pass it on to Tommy, but she could
not carry it to him herself, because—Why was
it? Oh, yes, because she hated him. So she
made a messenger of Corp, and warned him
against telling who had sent him with the
news.

Half enlightened, Tommy began to strut again. "You see there's something in me for all they say," he told Elspeth. "Listen to this. At the bursary examinations there was some English we had to turn into Latin, and it said, 'No man ever attained supreme eminence who worked for mere lucre; such efforts must ever be bounded by base mediocrity. None shall climb high but he who climbs for love, for in truth where the heart is, there alone shall the treasure be found.' Elspeth, it came ower me in a clink how true that was, and I sat saying it to myself, though I saw Gav Dishart and Willie Simpson and the rest beginning to put it into Latin at once, as little ta'en up wi' the words as if they had been about auld Hannibal. I aye kent, Elspeth, that I could never do much at the learning, but I didna see the reason till I read that. Syne I kent that playing so real-like in the Den, and telling about my fits when it wasna me that had them but Corp, and mourning for Lewis Doig's father, and writing letters for folk so grandly, and a' my other queer ploys that ended in Cathro's calling me Sentimental Tommy, was what my heart was in, and I saw in a jiffy that if thae things were work, I should soon rise to supreme eminence."

"But they're no," said Elspeth, sadly.

"No," he admitted, his face falling, "but, Elspeth, if I was to hear some day of work I could put my heart into as if it were a game! I wouldna be lang in finding the treasure syne. Oh, the blatter I would make!"

"I doubt there's no sic work," she answered,

but he told her not to be so sure. "I thought there wasna mysel'," he said, "till now, but sure as death my heart was as ta'en up wi' hunting for the right word as if it had been a game, and that was how the time slipped by so quick. Yet it was paying work, for the way I did it made Mr. Ogilvy see I should have got the prize, and a' body kens there's more clever-ness in him than in a cart-load o' ministers."

"But, but there are no more Hugh Black-adders to try for, Tommy!"

"That's nothing, there maun be other work o' the same kind. Elspeth, cheer up, I tell you, I'll find a wy!"

"But you didna ken yoursel' that you should have got the Hugh Blackadder?"

He would not let this depress him. "I ken now," he said. Nevertheless, why he should have got it was a mystery which he longed to fathom. Mr. Ogilvy had returned to Glen Quharity, so that an explanation could not be drawn from him even if he were willing to supply it, which was improbable; but Tommy caught Grizel in the Banker's Close and com-pelled her to speak.

"I won't tell you a word of what Mr. Ogilvy said," she insisted, in her obstinate way, and, oh, how she despised Corp for breaking his promise.

"Corp didna ken he telled me," said Tommy, less to clear Corp than to exalt him-self. "I wriggled it out o' him;" but even this did not bring Grizel to a proper frame of mind, so he said, to annoy her,

"At any rate you're fond o' me."

"I am not," she replied, stamping; "I think you are horrid."

"What else made you send Corp to me?"

"I did that because I heard you were calling yourself a blockhead."

"Oho," said he, "so you have been speiring about me though you winna speak to me!"

Grizel looked alarmed, and thinking to weaken his case, said, hastily, "I very nearly kept it from you, I said often to myself 'I won't tell him.'"

"So you have been thinking a lot about me!" was his prompt comment.

"If I have," she retorted, "I did not think nice things. And what is more, I was angry with myself for telling Corp to tell you."

Surely this was crushing, but apparently Tommy did not think so, for he said, "You did it against your will! That means I have a power over you that you canna resist. Oho, oho!"

Had she become more friendly so should he, had she shed one tear he would have melted immediately; but she only looked him up and down disdainfully, and it hardened him. He said with a leer, "I ken what makes you hold your hands so tight, it's to keep your arms frae wagging;" and then her cry, "How do you know?" convicted her. He had not succeeded in his mission, but on his way home he muttered, triumphantly, "I did her, I did her!" and once he stopped to ask himself the question, "Was it

D D

because my heart was in it?" It was their last
meeting till they were man and woman.

A blazing sun had come out on top of heavy
showers, and the land reeked and smelled as of
the wash-tub. The smaller girls of Monypenny
were sitting in passages playing at fivey, just as
Sappho, for instance, used to play it; but they
heard the Dubb of Prosen cart draw up at Aaron
Latta's door, and they followed it to see the last
of Tommy Sandys. Corp was already there,
calling in at the door every time he heard a sob;
"Dinna Elspeth, dinna, he'll find a wy," but
Grizel had refused to come, though Tommy
knew that she had been asking when he started
and which road the cart would take. Well, he
was not giving her a thought at any rate; his
box was in the cart now, and his face was
streaked with tears that were all for Elspeth.
She should not have come to the door, but she
came, and—it was such a pitiable sight that
Aaron Latta could not look on. He went
hurriedly to his workshop, but not to warp, and
even the carter was touched and he said to
Tommy, "I tell you what, man, I have to go
round by Causeway End smiddy, and you and
the crittur have time, if you like, to take the
short cut and meet me at the far corner o'
Caddam wood."

So Tommy and Elspeth, holding each other's
hands, took the short cut and they came to the
far end of Caddam, and Elspeth thought they
had better say it here before the cart came; but
Tommy said he would walk back with her

through the wood as far as the Toom Well, and they could say it there. They tried to say it at the Well, but—Elspeth was still with him when he returned to the far corner of Caddam, where the cart was now awaiting him. The carter was sitting on the shaft, and he told them he was in no hurry, and what is more, he had the delicacy to turn his back on them and struck his horse with the reins for looking round at the sorrowful pair. They should have said it now, but first Tommy walked back a little bit of the way with Elspeth, and then she came back with him, and that was to be the last time, but he could not leave her, and so, there they were looking woefully at each other, and it was not said yet.

They had said it now, and all was over; they were several paces apart. Elspeth smiled, she had promised to smile because Tommy said it would kill him if she was greeting at the very end. But what a smile it was! Tommy whistled, he had promised to whistle to show that he was happy as long as Elspeth could smile. She stood still, but he went on, turning round every few yards to—to whistle. " Never forget, day nor night, what I said to you," he called to her. " You're the only one I love, and I care not a hair for Grizel."

But when he disappeared, shouting to her, " I'll find a wy, I'll find a wy," she screamed and ran after him. He was already in the cart, and it had started. He stood up in it and waved his hand to her, and she stood on the dyke and waved to him, and thus they stood waving till a hollow in the road swallowed cart and man and boy. Then Elspeth put her hands to her eyes and went sobbing homeward.

When she was gone, a girl who had heard all that had passed between them rose from among the broom of Caddam and took Elspeth's place on the dyke, where she stood motionless waiting for the cart to reappear as it climbed the other side of the hollow. She wore a black frock and a blue bonnet with white strings, but the cart was far away, and Tommy thought she was Elspeth, and springing to his feet again in the cart he waved and waved. At first she did not respond, for had she not heard him say " You're the only one I love, and I care not a hair for Grizel " ? And she knew he was mistaking her for Elspeth. But by and by it struck her that he would be more unhappy if he thought Elspeth was too overcome by grief to wave to him. Her arms rocked passionately ; no, no, she would not lift them to wave to him, he could be as unhappy as he chose. Then in a spirit of self-abnegation that surely raised her high among the daughters of men, though she was but a painted lady's child, she waved to him to save him pain, and he, still erect in the cart, waved back until nothing could be seen by either of them save wood and fields and a long, deserted road.

THE END

PRINTED BY CASSELL & COMPANY, LIMITED, LA BELLE SAUVAGE, LONDON, E.C.

By MAX PEMBERTON.

A Puritan's Wife. Illustrated. *Just published.* 6s.

"A Puritan's Wife" is a love story, that deals with the history of a Puritan who returns to England at the time of the Restoration, but is not included in the amnesty granted by Charles II. It is written in the quaint style which distinguishes the literature of the period.

The Impregnable City. *2nd Edition.* 6s.

"Those of us who are willing, and fain, to keep young as long as possible will read Mr. Pemberton's latest romance, 'The Impregnable City,' with the keenest delight."—*The Sketch.*

The Sea Wolves. *3rd Edition.* 6s.

"A story easy to begin and difficult, if not impossible, to leave off."—*Daily Chronicle.*

The Iron Pirate. *4th Edition.* 5s.

"One of the most thrilling books of adventure we have met with for some time."—*Athenæum.*

The Little Huguenot. *Third Edition.*

"Many readers will prefer Mr. Pemberton in the delicate and beautiful idyll he has just issued under the title of 'The Little Huguenot.'"—*British Weekly.*

By RIDER HAGGARD.

King Solomon's Mines. *100th Thousand.* 3s. 6d.

"To tell the truth, we would give many novels, say eight hundred (that is about the yearly harvest), for such a book."—*Saturday Review.*

By ANTHONY HOPE.

Father Stafford. *5th Edition.* 3s. 6d.

"The book will be heartily enjoyed by everyone who reads it, and will enhance its author's reputation."—*Scotsman.*

By BERTRAM MITFORD.

The White Shield. *4th Thousand.* 6s.

A new work, in which this popular author relates startling adventures amongst the Zulus and other tribes of South Africa.

By E. W. HORNUNG.

"Tiny Luttrell." 6s.

"'Tiny Luttrell' has a young Australian lady for its heroine—a charming incorporation of contradictions and inconsistencies."—*Daily Telegraph.*

The Rogue's March. Cloth gilt, 6s.

A powerful and exciting story dealing with the Prison and Transport System of sixty years ago. The reading of many books and of Parliamentary Papers of the period has supplied the author with his material.

By FRANK STOCKTON.

Mrs. Cliff's Yacht. *Just published.* 6s.

Stirring adventure and genuine humour characterise this new work from Mr. Stockton's pen. It is charmingly illustrated.

The Adventures of Captain Horn. *4th Edition.* 6s.

"Mr. Frank Stockton has prepared for his many admirers a great surprise and a surpassing treat."—*The Speaker.*

Pomona's Travels. 5s.

"Written with the happy blending of quaint naïveté and saturnine humour that is a familiar and ever-entertaining characteristic of Mr. Frank Stockton's fictional works."—*Daily Telegraph.*

By G. B. BURGIN.

Tuxter's Little Maid. 6s.

"'Tuxter's Little Maid,' by G. B. Burgin, is one of those rare fictitional masterpieces upon which the judicious critic feels inclined to lavish his whole stock of laudatory terms."—*Daily Telegraph.*

By JOHN BLOUNDELLE-BURTON.

The Hispaniola Plate. *3rd Thousand.* 6s.

"This cleverly constructed and vigorously written book is a tale of piracy and treasure-seeking, heaped up, pressed down, and running over with buccaneers, sharks, and foul weather."—*Scotsman.*

By J. MACLAREN COBBAN.

The Avenger of Blood. 3s. 6d.

"Mr. Maclaren Cobban's spirited romance commends itself at once to the moralist and the pleasure-seeking reader."—*Athenæum.*

By A. CONAN DOYLE.

The Doings of Raffles Haw. 3s. 6d.

"So full of life and variety that it is difficult to lay it down before the end is reached."—*Liverpool Mercury.*

By W. CLARK RUSSELL.

What Cheer! Dedicated by permission to H.R.H. The Duke of York. Cloth gilt, 6s.

List, ye Landsmen! A Romance of Incident. 6s.

"Never has he more cunningly contrived a tale full of romance and adventure. The breeze in which he delights rushes through his descriptions of wild plotting."—*Globe.*

Works by Q.

Ia : A Love Story. *2nd Edition.* 3s. 6d.

"'Ia,' a Cornish tale, will rank as one of the strongest of Q's short stories."—*Pall Mall Gazette.*

Wandering Heath. *2nd Edition.* 6s.

A Selection of Short Stories, uniform with "Noughts and Crosses" and "The Delectable Duchy."

Dead Man's Rock. A Romance. *17th Thousand.* 5s.

"A fascinating story which may be confidently recommended to those who have a taste for romance of the weird, mystic, and thrilling kind."—*Daily News.*

"I Saw Three Ships"; and Other Winter's Tales. *4th Edition.* 5s.

"Q has never written anything more fresh or lively than 'I Saw Three Ships'; and everyone who enjoys a breezy, humorous, and fiery story should make haste to read it."—*Scotsman.*

A Blot of Ink. 3s. 6d.

"Q has given us a delightful translation of M. Bazin's pleasant little story. It is only a trifle, delicate as a soap-bubble, but the colours of the sketch are laid on with masterly skill, and an atmosphere of brilliant sunshine pervades the whole book."—*Speaker.*

Noughts and Crosses : Stories, Studies, and Sketches. *4th Edition.* 5s.

"'Noughts and Crosses' is a book of altogether exceptional attractiveness and value."—*Globe.*

The Splendid Spur. *11th Thousand.* 5s.

"'The Splendid Spur' is decidedly Q's most successful effort, and we do not scruple to say that it raises its author to a high place in the new school of novelists—the school of action."—*The Times.*

The Blue Pavilions. *4th Edition.* 5s.

"'The Blue Pavilions,' by Q, is about as good a tale of dramatic and exciting adventure as the Baron remembers to have read—for some time, at least. . . . As a one-barrel novel, this ought to score a gold right in the centre."—*Punch.*

The Astonishing History of Troy Town. *5th Edition.* 5s.

"Original, amusing, and well carried out."—*Morning Post.*

"The book is singularly fresh, taking, and spirited."—*St. James's Gazette.*

The Delectable Duchy. Stories, Studies, and Sketches. *4th Edition.* 5s.

"Open this book where you may, you will light upon something that attracts and holds."—*Globe.*

CASSELL & COMPANY, Limited, *London; Paris & Melbourne.*

A SELECTED LIST

OF

CASSELL & COMPANY'S

PUBLICATIONS.

Illustrated, Fine Art, and other Volumes.

Abbeys and Churches of England and Wales, The: Descriptive, Historical, Pictorial. Series II. 21s.

Adventure, The World of. Fully Illustrated. Complete in Three Vols. 9s. each.

Adventures in Criticism. By A. T. QUILLER-COUCH. 6s.

Africa and its Explorers, The Story of. By Dr. ROBERT BROWN, F.R.G.S., &c. With about 800 Original Illustrations. Complete in 4 Vols. 7s. 6d. each.

Allon, Henry, D.D.: Pastor and Teacher. The Story of his Ministry, with Selected Sermons and Addresses. By the Rev. W. HARDY HARWOOD. 6s.

American Life. By PAUL DE ROUSIERS. 12s. 6d.

Animal Painting in Water Colours. With Coloured Plates. 5s.

Animals, Popular History of. By HENRY SCHERREN, F.Z.S. With 13 Coloured Plates and other Illustrations. 7s. 6d.

Architectural Drawing. By R. PHENÉ SPIERS. Illustrated. 10s. 6d.

Art, The Magazine of. Yearly Volume. With about 400 Illustrations, 14 Etchings or Photogravures, and a Series of Full-page Plates. 21s.

Artistic Anatomy. By Prof. M. DUVAL. *Cheap Edition*, 3s. 6d.

Astronomy, The Dawn of. A Study of the Temple Worship and Mythology of the Ancient Egyptians. By Professor J. NORMAN LOCKYER, C.B., F.R.S., &c. Illustrated. 21s.

Atlas, The Universal. A New and Complete General Atlas of the World. List of Maps, Prices, and all particulars on application.

Ballads and Songs. By WILLIAM MAKEPEACE THACKERAY. With Original Illustrations. 6s.

Barber, Charles Burton, The Works of. With Forty-one Plates and Portraits, and Introduction by HARRY FURNISS. 21s. net.

Battles of the Nineteenth Century. An entirely New and Original Work, with Several Hundred Illustrations. Complete in Two Vols., 9s. each.

"Belle Sauvage" Library, The. Cloth, 2s. (*A complete list of the volumes post free on application.*)

Beetles, Butterflies, Moths, and other Insects. By A. W. KAPPEL, F.L.S., F.E.S., and W. EGMONT KIRBY. With 12 Coloured Plates. 3s. 6d.

Biographical Dictionary, Cassell's New. Containing Memoirs of the Most Eminent Men and Women of all Ages and Countries. *Cheap Edition*. 3s. 6d.

Birds' Nests, British: How, Where, and When to Find and Identify Them. By R. KEARTON. With nearly 130 Illustrations of Nests, Eggs, Young, etc., from Photographs by C. KEARTON. 21s.

Birds' Nests, Eggs, and Egg-Collecting. By R. KEARTON. Illustrated with 16 Coloured Plates of Eggs. *Fifth and Enlarged Edition.* 5s.

Black Watch, The. A Vivid Descriptive Account of this Famous Regiment. By ARCHIBALD FORBES. 6s.

Britain's Roll of Glory; or, the Victoria Cross, its Heroes, and their Valour. By D. H. PARRY. Illustrated. 7s. 6d.

British Ballads. 275 Original Illustrations. Two Vols. Cloth, 15s.

British Battles on Land and Sea. By JAMES GRANT. With about 800 Illustrations. Four Vols., 4to, £1 16s.; *Library Edition*, Four Vols., £2.

Building World. Half-yearly Volumes, I. and II. 4s. each.

Butterflies and Moths, European. By W. F. KIRBY. With 61 Coloured Plates. 35s.

Canaries and Cage-Birds, The Illustrated Book of. By W. A. BLAKSTON, W. SWAYSLAND, and A. F. WIENER. With 56 Facsimile Coloured Plates. 35s.

Captain Horn, The Adventures of. By FRANK STOCKTON. 6s.

Capture of the "Estrella," The. By COMMANDER CLAUD HARDING, R.N. *Cheap Illustrated Edition.* 3s. 6d.

Cassell's Family Magazine. Yearly Volume. Illustrated. 7s. 6d.

Cathedrals, Abbeys, and Churches of England and Wales. Descriptive, Historical, Pictorial. *Popular Edition.* Two Vols. 25s.

Cats and Kittens. By HENRIETTE RONNER. With Portrait and 13 magnificent Full-page Photogravure Plates and numerous Illustrations. 4to, £2 10s.

China Painting. By FLORENCE LEWIS. With Sixteen Coloured Plates, &c. 5s.

Choice Dishes at Small Cost. By A. G. PAYNE. *Cheap Edition*, 1s.

Chums. The Illustrated Paper for Boys. Yearly Volume, 8s.

Cities of the World. Four Vols. Illustrated. 7s. 6d. each.

Civil Service, Guide to Employment in the. *Entirely New Edition.* Paper, 1s.; cloth, 1s. 6d.

Clinical Manuals for Practitioners and Students of Medicine. (*A List of Volumes forwarded post free on application to the Publishers.*)

Cobden Club, Works published for the. (*A Complete List on application.*)

Colour. By Prof. A. H. CHURCH. *New and Enlarged Edition*, 3s. 6d.

Combe, George, The Select Works of. Issued by Authority of the Combe Trustees. *Popular Edition*, 1s. each, net.

> The Constitution of Man. Moral Philosophy. Science and Religion.
> Discussions on Education. American Notes.

Conning Tower, In a; or, How I Took H.M.S. "Majestic" into Action. By H. O. ARNOLD-FORSTER, M.P. *Cheap Edition.* Illustrated. 6d.

Conquests of the Cross. Edited by EDWIN HODDER. With numerous Original Illustrations. Complete in Three Vols. 9s. each.

Cook, The Thorough Good. By GEORGE AUGUSTUS SALA. With 900 Recipes. 21s.

Cookery, Cassell's Dictionary of. With about 9,000 Recipes, and Key to the Principles of Cookery. 5s.

Cookery, A Year's. By PHYLLIS BROWNE. *New and Enlarged Edition*, 3s. 6d.

Cookery Book, Cassell's New Universal. By LIZZIE HERITAGE. With 12 Coloured Plates and other Illustrations. 1,344 pages, strongly bound in leather gilt, 6s.

Cookery, Cassell's Popular. With Four Coloured Plates. Cloth gilt, 2s.

Cookery, Cassell's Shilling. 125*th Thousand*. 1s.

Cookery, Vegetarian. By A. G. PAYNE. 1s. 6d.

Cooking by Gas, The Art of. By MARIE J. SUGG. Illustrated. Cloth, 2s.

Cottage Gardening. Edited by W. ROBINSON, F.L.S. Illustrated. Half-yearly Vols., 2s. 6d. each.

Countries of the World, The. By DR. ROBERT BROWN, F.L.S. In Six Vols., with about 750 Illustrations. 7s. 6d. each. Cheap Edition. Vols. I., II. and III., 6s. each.

Cyclopædia, Cassell's Concise. Brought down to the latest date. With about 600 Illustrations. 7s. 6d.

Cyclopædia, Cassell's Miniature. Containing 30,000 Subjects. Cloth, 2s. 6d.; half-roxburgh, 4s.

David Balfour, The Adventures of. By R. L. STEVENSON. Illustrated. Two Vols. 6s. each.

> Part 1.—Kidnapped.   Part 2.—Catriona.

Dictionaries. (For description, see alphabetical letter.) Religion, Biographical, Encyclopædic, Concise Cyclopædia, Miniature Cyclopædia, Mechanical, English, English History, Phrase and Fable, Cookery, Domestic. (French, German, and Latin, see with *Educational Works*.)

Diet and Cookery for Common Ailments. By a Fellow of the Royal College of Physicians, and PHYLLIS BROWNE. *Cheap Edition.* 2s. 6d.

Dog, Illustrated Book of the. By VERO SHAW, B.A. With 28 Coloured Plates. Cloth bevelled, 35s.; half-morocco, 45s.

Domestic Dictionary, The. An Encyclopædia for the Household. Cloth, 7s. 6d.

Doré Don Quixote, The. With about 400 Illustrations by GUSTAVE DORÉ. *Cheap Edition*, bevelled boards, gilt edges, 10s. 6d.

Doré Gallery, The. With 250 Illustrations by GUSTAVE DORÉ. 4to, 42s.

Doré's Dante's Inferno. Illustrated by GUSTAVE DORÉ. *Popular Edition.* With Preface by A. J. BUTLER. Cloth gilt or buckram, 7s. 6d.

Doré's Dante's Purgatory and Paradise. Illustrated by GUSTAVE DORÉ. *Cheap Edition.* 7s. 6d.

Doré's Milton's Paradise Lost. Illustrated by GUSTAVE DORÉ. 4to, 21s. *Popular Edition.* Cloth gilt, or buckram gilt. 7s. 6d.

Earth, Our, and its Story. Edited by Dr. ROBERT BROWN, F.L.S. With 36 Coloured Plates and 740 Wood Engravings. Complete in Three Vols. 9s. each.

Edinburgh, Old and New, Cassell's. With 600 Illustrations. Three Vols. 9s. each; library binding, £1 10s. the set.

Egypt: Descriptive, Historical, and Picturesque. By Prof. G. EBERS. Translated by CLARA BELL, with Notes by SAMUEL BIRCH, LL.D., &c. Two Vols. 42s.

Electric Current, The. How Produced and How Used. By R. MULLINEUX WALMSLEY, D.Sc., &c. Illustrated. 10s. 6d.

Electricity, Practical. By Prof. W. E. AYRTON. Illustrated. Cloth, 7s. 6d.

Electricity in the Service of Man. A Popular and Practical Treatise. With upwards of 950 Illustrations. *New and Revised Edition*, 10s. 6d.

Employment for Boys on Leaving School, Guide to. By W. S. BEARD, F.R.G.S. 1s. 6d.

Encyclopædic Dictionary, The. Complete in Fourteen Divisional Vols., 10s. 6d. each; or Seven Vols., half-morocco, 21s. each; half-russia, 25s. each.

England, Cassell's Illustrated History of. With upwards of 2,000 Illustrations. *New and Revised Edition.* Complete in Eight Vols., 9s. each; cloth gilt, and embossed gilt top and headbanded, £4 net the set.

English Dictionary, Cassell's. Containing Definitions of upwards of 100,000 Words and Phrases. *Cheap Edition*, 3s. 6d. ; *Superior Edition*, 5s.

English History, The Dictionary of. Edited by SIDNEY LOW, B.A., and Prof. F. S. PULLING, M.A., with Contributions by Eminent Writers. *Cheap Edition.* 10s. 6d.

English Literature, Library of. By Prof. H. MORLEY. In 5 Vols. 7s. 6d. each.

English Literature, Morley's First Sketch of. *Revised Edition*, 7s. 6d.

English Literature, The Story of. By ANNA BUCKLAND. 3s. 6d.

English Writers from the Earliest Period to Shakespeare. By HENRY MORLEY. Eleven Vols. 5s. each.

Æsop's Fables. Illustrated by ERNEST GRISET. *Cheap Edition.* Cloth, 3s. 6d. ; bevelled boards, gilt edges, 5s.

Etiquette of Good Society. *New Edition.* Edited and Revised by LADY COLIN CAMPBELL. 1s. ; cloth, 1s. 6d.

Europe, Cassell's Pocket Guide to. Leather, 6s.

Fairy Tales Far and Near. Retold by Q. Illustrated. 3s. 6d.

Fairway Island. By HORACE HUTCHINSON. *Cheap Edition.* 2s. 6d.

Family Physician. By Eminent PHYSICIANS and SURGEONS. Cloth, 21s. ; roxburgh, 25s.

Fiction, Cassell's Popular Library of. 3s. 6d. each.

The Snare of the Fowler. By Mrs. ALEX-ANDER.	"La Bella," and others. By EGERTON CASTLE.
Out of the Jaws of Death. By FRANK BARRETT.	A Blot of Ink. Translated by Q. and PAUL M. FRANCKE. 5s.
Fourteen Ito One, &c. By ELIZABETH STUART PHELPS.	The Avenger of Blood. By J. MACLAREN COBBAN.
The Medicine Lady. By L. T. MEADE.	A Modern Dick Whittington. By JAMES PAYN.
Leona. By Mrs. MOLESWORTH.	
Father Stafford. A Novel. By ANTHONY HOPE.	The Man in Black. By STANLEY WEYMAN.
	The Doings of Raffles Haw. By A. CONAN DOYLE.
Dr. Dumány's Wife. By MAURUS JÓKAI.	

Field Naturalist's Handbook, The. By Revs. J. G. WOOD and THEODORE WOOD. *Cheap Edition*, 2s. 6d.

Figuier's Popular Scientific Works. With Several Hundred Illustrations in each. 3s. 6d. each.

The Insect World.	Reptiles and Birds.	The Vegetable World.
The Human Race.	Mammalia.	Ocean World.
	The World before the Deluge.	

Figure Painting in Water Colours. With 16 Coloured Plates. 7s. 6d.

Flora's Feast. A Masque of Flowers. Penned and Pictured by WALTER CRANE. With 40 pages in Colours. 5s.

Flower Painting, Elementary. With Eight Coloured Plates. 3s.

Flowers, and How to Paint Them. By MAUD NAFTEL. With Coloured Plates. 5s.

Football: the Rugby Union Game. Edited by Rev. F. MARSHALL. Illustrated. *New and Enlarged Edition.* 7s. 6d.

For Glory and Renown. By D. H. PARRY. Illustrated. *Cheap Edition.* 3s. 6d.

Fossil Reptiles, A History of British. By Sir RICHARD OWEN, F.R.S., &c. With 268 Plates. In Four Vols. £12 12s.

France, From the Memoirs of a Minister of. By STANLEY WEYMAN. 6s.

Franco-German War, Cassell's History of the. Complete in Two Vols., containing about 500 Illustrations. 9s. each.

Free Lance in a Far Land, A. By HERBERT COMPTON. 6s.

Garden Flowers, Familiar. By SHIRLEY HIBBERD. With Coloured Plates by F. E. HULME, F.L.S. Complete in Five Series. Cloth gilt, 12s. 6d. each.

Gazetteer of Great Britain and Ireland, Cassell's. With numerous Illustrations and Maps in Colours. Vols. I., II. and III. 7s. 6d. each.

Gladstone, The Right Hon. W. E., M.P., Life of. Profusely Illustrated. 1s.

Gleanings from Popular Authors. Two Vols. With Original Illustrations. 9s. each. Two Vols. in One, 15s.

Gulliver's Travels. With 88 Engravings. Cloth, 3s. 6d. ; cloth gilt, 5s.

Gun and its Development, The. By W. W. GREENER. Illustrated. 10s. 6d.

Guns, Modern Shot. By W. W. GREENER. Illustrated. 5s.

Health, The Book of. By Eminent Physicians and Surgeons. Cloth, 21s.

Heavens, The Story of the. By Sir ROBERT STAWELL BALL, LL.D., F.R.S. With Coloured Plates and Wood Engravings. *Popular Edition*, 12s. 6d.

Hiram Golf's Religion; or, the Shoemaker by the Grace of God. 2s.

Hispaniola Plate. A Romance. By JOHN BLOUNDELLE-BURTON. 6s.

History, A Footnote to. Eight Years of Trouble in Samoa. By R. L. STEVENSON. 6s.

Home Life of the Ancient Greeks, The. Translated by ALICE ZIMMERN. Illustrated. *Cheap Edition.* 5s.

Horse, The Book of the. By SAMUEL SIDNEY. With 17 Full-page Collotype Plates of Celebrated Horses of the Day, and numerous other Illustrations. Cloth, 15s.

Horses and Dogs. By O. EERELMAN. With Descriptive Text. Translated from the Dutch by CLARA BELL. With Author's portrait and Fifteen Full-page and other Illustrations. 25s. net.

Houghton, Lord : The Life, Letters, and Friendships of Richard Monckton Milnes, First Lord Houghton. By Sir WEMYSS REID. Two Vols. 32s.

Household, Cassell's Book of the. Illustrated. Complete in Four Vols. 5s. each; or Four Vols. in Two, half-morocco, 25s.

Hygiene and Public Health. By B. ARTHUR WHITELEGGE, M.D. Illustrated. *New and Revised Edition.* 7s. 6d.

Ia : A Love Story. By Q. Illustrated. 3s. 6d.

Impregnable City, The. By MAX PEMBERTON. 6s.

In-door Amusements, Card Games, and Fireside Fun, Cassell's Book of. With numerous Illustrations. *Cheap Edition.* Cloth, 2s.

Iron Pirate, The. By MAX PEMBERTON. Illustrated. 5s.

Island Nights' Entertainments. By R. L. STEVENSON. Illustrated, 6s.

Italy from the Fall of Napoleon I. in 1815 to 1890. By J. W. PROBYN. 3s. 6d.

Kennel Guide, Practical. By Dr. GORDON STABLES. Illustrated. *Cheap Edition*, 1s.

Khiva, A Ride to. By Col. FRED BURNABY. *New Edition.* Illustrated. 3s. 6d.

King George, In the Days of. By COL. PERCY GROVES. Illustrated. 1s. 6d.

King's Hussar, A. Memoirs of a Troop Sergeant-Major of the 14th (King's) Hussars. Edited by HERBERT COMPTON. 3s. 6d.

Ladies' Physician, The. By a London Physician. *Cheap Edition, Revised and Enlarged.* 3s. 6d.

Lady's Dressing Room, The. Translated from the French by LADY COLIN CAMPBELL. *Cheap Edition.* 2s. 6d.

Lady Biddy Fane, The Admirable. By FRANK BARRETT. *New Edition.* With 12 Full-page Illustrations. 6s.

Lake Dwellings of Europe. By ROBERT MUNRO, M.D., M.A. Cloth, 31s. 6d.

Letters, The Highway of; and its Echoes of Famous Footsteps. By THOMAS ARCHER. *Cheap Edition*, Illustrated, 5s.

Letts's Diaries and other Time-saving Publications are now published exclusively by CASSELL & COMPANY. (*A List sent post free on application.*)

Lights of Sydney, The. By LILIAN TURNER. With Eight Illustrations. 3s. 6d.

Little Minister, The. By J. M. BARRIE. *Illustrated Edition*, 6s.

Lobengula, Three Years with, and Experiences in South Africa. By J. COOPER-CHADWICK. *Cheap Edition.* 2s. 6d.

Locomotive Engine, The Biography of a. By HENRY FRITH. 3s. 6d.

Loftus, Lord Augustus, P.C., G.C.B., The Diplomatic Reminiscences of. First Series. With Portrait. Two Vols. 32s. Second Series. Two Vols. 32s.

London, Cassell's Guide to. With Numerous Illustrations. 6d.

London, Greater. By EDWARD WALFORD. Two Vols. With about 400 Illustrations. 9s. each. *Library Edition.* Two Vols. £1 the set.

London, Old and New. By WALTER THORNBURY and EDWARD WALFORD. Six Vols., with about 1,200 Illustrations. Cloth, 9s. each. *Library Edition*, £3.

London, The Queen's. With nearly 400 Superb Views. 9s.

Loveday : A Tale of a Stirring Time. By A. E. Wickham. Illustrated. 6s.

Manchester, Old and New. By WILLIAM ARTHUR SHAW, M.A. With Original Illustrations. Three Vols., 31s. 6d.

Medical Handbook of Life Assurance. By JAMES EDWARD POLLOCK, M.D., and JAMES CHISHOLM. *New and Revised Edition.* 7s. 6d.

Medicine, Manuals for Students of. (*A List forwarded post free on application.*)

Modern Europe, A History of. By C. A. FYFFE, M.A. *Cheap Edition in One Volume*, 10s. 6d.; *Library Edition, Illustrated*, 3 vols., 7s. 6d. each.

Mrs. Cliff's Yacht. By FRANK STOCKTON. Illustrated. 6s.

Music, Illustrated History of. By EMIL NAUMANN. Edited by the Rev. Sir F. A. GORE OUSELEY, Bart. Illustrated. Two Vols. 31s. 6d.

National Library, Cassell's. Consisting of 214 Volumes. Paper covers, 3d.; cloth, 6d. (*A Complete List of the Volumes post free on application.*)

Natural History, Cassell's Concise. By E. PERCEVAL WRIGHT, M.A., M.D., F.L.S. With several Hundred Illustrations. 7s. 6d.; also kept half-bound.

Natural History, Cassell's New. Edited by P. MARTIN DUNCAN, M.B., F.R.S., F.G.S. Complete in Six Vols. With about 2,000 Illustrations. Cloth, 9s. each.

Nature's Wonder Workers. By KATE R. LOVELL. Illustrated. 2s. 6d.

Nelson, The Life of. By ROBERT SOUTHEY. Illustrated with Eight Plates. 3s. 6d.

New Zealand, Pictorial. With Preface by Sir W. B. PERCEVAL, K.C.M.G. Illust. 6s.

Nursing for the Home and for the Hospital, A Handbook of. By CATHERINE J. WOOD. *Cheap Edition*, 1s. 6d.; cloth, 2s.

Nursing of Sick Children, A Handbook for the. By CATHERINE J. WOOD. 2s. 6d.

Old Maids and Young. By ELSA D'ESTERRE-KEELING. 6s.

Old Boy's Yarns, An. By HAROLD AVERY. With 8 Plates. 3s. 6d.

Our Own Country. Six Vols. With 1,200 Illustrations. Cloth, 7s. 6d. each.

Painting, The English School of. By ERNEST CHESNEAU. *Cheap Edition*, 3s. 6d.

Paris, Old and New. Profusely Illustrated. Complete in Two Volumes. 9s. each, or gilt edges, 10s. 6d. each.

Parliament, A Diary of the Home Rule, 1892-95. By H. W. LUCY. 10s. 6d.

Peoples of the World, The. By Dr. ROBERT BROWN, F.L.S. Complete in Six Vols. With Illustrations. 7s. 6d. each.

Photography for Amateurs. By T. C. HEPWORTH. Illustrated, 1s.; cloth, 1s. 6d.

Phrase and Fable, Dr. Brewer's Dictionary of. *Entirely New and largely increased Edition.* 10s. 6d. Also in half-morocco.

Physiology for Students, Elementary. By ALFRED T. SCHOFIELD, M.D., M.R.C.S. With Two Coloured Plates and numerous Illustrations. *New Edition.* 5s.

Picturesque America. Complete in Four Vols., with 48 Exquisite Steel Plates, and about 800 Original Wood Engravings. £12 12s. the set. *Popular Edition*, Vols. I., II. and III., price 18s. each.

Picturesque Australasia, Cassell's. With upwards of 1,000 Illustrations. In Four Vols., 7s. 6d. each.

Picturesque Canada. With about 600 Original Illustrations. Two Vols. £9 9s. the set.

Picturesque Europe. Complete in Five Vols. Each containing 13 Exquisite Steel Plates, from Original Drawings, and nearly 200 Original Illustrations. £21. *Popular Edition.* In Five Vols. 18s. each.

Picturesque Mediterranean, The. With a Series of Magnificent Illustrations from Original Designs by leading Artists of the day. Two Vols. Cloth, £2 2s. each.

Pigeon Keeper, The Practical. By LEWIS WRIGHT. Illustrated. 3s. 6d.

Pigeons, Fulton's Book of. Edited by LEWIS WRIGHT. Revised, Enlarged, and Supplemented by the Rev. W. F. LUMLEY. With 50 Full-page Illustrations. *Popular Edition.* In One Vol., 10s. 6d. *Original Edition*, with 50 Coloured Plates and numerous Wood Engravings. 21s.

Planet, The Story of Our. By the Rev. Prof. BONNEY, F.R.S., &c. With Coloured Plates and Maps and about 100 Illustrations. *Cheap Edition.* 10s. 6d.

Playthings and Parodies. Short Stories, Sketches, &c. By BARRY PAIN. 3s. 6d.

Pocket Library, Cassell's. Cloth, 1s. 4d. each.

A King's Diary. By PERCY WHITE.	The Little Huguenot. By MAX PEMBERTON.
A White Baby. By JAMES WELSH.	A Whirl Asunder. By GERTRUDE ATHERTON.
Lady Bonnie's Experiment. By TIGHE HOPKINS.	The Paying Guest. By GEO. GISSING.

Polytechnic Series, The. Practical Illustrated Manuals. (*A List will be sent on application.*)

Pomona's Travels. By FRANK R. STOCKTON. Illustrated. 5s.

Portrait Gallery, Cassell's Universal. Containing 240 Portraits of Celebrated Men and Women of the Day. Cloth, 6s.

Portrait Gallery, The Cabinet. Complete in Five Series, each containing 36 Cabinet Photographs of Eminent Men and Women of the day. 15s. each.

Poultry Keeper, The Practical. By LEWIS WRIGHT. Illustrated. 3s. 6d.

Poultry, The Book of. By LEWIS WRIGHT. *Popular Edition.* Illustrated. 10s. 6d.

Poultry, The Illustrated Book of. By LEWIS WRIGHT. With Fifty Exquisite Coloured Plates, and numerous Wood Engravings. *Revised Edition.* Cloth, gilt edges, 21s. ; half-morocco (*price on application*).

"Punch," The History of. By M. H. SPIELMANN. With nearly 170 Illustrations, Portraits, and Facsimiles. Cloth, 16s. ; *Large Paper Edition*, £2 2s. net.

Prison Princess, A. By MAJOR ARTHUR GRIFFITHS. 6s.

Puritan's Wife, A. By MAX PEMBERTON. Illustrated. 6s.

Q's Works, Uniform Edition of. 5s. each.

Dead Man's Rock.	The Astonishing History of Troy Town.
The Splendid Spur.	"I Saw Three Ships," and other Winter's Tales.
The Blue Pavilions.	Noughts and Crosses.

The Delectable Duchy. Stories, Studies, and Sketches.

Queen Summer; or, The Tourney of the Lily and the Rose. Penned and Portrayed by WALTER CRANE. With 40 pages in Colours. 6s.

Queen, The People's Life of their. By Rev. E. J. HARDY, M.A. 1s.

Queen Victoria, The Life and Times of. By ROBERT WILSON. Complete in 2 Vols. With numerous Illustrations. 9s. each.

Queen's Scarlet, The. By G. MANVILLE FENN. Illustrated. 3s. 6d.

Rabbit-Keeper, The Practical. By CUNICULUS. Illustrated. 3s. 6d.

Railway Guides, Official Illustrated. With Illustrations on nearly every page. Maps, &c. Paper covers, 1s.; cloth, 2s.

London and North Western Railway.	Great Eastern Railway.
Great Western Railway.	London and South Western Railway.
Midland Railway.	London, Brighton and South Coast Railway.
Great Northern Railway.	South Eastern Railway.

Railway Guides, Official Illustrated. Abridged and Popular Editions. Paper covers, 3d. each.

Great Eastern Railway.	Great Western Railway.
London and North Western Railway.	Midland Railway.
London and South Western Railway.	Great Northern Railway.
London, Brighton and South Coast Railway.	South Eastern Railway.

Railways, Our. Their Origin, Development, Incident, and Romance. By JOHN PENDLETON. Illustrated. 2 Vols., 12s.

Rivers of Great Britain : Descriptive, Historical, Pictorial.

The Royal River: The Thames from Source to Sea. *Popular Edition*, 16s.
Rivers of the East Coast. With highly-finished Engravings. *Popular Edition*, 16s.

Robinson Crusoe. *Cassell's New Fine-Art Edition.* With upwards of 100 Original Illustrations. *Cheap Edition*, 3s. 6d. or 5s.

Rogue's March, The. By E. W. HORNUNG. 6s.

Romance, The World of. Illustrated. One Vol., cloth, 9s.

Ronner, Henriette, The Painter of Cat-Life and Cat-Character. By M. H. SPIELMANN. Containing a Series of beautiful Phototype Illustrations. 12s.

Royal Academy Pictures, 1896. With upwards of 200 magnificent reproductions of Pictures in the Royal Academy of 1896. 7s. 6d.

Russo-Turkish War, Cassell's History of. With about 500 Illustrations. Two Vols., 9s. each ; library binding, One Vol., 15s. *New Edition.* Vol. I., 9s.

Sala, George Augustus, The Life and Adventures of. By Himself. *Library Edition* in Two Vols. 32s. *Cheap Edition*, One Vol., 7s. 6d.

Saturday Journal, Cassell's. Illustrated throughout. Yearly Vol., 7s. 6d.

Science for All. Edited by Dr. ROBERT BROWN, M.A., F.L.S., &c. *Revised Edition.* With 1,500 Illustrations. Five Vols. 9s. each.

Science Series, The Century. Consisting of Biographies of Eminent Scientific Men of the present Century. Edited by Sir HENRY ROSCOE, D.C.L., F.R.S., M.P. Crown 8vo, 3s. 6d. each.

John Dalton and the Rise of Modern Chemistry. By Sir HENRY E. ROSCOE, F.R.S.
Major Rennell, F.R.S., and the Rise of English Geography. By CLEMENTS R. MARKHAM, C.B., F.R.S., President of the Royal Geographical Society.
Justus Von Liebig: His Life and Work. By W. A. SHENSTONE.
The Herschels and Modern Astronomy. By Miss AGNES M. CLERKE.
Charles Lyell and Modern Geology. By Professor T. G. BONNEY, F.R.S.
J. Clerk Maxwell and Modern Physics. By R. T. GLAZEBROOK, F.R.S.
Humphry Davy, Poet and Philosopher. By T. E. THORPE, F.R.S.
Charles Darwin and the Theory of Natural Selection. By EDWARD B. POULTON, M.A., F.R.S.

Scotland, Picturesque and Traditional. By G. E. EYRE-TODD. 6s.

Sea, The Story of the. An Entirely New and Original Work. Edited by Q. Illustrated. Complete in Two Vols., 9s. each.

Sea-Wolves, The. By MAX PEMBERTON. Illustrated. **6s.**

Sentimental Tommy. By J. M. BARRIE. 6s.

Shaftesbury, The Seventh Earl of, K.G., The Life and Work of. By EDWIN HODDER. Illustrated. *Cheap Edition,* 3s. 6d.

Shakespeare, Cassell's Quarto Edition. Edited by CHARLES and MARY COWDEN CLARKE, and containing about 600 Illustrations by H. C. SELOUS. Complete in Three Vols., cloth gilt, £3 3s.—Also published in Three separate Vols., in cloth, viz. :—The COMEDIES, 21s. ; The HISTORICAL PLAYS, 18s. 6d. ; The TRAGEDIES, 25s.

Shakespeare, The England of. *New Edition.* By E. GOADBY. With Full-page Illustrations. Crown 8vo, 224 pages, 2s. 6d.

Shakespeare, The Plays of. Edited by Prof. HENRY MORLEY. Complete in 13 Vols., cloth, in box, 21s. ; also 39 Vols., cloth, in box, 21s. ; half-morocco, cloth sides, 42s.

Shakspere, The International. *Édition de luxe.*

King Henry VIII. By Sir JAMES LINTON, P.R.I. (*Price on application.*)
Othello. Illustrated by FRANK DICKSEE, R.A. £3 10s.
King Henry IV. Illustrated by Herr EDUARD GRÜTZNER. £3 10s.
As You Like It. Illustrated by the late Mons. ÉMILE BAYARD. £3 10s.

Shakspere, The Leopold. With 400 Illustrations, and an Introduction by F. J. FURNIVALL. *Cheap Edition,* 3s. 6d. Cloth gilt, gilt edges, 5s. ; roxburgh, 7s. 6d.

Shakspere, The Royal. With Exquisite Steel Plates and Wood Engravings. Three Vols. 15s. each.

Sketches, The Art of Making and Using. From the French of G. FRAIPONT. By CLARA BELL. With Fifty Illustrations. 2s. 6d.

Social England. A Record of the Progress of the People. By various writers. Edited by H. D. TRAILL, D.C.L. Vols. I., II., and III., 15s. each. Vols. IV. and V., 17s. each. Vol. VI., 18s.

Scarlet and Blue, or Songs for Soldiers and Sailors. By JOHN FARMER. 5s. Words only, 6d.

Sorrow, The Highway of. By HESBA STRETTON and a well-known Russian exile. 6s.

Sports and Pastimes, Cassell's Complete Book of. *Cheap Edition,* 3s. 6d.

Squire, The. By MRS. PARR. *Cheap Edition,* 3s. 6d.

Star-Land. By Sir ROBERT STAWELL BALL, LL.D., &c. Illustrated. 6s.

Story of Francis Cludde, The. A Novel. By STANLEY J. WEYMAN. 6s.

Story of My Life, The. By SIR RICHARD TEMPLE. Two Vols., 21s.

Sun, The Story of the. By Sir ROBERT STAWELL BALL, LL.D., F.R.S., F.R.A.S. With Eight Coloured Plates and other Illustrations. 21s.

Sunshine Series, Cassell's. In Vols. 1s. each. *A List post free on application.*

Taxation, Municipal, at Home and Abroad. By J. J. O'MEARA. 7s. 6d.

Thames, The Tidal. By GRANT ALLEN. With India Proof Impressions of 20 Magnificent Full-page Photogravure Plates, and many other Illustrations, after original drawings by W. L. WYLLIE, A.R.A. *New Edition,* cloth, 42s. net. Also in half-morocco (*price on application*).

Things I have Seen and People I have Known. By G. A. SALA. With Portrait and Autograph. 2 Vols. 21s.

Three Homes. By the VERY REV. DEAN FARRAR, D.D., F.R.S. *New Edition.* With 8 Full-page Illustrations. 6s.

To the Death. By R. D. CHETWODE. With Four Plates. 5s.

"Treasure Island" Series, The. *Cheap Illustrated Edition.* Cloth, 3s. 6d. each.
Treasure Island. By ROBERT LOUIS STEVENSON.
The Master of Ballantrae. By ROBERT LOUIS STEVENSON.
The Black Arrow: A Tale of the Two Roses. By ROBERT LOUIS STEVENSON.
King Solomon's Mines. By H. RIDER HAGGARD.

Treatment, The Year-Book of, for 1897. A Critical Review for Practitioners of Medicine and Surgery. Thirteenth Year of Issue. 7s. 6d.

Trees, Familiar. By Prof. G. S. BOULGER, F.L.S., F.G.S. Two Series. With Forty Coloured Plates in each. (*Price on application.*)

Tuxter's Little Maid. By G. B. BURGIN. 6s.

Uncle Tom's Cabin. By HARRIET BEECHER STOWE. With upwards of 100 Original Illustrations. *Fine Art Memorial Edition.* 7s. 6d.

"Unicode": The Universal Telegraphic Phrase Book. Pocket or Desk Edition. 2s. 6d. each.

United States, Cassell's History of the. By EDMUND OLLIER. With 600 Illustrations. Three Vols. 9s. each.

Universal History, Cassell's Illustrated. With nearly ONE THOUSAND ILLUSTRATIONS. Vol. I. Early and Greek History.—Vol. II. The Roman Period.—Vol. III. The Middle Ages.—Vol. IV. Modern History. 9s. each.

Verses, Wise or Otherwise. By ELLEN THORNEYCROFT FOWLER. 3s. 6d.

Wandering Heath. Short Stories. By Q. 6s.

War and Peace, Memories and Studies of. By ARCHIBALD FORBES. *Original Edition*, 16s. *Cheap Edition*, 6s.

Water-Colour Painting, A Course of. With Twenty-four Coloured Plates by R. P. LEITCH, and full Instructions to the Pupil. 5s.

Westminster Abbey, Annals of. By E. T. BRADLEY (Mrs. A. MURRAY SMITH). Illustrated. With a Preface by The DEAN OF WESTMINSTER. 63s.

What Cheer ! By W. CLARK RUSSELL. 6s.

White Shield, The. By BERTRAM MITFORD. 6s.

Wild Birds, Familiar. By W. SWAYSLAND. Four Series. With 40 Coloured Plates in each. (In sets only, price on application.)

Wild Flowers, Familiar. By F. E. HULME, F.L.S., F.S.A. Five Series. With 40 Coloured Plates in each. (In sets only, price on application.)

Wild Flowers Collecting Book. In Six Parts, 4d. each.

Wild Flowers Drawing and Painting Book. In Six Parts. 4d. each.

Windsor Castle, The Governor's Guide to. By the Most Noble the MARQUIS OF LORNE, K.T. Profusely Illustrated. Limp cloth, 1s. Cloth boards, gilt edges. 2s.

World of Wit and Humour, Cassell's New. With New Pictures and New Text. Complete in Two Vols., 6s. each.

With Claymore and Bayonet. By Col. PERCY GROVES. With 8 Plates. 3s. 6d

Work. The Illustrated Journal for Mechanics. Half-Yearly Vols. 4s. each.

"Work" Handbooks. A Series of Practical Manuals prepared under the Direction of PAUL N. HASLUCK, Editor of *Work.* Illustrated. Cloth, 1s. each.

World of Wonders, The. With 400 Illustrations. *Cheap Edition.* Vol. I. 4s. 6d.

Wrecker, The. By R. L. STEVENSON and LLOYD OSBOURNE. Illustrated. 6s.

ILLUSTRATED MAGAZINES.

The Quiver, for Sunday and General Reading. Monthly, 6d.

Cassell's Family Magazine. Monthly, 6d.

" Little Folks" Magazine. Monthly, 6d.

The Magazine of Art. Monthly, 1s. 4d.

Cassell's Saturday Journal. Weekly, 1d. ; Monthly, 6d.

Chums. The Illustrated Paper for Boys. Weekly, 1d.; Monthly, 6d.

Work. Illustrated Journal for Mechanics. Weekly, 1d.; Monthly, 6d.

Building World. The New Practical Journal on Building and Building Trades. Weekly, 1d. ; Monthly, 6d.

Cottage Gardening. Illustrated. Weekly, ½d. ; Monthly, 3d.

** *Full particulars of* CASSELL & COMPANY'S **Monthly Serial Publications** *will be found in* CASSELL & COMPANY'S COMPLETE CATALOGUE.

Catalogues of CASSELL & COMPANY'S PUBLICATIONS, which may be had at all Booksellers', or will be sent post free on application to the Publishers :—

CASSELL'S COMPLETE CATALOGUE, containing particulars of upwards of One Thousand Volumes.

CASSELL'S CLASSIFIED CATALOGUE, in which their Works are arranged according to price, from *Threepence to Fifty Guineas.*

CASSELL'S EDUCATIONAL CATALOGUE, containing particulars of CASSELL & COMPANY'S Educational Works and Students' Manuals.

CASSELL & COMPANY, LIMITED, *Ludgate Hill, London.*

Bibles and Religious Works.

Bible Biographies. Illustrated. 1s. 6d. each.

The Story of Joseph. Its Lessons for To-Day. By the Rev. GEORGE BAINTON.
The Story of Moses and Joshua. By the Rev. J. TELFORD.
The Story of Judges. By the Rev. J. WYCLIFFE GEDGE.
The Story of Samuel and Saul. By the Rev. D. C. TOVEY.
The Story of David. By the Rev. J. WILD.

The Story of Jesus. In Verse. By J. R. MACDUFF, D.D.

Bible, Cassell's Illustrated Family. With 900 Illustrations. Leather, gilt edges, £2 10s. ; full morocco, £3 10s.

Bible, Cassell's Guinea. With 900 Illustrations and Coloured Maps. Royal 4to. Leather, 21s. net. Persian antique, with corners and clasps, 25s. net.

Bible Educator, The. Edited by E. H. PLUMPTRE, D.D. With Illustrations, Maps, &c. Four Vols., cloth, 6s. each.

Bible Dictionary, Cassell's Concise Illustrated. By the Rev. ROBERT HUNTER, LL.D. 7s. 6d.

Bible Student in the British Museum, The. By the Rev. J. G. KITCHIN, M.A. *Entirely New and Revised Edition*, 1s. 4d.

Bunyan, Cassell's Illustrated. With 200 Original Illustrations. *Cheap Edition,* 7s. 6d.

Bunyan's Pilgrim's Progress (Cassell's Illustrated). 4to. *Cheap Edition,* 3s. 6d.

Child's Bible, The. With 200 Illustrations. Demy 4to, 830 pp. 150th Thousand. *Cheap Edition,* 7s. 6d. *Superior Edition,* with 6 Coloured Plates, gilt edges, 10s. 6d.

Child's Life of Christ, The. Complete in One Handsome Volume, with about 200 Original Illustrations. *Cheap Edition,* cloth, 7s. 6d. ; or with 6 Coloured Plates, cloth, gilt edges, 10s. 6d. Demy 4to, gilt edges, 21s.

Commentary, The New Testament, for English Readers. Edited by the Rt. Rev. C. J. ELLICOTT, D.D., Lord Bishop of Gloucester and Bristol. In Three Vols. 21s. each.

> Vol. I.—The Four Gospels.
> Vol. II.—The Acts, Romans, Corinthians, Galatians.
> Vol. III.—The remaining Books of the New Testament.

Commentary, The Old Testament, for English Readers. Edited by the Rt. Rev. C. J. ELLICOTT, D.D., Lord Bishop of Gloucester and Bristol. Complete in 5 Vols. 21s. each.

Vol. I.—Genesis to Numbers. | Vol. III.—Kings I. to Esther.
Vol. II.—Deuteronomy to Samuel II. | Vol. IV.—Job to Isaiah.
Vol. V.—Jeremiah to Malachi.

Commentary, The New Testament. Edited by Bishop ELLICOTT. Handy Volume Edition. Suitable for School and General Use.

St. Matthew. 3s. 6d.	Romans. 2s. 6d.	Titus, Philemon, Hebrews,
St. Mark. 3s.	Corinthians I. and II. 3s.	and James. 3s.
St. Luke. 3s. 6d.	Galatians, Ephesians, and	Peter, Jude, and John. 3s.
St. John. 3s. 6d.	Philippians. 3s.	The Revelation. 3s.
The Acts of the Apostles.	Colossians, Thessalonians,	An Introduction to the New
3s. 6d.	and Timothy. 3s.	Testament. 2s. 6d.

Commentary, The Old Testament. Edited by Bishop ELLICOTT. Handy Volume Edition. Suitable for School and General Use.

Genesis. 3s. 6d.	Leviticus. 3s.	Deuteronomy. 2s. 6d.
Exodus. 3s.	Numbers. 2s. 6d.	

Dictionary of Religion, The. An Encyclopædia of Christian and other Religious Doctrines, Denominations, Sects, Heresies, Ecclesiastical Terms, History, Biography, &c. &c. By the Rev. WILLIAM BENHAM, B.D. *Cheap Edition,* 10s. 6d.

Doré Bible. With 230 Illustrations by GUSTAVE DORÉ. *Original Edition.* Two Vols., best morocco, gilt edges, £15. *Popular Edition.* With Full-page Illustrations. In One Vol. 15s. Also in leather binding. *(Price on application.)*

Early Days of Christianity, The. By the Very Rev. Dean FARRAR, D.D., F.R.S. LIBRARY EDITION. Two Vols., 24s. ; morocco, £2 2s.
POPULAR EDITION. Complete in One Vol., cloth, 6s. ; cloth, gilt edges, 7s. 6d. ; Persian morocco, 10s. 6d. ; tree-calf, 15s.

Family Prayer-Book, The. Edited by the Rev. Canon GARBETT, M.A., and the Rev. S. MARTIN. With Full-page Illustrations. *New Edition.* Cloth, 7s. 6d.

Gleanings after Harvest. Studies and Sketches. By the Rev. JOHN R. VERNON, M.A. Illustrated. *Cheap Edition.* 5s.

"Graven in the Rock;" or, the Historical Accuracy of the Bible confirmed by reference to the Assyrian and Egyptian Sculptures in the British Museum and elsewhere. By the Rev. Dr. SAMUEL KINNS, F.R.A.S., &c. &c. Illustrated. *Library Edition*, in Two Volumes, cloth, with top edges gilded, 15s.

"Heart Chords." A Series of Works by Eminent Divines. In cloth, 1s. each.

My Father. By the Right Rev. Ashton Oxenden, late Bishop of Montreal.
My Bible. By the Rt. Rev. W. Boyd Carpenter, Bishop of Ripon.
My Work for God. By the Right Rev. Bishop Cotterill.
My Object in Life. By the Very Rev. Dean Farrar, D.D.
My Aspirations. By the Rev. G. Matheson, D.D.
My Emotional Life. By Preb. Chadwick, D.D.
My Body. By the Rev. Prof. W. G. Blaikie, D.D.
My Soul. By the Rev. P. B. Power, M.A.

My Growth in Divine Life. By the Rev. Prebendary Reynolds, M.A.
My Hereafter. By the Very Rev. Dean Bickersteth.
My Walk with God. By the Very Rev. Dean Montgomery.
My Aids to the Divine Life. By the Very Rev. Dean Boyle.
My Sources of Strength. By the Rev. E. E. Jenkins, M.A.
My Comfort in Sorrow. By Hugh Macmillan, D.D.

Helps to Belief. A Series of Helpful Manuals on the Religious Difficulties of the Day. Edited by the Rev. TEIGNMOUTH SHORE, M.A., Canon of Worcester, and Chaplain-in-Ordinary to the Queen. Cloth, 1s. each.

CREATION. By Harvey Goodwin, D.D., late Lord Bishop of Carlisle.
MIRACLES. By the Rev. Brownlow Maitland, M.A.
PRAYER. By the Rev. Canon Shore, M.A.

THE DIVINITY OF OUR LORD. By the Lord Bishop of Derry.
THE ATONEMENT. By William Connor Magee, D.D., Late Archbishop of York.

Holy Land and the Bible, The. A Book of Scripture Illustrations gathered in Palestine. By the Rev. CUNNINGHAM GEIKIE, D.D., LL.D. (Edin.). *Cheap Edition*, with 24 Collotype Plates, 12s. 6d.

Life of Christ, The. By the Very Rev. Dean FARRAR, D.D., F.R.S., Chaplain-in-Ordinary to the Queen.
CHEAP EDITION. With 16 Full-page Plates. Cloth gilt, 3s. 6d.
POPULAR EDITION. Cloth, 7s. 6d. Persian morocco, gilt edges, 10s. 6d.
ILLUSTRATED EDITION. Cloth, 7s. 6d. Cloth, full gilt, gilt edges, 10s. 6d.
LIBRARY EDITION. Two Vols. Cloth, 24s.; morocco, 42s.

Moses and Geology; or, the Harmony of the Bible with Science. By the Rev. SAMUEL KINNS, Ph.D., F.R.A.S. Illustrated. *Library Edition*, revised to date, 10s. 6d.

My Last Will and Testament. By HYACINTHE LOYSON (PÈRE HYACINTHE). Translated by FABIAN WARE. 1s.; cloth, 1s. 6d.

New Light on the Bible and the Holy Land. By BASIL T. A. EVETTS, M.A. Illustrated. Cloth, 7s. 6d.

Old and New Testaments, Plain Introductions to the Books of the. Containing Contributions by many Eminent Divines. In Two Vols., 3s. 6d. each.

Plain Introductions to the Books of the Old Testament. 336 pages. Edited by the Right Rev. C. J. ELLICOTT, D.D., Lord Bishop of Gloucester and Bristol. 3s. 6d.

Plain Introductions to the Books of the New Testament. 304 pages. Edited by the Right Rev. C. J. ELLICOTT, D.D., Lord Bishop of Gloucester and Bristol. 3s. 6d.

Protestantism, The History of. By the Rev. J. A. WYLIE, LL.D. Containing upwards of 600 Original Illustrations. Three Vols., 27s.

"Quiver" Yearly Volume, The. With about 600 Original Illustrations and Coloured Frontispiece. 7s. 6d. Also Monthly, 6d.

St. George for England; and other Sermons preached to Children. *Fifth Edition.* By the Rev. T. TEIGNMOUTH SHORE, M.A., Canon of Worcester. 5s.

St. Paul, The Life and Work of. By the Very Rev. Dean FARRAR, D.D., F.R.S.
LIBRARY EDITION. Two Vols., cloth, 24s.; calf, 42s.
ILLUSTRATED EDITION, One Vol., £1 1s.; morocco, £2 2s.
POPULAR EDITION. One Vol., 8vo, cloth, 6s.; Persian morocco, 10s. 6d.; tree-calf, 15s.

Searchings in the Silence. By Rev. GEORGE MATHESON, D.D. 3s. 6d.

Shall We Know One Another in Heaven? By the Rt. Rev. J. C. RYLE, D.D., Bishop of Liverpool. *New and Enlarged Edition.* Paper covers, 6d.

Shortened Church Services and Hymns, suitable for use at Children's Services. Compiled by the Rev. T. TEIGNMOUTH SHORE, M.A., Canon of Worcester. *Enlarged Edition.* 1s.

Signa Christi: Evidences of Christianity set forth in the Person and Work of Christ. By the Rev. JAMES AITCHISON. 2s. 6d.

"Sunday:" Its Origin, History, and Present Obligation. By the Ven. Archdeacon HESSEY, D.C.L. *Fifth Edition,* 7s. 6d.

Twilight of Life, The: Words of Counsel and Comfort for the Aged. By JOHN ELLERTON, M.A. 1s. 6d.

Educational Works and Students' Manuals.

Agricultural Text-Books, Cassell's. (The "Downton" Series.) Fully Illustrated. Edited by JOHN WRIGHTSON, Professor of Agriculture. **Soils and Manures.** By J. M. H. Munro, D.Sc. (London), F.I.C., F.C.S. 2s. 6d. **Farm Crops.** By Professor Wrightson. 2s. 6d. **Live Stock.** By Professor Wrightson. 2s. 6d.

Alphabet, Cassell's Pictorial. Mounted on Linen, with rollers. 3s. 6d.

Arithmetic:—Howard's Art of Reckoning. By C. F. HOWARD. Paper, 1s. ; cloth, 2s. *Enlarged Edition*, 5s.

Arithmetics, The "Belle Sauvage." By GEORGE RICKS, B.Sc. Lond. With Test Cards. (*List on application.*)

Atlas, Cassell's Popular. Containing 24 Coloured Maps. 1s. 6d.

Book-Keeping. By THEODORE JONES. FOR SCHOOLS, 2s. ; or cloth, 3s. FOR THE MILLION, 2s. ; or cloth, 3s. Books for Jones's System, Ruled Sets of, 2s.

British Empire Map of the World. New Map for Schools and Institutes. By G. R. PARKIN and J. G. BARTHOLOMEW, F.R.G.S. Mounted on cloth, varnished, and with Rollers or Folded. 25s.

Chemistry, The Public School. By J. H. ANDERSON, M.A. 2s. 6d.

Cookery for Schools. By LIZZIE HERITAGE. 6d.

Dulce Domum. Rhymes and Songs for Children. Edited by JOHN FARMER, Editor of "Gaudeamus," &c. Old Notation and Words, 5s. N.B.—The Words of the Songs in "Dulce Domum" (with the Airs both in Tonic Sol-Fa and Old Notation) can be had in Two Parts, 6d. each.

English Literature, A First Sketch of, from the Earliest Period to the Present Time. By Prof. HENRY MORLEY. 7s. 6d.

Euclid, Cassell's. Edited by Prof. WALLACE, M.A. 1s.

Euclid, The First Four Books of. *New Edition.* In paper, 6d. ; cloth, 9d.

French, Cassell's Lessons in. *New and Revised Edition.* Parts I. and II., each, 2s. 6d. ; complete, 4s. 6d. Key, 1s. 6d.

French-English and English-French Dictionary. *Entirely New and Enlarged Edition.* 1,150 pages, 8vo, cloth, 3s. 6d. ; half-morocco, 5s.

French Reader, Cassell's Public School. By GUILLAUME S. CONRAD. 2s. 6d.

Galbraith and Haughton's Scientific Manuals.
Plane Trigonometry. 2s. 6d. **Euclid.** Books I., II., III. 2s. 6d. Books IV., V., VI. 2s. 6d. **Mathematical Tables.** 3s. 6d. **Mechanics.** 3s. 6d. **Optics.** 2s. 6d. **Hydrostatics.** 3s. 6d. **Algebra.** Part I., cloth, 2s. 6d. Complete, 7s. 6d. **Tides and Tidal Currents,** with Tidal Cards, 3s.

Gaudeamus. Songs for Colleges and Schools. Edited by JOHN FARMER. 5s. Words only, paper, 6d. ; cloth, 9d.

Geometrical Drawing for Army Candidates. By H. T. LILLEY, M.A. 2s. 6d.

Geometry, First Elements of Experimental. By PAUL BERT. Illustrated. 1s. 6d.

Geometry, Practical Solid. By Major ROSS, R.E. 2s.

German Dictionary, Cassell's New. German-English, English-German. *Cheap Edition*, cloth, 3s. 6d. ; half-morocco, 5s.

German Reading, First Lessons in. By A. JAGST. Illustrated. 1s.

Hand and Eye Training. By GEORGE RICKS, B.Sc., and JOSEPH VAUGHAN. Illustrated. Vol. I. Designing with Coloured Papers. Vol. II. Cardboard Work. 2s. each. Vol. III. Colour Work and Design, 3s.

Hand and Eye Training. By G. RICKS, B.Sc. Two Vols., with 16 Coloured Plates in each Vol. Crown 4to, 6s. each.

"Hand and Eye Training" Cards for Class Work. Five sets in case. 1s. each.

Historical Cartoons, Cassell's Coloured. Size 45 in. × 35 in., 2s. each. Mounted on canvas and varnished, with rollers, 5s. each. (Descriptive pamphlet, 16 pp., 1d.)

Italian Lessons, with Exercises, Cassell's. In One Vol. 3s. 6d.

Latin Dictionary, Cassell's New. (Latin-English and English-Latin.) Revised by J. R. V. MARCHANT, M.A., and J. F. CHARLES, B.A. 3s. 6d. ; half-morocco, 5s.

Latin Primer, The New. By Prof. J. P. POSTGATE. 2s. 6d.

Latin Primer, The First. By Prof. POSTGATE. 1s.

Latin Prose for Lower Forms. By M. A. BAYFIELD, M.A. 2s. 6d.

Laws of Every-Day Life. For the Use of Schools. By H. O. ARNOLD-FORSTER, M.P. 1s. 6d. *Special Edition* on green paper for those with weak eyesight, 1s. 6d.

Lessons in Our Laws ; or, Talks at Broadacre Farm. By H. F. LESTER, B.A. Part I. : THE MAKERS AND CARRIERS-OUT OF THE LAW. Part II. : LAW COURTS AND LOCAL RULE, &c. 1s. 6d. each.

Little Folks' History of England. By ISA CRAIG-KNOX. Illustrated. 1s. 6d.

Making of the Home, The. By Mrs. SAMUEL A. BARNETT. 1s. 6d.

Marlborough Books :—Arithmetic Examples. 3s. French Exercises. 3s. 6d. French Grammar. 2s. 6d. German Grammar. 3s. 6d.

Mechanics for Young Beginners, A First Book of. By the Rev. J. G. EASTON, M.A. *Cheap Edition,* 2s. 6d.

Mechanics and Machine Design, Numerical Examples in Practical. By R. G. BLAINE, M.E. *New Edition, Revised and Enlarged.* With 79 Illustrations. Cloth, 2s. 6d.

Natural History Coloured Wall Sheets, Cassell's New. Consisting of 16 subjects. Size, 39 by 31 in. Mounted on rollers and varnished. 3s. each.

Object Lessons from Nature. By Prof. L. C. MIALL, F.L.S., F.G.S. Fully Illustrated. *New and Enlarged Edition.* Two Vols. 1s. 6d. each.

Physiology for Schools. By ALFRED T. SCHOFIELD, M.D., M.R.C.S., &c. Illustrated. 1s. 9d. Three Parts, paper covers, 5d. each ; or cloth limp, 6d. each.

Poetry Readers, Cassell's New. Illustrated. 12 Books. 1d. each. Cloth, 1s. 6d.

Popular Educator, Cassell's New. With Revised Text, New Maps, New Coloured Plates, New Type, &c. Complete in Eight Vols., 5s. each ; or Eight Vols. in Four, half-morocco, 50s.

Readers, Cassell's "Belle Sauvage." An Entirely New Series. Fully Illustrated. Strongly bound in cloth. (*List on application.*)

Reader, The Citizen. By H. O. ARNOLD-FORSTER, M.P. Cloth, 1s. 6d. ; also a Scottish Edition, cloth, 1s. 6d.

Reader, The Temperance. By Rev. J. DENNIS HIRD. 1s. 6d.

Readers, Cassell's "Higher Class." (*List on application.*)

Readers, Cassell's Readable. Illustrated. (*List on application.*)

Readers for Infant Schools, Coloured. Three Books. 4d. each.

Readers, Geographical, Cassell's New. With Numerous Illustrations in each Book. (*List on application.*)

Readers, The Modern Geographical. Illustrated throughout. (*List on application.*)

Readers, The Modern School. Illustrated. (*List on application.*)

Reading and Spelling Book, Cassell's Illustrated. 1s.

Round the Empire. By G. R. PARKIN. With a Preface by the Rt. Hon. the Earl of Rosebery, K.G. Fully Illustrated. 1s. 6d.

Science Applied to Work. By J. A. BOWER. Illustrated. 1s.

Science of Every-Day Life. By J. A. BOWER. Illustrated. 1s.

Sculpture, A Primer of. By E. ROSCOE MULLINS. Illustrated. 2s. 6d.

Shade from Models, Common Objects, and Casts of Ornament, How to. By W. E. SPARKES. With 25 Plates by the Author. 3s.

Shakspere's Plays for School Use. Illustrated. 9 Books. 6d. each.

Spelling, A Complete Manual of. By J. D. MORELL, LL.D. 1s.

Technical Educator, Cassell's New. An entirely New Cyclopædia of Technical Education, with Coloured Plates and Engravings. Complete in Six Vols., 5s. each.

Technical Manuals, Cassell's. Illustrated throughout. 16 Vols., from 2s. to 4s. 6d. (*List free on application.*)

Technology, Manuals of. Edited by Prof. AYRTON, F.R.S., and RICHARD WORMELL, D.Sc., M.A. Illustrated throughout. (*List on application.*)

Things New and Old ; or, Stories from English History. By H. O. ARNOLD-FORSTER, M.P. Fully Illustrated. Strongly bound in Cloth. Standards I. and II., 9d. each ; Standard III., 1s. ; Standard IV., 1s. 3d. ; Standards V. and VI., 1s. 6d. each ; Standard VII., 1s. 8d.

World of Ours, This. By H. O. ARNOLD-FORSTER, M.P. Fully Illustrated. 3s. 6d.

Books for Young People.

"Little Folks" Half-Yearly Volume. Containing 480 pages of Letterpress, with Pictures on nearly every page, together with Six Full-page Plates printed in Colours. Coloured boards, 3s. 6d.; or cloth gilt, gilt edges, 5s.

Bo-Peep. A Book for the Little Ones. With Original Stories and Verses. Illustrated with beautiful Pictures on nearly every page, and Four Full-page Plates in Colours. Yearly Vol. Elegant picture boards, 2s. 6d.; cloth, 3s. 6d.

Beneath the Banner. Being Narratives of Noble Lives and Brave Deeds. By F. J. CROSS. Illustrated. Limp cloth, 1s.; cloth boards, gilt edges, 2s.

Good Morning! Good Night! Morning and Evening Readings for Children, by the Author of "Beneath the Banner." Fully Illustrated. Limp cloth, 1s., or cloth boards, gilt edges, 2s.

Five Stars in a Little Pool. By EDITH CARRINGTON. Illustrated. *Cheap Edition,* 3s. 6d.

Merry Girls of England. By L. T. MEADE. 3s. 6d.

Beyond the Blue Mountains. By L. T. MEADE. Illustrated. 5s.

The Cost of a Mistake. By SARAH PITT. Illustrated. *New Edition.* 2s. 6d.

The Peep of Day. Cassell's Illustrated Edition. 2s. 6d.

A Book of Merry Tales. By MAGGIE BROWNE, SHEILA, ISABEL WILSON, and C. L. MATÉAUX. Illustrated. 3s. 6d.

A Sunday Story-Book. By MAGGIE BROWNE, SAM BROWNE, and AUNT ETHEL. Illustrated. 3s. 6d.

A Bundle of Tales. By MAGGIE BROWNE, SAM BROWNE, & AUNT ETHEL. 3s. 6d.

Story Poems for Young and Old. By E. DAVENPORT. 3s. 6d.

Pleasant Work for Busy Fingers. By MAGGIE BROWNE. Illustrated. *Cheap Edition.* 2s. 6d.

Magic at Home. By Prof. HOFFMAN. Fully Illustrated. A Series of easy and startling Conjuring Tricks for Beginners. Cloth gilt, 3s. 6d.

Schoolroom and Home Theatricals. By ARTHUR WAUGH. With Illustrations by H. A. J. MILES. *New Edition.* Cloth, 1s. 6d.

Little Mother Bunch. By Mrs. MOLESWORTH. Illustrated. *New Edition.* 2s. 6d.

Heroes of Every-Day Life. By LAURA LANE. With about 20 Full-page Illustrations. 256 pages, crown 8vo, cloth, 2s. 6d.

Ships, Sailors, and the Sea. By R. J. CORNEWALL-JONES. Illustrated throughout, and containing a Coloured Plate of Naval Flags. *Cheap Edition,* 2s. 6d.

Gift Books for Young People. By Popular Authors. With Four Original Illustrations in each. Cloth gilt, 1s. 6d. each.

The Boy Hunters of Kentucky. By Edward S. Ellis.	Jack Marston's Anchor.
Red Feather: a Tale of the American Frontier. By Edward S. Ellis.	Frank's Life-Battle.
Fritters; or, "It's a Long Lane that has no Turning."	Major Monk's Motto; or, "Look Before you Leap."
Trixy; or, "Those who Live in Glass Houses shouldn't throw Stones."	Tim Thomson's Trial; or, "All is not Gold that Glitters."
The Two Hardcastles.	Ursula's Stumbling-Block.
Seeking a City.	Ruth's Life-Work; or, "No Pains, no Gains."
Rhoda's Reward.	Rags and Rainbows.
	Uncle William's Charge.
	Pretty Pink's Purpose.

Golden Mottoes" Series, The. Each Book containing 208 pages, with Four full-page Original Illustrations. Crown 8vo, cloth gilt, 1s. each.

"Nil Desperandum." By the Rev. F. Langbridge, M.A.	"Honour is my Guide." By Jeanie Hering (Mrs. Adams-Acton).
' Bear and Forbear." By Sarah Pitt.	"Aim at a Sure End." By Emily Searchfield.
"Foremost if I Can." By Helen Atteridge.	"He Conquers who Endures." By the Author of "May Cunningham's Trial," &c.

"Cross and Crown" Series, The. With Four Illustrations in each Book. Crown 8vo, 256 pages, 2s. 6d. each.

Heroes of the Indian Empire; or, Stories of Valour and Victory. By Ernest Foster.	By Fire and Sword: A Story of the Huguenots. By Thomas Archer.
Through Trial to Triumph; or, "The Royal Way." By Madeline Bonavia Hunt.	Adam Hepburn's Vow: A Tale of Kirk and Covenant. By Annie S. Swan.
In Letters of Flame: A Story of the Waldenses. By C. L. Matéaux.	No. XIII.; or, The Story of the Lost Vestal. A Tale of Early Christian Days. By Emma Marshall.
Strong to Suffer: A Story of the Jews. By E. Wynne.	Freedom's Sword: A Story of the Days of Wallace and Bruce. By Annie S. Swan.

Albums for Children. Price 3s. 6d. each.

The Album for Home, School, and Play. Set in bold type, and illustrated throughout.

My Own Album of Animals. Illustrated. Picture Album of All Sorts. Illustrated.

The Chit-Chat Album. Illustrated.

"Wanted—a King" Series. *Cheap Edition.* Illustrated. 2s. 6d. each.

Great-Grandmamma. By Georgina M. Synge.
Fairy Tales in Other Lands. By Julia Goddard.

Wanted—a King; or, How Merle set the Nursery Rhymes to Rights. By Maggie Browne.

Robin's Ride. By Ellinor Davenport Adams.

"Peeps Abroad" Library. *Cheap Editions.* Cloth gilt, 2s. 6d. each.

Rambles Round London. By C. L. Matéaux. Illustrated.
Around and About Old England. By C. L. Matéaux. Illustrated.
Paws and Claws. By one of the Authors of "Poems Written for a Child." Illustrated.
Decisive Events in History. By Thomas Archer. With Original Illustrations.
The True Robinson Crusoes.
Peeps Abroad for Folks at Home. Illustrated throughout.

Wild Adventures in Wild Places. By Dr. Gordon Stables, R.N. Illustrated.
Modern Explorers. By Thomas Frost. Illustrated. *New and Cheaper Edition.*
Early Explorers. By Thomas Frost.
Home Chat with our Young Folks. Illustrated throughout.
Jungle, Peak, and Plain. Illustrated throughout.

Three-and-Sixpenny Books for Young People. With Original Illustrations.
Cloth gilt, 3s. 6d. each.

Told Out of School. By A. J. Daniels.
† Red Rose and Tiger Lily. By L. T. Meade.
The Romance of Invention. By James Burnley.
‖ Bashful Fifteen. By L. T. Meade.
The King's Command. A Story for Girls. By Maggie Symington.
† A Sweet Girl Graduate. By L. T. Meade.

† The White House at Inch Gow. By Sarah Pitt.
† Polly. By L. T. Meade.
† The Palace Beautiful. By L. T. Meade.
"Follow my Leader."
For Fortune and Glory.
Lost among White Africans.
† A World of Girls. By L. T. Meade.

Books marked thus † can also be had in extra cloth gilt, gilt edges, 5s. each.

Books by Edward S. Ellis. Illustrated. Cloth, 2s. 6d. each.

The Phantom of the River.
Shod with Silence.
The Great Cattle Trail.
The Path in the Ravine.
The Hunters of the Ozark.
The Camp in the Mountains.
Ned in the Woods. A Tale of Early Days in the West.

Down the Mississippi.
The Last War Trail.
Ned on the River. A Tale of Indian River Warfare.
Footprints in the Forest.
Up the Tapajos.
Ned in the Block House. A Story of Pioneer Life in Kentucky.

The Young Ranchers.
The Lost Trail.
Camp-Fire and Wigwam.
Lost in the Wilds.
Lost in Samoa. A Tale of Adventure in the Navigator Islands.
Tad; or, "Getting Even" with Him.

Cassell's Picture Story Books. Each containing 60 pages. 6d. each.

Little Talks.
Bright Stars.
Nursery Joys.
Pet's Posy.
Tiny Tales.

Daisy's Story Book.
Dot's Story Book.
A Nest of Stories.
Good Night Stories.
Chats for Small Chatterers.

Auntie's Stories.
Birdie's Story Book.
Little Chimes.
A Sheaf of Tales.
Dewdrop Stories.

Illustrated Books for the Little Ones. Containing interesting Stories. All
Illustrated. 1s. each; or cloth gilt, 1s. 6d.

Bright Tales and Funny Pictures.
Merry Little Tales.
Little Tales for Little People.
Little People and Their Pets.
Tales Told for Sunday.
Sunday Stories for Small People.
Stories and Pictures for Sunday.

Bible Pictures for Boys and Girls.
Firelight Stories.
Sunlight and Shade.
Rub-a-dub Tales.
Fine Feathers and Fluffy Fur.
Scrambles and Scrapes.
Tittle Tattle Tales.
Dumb Friends.
Indoors and Out.
Some Farm Friends.

Those Golden Sands.
Little Mothers and their Children.
Our Pretty Pets.
Our Schoolday Hours.
Creatures Tame.
Creatures Wild.
Up and Down the Garden.
All Sorts of Adventures.
Our Sunday Stories.
Our Holiday Hours.
Wandering Ways.

Shilling Story Books. All Illustrated, and containing Interesting Stories.

Seventeen Cats.
Bunty and the Boys.
The Heir of Elmdale.
The Mystery at Shoncliff School.
Claimed at Last, and Roy's Reward.
Thorns and Tangles.

The Cuckoo in the Robin's Nest.
John's Mistake.
Diamonds in the Sand.
Surly Bob.
The History of Five Little Pitchers.
The Giant's Cradle.
Shag and Doll.

Aunt Lucia's Locket.
The Magic Mirror.
The Cost of Revenge.
Clever Frank.
Among the Redskins.
The Ferryman of Brill.
Harry Maxwell.
A Banished Monarch.

Eighteenpenny Story Books. All Illustrated throughout.

Wee Willie Winkie.
Ups and Downs of a Donkey's Life.
Three Wee Ulster Lassies.
Up the Ladder.
Dick's Hero; & other Stories.
The Chip Boy.

Raggles, Baggles, and the Emperor.
Roses from Thorns.
Faith's Father.
By Land and Sea.
The Young Berringtons.
Jeff and Leff.

Tom Morris's Error.
Worth more than Gold.
"Through Flood—Through Fire."
The Girl with the Golden Locks.
Stories of the Olden Time.

Library of Wonders. Illustrated Gift-books for Boys. Cloth, 1s. 6d.

Wonderful Escapes.
Wonders of Animal Instinct.

Wonderful Balloon Ascents.
Wonders of Bodily Strength and Skill.

The "World in Pictures" Series. Illustrated throughout. *Cheap Edition.* 1s. 6d. each.

A Ramble Round France.
All the Russias.
Chats about Germany.
Peeps into China.
The Land of Pyramids (Egypt).

The Eastern Wonderland (Japan).
Glimpses of South America.
Round Africa.
The Land of Temples (India).
The Isles of the Pacific.

Two-Shilling Story Books. All Illustrated.

Margaret's Enemy.
Stories of the Tower.
Mr. Burke's Nieces.
May Cunningham's Trial.
The Top of the Ladder: How to Reach it.
Little Flotsam.

Madge and her Friends.
The Children of the Court.
Maid Marjory.
The Four Cats of the Tippertons.
Marion's Two Homes.
Little Folks' Sunday Book.

Two Fourpenny Bits.
Poor Nelly.
Tom Heriot.
Aunt Tabitha's Waifs.
In Mischief Again.
Through Peril to Fortune.
Peggy, and other Tales.

Half-Crown Story Books.

In Quest of Gold; or, Under the Whanga Falls.
On Board the *Esmeralda*; or, Martin Leigh's Log.

Esther West.
For Queen and King.
Perils Afloat and Brigands Ashore.

Working to Win.
At the South Pole.
Pictures of School Life and Boyhood.

Cassell's Pictorial Scrap Book. In Twenty-four Books, each containing 32 pages, 6d. each.

Books for the Little Ones. Fully Illustrated.

Rhymes for the Young Folk. By William Allingham. Beautifully Illustrated. 1s. 6d.

The Sunday Scrap Book. With Several Hundred Illustrations. Boards, 3s. 6d.; cloth, gilt edges, 5s.

Cassell's Robinson Crusoe. With 100 Illustrations. Cloth, 3s. 6d.; gilt edges, 5s.
The Old Fairy Tales. With Original Illustrations. Cloth, 1s.
Cassell's Swiss Family Robinson. Illustrated. Cloth, 3s. 6d.; gilt edges, 5s.

The New "Little Folks" Painting Book. Containing nearly 350 Outline Illustrations suitable for Colouring. 1s.

The World's Workers. A Series of New and Original Volumes by Popular Authors. With Portraits printed on a tint as Frontispiece. 1s. each.

John Cassell. By G. Holden Pike.
Charles Haddon Spurgeon. By G. Holden Pike.
Dr. Arnold of Rugby. By Rose E. Selfe.
The Earl of Shaftesbury.
Sarah Robinson, Agnes Weston, and Mrs. Meredith.
Thomas A. Edison and Samuel F. B. Morse.
Mrs. Somerville and Mary Carpenter.
General Gordon.
Charles Dickens.
Florence Nightingale, Catherine Marsh, Frances Ridley Havergal, Mrs. Ranyard ("L. N. R.").

Dr. Guthrie, Father Mathew, Elihu Burritt, Joseph Livesey.
Sir Henry Havelock and Colin Campbell Lord Clyde.
Abraham Lincoln.
David Livingstone.
George Muller and Andrew Reed.
Richard Cobden.
Benjamin Franklin.
Handel.
Turner the Artist.
George and Robert Stephenson.
Sir Titus Salt and George Moore.

** The above Works can also be had Three in One Vol., cloth, gilt edges, 3s.

CASSELL & COMPANY, Limited, Ludgate Hill, London; Paris & Melbourne.

P93 "O God. if I was sure I were to die tonight I would repent at once".

P444 "God is fonder of lonely lasses than of any other kind, + every time you greet it makes Him greet. + when you're cheerful it makes Him cheerful too". Tommy to Elspeth.